Novels by Vince Flynn

And by Kyle Mills

VINCE FLYNN

LETHAL AGENT

A MITCH RAPP NOVEL
BY KYLE MILLS

POCKET BOOKS

New York   London   Toronto   Sydney   New Delhi

Pocket Books
An Imprint of Simon & Schuster, Inc.
1230 Avenue of the Americas
New York, NY 10020

This book is a work of fiction. Any references to historical events, real people, or real places are used fictitiously. Other names, characters, places, and events are products of the author's imagination, and any resemblance to actual events or places or persons living or dead is entirely coincidental.

This Pocket Books paperback edition September 2020

POCKET and colophon are registered trademarks of Simon & Schuster, Inc.

For information about special discounts for bulk purchases, please contact Simon & Schuster Special Sales at 1-866-506-1949 or business@simonandschuster.com.

The Simon & Schuster Speakers Bureau can bring authors to your live event. For more information, or to book an event, contact the Simon & Schuster Speakers Bureau at 1-866-248-3049 or visit our website at www.simonspeakers.com.

Manufactured in the United States of America

10   9   8   7   6   5   4   3   2   1

ISBN 978-1-5011-9063-6
ISBN 978-1-5011-9064-3 (ebook)

ACKNOWLEDGMENTS

Sitting alone in your basement all year can make producing a book seem like a solo effort. Nothing could be further from the truth. Thankfully, I've managed to fall in with a good crowd.

Emily Bestler and Sloan Harris were always there for Vince and they've been every bit as supportive of me. Lara Jones keeps me on track. Simon Lipskar and Celia Taylor Mobley keep me from getting tangled in the complex web I've created over the last twenty years. David Brown leaves no marketing stone unturned. Ryan Steck props me up with his enthusiasm and unparalleled knowledge of the Rappverse. My mother and wife are my first editorial stop, providing early criticism and ideas. Rod Gregg has become a recurring character—making sure I don't make any fatal firearms errors.

Without all of you, I'd just be staring at a blank computer screen . . .

AUTHOR'S NOTE

In *Transfer of Power*, Vince wrote that he intention-
ally omitted details relating to the White House and
Secret Service. I find myself in a similar position with
Lethal Agent.

Because of the sensitivity of border security at the
time of writing, I've kept the details of crossings vague.
Further, I either omitted or obscured the details of
anthrax production.

LETHAL
AGENT

PRELUDE

THE cave was more than ten meters square, illuminated with a handful of battery-powered work lights. The glare and heat from them was centered on two rows of men kneeling on colorful cushions. Armed guards lurked near the jagged walls, barely visible in the shadows.

Mullah Sayid Halabi sat cross-legged, gazing down from a natural stone platform. Most of the men lined up in front of him were in their middle years—former junior officers from Saddam Hussein's disbanded army. Their commanders had been either captured or killed over the years, but these simpler soldiers were in many ways more useful. Their superiors had left the details of war to them while they focused on the much more critical activity of currying favor with Hussein.

The prior leader of ISIS had recruited these men in an effort to turn his motivated but undisciplined forces into an army capable of holding and administering territory. After his death in a drone strike, Halabi had taken over the organization with a much more ambitious goal: building a military capacity that could stand against even the Americans. Unfortunately, it was proving to be an infuriating, slow, and expensive process.

His men, generally prone to bickering and loud displays of fealty, had fallen silent in order to contemplate the rhythm of approaching footsteps. Halabi did the same, turning his attention to an inky black tunnel in the wall facing him. A few moments later, Aali Nassar appeared.

His expensive clothing was torn and covered in the dust that made up this part of Iraq. His physical suffering was admirably absent from his expression but evident in both his posture and the broken section of collarbone pressing against the luxurious cotton of his shirt.

Only hours ago, he had been the highly respected and greatly feared director of Saudi intelligence. A man who had never failed to prove himself—first in the Saudi Special Forces and then during his meteoric rise through the ranks of his country's intelligence apparatus. He had the ear of the king, a devoted family, and a lifestyle marked by privilege and power.

But now all that was gone. His plot to overthrow the Saudi royalty had been discovered and he'd been forced to flee the country. The great Aali Nassar was now alone, injured, and standing in a cave with nothing more than the clothes on his back and the contents of his pockets. It was the latter that he hoped to exchange for protection and a position in the ISIS hierarchy.

"Welcome, Aali," Halabi said finally. "I trust your journey wasn't too uncomfortable."

"Not at all," he said, revealing only a hint of the pain that speaking caused him.

"I understand that you have something for me?"

The thumb drive Nassar was carrying had been discovered when he'd been searched for tracking devices in Mecca. He'd been allowed to keep it and now retrieved it from his pocket. When he stepped forward to hand it to Halabi, the men at the edges of the cave stirred.

"Don't give it to me." The ISIS leader pointed at a man to Nassar's right. "Give it to him."

He did as he was told and the man slipped the drive into a laptop.

"It's asking for a password."

"Of course it is," Halabi said. "But I suspect that Director Nassar will be reluctant to give us that password."

Prior to his escape from Saudi Arabia, Nassar had downloaded an enormous amount of information on that country's security operations, government officials, and clandestine financial dealings.

"The intelligence and bank account information on that drive are yours," Nassar said.

Halabi smiled. "A meaningless response. Perhaps politics was your true calling."

"Perhaps."

"Can we break his encryption?" Halabi asked.

His very capable technological advisor shook his head. "Unlikely. Torturing him for it would have a higher probability of success."

"I wonder," Halabi said thoughtfully. "It seems likely that there's a password that would put the information forever out of our reach. Isn't that so, Aali?"

"It is."

Halabi rubbed his palms together in front of his face. "The money that drive gives us access to will quickly slip through our fingers and the intelligence will just as quickly become dated. Is it the information it contains that's valuable or is it the cunning and experience of the man who brought it here?"

The question was clearly rhetorical, but one Halabi's people answered anyway. "Do those qualities make him valuable or do they make him dangerous? He's betrayed his king and country. Why? For the cause? For Allah? Or is it for personal gain? Can he be trusted, Mullah Halabi? Is he here to assist you or is he here to replace you?"

"I had power," Nassar responded. "I had wealth. I had the respect of the king and the Americans. But I jeopardized it all. I—"

"The king is old and weak," the man interrupted. "You feared the collapse of the kingdom and were playing both sides. The Americans discovered your treachery and now you've had to run."

Nassar fell silent for a moment before speaking again.

"They discovered my allegiance to Mullah Halabi, yes. Regrettable, because while I can be of great assistance to you from here, I would have been much more effective at the king's side. The effort that went into gaining his confidence isn't something that I'd expect a simple soldier to understand."

The man stiffened at the insult, but Nassar continued. "I've worked closely with the Americans on their homeland security protocols and preventing terrorist attacks on their soil. It's given me an intimate knowledge of their borders and immigration policy, their power grid and nuclear plants. Even their water supply. If we strike surgically, we can turn the tide of the war. We can make the Americans lash out against all Muslims and turn your thirty thousand soldiers into a billion."

Halabi stared down at Nassar, who averted his eyes in an obviously insincere gesture of fealty.

Then his forehead exploded outward.

In the split second of stillness that followed, Halabi saw a bearded face flicker into view at the tunnel entrance. It was the face of the devil that had been burned so indelibly onto his mind and soul. The face of Mitch Rapp.

And then everything was in motion. Members of Halabi's guard charged toward him while others fired into the tunnel. Three of his men began dragging him toward a small opening at the back of the cavern as the roar of gunfire and acrid stench of gunpowder became overwhelming.

A blinding flash preceded the sensation of shrapnel tearing through his lower leg. The man behind him took the brunt of the blast, slamming into Halabi from behind and driving him to the ground. The lights were immediately extinguished and debris began cascading from the ceiling. The men with him were either dead or unconscious, and Halabi struggled to get out from beneath the weight of the one sprawled across his back.

As he did so, the extent of his injuries became clear. His right arm was useless and completely numb. His left leg felt as though it was on fire and a dagger-like pain in his side made it difficult to breathe. The warm, wet sensation of flowing blood seemed to cover nearly his entire body, but it was impossible to know if it was his or that of his men.

A few muffled shouts became audible but were quickly drowned out by a collapse somewhere not far from him. A rush of air washed over him, filling the cavern with a choking cloud of dust and pulverized rock. He buried his face in his blood-soaked tunic and fought to stay conscious.

It couldn't end this way. God wouldn't allow it. He wouldn't allow his faithful disciple to die at the hands of Satan's representative on earth. Not before His work was done.

A test. That had to be the explanation. It was a test of his strength. His worthiness. His devotion.

Bolstered by that realization, Halabi managed to drag himself from beneath his man. The darkness was now absolute, but he was able to find the back wall of the cave and feel along it as the last weak shouts around him fell silent. Finally, he located the narrow opening he was looking for and, by the grace of God, it was still passable.

Reports were that it was six hundred meters long and varied from three meters in diameter to barely wide enough for a full-grown man. He dragged himself through the broken rock, feeling his way forward. In places the passage seemed blocked, but after a few moments of blind exploration, he always managed to progress a few more meters.

Finally the walls narrowed to the point that it was impossible to continue. He tried to retreat but found himself trapped.

The world seemed to disappear, adding to his

confusion and amplifying the pain that racked his body. For a time, there was little else. No sound that wasn't produced by him. No light that his eyes could process. Only the pain, the taste of earth, and the swirl of his own thoughts.

The elation he'd felt when he'd concluded this was a test became lost in the realization that what he was experiencing felt more like a punishment. What had he done to deserve Allah's wrath?

He slipped in and out of consciousness, though in the darkness it was difficult to differentiate the two. He saw America. The gleaming buildings. The mass of humanity pursuing pleasure and comfort as a replacement for God. He saw the glorious collapse of the World Trade Center and the horror and vulnerability that attack had instilled in the American people. An incredible victory wasted by Osama bin Laden, who had turned to blithering endlessly about Islam on hazy video.

He saw the rise of ISIS fueled by its grasp of social media and intimate understanding of what motivated young men throughout the world. And, finally, he saw its battlefield victories and ability to terrify the Americans in a way that even September 11 hadn't.

He tried to pull himself forward again and again collapsed into the bed of shattered rock beneath him. The darkness and silence was deeper than anything he'd ever experienced. It blurred not only the lines between consciousness and lucidity but between life and death. Only the pain and sound of his own breathing assured him that he hadn't crossed over.

He didn't know how long he lay there but finally the darkness began to recede. He opened his eyes but didn't see the earthen tunnel around him. Only the blinding white light of God. It was then that he understood. It was his own arrogance that had brought him to this place. He had allowed his own hate and thirst for victory to deflect him from the work God had charged him with. He had become seduced by the power he wielded over his followers and the fear he commanded from his enemies. By visions of a new caliphate with him at its head, locked in righteous battle with the forces of the West.

He felt the panic rising in him, growing to a level that was nearly unbearable. The life he'd lived was a lie and God had finally shown him that fact. He had served only himself. Only his own vanity and hate.

Halabi clawed at the walls around him, unwilling to die in this graceless state. He felt something in his shoulder tear, but ignored it and was finally rewarded with a cascade of rock that created a path forward.

He was free.

CHAPTER 1

MITCH Rapp started to move again, weaving through an expansive boulder field before dropping to his stomach at its edge. A quick scan of the terrain through his binoculars provided the same result it had every time before: reddish dirt covering an endless series of pronounced ridges. No water. No plant life. A burned-out sky starting to turn orange in the west. If it were ninety-five below zero instead of ninety-five above, he could have been on Mars.

Rapp shifted his gaze to the right, concentrating for a good fifteen seconds before spotting a flash of movement that was either Scott Coleman or one of his men. All were wearing camo made from cloth specifically selected and dyed for this op by Charlie Wicker's girlfriend. She was a professional textile designer and a flat-out genius at matching colors and textures. If you gave her a few decent photos of your operating theater, she'd make you disappear.

A couple of contrails appeared above and he followed them with his eyes. Saudi jets on their way to bomb urban targets to the west. This sparsely populated part of Yemen had become the exclusive territory of ISIS and al Qaeda, but the Saudis largely ignored it. Viable targets were hard to engage from the air and the Kingdom didn't have the stomach to get bloody on the ground. That job had once again landed in his lap.

Satisfied they weren't being watched, Rapp started forward in a crouch. Coleman and his team would follow, watching his back at perfect intervals like they had in Iraq. And Afghanistan. And Syria. And just about every other shithole the planet had to offer.

The Yemeni civil war had broken out in 2015 between Houthi rebels and government forces. Predictably, other regional powers had been drawn in, most notably Iran backing the rebels and Saudi Arabia getting behind the government. The involvement of those countries had intensified the conflict, creating a humanitarian disaster impressive even by Middle Eastern standards.

In many ways, it was a forgotten war. The world's dirty little secret. Even among U.S. government officials and military commanders, it would be hard to find anyone aware that two-thirds of Yemen's population was surviving on foreign aid and another eight million were slowly starving. They also wouldn't be able to tell you that hunger and the loss of basic services were causing disease to run rampant through the country. Cholera, antibiotic-resistant bacteria, and even diphtheria were surging to levels unheard-of in the modern era.

And anyplace that could be described using words like "forgotten," "rampant," and "war" eventually became a magnet for terrorists. They were yet another disease that infected the weakened and wounded.

An unusually high ridge became visible to the northwest, and Rapp dropped to the ground again, studying it through his lenses. He could make out a gap just large enough for a human about three hundred yards away.

"Whatcha got?" Coleman said over his earpiece.

"The cave entrance. Right where they said it would be."

"Are we moving?"

"No, it's backlit. We'll let the sun drop over the horizon."

"Roger that. Everybody copy?"

Bruno McGraw, Joe Maslick, and Charlie Wicker all acknowledged. The four men made up about half the people in the world Rapp trusted. Probably a sad state of affairs, but one that had kept him alive for a lot longer than anyone would have predicted.

He fine-tuned the focus on his binoculars, refining his view of the dark hole in the cliff face. It was hard to believe that Sayid Halabi was still alive. If Rapp had been any closer with that grenade, it would have gotten jammed in the ISIS leader's throat. But even if his aim had been way off, it shouldn't have mattered. The blast had brought down a significant portion of the cavern he'd been hiding out in.

The collapse had been extensive enough that Rapp himself had been trapped in it. In fact, he'd have died slowly in the darkness if Joe Maslick wasn't a human wrecking ball who had spent much of his youth digging ditches on a landscaping crew. Oxygen had been getting pretty scarce when Mas finally broke through and dragged him from the grave he'd made for himself.

Despite all that, the intel on Halabi seemed reasonably solid. A while back, someone at NSA had decrypted a scrambled Internet video showing the man standing in the background at an al Qaeda meeting. The initial take had been that it was archival footage dredged up to keep the troops motivated. Deeper analysis, though, suggested that the images may have been taken six months *after* the night Rapp thought he'd finally ground his boot into that ISIS cockroach.

The video had led to the capture of one of the people at that meeting, and his interrogation led Rapp to this burned-out plain. The story was that Halabi had been severely injured by that grenade and was hiding out here convalescing. The sixty-four-thousand-dollar question was whether it was true. And if it was true, was he *still* here. Clearly, he was healthy enough to be going to meetings and starting the process of rebuilding ISIS after the beating it had taken in his absence.

The sun finally hit the horizon, causing an immediate drop in temperature and improvement in visibility. Waiting for full darkness was an option, but it seemed unnecessary. He hadn't seen any sign of exterior guards and night versus day would have little meaning once he passed into that cave.

"We're on," he said into his throat mike.

"Copy that," came Coleman's response.

Rapp angled left, moving silently across the rocky terrain until he reached a stone wall about twenty yards from the cavern entrance. Staying low, he crept along the wall's base until he reached its edge. Still no sign of ISIS enforcers. Behind him, the terrain was similarly empty, but that was to be expected. Coleman and his team would remain invisible until they were needed. It was impossible to anticipate the environment inside the cave, and Rapp was concerned that it could get tight enough to make a force of more than one man counterproductive.

When he finally slipped inside, the only evidence that it was inhabited was the churned dirt beneath his feet. He held his weapon in front of him as he eased along a passage about three feet wide and ten feet high. The familiar weight of his Glock had been replaced with that of an early-model Mission crossbow. His weapons tech had modified it for stealth, pushing the decibel level below eighty-five at the bow. Even better, the pitch had been lowered to the point that it sounded nothing like a weapon. Even to Rapp's practiced ear, it came off more like a bag of sand dropping onto a sidewalk.

Crossbows weren't the fastest things to reload and there hadn't been much time to train with it, but he still figured it was the best tool for the job. The quietest pistol he owned—a Volquartsen .22 with a Gemtech suppressor—was strapped to his thigh, but it would be held in reserve. While it was impressively stealthy, the sharp crack it made was too loud and recognizable for this operating environment.

The darkness deepened the farther he penetrated, forcing him to move slowly enough for his eyes to keep pace. Based on what had happened last time he'd chased Sayid Halabi into a hole, it made sense to prioritize caution over speed. Mas might have forgotten his shovel.

A faint glow became visible at the end of the passage and Rapp inched toward it, avoiding the rocks beneath his feet and staying on the soft earth. As he got closer, he could see that the corridor came to a T. The branch going right dead-ended after a few feet but the one to the left continued. A series of tiny bulbs wired to a car battery was the source of the glow.

One of the downsides of LED technology was that it made hiding out in caves a lot easier. A single battery could provide light for days. But it also created a vulnerability. Power supplies tended not to be as widely distributed and redundant as they used to be.

Rapp reached down and flipped the cable off the battery, plunging the cavern into darkness.

Shouts became audible almost immediately, but sounded more annoyed than alarmed. Rapp could tell that the voices belonged to two male Arabic speakers, but picking out exactly what they were saying was difficult with the echo. Basically a little name-calling and arguing about whose turn it was to fix the problem. When all your light came from a single improvised source, occasional outages were inevitable.

One of the men appeared a few seconds later, swinging a flashlight in his right hand but never lifting it high enough to give detail to his face. It didn't matter. From his youthful gait and posture, it was clear that it wasn't Halabi. Just one of his stooges.

Rapp aimed around the corner and gently squeezed the trigger. The sound profile of the crossbow and the projectile's impact were both outstanding. Unfortunately, the accuracy at this range was less so. The man was still standing, seemingly perplexed by the fletching protruding beneath his left clavicle.

Rapp let go of his weapon and sprinted forward,

getting one arm around the Arab's neck and clamping a hand over his mouth and nose. The man fought as he was dragged back around the corner, but the sound of their struggle was attenuated by soft ground. Finally, Rapp dropped and wrapped his legs around him to limit his movement. There wasn't enough leverage to choke him out, but the hand over his face was doing a pretty good job of suffocating him. The process took longer than he would have liked and he was gouged a few times by the protruding bolt, but the Arab finally lost consciousness. A knife to the base of his skull finished the job.

Rapp slid from beneath the body and was recocking the crossbow when another shout echoed through the cavern.

"Farid! What are you doing, idiot? Turn the lights back on!"

Rapp yelled back that he couldn't get them working, counting on the acoustics to make it difficult to distinguish one Arabic-speaking male from another. He loaded a bolt into his weapon and ran to the battery, putting the flashlight facedown in the dirt before crouching. The illumination was low enough that anyone approaching wouldn't be able to see much more than a vague human outline.

A stream of half-baked electrical advice preceded the sound of footsteps and then another young man appeared. He didn't seem at all concerned, once again proving the grand truth of all things human: people saw what they wanted and expected to see.

Rapp let the terrorist get to within fifteen feet before snatching up the crossbow. This time he compensated by aiming low and left, managing to put the projectile center of mass. No follow-up was necessary. The man fell forward, landing face-first in the dirt.

Certain that he wasn't getting up again, Rapp reconnected the battery. He was likely going to need the light. Things had gone well so far but, in his experience, good luck never came in threes.

Support for that hypothesis emerged when a man who was apparently distrustful of the sound of falling sand bags sprinted around the corner. Rapp's .22 was in an awkward position to draw, so instead he grabbed one of the bolts quivered on the crossbow.

The terrorist had been a little too enthusiastic in his approach and his momentum bounced him off one of the cave's walls. Rapp took advantage of his compromised balance and lunged, driving the bladed head into his throat.

Not pretty, but effective enough to drop the man. As he fell, though, a small pipe sprouting wires rolled from his hand.

Not again.

Rapp used his boot to kick the IED beneath the man's body and then ran in the opposite direction, making it about twenty feet before diving into a shallow dip in the ground. The explosion sent hot gravel washing over him and he heard a few disconcertingly loud cracks from above, but that was it. The rock held. He rolled onto his back, pulling his shirt over his mouth and nose to protect his lungs from the dust. The smart money would be to turn tail and call in a few bunker busters, but he couldn't bring himself to do it. If Halabi was there, Rapp was going to see him dead. Even if they entered the afterlife together with their hands around each other's throats.

The sound of automatic fire started up outside but Rapp ignored it, pulling the Volquartsen and using a penlight to continue deeper into the cavern. Coleman and his boys could handle themselves.

The cave system turned out to be relatively simple—a lot of branches, but almost all petered out after a few feet. The first chamber of any size contained a cot and some rudimentary medical equipment—an IV cart, monitors, and a garbage can half full of bloody bandages. All of it looked like it had been there for a while.

The second chamber appeared to have been set up for surgical procedures but wasn't much more advanced than something from World War I. A gas cylinder that looked like it came from a welder, a tray with a few instruments strewn across it, and a make-shift operating table streaked with dried blood.

And that was the end of the line. The cave system dead-ended just beyond.

"Shit!" Rapp shouted, his voice reverberating down the corridor and bouncing back to him.

The son of a bitch had been there. They'd brought him to treat the injuries he'd sustained in Iraq and to give him time to heal. A month ago, Rapp might have been able to look into his eyes, put a pistol between them, and pull the trigger. But now he was long gone. Sayid Halabi had slipped through his fingers again.

CHAPTER 2

SAYID Halabi carefully lowered himself into a chair facing a massive hole in the side of the building he was in. Shattered concrete and twisted rebar framed his view of the cityscape stretching into the darkness. A half-moon made it possible to make out the shapes of destroyed vehicles, collapsed homes, and scattered cinder blocks. No light beyond that provided by God burned anywhere in sight. Power had once again been lost and the city's half a million residents were reluctant to light fires or use battery power out of fear that they could be targeted by the Saudis.

It hadn't always been so. In 2015, al Qaeda had taken advantage of the devastation brought by Saudi Arabia's air war in Yemen and mounted an attack on Al Mukalla. Government forces had barely even gone through the motions of fighting back. After a few brief skirmishes they'd run, abandoning not only a terrified populace but the modern weapons of war— battle tanks, American-made Humvees, and heavy artillery.

After that stunning victory, a glorious glimpse of what was possible had ensued. Strict Islamic law was imposed as al Qaeda took over the governance of the city. Roads were repaired, public order was restored, hospitals were built. Sin and destruction were replaced by order and service to God.

A year later, Emirati-backed soldiers had driven al Qaeda out, returning the city to the dysfunctional and corrupt Yemeni government. Since then, nothing had been done to rebuild, and the Saudis' indiscriminant bombing continued, slowly strangling hope. Hunger, disease, and violence were all that people had left.

A lone car appeared to the east, weaving slowly through the debris with headlights extinguished. Halabi followed it with his gaze for a time, wondering idly where the driver had managed to find fuel and listening for approaching Saudi jets. None materialized, though, and the car eventually faded from view.

The ISIS leader was finally forced to stand, the pain in his back making it impossible to remain in the chair any longer. Three cracked vertebrae were the least visible of his injuries, but by far the most excruciating. Mitch Rapp's attack on him in Iraq had taken its toll. Beyond the damage to his back, Halabi no longer had full use of his right leg and, in fact, had barely avoided its amputation. His left eye had been damaged beyond repair and was now covered with a leather patch. The shattered fingers on his left hand had been straightened and set, but lacked sensation.

He'd spent months hidden underground, submitting to primitive medical procedures, surviving various infections and extended internal bleeding. All the while wondering if the Americans knew he'd survived. If, at any moment, Rapp would once again appear.

After a time those fears had faded and he began to heal both physically and psychologically. Once he was able, he'd devoted himself to prayer and study. He'd spent endless hours watching newsfeeds from throughout the world, reading history and politics, and studying military strategy. During that time, he came to understand why God had allowed his most devoted servant to be attacked in such a way. Halabi had let his life become consumed with the battle. He'd pursued the fleeting pleasure of inflicting damage instead of dedicating himself to the far more arduous and unsatisfying task of securing a final victory.

Footsteps became audible behind him and he turned to watch his most loyal disciple approach.

Muhammad Attia was an American by birth, the son of Algerian immigrants. He'd expended his youth working at his parents' general store in New York and seeking the approval and acceptance of the Westerners around him. After high school, he'd attended a year of community college before taking a job as a civilian Arabic translator for the U.S. Army.

As a Muslim American, he'd already experienced the treachery and moral bankruptcy of his parents' adopted country, but it wasn't until he'd arrived in Iraq that he came to understand the magnitude of it.

His recruitment by al Qaeda had occurred less than six months into his tour and he spent almost five years as an agent for the organization before being discovered. He'd proved too clever for the Americans, though, and had escaped into the desert before they could come for him.

"Can we change?" Halabi said as the younger man approached. "Are my followers capable?"

"Everything is possible with Allah's help."

"But it's far more difficult than I imagined to garner that help."

"No man can see into the mind of God. We can only seek to play our small role in His plan."

Halabi nodded. "Are we ready?"

"We are."

The stairs had been cleared of debris, but the ISIS leader still needed help getting down them. The darkness deepened as they descended into what was left of the building's basement. Halabi felt a moment of panic when the door closed behind them and the blackness recalled the agonizing hours he'd spent dragging himself from the cavern in Iraq.

This time, though, the darkness didn't last. The dim glow of computer monitors coming to life pushed back the emptiness and he found himself standing in front of a series of screens, each depicting a lone male face.

The difference between this ISIS leadership meeting and his last one couldn't have been more stark. The former Iraqi soldiers who had lined up on the ground in front of him and the traitorous Aali Nassar were all dead now. Taken from him by God not as a punishment but because they were useless. He understood that and so much more now.

With his newfound clarity, Halabi saw his past actions as almost comically misguided. He'd put his faith in men who had already been defeated by the Americans once. They'd had no new ideas. No new capabilities. No knowledge or insight that hadn't existed for decades. The most that they could hope to do was bring order and discipline to ISIS's next failure.

A red light flashed on a camera in front of him and the faces on-screen gained resolve. Despite the hardening of their expressions, though, it was clear that none were soldiers. Some were well-groomed and clean-shaven while others had thick beards and unkempt hair. The youngest was barely twenty and the oldest hadn't yet reached his fortieth year of life. Two—one a pale-complected Englishman—didn't even speak rudimentary Arabic.

That diversity went deeper than appearance, extending to their areas of expertise. Computer programming. Marketing. Finance. The sciences. Perhaps most important was a young documentary filmmaker who had spent the last year working for Al Jazeera. The only common thread was that all had been educated in the West. It was something he now required of his inner circle.

While a far cry from the brutal and fanatical forces Halabi had once commanded, these men had the potential to be much more dangerous.

"There was a time when I believed that the movement had lost its way," Halabi said in English, his heavily accented words being transmitted over a secure satellite link. "But now I understand that there was never a path to victory. Osama bin Laden expected his actions in New York to begin the collapse of a society already faltering under the weight of its own moral decay. But what was really accomplished? Punishing but ultimately indecisive wars in Afghanistan and Iraq. A handful of minor follow-up attacks that were lost in America's culture of violence and mass murder. Bin Laden spent his final years bleating like a sheep and waiting for the Americans to find him."

Halabi paused and examined the faces on the screens before him. While these men were indeed different from the ones he'd commanded before, the fire in their eyes burned just as intensely. The movement was everything to them. It gave them purpose. It gave them a target for their fury, hate, and frustration. And it gave them peace.

"Al Qaeda failed because their leadership grew old and forgot what motivates young men," Halabi said flatly.

Osama bin Laden had feared the rise in brutality throughout the region, seeing it as counterproductive to recruitment. Unfortunately, he hadn't lived to see the truth. To see the slickly produced videos of chaotic, merciless victories. To hear the pumping music that accompanied them and the computer-generated imagery that enhanced them. To see thousands of young men, motivated by this propaganda, flood into the Middle East. Ready to fight. Ready to die.

"And ISIS did no better," Halabi continued. "I and my predecessors became intoxicated by the vision of a new caliphate. The Middle East was fractured and the West was tired of fighting wars that couldn't be decisively won. We deluded ourselves into believing that we were ready to come out of the shadows and stand against the U.S. military."

He paused, considering how much he wanted to say. In the end, though, this was the age of information. Withholding it from his inner circle would lead only to another defeat.

"It was all a waste of time and martyrs. The moment for that kind of action had not yet arrived."

"Has it arrived now?" one of the men said, his youthful impatience audible even over the cheap computer speakers. "America is as weak as it has been in a hundred and fifty years. Its people are consumed with hatred for each other. They see themselves as having been cheated by the rest of the world. Stolen from. Taken advantage of. The twenty-four-hour news cycle continues to reinforce these attitudes, as do the Russians' Internet propaganda efforts. And the upcoming presidential election is amplifying those divisions to the point that the country is being torn apart."

"It's not enough," Halabi said. "The Americans are people of extremes, prone to fits of rage and self-destructiveness, but also in possession of an inner strength that no one in history has been able to overcome."

The faces on the screens looked vaguely stunned at what they saw as adulation for their enemy. It was one of many lessons Halabi had learned in his time confined to a hospital bed deep underground: not to let hatred blind one to the strengths and virtues of one's enemies.

"If no one has been able to overcome it," the British man said, "how can we?"

It was the question that Halabi had been asking for almost his entire life. The question that God had finally answered.

"We'll continue to distract them by fanning the flames of their fear and division," he said.

"And after that?" the man pressed.

"After that we'll strike at them in a way that no one in history has ever even conceived of."

CHAPTER 3

THE port city still had more than two million residents, but at this point it was just because they didn't have anywhere else to go. Some buildings remained untouched, but others had taken hits from the Saudi air force and were now in various states of ruin. Almost nightly, bombing runs rewrote the map of Al Hudaydah, strewing tons of rubble across some streets while blasting others clean.

Rapp walked around a burned-out car and turned onto a pitted road that was a bit more populated. Knots of men had formed around wooden carts, buying and trading for whatever was available. Women, covered from head to toe in traditional dress, dotted the crowd, but only sparsely. They tended to be kept squirreled away in this part of the world, adding to the dysfunction.

One was walking toward Rapp, clinging to the arm of a male relative whose function would normally have been to watch over her. In this case, the roles had been reversed. He was carrying the AK-47 and ceremonial dagger that were obligatory fashion accessories in Yemen, but also suffering from one of the severe illnesses unleashed by the war. The woman was the only thing keeping him upright.

He stumbled and Rapp caught him, supporting his weight until he could get his feet under him again. When the woman mumbled her thanks, Rapp figured he'd take advantage of her gratitude. The map he'd been given by the CIA wasn't worth the paper it was printed on.

"Do you know where Café Pachachi is?"

Her eyes—the only part of her visible—widened and she took a hesitant step back.

It wasn't surprising. As ISIS lost territory, a lot of its unpaid and leaderless fighters were turning to extortion, drug trafficking, and sexual slavery to make a living. Rapp's physical appearance and Iraqi accent would likely mark him as one of those men.

"Café Pachachi?" he repeated.

She gave a jerky nod and a few brief instructions before skirting him and disappearing into the glare of the sun.

It took another thirty minutes, but he finally found it. The restaurant was housed in a mostly intact stone building with low plastic tables and chairs set up out front. A few makeshift awnings provided shade, and improvised barriers kept customers from falling into a bomb crater along the eastern edge.

Despite the war, business seemed good. The patio was filled with men leaning close to each other, speaking about politics, God, and death. Waiters hustled in and out of the open storefront, shuttling food and drinks, clearing dishes, and occasionally getting drawn into one of the passionate conversations going on around them.

It was hard to believe that this was pretty much the sum total of the CIA's presence in Yemen. It was one of the most lawless, terrorist-ridden countries in the world, and the United States had ceded its interests to the Saudis.

America's politicians were concerned with nothing but the perpetuation of their own power through the next election cycle. The sitting president was playing defense, trying not to do anything that could cause problems for his party in the upcoming presidential election. The primaries were in full swing, with the sleaziest, most destructive candidates on both sides in the lead. And the American people were laser-locked on all of it, goading the participants on like it was some kind of pro wrestling cage match.

With no one watching the store in Yemen, ISIS was starting to find its footing again—using the chaos as cover to regroup and evolve. It was a mistake the politicians couldn't seem to stop making. Or maybe it wasn't a mistake at all. Terrorism was great theater— full of sympathetic victims, courageous soldiers, and evil antagonists. It was the ultimate political prop. Perhaps America's elected officials weren't as anxious to give it up as their constituents thought. Solved problems didn't get out the vote.

"Allah has delivered you safely!" Shamir Karman exclaimed, weaving through the busy tables to embrace him. "Welcome, my friend!"

Rapp didn't immediately recognize the man. Karman always carried an extra twenty-five or so pounds in a gravity-defying ring around his waist. It was completely gone now and his bearded face looked drawn.

"It's good to see you again," Rapp said in the amiable tone expected by the diners around him.

"Come! There's no reason for us to stand among this riffraff. I keep the good food and coffee in the back."

Laughter rose up from his customers as he led Rapp into the dilapidated building. The human element had always been Karman's genius. The native Yemeni had been recruited by the CIA years ago, but it had been clear from the beginning that he'd never be a shooter. No, his weapon was that he was likable as hell. The kind of guy you told your deepest secrets to. That you wanted in your wedding party. That you invited to come stay indefinitely at your house. All within the first ten minutes of meeting him.

"There was another bombing last night," he said as they passed indoor tables that had been set aside for women to sit with their families.

"Did they get close?"

The Agency was working to keep the Saudis away from this neighborhood, but no one was anxious to tell them too much out of fear of a leak. It was the kind of tightrope walk that was Irene Kennedy's bread and butter, but there were no guarantees. One arrogant commander or confused pilot could turn Karman and his operation into a pillar of fire.

"No. The bastards were just dropping random bombs to hide their real target."

"Which was?"

"The sanitation facility we keep putting back together with spit and chewing gum. We're already dealing with one of the deadliest outbreaks of cholera in history, and they want to make it worse. If they can't bomb us into submission, they'll kill us with disease and hunger."

The anger in his voice wasn't just for the benefit of his cover. In truth, Karman's loyalties were a bit hard to pin down, but that's what made him so good at his job. He sincerely cared about his country, and anyone who met him could feel that sincerity.

"Did you come with family?" the Yemeni said.

It wasn't hard to figure out what he was asking. He was worried that Coleman and his men were in-country and would stand out like a sore thumb. Rapp shared that concern and had sent them to Riyadh. They were currently floating in the pool of a five-star resort at the American taxpayers' expense.

"No. I'm alone."

"You'll stay with me, of course. I can't offer you much luxury, but there's not a lot of that to be had in Yemen anymore."

"Thank you. You're very generous, my friend."

They entered the kitchen and instead of the pleasant odor of boiling saltah, Rapp was hit with the powerful stench of bleach.

"My success isn't just about my skills as a chef and my consistent supply of food," Karman said, reading his expression. "With the cholera outbreak, it's all about cleanliness. No one has ever gotten sick eating at my establishment." He increased the volume of his voice. "And no one ever will, right?"

The kitchen staff loudly assured him that was the case.

"Seriously," he said, pushing through a door at the

back. "Don't put anything in your mouth that doesn't come from here or you'll find yourself shitting and vomiting your guts out. And you'll be doing it on your own. The hospital's been bombed three times and still has hundreds of new patients flooding in every day. The sick and dying are covering every centimeter of floor there and spilling out into the parking lot. I don't know why. There's no medicine. Hardly any staff. Nothing."

The room they found themselves in was about eight feet square, illuminated by a bare bulb hanging from the celling. There was a folding table that served as a desk and a single plastic chair raided from the restaurant. Walls were stacked with boxes labeled with the word "bleach" in Arabic. A few notebooks that looked like business ledgers and a tiny potted plant rounded out the inventory.

According to Rapp's briefing, there was also a hidden chamber with communications equipment and a few weapons, but it was best to use it sparingly. If anyone discovered its existence, Karman's body would be hanging from one of his restaurant's ceiling beams inside an hour.

"Better than bleach . . ." the Yemeni said, rummaging in a box behind him, "is alcohol."

He retrieved a half-full bottle of Jack Daniel's and poured careful measures into two coffee cups before handing one to Rapp.

"Did your work go well?" he asked, keeping the conversation vague and in Arabic. He was well-liked and trusted in the area, but it was still a war zone. People were always listening. Always suspicious.

"No. I wasn't able to connect with our friend."

Karman's face fell. "I'm sorry for that. I did the best I could to schedule it, but you know how unpredictable he can be."

Rapp nodded and took a sip of his drink.

"I've become nothing more than a tea room gossip," Karman said in a hushed tone. "Trying to live off the pittance the restaurant makes and arguing politics with whoever sits down at one of my tables."

The message was clear. He was calling for resources. Unfortunately, the dipshits in Washington weren't in the mood to provide them.

"Really? Business looks good to me."

"An illusion. Customers are dwindling and talk has turned wild. Spies. Intrigue. Conspiracies. I spend my days listening to this and searching the sky for the Saudi missile that will kill me. Or looking behind me for the man who will put a knife in my back for the money in my pocket."

"Former ISIS fighters?" Rapp said.

Karman nodded. "They're heavily armed and purposeless. Young men full of hate, violence, and lust. All believing that their every whim is a directive from God. If Sayid Halabi is alive I would have expected him to move them toward the lawless middle of the country. But he doesn't seem interested. The rumor is that he's forming a much smaller group of well-educated, well-trained followers."

Karman brought his mug to his lips and closed his eyes as he swished the whiskey around in his mouth before swallowing. "People speak of him as though he's a ghost. As if he'd died and returned. They believe that God spoke to him and gave him the secret to defeating the infidels."

"Do you believe that's true?"

"No. But I think Halabi does. And I think that he's even more brilliant than he is twisted. What I can tell you for certain is that ISIS is evolving. And if he's behind that, I guarantee you he's not doing it for his entertainment. He's working toward something. Something big."

Again, Karman was using the cover of idle gossip to make a point: that something needed to be done before Halabi could assert his dominance over a reinvigorated jihadist movement. Unfortunately, he was preaching to the choir. Rapp and Kennedy spent a hell of a lot of time and effort making that precise case to politicians who seemed less interested every day.

Karman reached for a pack of cigarettes and lit one before speaking again. "There's nothing more for us here, my friend. I can't distinguish one day from another anymore. I serve food. I clean. I listen to loose talk. And I wait for death."

CHAPTER 4

THE boy curled up on the dirty cot, covering his mouth and bracing himself for the coughing fit that was to come. Dr. Victoria Schaefer watched helplessly as he convulsed, the sound of his choking muffled by the hazmat suit she was wearing. When it was over, he reached out a hand spattered with blood from his lungs.

She took it, squeezing gently through rubber gloves and fighting back the urge to cry. With the headgear she was wearing, there was no way to wipe the tears away. It was a lesson she'd learned over and over again throughout the years.

"It's going to be all right," she lied through her faceplate.

The respiratory disease she'd stumbled upon in that remote Yemeni village killed more than a third of the people who displayed symptoms. Soon he'd be added to that statistic. And there was nothing she could do about it.

He managed to say something as he pointed to another of the cots lined up in the tiny stone building.

She didn't understand the words—bringing her inter-preter into this makeshift clinic would have been too dangerous—but she understood their meaning. The woman lying by the door was his mother. After days of struggling for every breath, she'd lost her fight two hours ago.

"She's just sleeping," Schaefer said in as soothing a tone as she could manage.

The boy was young enough to have eyes still full of trust and hope. In contrast, the adults in the village had started to lose faith in her. And why not? Even before her medical supplies had dwindled, she'd been largely powerless. Beyond keeping victims as comfortable as possible and treating their secondary infections with antibiotics, there was little choice but to just let the virus run its course.

The boy lost consciousness and Schaefer walked through the gloom to a stool in the corner. The win-dows had been sealed and the door was closed tight against a jamb enhanced with rubber stripping. Light was provided by a hole in the roof covered with a piece of white cloth that was the best filter they could come up with.

The other three living people in the building were in various stages of the illness. One—ironically a man who estimated himself to be in his late sixties—was on his way to recovery. What that recovery would look like, though, she wasn't sure. Yemeni acute respira-tory syndrome, as they'd dubbed it, left about thirty percent of its survivors permanently disabled. It was almost certain that he would never be able to work again. The question was whether he would even be able to care for himself without assistance.

The ultimate fate of the other two victims was unknown. They were in the early stages and it was still too soon to tell. Both were strong and in their twenties, but that didn't seem to make any difference to YARS. It was an equal opportunity killer that took healthy adults at about the same rate it did children and the elderly.

The boy started to cough again, but this time she didn't go to him, instead staring down at his blood on her gloves. She'd leave his mother where he could see her and take comfort from her presence. The heat in the building was suffocating, but it didn't matter. He wouldn't last long enough for her to start to decompose.

"Vick—"

The satellite phone cut out and Schaefer shook it violently. Not the most high-tech solution, but it seemed to work. She was able to make out the last few words of her boss's sentence, but ignored them. Ken Dinh was the president of Doctors Without Borders, a good man and a personal friend. But he was sitting behind a desk in Toronto and she was on the ground in the middle-of-nowhere Yemen.

"Are you listening to what I'm saying, Vicky?"

No one was watching, so she allowed herself a guilty frown. At forty-two, she'd already been through a number of husbands, all of whom had roughly the same complaints. The top of the list was that she was obsessed with her job. Second was that she was—to use her last husband's words—always camped out in some war-torn, disease-ridden, third-world hellhole. The last one was something about never listening and instead just waiting to talk. She wasn't sure, though, because she hadn't really been listening.

"I heard you but I don't know what you want me to say. No worries? Hey, maybe it's not as bad as it looks? And what do you want me to tell the people in this village? Take two aspirin and call me in the morning?"

"This sarcasm isn't like you, Vicky."

"Seriously?"

"No. Obviously that was a joke."

"So now we're going to sit around telling jokes?"

Even from half a world away she could hear his deep sigh. "But it's *isolated*, right? You haven't seen or heard anything that points to an outbreak outside that village."

She'd walked about a third of a mile to make the call, stopping partway up a slope containing boulders big enough to provide shade. It was the place she came when she needed to be alone. When she needed to find a little perspective in a world that didn't offer much anymore.

The village below wasn't much to look at, a few buildings constructed of the same reddish stone and dirt that extended to the horizon in every direction. She surveyed it for a few moments instead of answering. Dinh was technically right. The disease she'd discovered appeared to be isolated to this forgotten place and its forty-three remaining inhabitants.

And because of that, no one cared. It had no strategic relevance to the Houthi rebels or government forces fighting for control of the country. The ISIS and al Qaeda forces operating in the area didn't consider it a sufficient prize to send the two or three armed men necessary to take it. And the Saudis had no reason to waste fuel and ordnance blowing it up.

The disease devastating the village had probably come from one of the bat populations living in caves set into the slope she was now calling from. But the specialists she'd consulted assured her that their range was nowhere near sufficient to make it to the closest population center—a similarly tiny village over forty hard miles to the east.

"It's isolated," she admitted finally. "But I don't know for how much longer. I'm containing it by giving these people food and health care so none of them have any reason to leave. And I'm counting on the fact that no one from outside has any reason to come. Is that what you want to hang your hat on?"

"You also told me that you thought the whole thing was a fluke, right? The war cut off the village's food supply and they started eating bats for the first time?"

"That's just a guess," she responded through clenched teeth. "We can't get anyone with the right expertise to come here to do the testing. Look, Ken, I'm here with one nurse and a microbiologist who's only interested in getting his name in the science journals. Twenty-five people in this village are dead. That's a third of the population."

"But you've stopped the spread, right? You've got it under control."

"We've got the last few identified victims quarantined and for now we've convinced the villagers to steer clear of the local bat population," she admitted. "But it's incredibly contagious, Ken. Not like anything I've seen in my lifetime. Even casual contact with someone who's sick comes with over a fifty percent infection rate. But the worst thing is how long the virus seems to be able to survive on surfaces. We have credible evidence of people getting sick after touching things handled by a victim seventy-two hours before. What if someone infected with this went through an airport? They could push a button on an elevator or touch the check-in counter and have people carry it all over the world. How could we stop it?"

"We stopped it last time," he said in an obvious reference to the SARS outbreak in the early 2000s.

"It's not the same thing and you know it! SARS is an order of magnitude less contagious and it broke out in Asia. We had time to mount a worldwide response in countries with modern medical systems. This is Yemen. They don't have the resources to do anything but stand back and pray. We could be talking about a pandemic that could kill a hundred million people. Are you a doctor or a politician, Ken? We—"

"Shut up, Vicky! Just shut your mouth for one minute if that's possible."

She fell silent at the man's uncharacteristic outburst.

"Do you have any idea what's happening in the rest of Yemen? Outside your little world? We're dealing with a cholera outbreak that's now officially the worst in modern history. NGOs are backing out because of the bombing and growing violence. Local medical personnel are either sick themselves or haven't been paid in months and are moving on to figure out how to feed themselves."

"Ken—"

"I'm not done! About a third of the country is slowly starving. We're seeing infections that none of our antibiotics work on. And there are rumors that there's going to be a major attack on Al Hudaydah. If that port closes, most of the imports into the country are going to dry up. No more humanitarian aid. No more food or medicine. No more fuel. On top of everything else, the country's going to slip into famine."

"But—" she tried to interject.

"Shut it!" he said and then continued. "All this and I can barely get governments or private donors to take my calls. Why? Because no one gives a crap about Yemen. They can't find it on a map and they're bone tired of pouring money into Middle East projects that get blown up before they're even finished. And that's leaving aside the U.S. presidential election that's already consuming every media outlet in the world. If an alien spaceship landed in Yemen tomorrow, it'd be lucky to make page nine in the *Times*."

"Ken—"

"Shut up, shut up, *shut up!*" he said. "Now, where was I? Oh, yeah. So, after all that's said, you want me to divert my almost nonexistent resources from the thousands of people dying in the cities to a little village of fifty people surrounded by an impassable sea of desert?"

"Screw you, Ken."

When he spoke again, his voice had softened. "Look. I really do understand what you're saying to me. Remember that before I sat down behind this desk I spent years doing exactly what you're doing. I want to help you. What you're dealing with terrifies me—"

"But you're going to do nothing."

"Oh, ye of little faith."

She perked up. "What does that mean?"

"I wish I could take credit for this, but in truth I had nothing to do with it. A couple weeks ago, a Saudi businessman I've never heard of contacted me. He said he'd seen something about you in a university newspaper and wanted to help. It kind of took me by surprise, so I just threw a number out there."

"What number?"

"Two hundred and fifty grand."

"And?"

"Long story, but he said yes."

"What?" Victoria stammered, unable to process what she was hearing after months of fighting for cast-offs and pocket change. "I . . . I don't even understand what that means."

"It means that I've got a team putting together a drop for you. Equipment, food, medicine. I might even have someone from the University of Wyoming who's willing to look at your bats. We'll lower the supplies down to you from a cargo chopper so we don't have to get anywhere near your patients. I'm working on permission from the Saudis now."

"Why didn't you tell me this when we started talking?"

"Because I wanted you to make an ass out of yourself. Now, listen to me. This isn't a bottomless well. I don't even know how to get in touch with this donor. He wanted to be anonymous and he's doing a good job of it. Get that village healthy and figure out a way to keep them that way."

"Ken. I'm sorry about—"

The line went dead and she dropped the phone, leaning against the rock behind her.

It was hard to remember everything that had

happened to get her to that particular place at that particular time. Her childhood outside of Seattle had been unremarkable. She'd never traveled much and she'd stayed in Washington through her early career as a physician. It wasn't until she was in her early thirties that she'd felt the pull of the outside world and the billions of desperate people who inhabited it.

Schaefer scooted away from the approaching rays of sun and focused on the village below. The door to their improvised clinic opened and a man in protective clothing appeared, shading his faceplate-covered eyes as he emerged. Otto Vogel was her no-nonsense German pillar of steel. They'd met in Ghana seven years ago and had been working together ever since. Not only was he the best nurse she'd ever met, but he was perhaps the most reliable person on the planet. There was no situation that he couldn't deal with, no disaster that could ruffle him, no objective danger that could scare him. They'd been through Haiti, Nigeria, and Laos together, to name only a few. And now here they were in Yemen. The world's forgotten humanitarian disaster.

He scanned the terrain, finally finding her hidden among the rocks. She'd told him that she was calling Ken Dinh and it wouldn't be hard for him to guess that she'd do it from the shade of her favorite boulder.

Vogel made an exaggerated motion toward his wrist. He wasn't actually wearing a watch, but she understood that it was a reference to the tardiness of their third musketeer. A man who was less a pillar of steel and more a pile of shit softened by the heat.

When Vogel disappeared around the corner to begin removing his contaminated clothing, she stood

and reluctantly started toward a building at the opposite edge of the village.

When she finally pushed through the door of the
stone structure she found a lone man scribbling in a
notebook. He was only partially visible behind the
battered lab equipment she'd borrowed from fleeing
NGOs. Usually while wearing a black turtleneck and
driving a van with the headlights turned off.

"You were supposed to relieve Otto more than a
half an hour ago," she said.

The initial reaction was an irritated frown—
intimidating to the grad students who hung on his
every word, but not as weighty in Yemen.

"I'm in the middle of something," he said. His
English was grammatically perfect, but he took pride
in maintaining a thick French accent. "I need to work
through it while my mind is fresh."

Gabriel Bertrand was a world-class prick but
unquestionably a brilliant one. He'd started his career
as a physician, but after discovering that he didn't like
being around sick people, he'd moved into research
and teaching.

"I appreciate that," she said, her good mood
managing to hold. "But we've got people dying in that
building. Otto and I can't handle—"

"Then let me help them, Victoria! You know
perfectly well that we don't know how to save those
people. What I'm doing here could prevent future
victims. It could—"

"Get you a big prize and invitations to all the right
Paris cocktail parties?"

That condescending frown again. This time aimed
over his reading glasses. "If this disease ever defeats

our containment measures, it's going to be *my* work that's important. Not what's being done in your little infirmary."

"Tell that to the people in the little infirmary."

"There's a bigger picture here. In fact, I'm guessing that a few minutes ago, you were trying to impress that very fact on Ken Dinh."

He stood from behind his improvised desk and moved a little too close, rubbing a hand over her bare shoulder. She was quite a bit older than the coeds he normally hit on, but she was still trim, with long blond hair and the tan that she'd always aspired to while growing up in the Pacific Northwest. More important, she was the only game in town.

"Your narrative can be featured prominently in my work. It would come off as very heroic. That wouldn't be bad for your career."

In her youth, she'd have probably gone for him. The brilliant, distinguished ones had always gotten to her. But not anymore. She'd seen way too much.

"Ten minutes, Bert," she said using the shortened version of his name that he despised. "After that, I'm going to have Otto drag you out of here."

CHAPTER 5

"Two orders of saltah," Shamir Karman shouted through the open door of the restaurant. "And do we still have any bottled cola?"

Rapp was sitting alone at one of the tables outside, drinking coffee and working through the pack of cigarettes he always traveled with in this part of the world. It was still early and the sun was at a steep enough angle to shade the improvised terrace. Around him, about a quarter of the tables were occupied by men sipping from steaming cups, gossiping, and shooting occasional jealous glances at Rapp's smokes.

If he ignored the bomb crater behind him and the collapsed buildings in front, it all seemed pretty normal. Not much different than a thousand other cafes Rapp had eaten in over the last twenty years of his life. According to Karman, though, the illusion of business as usual would disappear sometime around lunch.

Apparently, his restaurant—along with all the other struggling businesses in the area—was being shaken down by an organized crime outfit made up of former ISIS fighters. The gang had their hands in just about every dirty enterprise going on in Al Hudaydah, but that wasn't what had attracted Rapp's attention. No, his interest was in the whispers that they were still connected to Sayid Halabi.

The question was whether those rumors were true or just marketing. Staying in the glow of the ISIS leader's legend would be good for the images of men who were now nothing more than unusually sadistic criminals. Anything they could do to amplify the fear of the desperate people they preyed upon worked in their favor.

If it was true that Halabi was trying to build a smarter, more agile organization, it was possible that he'd completely severed his ties with the morons terrorizing Al Hudaydah. On the other hand, men willing to martyr themselves could be extremely powerful weapons. Maybe too powerful for Halabi to give up.

After four more hours, all the tables were full and the conversations had turned into an indecipherable roar. Waiters weaved skillfully through the customers, serving coffee, tea, and dishes prepared by Karman's harried kitchen staff. Tattered umbrellas had gone up and people huddled beneath them, trying to escape the increasingly powerful sun.

Rapp was almost through his bowl of marak temani when the buzz of conversation began to falter. He glanced behind him and quickly picked out the cause of the interruption: two hard-looking young men approaching. They were armed with AKs like just about every other Yemeni male, but these weren't fashion accessories. They were slung at the ready across their torsos with fingers on the trigger guards.

That, combined with their sweeping eyes and cruel expressions, suggested they weren't there for the food.

Rapp waited for them to enter the restaurant before
following. The sparsely populated interior had gone
dead silent except for Karman, who was standing in
the kitchen door inviting the men inside.

Again, Rapp followed, slipping into the hectic
kitchen in time to see his old friend lead one of the
men to his office. The other stood near the open door,
chewing khat and scanning for threats.

Not ready to be identified as yet, Rapp angled
toward an employee bathroom at the far end of the
kitchen. After pretending to test the door and find it
locked, he pressed his back against the wall and lit
another cigarette.

It was hard to see into the office but there was just
enough light for Rapp to make out Karman opening
a small lockbox. The Yemeni started calmly counting bills onto the table as the other man speculated
loudly about the success of the restaurant and whether
he was being paid fairly. In the end, the calculations
proved too taxing and he just snatched a little extra
from the box before scooping up the stack Karman
had dealt out. A hard shove sent the CIA informant
stumbling backward into his chair with enough force
that it almost flipped.

The kitchen staff bowed their heads as the two men
left, careful to not make eye contact. Rapp didn't follow suit, instead staring intently at them. Neither
noticed. They were too busy arguing about how they
were going to split the unexpected bonus cash.

After they disappeared back out into the dining
room, Rapp tossed his half-smoked cigarette on the

floor and started after them. By the time he stepped into the blinding sun, the men had a twenty-yard lead. He let that extend a bit as he swung by his table and slammed back the rest of what might have been the best cup of coffee he'd ever had.

They led him through the sparsely populated maze of streets, finally arriving at a bustling market. The stench of sweat and raw sewage filled Rapp's nostrils as he watched the men work their way through the stands, extorting money from each of their cowering proprietors.

The sun was sinking low on the horizon by the time the men finished their rounds through the business district and started toward a more desperate area of town. Rapp was getting hungry and thirsty, but the occasional corpse of a cholera victim awaiting removal kept him from doing anything about it.

The dust caked in his throat and the empty stomach just added to the anger that had been building in him all day. Watching these men steal from people who had virtually nothing was something he'd seen before, but it never got any more pleasant. Rapp had dedicated his life to eradicating this kind of scum from the earth, but there seemed to be an endless supply.

They finally stopped at a house that had been repaired with tarps and other scrounged materials. Rapp assumed they were done for the day and had led him to their base of operations, but he turned out to be wrong.

A halfhearted kick from one of the men knocked in what was left of a wooden door and they disappeared inside. Weak shouts and the screams of children flowed through the empty window frames as Rapp moved into a shadowed position that still gave him a solid line of sight.

The ISIS men reappeared a few minutes later with a girl of about fourteen in tow. She was struggling and screaming, trying futilely to break free and retreat back into the house. A moment later a man Rapp assumed was her father came after her, grabbing one of the men, but then collapsing to the ground. The remaining glow from the sun glistened off his sweat-soaked skin, highlighting its pallor and dark, sunken eyes. Another victim of Al Hudaydah's nonfunctional sanitation system and lack of medicine. The ISIS men just laughed and continued dragging his daughter up the street.

What followed was easily predicted: the journey to a somewhat more affluent part of town. The dull stares of the people along the route, their lives too close to the edge to interfere. The delivery to a man who paid in cash. Her screams penetrating the walls of the house and echoing up the street.

Rapp followed the men, trying to block out the girl's cries for help. He'd been in a similar situation in Iraq and it was one of the few episodes in his life that wouldn't leave him alone. His stride faltered and he considered going back, but knew that it was impossible. She was one of thousands. The mission wasn't one girl. It couldn't be.

The night was starting to get cold when the two men led him to a block of commercial buildings that had been spared from bombing. They disappeared into a small warehouse and Rapp came to a stop, staring blankly at the stone structure. What he wanted to do was walk in there and execute every son of a bitch inside.

It would be so easy. Men like that had no real skill or training and they became accustomed to everyone being too afraid or weak to move against them. While they expected to die one day in a battle or a drone strike, the idea of one man acting against them was unfathomable. If Rapp's experience was any indicator, they'd just sit there like a bunch of idiots while he emptied his Glock into their skulls.

A beautiful fantasy, but like the empty heroism of saving the girl, an impossible one. This was the real world—a dirty, violent place, where wins came at a high price. Even capturing and interrogating them would be of limited value. Far more useful would be figuring out how many men were in there, getting photos that the CIA might be able to connect with names, and compromising their communications.

Halabi was out there and he was going to hunt that bastard down and stick a knife in his eye socket—even if it meant he had to do the thing he hated most in life.

Wait.

CHAPTER 6

THE late afternoon sun cast virtually no shadows because there was little to create them. The terrain here consisted of nothing but blunt ridges, rocky desert soil, and a single, poorly defined road disappearing over the slope ahead. Mullah Sayid Halabi didn't see any of it, though. Instead, he focused on the sky. The Americans were up there. As were the Saudis. Watching. Analyzing. Waiting for an opportunity to strike.

Normally he didn't emerge during the day. His life was lived almost entirely underground now, an existence of darkness broken by dim, artificial light, and the occasional transfer beneath the stars. The risk he was running now was unacceptably high and taken for what seemed to be the most absurd reason imaginable. One of his young disciples had said that this was the time of day that the light was most attractive.

It was indeed a new era.

He was positioned in the center of a small convoy consisting of vehicles taken from the few charitable organizations still working in the country. A bulky

SUV led the way and a supply truck trailed them at a distance of twenty meters, struggling with the rutted track.

The Toyota Land Cruiser he was in was the most comfortable of the three, with luxurious leather seats, air-conditioning, and the blood of its former driver painted across the dashboard.

The men crammed into the vehicles represented a significant percentage of the forces under his direct command. It was another disorienting change. He'd once led armies that had rolled across the Middle East in the modern instruments of war. His fanatical warriors had taken control of huge swaths of land, sending thousands of Western trained forces fleeing in terror. He had built the foundation of a new caliphate that had the potential to spread throughout the region.

And then he had lost it.

That defeat and his months convalescing from Mitch Rapp's attack had left him with a great deal of time to think. About his victories. His defeats. His weaknesses as a leader and failings as a disciple of the one true God. Ironically, the words that had been the seed of his new strategy were said to have come from an agnostic Jew.

The definition of insanity is doing the same thing over and over and expecting a different result.

While his current forces were limited in number, they were substantially different than those that came before. All would give their lives for him and the cause, of course. But the region was full of such fighters. What set the men with him apart was their level of education and training. All could read, write, and speak at least functional English. All were former

soldiers trained by the Americans or other Westerners. And all had long, distinguished combat records.

His problems had come to parallel the ones that
plagued the American military and intelligence
community: finding good men and managing them
effectively. The well-disciplined soldiers with him
today were relatively easy to deal with—all were accustomed to the rigid command structure he'd created.
The technical people spread across the globe, though,
posed a different challenge. They were temperamen-
tal, fearful, and unpredictable. Unfortunately, they
were also the most critical part in the machine he was
building.

The lead vehicle came to a stop and Halabi rolled
down his window, leaning out to read a large sign
propped in a pile of rocks. It carried the Doctors
Without Borders logo as well as a skull and cross-
bones and biohazard symbol. In the center was text in
various languages explaining the existence of a severe
disease in the village ahead and warning off anyone
approaching. Punctuating those words was a line of
large rocks blocking the road.

Muhammad Attia, his second in command, leapt
from the lead vehicle and directed the removal of the
improvised barrier.

It was a strangely disturbing scene. They worked
with a precision that could only be described as Western. The economy of their movements, combined with
their camouflage uniforms, helmets, and goggles,
made them indistinguishable from the American
soldiers that Halabi despised. The benefits of adopting
the methods of his enemy, though, were undeniable.
In less than three minutes they were moving again.

The village revealed itself fifteen minutes later, looking exactly as expected from the reconnaissance photos his team had gathered. A few people were visible moving through the spaces between stone buildings, but he was much more interested in the ones running up the road toward him. The blond woman was waving her arms in warning while the local man behind her struggled to keep up.

She stopped directly in front of their motorcade, shouting and motioning them back. When the lead car stopped, she jogged to its open side window. Halabi was surprised by the intensity of his anticipation as he watched her speak with the driver through her translator.

Of course, Halabi knew everything about her. He'd had a devoted follower call Doctors Without Borders and, in return for a sizable donation to her project, the organization's director had been willing to answer any question he was asked. In addition, Halabi's computer experts had gained access to her social media and email accounts, as well as a disused blog she'd once maintained.

Victoria Schaefer had spent years with the NGO, largely partnered with a German nurse named Otto Vogel. Though she was a whore who had been through multiple husbands, there was no evidence of a relationship between her and the German that went beyond friendship and mutual respect. She was ostensibly in charge of the management of the operation there, but it was the as-yet-unseen Frenchman who was the driving force behind the research being done.

Her relationship with Dr. Gabriel Bertrand was somewhat more complex. Based on intercepted messages sent to family members, she despised the man but acknowledged his genius and indispensability. Bertrand's own Internet accounts were even more illuminating, portraying an obsessive, arrogant, and selfish man dedicated largely to the pursuit of his own ambition. He had no family he remained in regular contact with and was blandly noncommittal in his responses to correspondence sent by the various women he had relationships with in Europe.

Schaefer began stalking toward Halabi's vehicle with her translator in tow, apparently unsatisfied by the response she was getting from the lead car.

"We speak English," Halabi said, noting the frustration in her expression as she came alongside.

"Then what in God's name are you doing here? Didn't you see the sign? Why did you move the rocks we put up?"

Halabi gave a short nod and his driver fired a silenced pistol through the window. The round passed by the woman and struck her translator in the chest. He fell to the ground and she staggered back, stunned. A moment later, her instincts as a physician took over and she dropped to her knees, tearing his shirt open. When she saw the irreparable hole over his heart, she turned back toward them. Surprisingly, there was no fear in her eyes. Just hate.

Only when Halabi's driver threw his door open did she run. Chasing her down was a trivial matter, and she was bound with the same efficiency that had been deployed to clear the rock barrier. Once she was safely in the SUV's backseat, Halabi's men spread out, mounting a well-ordered assault on their target.

The handful of villagers outside realized what was happening and began to run just as the woman had. All were taken out in the same way as the translator— with a single suppressed round. It was an admittedly impressive display. The last victim, a child of around ten, was dead before the first victim had hit the ground. It was unlikely that America's SEALs or Britain's SAS could have acted more quickly or silently.

His driver stopped fifty meters from the first building and Halabi watched the operation through the dusty windshield.

Two men went directly for the building that their spotter confirmed was currently occupied by both Gabriel Bertrand and Otto Vogel. The other men penetrated the tiny village to carry out a plan developed by Muhammad Attia.

Each carried a battery-powered nail gun and they moved quickly through the tightly packed stone dwellings, firing nails through the wood doors and frames, sealing the people in their homes. As anticipated, the entire operation took less than four minutes. The muffled shouts of confused inhabitants started as they tried futilely to open their doors. One woman opened shutters that had been closed against the heat and was hit in the forehead by another perfectly aimed bullet. The round wasn't audible from Halabi's position, but the shouts of her husband and shrieks of her children penetrated the vehicle easily.

As the Frenchman and German were dragged from the lab, Halabi's men began prying open shutters and throwing purpose-built incendiary devices into the homes and other buildings, carefully avoiding the structure that had been repurposed as a hospital. The screams of the inhabitants became deafening as they began to burn.

Halabi finally stepped from the vehicle, walking toward the village as a man followed along, filming with an elaborate high-definition camera. He focused on Halabi's face for a moment, drawing in on the patch covering his useless left eye—a battle scar all the more dramatic for having been inflicted by the infamous Mitch Rapp. Halabi's awkward use of a cane to help him walk, on the other hand, would be artistically obscured. While that too was a result of Rapp's attack, it made him appear old and physically weak—things that were unacceptable in this part of the world.

Smoke billowed dramatically over him as he gazed into the flames. A woman managed to shove a crying child through a window but he was shot before he could even get to his feet. The Frenchman was blubbering similarly, lying on the ground in front of his still-intact lab while the woman and the German were pushed down next to him.

Halabi took a position next to them and his videographer crouched to frame the bound Westerners with the mullah towering over them. Halabi looked down at the helpless people at his feet and then back at the camera.

"Now I have your biological weapons experts," he said in practiced English. "Now I have the power to use your weapons against you."

The man with the camera seemed a bit dazed by the brutal reality of the operation, but gave a weak thumbs-up. In postproduction he would add music, terrifying stock images, and whatever else was necessary to turn the footage into a propaganda tool far more potent than any IED or suicide bomber.

A few moments later, Muhammad Attia took Halabi by the arm and helped him back to the vehicle. His driver already had the door open, but Halabi resisted being assisted inside.

"The smoke could attract the attention of the Saudis," Attia warned. "We need to be far from this place before that happens."

Halabi nodded as the medical people were dragged to another of the vehicles.

"Be that as it may, your men will stay."

"Stay? Why? I don't understand."

"Because he's coming, Muhammad."

"Who?"

"Rapp."

One of his men had survived the recent assault on the cave where Halabi had recovered from his injuries. The description of the attackers could be no one but Rapp and the former American soldiers he worked with.

"He missed you in the cave," Attia protested. "Why would he still be in Yemen?"

"Because he doesn't give up, Muhammad. He's still here. I can feel him. And when he finds out I was in this village, he'll come."

"Even if that's true, we can't spare—"

"Tell your men not to kill him," Halabi interjected. "I want him captured."

"Captured? Why?"

Halabi didn't answer, instead lowering himself into the Land Cruiser.

Why? It was simple. He wanted to break Rapp. Over months. Perhaps even years. He'd make the CIA man beg. Crawl. Turn him into a pet, naked and helpless in his cage, looking with fear and longing into the eyes of his master.

CHAPTER 7

SENATOR Christine Barnett continued to hold the phone to her ear but had stopped listening more than a minute ago. Instead she leaned back in her chair and gazed disinterestedly around her office. The heavy, polished wood. The photos of her with powerful people throughout the world. The awards and recognition she'd received over a lifetime of successes.

There was a pause in the dialogue, and she voiced a few practiced platitudes that set the man to talking again. He was an important donor who expected this kind of personal access, but also one of the most tedious pricks alive. He'd grown up in the shadow of World War II and was still a true believer—in America, in God, in objective truth. A doddering old fool trapped in a web of things that no longer mattered.

There was a no-nonsense knock on her door and a moment later someone more interesting entered.

Kevin Gray wore the slightly disheveled suit and overly imaginative tie that everyone in Washington had come to associate with him. He was only in his mid-thirties but still had managed to rack up a series of successes that nearly rivaled her own. A Harvard master's degree, a brief career with a top marketing firm, and finally a splashy entry into the world of politics.

He struggled sometimes to focus, but was unquestionably a creative genius—a man who could communicate with equal facility to all demographic groups and who always seemed to know what was coming next. Every new platform, every new style of messaging, and every cultural shift seemed to settle into his mind six months before anyone else even had an inkling. That, combined with his ability to act decisively on those abstractions, had made it possible for him to get a number of ostensibly unelectable people comfortable seats in Congress.

Her campaign was completely different, of course. The comfortable seat she was looking for was in the Oval Office and, with the exception of being a woman, she was eminently electable. A number of people in her party thought she'd been insane to hire Gray— dismissing him as a bottom feeder who relied on tricks and barely ethical tactics to salvage failed campaigns.

As usual, they'd been wrong and she'd been right. With a strong candidate to work with, the Gray magic became even more powerful. She was now thirty points ahead in the primary race and had become her party's de facto candidate for the election that was already consuming the nation.

A few of her primary opponents were staying in the race, but more to position themselves for a place in her administration than any hope they could overtake her in the polls. She would be the nominee. And based on the weakness of her likely opponent in the general election, she would become the first female president of the United States.

At least that was the opinion of the idiot pollsters and television pundits. But if she'd learned anything as a woman in the most cutthroat business in the world, it was to not take anything for granted.

Gray sat in front of her desk and crossed his legs, bouncing his loafer-clad foot in a way that she'd come to recognize as a sign of impatience. The call was winding down, but she asked an open-ended question to the man on the other end of the line to prolong it. This was her office and her campaign. Gray needed to remember that.

After another five minutes, she felt like she'd made her point and wrapped up the call. "I understand — exactly what you're talking about, Henry. It's why I'm running for president. And it's why I'm going to win."

Gray held up a thumb drive before she could even get the handset back in its cradle.

"Have you seen it?"

She had no idea what he was talking about but whatever *it* was must have been important. Normally the first words out of Gray's mouth when she hung up with a donor were "How much?"

"I haven't seen anything other than the inside of this office. And I haven't talked about anything but taxes, guns, and environmental regulations. What is it?"

"Mullah Sayid Halabi."

"What do I care about a dead terrorist?"

A smile spread slowly across his face. "You care that he's not actually dead."

"What are you talking about?"

He slipped the drive into his tablet and transmitted its contents to a television hanging on the wall.

Barnett watched in stunned silence as a slickly produced propaganda piece played out on the screen. Dramatic historical images of Halabi and ISIS victories accompanied by a voice-over diatribe about America and the West. In accented English and with a background of modern Arab music, he called on Muslim people throughout the world to unite against the infidels.

Just after that plea, the video stabilized, depicting him standing in front of a primitive village that was being consumed by fire. He appeared and disappeared in the smoke like a ghost, accusing the villagers of helping the Americans develop biological weapons to be used against the Muslim people.

Quick image cuts to bacteria squirming under magnification, overflowing hospitals, and diseased human flesh followed before returning to Halabi. Heavy-handed, but unquestionably effective.

The camera angle widened to encompass three people bound at the ISIS leader's feet.

"Now I have your biological weapons experts," he said, staring directly into the lens. "Now I have the power to use your weapons against you."

The screen faded to black and Christine Barnett just stared at it, her mind bogging down on the almost infinite political possibilities Halabi's survival provided.

"That video hit the Internet a few hours ago in Arabic and English," Gray said. "And it's expanding into other languages every few minutes."

"Are we sure that the footage of Halabi isn't old? From before Mitch Rapp supposedly killed him?"

"One hundred percent. According to the CIA, that video from that burning village was taken three days ago in Yemen."

Barnett felt her mouth start to go dry. "Who are the people tied up?"

"Doctors Without Borders. They were there treating the villagers for some respiratory infection."

"Do any of them really know anything about bioweapons?"

"One of them is a microbiologist from the Sorbonne in France. Obviously, his field isn't bioweapons, but he certainly has that kind of expertise. The woman is an American doctor and the other man is a nurse."

Barnett stood and began pacing around the spacious office. At this point the kidnapped doctors were a secondary consideration. Window dressing for the real issue at hand. Mitch Rapp and Irene Kennedy had screwed up. Badly.

"So Halabi isn't dead like the Agency told us."

"Actually, they said that Rapp threw a grenade at him but they couldn't confirm the kill because of the collapse of the cave system."

"The American people don't do nuance and they have the attention span of a goldfish. What they're going to remember is President Alexander telling them that we hit him with a bomb and that we haven't heard from him since. Now we find out he's been around all along. Hiding. Planning. And now capturing a Frenchman capable of building a bioweapon. All right under the noses of Irene Kennedy and Mitch

Rapp." She spun toward Gray. "I assume the video's starting to get traction in the media?"

"It started on the jihadist sites and now it's all over Al Jazeera. The U.S. stations are just starting to pick it up. Of course the Internet is way ahead of all of them. It's lighting up with hysterical predictions and partisan finger pointing. Half the trolls are saying we brought this on ourselves and the other half are proposing war with every country in the Middle East."

She started pacing again, turning what she'd been told over in her head. Alexander had been in power for almost eight years, with only one moderately successful attack on the United States and a number thwarted—largely by some combination of Rapp and Kennedy. The economy was solid with a deficit that was starting to decline. And the president was a generally well-liked former University of Alabama quarterback. It didn't leave much room to generate the kind of fear, rage, and sense of victimization that was necessary to win an election. Up to now, she'd been forced to focus on humanity's natural tendency toward tribalism to fuel her campaign. And while it had been effective thus far, it was really just smoke that could dissipate at the slightest breeze.

"Could this be it, Kevin? Could this be our issue?"

"It's not an attack, Senator. It's just a video. A good one for sure, but—"

"The danger exists now, though. It's not theoretical. It's right there. On TV. This administration failed to kill Halabi and now he has bioweapon technology. Maybe the only reason there hasn't been a successful attack on U.S. soil is because ISIS was concentrating on the Middle East. But now they're focused on us and the CIA has no idea what to do about it."

Gray folded his arms across his chest and stared out the window for a few seconds before speaking. "The American people like their safety. It's an issue that cuts across partisan lines and resonates with the un-decideds. And it's something real to go after Alexander on. This happened on his watch."

She nodded. Alexander's vice president was likely going to be the nominee and he wasn't much of a threat in and of himself—a seventy-two-year-old blue-blood with an increasing tendency to babble about the past. It was Alexander's support for him that made the man dangerous. Halabi's survival, though, could take the president's legs out from under him. If he could be forced to focus on his own political survival and legacy, there wouldn't be much capital left for him to expend supporting his party's candidate.

"Can we use this to bring down Alexander? Maybe even make him a liability?"

"I'm not sure," Gray hedged. "There hasn't—"

"Bullshit, you're not sure. With the right message, repeated enough times on enough media outlets, you could turn the American people against Jesus Christ himself."

He frowned. "You shouldn't blaspheme."

"When did you turn into a Boy Scout?"

"One of these days you're going to slip and say something like that on a hot mike."

"Don't try to change the subject. How hard can this be? Halabi's churning out propaganda videos left and right. The media's going to eat it up and the Internet is going to turn it toxic. All we have to do is make sure it hits our target."

His enthusiasm for her idea seemed unusually muted. The man loved manipulating people. The strange truth was that he didn't care about the trappings of power, just the exercise of it. He wanted to bend people to his will. To force them to turn away from reality and replace it with his carefully crafted speeches, tweets, and ads. Instead of the calculating excitement she'd expected, though, he looked worried.

"What?" she said.

"Do you think Halabi could actually succeed in an attack?"

She didn't answer, instead walking to the window and pretending to look out. In truth, she was focused on her own reflection, searching her carefully curated appearance for anything that didn't seem presidential. At fifty-two, she was still an extremely attractive woman—a product of good genetics, a rigid workout schedule, and a few discreet cosmetic procedures. The blue suit was conservative in style but fit her curves in a way that treaded the line between sex and power. Her still largely unlined face was framed by dark hair that could be used as a surprisingly versatile prop depending on her audience.

As always, everything was perfect. Despite that, it was still almost impossible to believe that she was about to become the most powerful person in the world. She had been neither born to power nor groomed for it. Her entry into politics had been largely at the whim of her tech billionaire husband. It was he who had suggested that she leave her law practice and run for an open seat in the Senate.

His company had been under heavy scrutiny by the Securities and Exchange Commission and other regulatory agencies for improprieties that had the potential to cause both of them serious problems. He'd backed her candidacy with virtually unlimited funds, and when she'd won, she'd used her new political clout to make their problems go away.

But it hadn't ended there. Her gift for politics had been immediately obvious, and over the course of fifteen short years she'd risen to become the chair of the Senate Intelligence Committee. Now she was poised to take the Oval Office.

Her husband, on the other hand, had been relegated to an increasingly secondary role. While still successful as a venture capitalist, he now lived a relatively anonymous life in Chicago, where her two children were in college. They saw each other often enough to keep the press happy, but otherwise their family functioned more as a business than anything else. Her husband continued to provide her campaign heavy financial support in return for the quiet privileges she could provide and her daughters toed the line to keep their trust funds flowing.

"Your silence is worrying me," Gray said finally.

She turned back toward him. "Could Halabi succeed in an attack? I have no idea. Can I assume we're demanding a briefing?"

"I have multiple calls into the White House. They said they're working on it and they'll get back to us."

She returned to the window, this time gazing past her reflection and into the American capital. In reality, a limited biological attack would be an ideal scenario for her. There was no way Alexander and his party could ride something like that out this close to the election. It would be a deathblow.

"We're going to have to deal with the fact that you've always been strongly opposed to our involvement in the Middle East in general and Yemen in particular," Gray continued.

"Because I was told that Halabi was dead. That ISIS was defeated."

He looked skeptical. "You staked out that position before ISIS even existed and I don't remember Irene Kennedy ever saying that ISIS was defeated or confirming that Halabi had been killed."

She took a seat behind her desk again. "The American people don't give a crap about political positions and they care even less about the truth. What they want is fireworks. They want a show and we've just been handed the script. While the other side talks about health care and the economy, we'll be talking about Islamic terrorists unleashing a plague that could wipe our country out. About watching your children die while Irene Kennedy covers her ass and Mitch Rapp chases his tail. This is a gift, Kevin. Use it."

CHAPTER 8

"**B**UT it's your last one," the man said, staring longingly at the slightly bent cigarette Rapp was offering him.

Over the last five days, Rapp had graduated from sitting alone near the edge of the terrace to being crowded around a long table near its center. In that time, he'd gone through more than thirty cups of tea, twenty cups of coffee, every food product Yemen had to offer, and way too many cigarettes. It was a good way to blend in and make friends, but at this rate cancer was going to kill him before ISIS did.

"You'd be doing me a favor, Jihan. My youngest wife has been begging me to quit."

"This new generation," the man responded with a disapproving shake of his head. "They think they can live forever."

There was a murmur of general agreement from the men around them.

"Tell me. How old is she?"

"Sixteen," Rapp responded.

After another few seconds of thought, Jihan

accepted the cigarette. "Then I'll smoke it. You need your strength."

The table burst into laughter and Rapp joined in, crumpling the empty pack and tossing it on the ground as the conversation resumed. The men wandered through the topics of the day—the Saudi bombings of the night before. The Iranians' backing of the rebels. The continued spread of disease and famine. And, finally, America's role in it all. Rapp tuned it all out, watching the discarded cigarette pack blow around on sun-heated cobbles.

The Agency had implemented round-the-clock overhead surveillance on the building full of former ISIS soldiers that Rapp had found. And the NSA had cracked all their communications with the exception of a couple of burner phones they couldn't get a bead on. Unfortunately, all that had been accomplished was to confirm his first impression. Those men were nothing more than a bunch of violent dipshits whom Halabi would have no use for other than maybe to stop bullets.

Rapp let himself be drawn back into the conversation, but it was a waste of time. There was no solid intel to be gained from restaurant gossip—particularly in a country where no one drank alcohol. Either the politicians needed to let the Agency commit resources to this part of the world or they needed to get out. Half measures against a man like Sayid Halabi were pointless. He was all-in, and anyone going up against him had better be the same.

The conversation had just turned to Syria when the voices around Rapp began to falter. He followed the gazes of the men around him to an old CRT television set up in the shade. The endless stream of Arab music videos had been interrupted by something that seemed almost like a twisted homage to them. Images of young people dancing and singing were replaced by ones of violence and death, with a sound track voiced over by none other than Sayid Halabi.

Rapp had seen the prior version of the video, but not this update. The backing music was more somber and the footage of the assault on the village more extensive. Halabi droned on about Muslim unity and combining forces against the West, but Rapp focused on the footage of the ISIS team tearing through the village. The men couldn't have been more different than the ones he was keeping tabs on in Al Hudaydah. They moved more like SEALs than the undisciplined psychos he'd come to expect from ISIS. More evidence of Halabi's efforts to turn his organization into a tighter, more modern force.

The video ended and was replaced by a CNN interview with Christine Barnett. The men around him began an animated discussion of Halabi's role in the region but Rapp remained focused on the television. The flow of the interview was pretty much what he would have predicted, with the head of the Senate Intelligence Committee insisting that she'd been assured that Halabi had been taken out.

So after managing to flail her way to a massive lead in the polls, Barnett had finally found her message: that the current administration had lied about Halabi's death for political gain while leaving the American people completely unprotected from the threat ISIS posed.

It was a demonstrable lie, but she'd probably get

away with it. Sure, there was endless footage of Irene Kennedy saying that Halabi's body had never been found, but why would the press want to dredge that up? They knew a ratings grabber when they saw one.

Barnett went on to blame the very security agencies she'd been hamstringing for failing to utterly eradicate terrorism from the face of the earth. And, of course, she rounded out the interview the way all politicians did—by implying that she, and only she, had the answer. All the American people had to do was elect her president and they'd be guaranteed safety, wealth, a hot spouse, and six-pack abs.

The scene cut again, this time to a couple of know-nothing pundits speculating about the type of attack that the kidnapped medical team could conjure up. The debate had devolved into nonsensical shouting about Ebola and plague when Shamir Karman came up behind Rapp and whispered in his ear.

"A call for you just came in. Use the phone in the office."

Rapp took a seat behind Karman's desk and made sure the door had swung all the way shut before he picked up the handset.

"Go ahead," he said in Arabic.

His greeting was met with silence on the other end and he suspected he knew why. Since taking over logistics for Scott Coleman's company, Claudia Gould had been diligently trying to learn Arabic. Unfortunately, she was still in the "See Dick run" stage. Partially it was his fault. She was also the woman he lived with, but he always found a reason not to get involved in her language education. Patience wasn't his strong suit.

"Hello," he said, simplifying his Arabic. There was no way he could use the English or French she was fluent in. One overheard word and he might as well tattoo *CIA* to his forehead.

"It's good to hear your voice, Mitch."

He hated to admit it, but it was good to hear hers, too. The soft lilt was a reminder that, for one of the few times in his life, he had something to go home to.

"First," she continued. "Are you okay?"

"Yes," he said, keeping his responses basic.

"Don't worry. I didn't call just to ask that question."

"Then why?"

"I assume you've been watching the news and you're aware of Halabi's videos?"

He grunted an affirmation.

"The Saudis have located the village he burned. It's in central Yemen about five hundred kilometers east of you."

"And the people?"

"The ones he kidnapped? The reporting has been pretty accurate about them. What *hasn't* hit the networks is that they were there caring for the victims of a respiratory disease similar to SARS. Based on the Agency's analysis of Halabi's videos, he must have known about it. He went in when none of the medical personnel were in the infirmary they'd set up and his people burned everything without coming in contact with the villagers."

"And?"

"The Saudis want to incinerate the village from the air as an additional safety measure. It appears that they're already making plans but they're not sharing the details with the Agency. I don't think there's any point to you going there. It seems high risk, low return."

While her assessment was hard to argue with, *high risk, low return* was a front-runner for the engraving on his tombstone. Currently in third place behind *Do you think they'll be able to stitch that up?* and *Does anyone else hear ticking?*

It was a thin lead but it was better than sitting around Al Hudaydah giving himself emphysema. There was always a chance that Halabi or one of his men had left something useful behind.

"Can I assume you disagree with my analysis and insist on going?" Claudia said, filling the silence between them.

"Yes."

"I thought you'd say that, so I sent the village's coordinates to Scott in Riyadh. They know a Saudi chopper pilot who's willing to pick you up and take you to the village."

"Where and when?"

"Before I tell you that, you have to listen me. I know you always want to charge in, but are you sure it's worth it to spend a couple of hours looking around a burned village? Al Qaeda and ISIS control that area. We have no eyes there and no idea of their strength or distribution."

"Understood," he said, swallowing his natural urge to just bark orders. It was the main drawback to having the woman he was sleeping with handling his logistics. The upside was that she was one of the best in the business.

"I'm not finished."

His jaw clenched, but he managed to get *go ahead* out in a relatively even tone.

"The Saudi pilot isn't one of ours. He has a solid reputation, but he's not Fred and he's not loyal to us."

"He'll be fine."

There was a brief pause as she translated his words in her head.

"One last thing. Doctors Without Borders gave us information about the virus that the medical team was dealing with and it sounds terrifying. Without going into detail—"

"This is your definition of not going into detail?"

She had no idea what he'd said but chose to ignore it based on his tone. "It's incredibly dangerous, Mitch. And more important, it can survive on surfaces for days. Don't take the idea that the fire killed it for granted. You need to use the biohazard protocols you've been trained in. I'm serious. If there's even a vague possibility that you or one of Scott's men has been exposed to this, you'll have to be quarantined and you'll probably die."

He was starting to think that she was enjoying his inability to give anything more than one-word answers. "Understood."

"So, you promise to be careful and not touch anything?"

"Yes."

"Okay then. The chopper will pick you up outside of town at exactly 2 a.m. I'll send the coordinates to your phone."

CHAPTER 9

SAYID Halabi stood on the ancient minaret looking out over the landscape hundreds of meters below. The village's tightly packed stone buildings dominated the top of the peak, offering 360-degree views of mountains dotted with cloud shadows. Steep slopes had been terraced for agriculture over the centuries, and some were still green with the coffee plants that Yemen had once been so famous for.

Up until about a year ago, this place had been home to a community of farmers who had contracted with an American company to produce and export coffee beans. The hope had been that the industry would regain its economic foothold and stabilize the region.

The foreign businessmen had quickly recognized the realities of trying to carve a secular commercial paradise from this war-torn country and given up on the enterprise. Most of the farmers and other workers had moved on shortly thereafter, leaving a core group of thirty villagers who were either too rooted to this place to abandon it or had nowhere else to go.

Their bodies were now piled in a low building to

the southeast. Halabi couldn't see it from his vantage point, but knew from reports that the work bricking up the windows and doors was nearly complete. By the end of the day, the godless collaborators would be sealed in the tomb where they would stay for all eternity. Forgotten by their families, by history, and by Allah.

He limped to the other side of the minaret and looked into the narrow street below. Two of his men were visible, one dressed in traditional Yemeni garb and the other in a chador. It was a bit of an indignity for the battle-hardened soldier, but an unavoidable one. The Saudis and Americans were always watching from above and they couldn't be permitted to see anything but the normal rhythms of rural Yemeni life.

The wind began to gust and he closed his eyes, feeling the presence of God on the cool, dry air. The path to victory became clearer every day as Allah blessed him with an increasingly detailed understanding of His plan. The objective, so indistinct before, now seemed as well defined as the landscape around him.

Halabi finally turned and began descending the spiral steps that provided access to the minaret. His injuries forced him to use the stone walls to steady himself, but he was grateful for the struggle. Every stabbing pain, unbalanced step, and constricted breath reminded him of his arrogance and God's punishment for it.

As expected, Muhammad Attia was waiting patiently for him on the mosque's main floor.

"What of Mitch Rapp?" Halabi asked as Attia fell in alongside him.

"There's still no sign of him, and our sources say

that the Saudis are planning to bomb the area out of concern over the biothreat. I've been forced to move our men into the hills immediately surrounding the village."

"Do I detect disapproval in your voice, Muhammad?"

"Disapproval? No. But concern. Our resources are limited and risking the few reliable men we have in hopes that Rapp will appear in an empty, burned-out village . . ."

"He'll come," Halabi assured him.

"Even if he does, how much are we willing to risk over one man?"

Halabi didn't answer, instead exiting the mosque and winding through the narrow cobbled paths between buildings. Near the center of the village, they entered a tall, slender structure with rows of arched windows and a ground floor lined with diesel generators. After descending another set of stone steps, they crossed into a room that had been built inside a natural cavern.

Despite the fact that he'd been personally involved in its design, the environment inside the room was disorientingly foreign. It was a long, rectangular space, with smooth white walls and rows of overhead LEDs that glinted dully off stainless steel biotech equipment arranged beneath.

The machinery had been extremely difficult to acquire and transport but the effect was exactly as he'd envisioned. The impression was of a medical research lab that would look at home in London, Berlin, or New York. Videos made in this room would be disseminated online, fanning the West's fear into full-fledged panic and intensifying the chaos already present in America's political system.

He turned his attention to the only thing in the room that wasn't modern and polished—a sheep's diseased carcass lying on a cart near the center of the room. As promised, the matted hair and dried blood around its nose and mouth contrasted terrifyingly with the sterile environment.

Halabi's cane thudded dully as he walked the length of the room, finally finding the three Western-ers near the back. They were huddled together on the floor beneath the watchful eye of an armed guard. None made a move to stand as he approached, instead staring up at him with expressions that were easily read. The German's face reflected calm resignation. Bertrand's, in contrast, projected desperation and ter-ror. Finally, the American woman was consumed with hate.

It was exactly the reaction he'd expected. While social media was one of the most powerful weapons ever devised by man, it wasn't that platform's abil-ity to disseminate false information that was useful to him at the moment. It was other people's willing-ness to use it to strip themselves of their secrets. The intimate knowledge he had of these three infidels would have been impossible only a few years ago. Or-ganizations like the FBI, Stasi, and KGB had spent billions on wiretaps, physical surveillance, and in-formants to learn less than he could with a few key-strokes.

Halabi understood their hopes and motivations. Their strengths and weaknesses. Their allegiances and the subtle dynamics within those allegiances. Enough to assign each of them a very specific role in the drama that was unfolding.

"Who are you? Why are you keeping us here?"

As expected, Victoria Schaefer was the first to speak. And while he had a strong distaste for dealing with women, there was no alternative in this case.

"I am Sayid Halabi."

The recognition was immediate. Some of the defiance drained from the woman's eyes, and the Frenchman appeared to be on the verge of fainting. The German, as was his nature, seemed unaffected.

Halabi swept a hand around the room. "All this is for you. So that you can build a biological weapon."

"A biological weapon?" Schaefer said after a brief silence. "I'm a doctor. Otto's a nurse. And Gabriel's a scientist who researches how to *stop* diseases. Not how to cause them."

"The skills are the same," Halabi said, and then pointed at the dead sheep. "It was taken from a flock infected with anthrax. The bacteria are simple to incubate and weaponize. It's my understanding that a second-year biology student could do it."

She stared at him for a few seconds and then began slowly shaking her head. "No way in hell."

There was a time when he would have immediately turned to violence in order to coerce them. Now, though, he understood that this tendency was just another facet of his arrogance. Less an opportunity to carry out God's plans than to vent his own hate. And while the time for savagery would undoubtedly come, it hadn't yet arrived. Manipulation was the secret to victory in the modern world. Not force.

He turned his attention to Gabriel Bertrand, the

weakest and most knowledgeable of the three. "I assume you're aware that while anthrax is a simple weapon to create, it's not particularly effective. In order to contract a deadly form of it, you'd have to inhale the spores and then not seek the widely available antibiotics capable of curing it. I'm a terrorist, yes? Isn't that how your government and media portrays me? If this is true, then it's my goal to spread terror, not death. I'll use you and this equipment to create propaganda videos—"

"Like the one you made in the village," the woman said, cutting him off. "You sealed innocent women and children in their homes and burned them alive. And now you want us to believe that all you want to do is a little marketing?"

"What you believe isn't important to me. Only what you do."

After a life dedicated to battle, the scene playing out in front of Halabi seemed laughably banal. The Crimean documentary filmmaker whose artistry had thus far exceeded all expectations was now entirely in his element. He had the three Westerners dressed up in elaborate hazmat suits and was orchestrating their every movement as they dissected the sheep. Lighting was constantly adjusted, camera angles were tested, close-ups were taken and retaken. He'd even experimented with some rudimentary dialogue, though it was unclear whether he thought it would be dramatic enough to make the final cut.

For their part, the three Westerners seemed content to play along. And why not? In their minds, nothing they were doing was real. Much of the equipment, while impressive looking, wasn't fully assembled or even relevant to the task of producing anthrax. The elaborate computer terminal they were pretending to consult wasn't plugged in. For now, they would be allowed to believe that they were nothing more than actors trading performances for survival.

The truth, though, was so much grander.

With biology, God had created a class of weapon infinitely more powerful than anything ever devised by man. Halabi now understood that pathogens and the skillful manipulation of information were the only weapons that mattered in the modern era. While the Western powers spent trillions maintaining massive armies and involving them in meaningless skirmishes, he had assembled the tools necessary to set fire to the earth.

CHAPTER 10

CONDITIONS were solid, with a half-moon, a sky full of stars, and light winds. Rapp's Saudi pilot was keeping the chopper high, making it unlikely that they'd be noticed by the scattered al Qaeda and ISIS forces that controlled the area.

Rapp scanned the dark terrain through the open door but couldn't pick up so much as a cooking fire. Maybe they'd get lucky and this operation would go quickly and smoothly. The best intel they had suggested that the village they were on their way to was completely devoid of human activity. Sayid Halabi's men had been admittedly efficient at turning it into a tomb, leaving nothing but the charred bodies of its inhabitants sealed in their burned homes.

The main dangers they expected to face were a few potential booby traps and the germs that Claudia was so afraid of. Time on the ground would have to be limited, so if they were going to come up with any clues as to where Halabi had taken the medical team, they'd have to do it fast. The Saudis were definitely committed to wiping what was left of this village off the face of the planet, but were being cagey as to exactly when. Better not to be standing in the middle of it when the bombers showed up.

The wind gusting through the door intensified and he pulled back, turning his attention to the dim cabin and the men sharing it with him. Scott Coleman, Joe Maslick, Charlie Wicker, and Bruno McGraw were all sitting calmly, lost in their own thoughts or lightly dozing. They'd been with him almost since the beginning. Long enough to accumulate a few too many years and a few too many injuries. It didn't matter, though. The kind of trust they'd developed over that time couldn't be replaced by one of the standout SEALs or Delta kids that Coleman occasionally got wind of.

This team had always been there for him and not a single one of them was replaceable as far as Rapp was concerned. He knew what they would do before they did it. He knew that every one of them was one hundred percent loyal to him and to each other. And he knew that not one of them would stop until five minutes after they were dead.

"Everyone's clear on the drill," Rapp said over the microphone hanging in front of his face. "We're looking for anything that could even have a chance of being useful—equipment left behind, shell casings, tire tracks. The guys in Langley said they'd take gum wrappers if that's all we can find. Get pictures of everything, and you're authorized to use flash. We don't have any choice, and I don't think anyone in that village is going to mind. The far building to the west is what they were using as a hospital. Don't get any closer than thirty feet. Hazmat protocols are in effect for the entire op, and anything we collect goes in the bags."

"What if we find a survivor?"

"Keep a twenty-foot interval and get 'em on the ground. We'll question them like that and call in an army medical team to make sure they're not sick."

"And if they don't follow directions?" Coleman asked.

"If they get inside that twenty-foot perimeter, give them one warning shot, and if they still don't get the message, put 'em down. Then we burn the body."

The shadowed faces around him seemed slightly more nervous than normal. Stand-up fights were one thing but bacteria and viruses were another. They'd all been there. Smoldering with fever in some god-forsaken jungle. Trying to be quiet while puking your guts out behind enemy lines. Dengue. Malaria. Dysentery. Infected wounds oozing pus. Everyone's least favorite part of the job.

The nose of the aircraft dipped and the pilot announced that they were on their final approach. The plan was to never let the runners touch the ground. As soon as they were out, the chopper would climb to a safe height and wait for them to call it back in. There was no reason for ISIS or al Qaeda to be hanging around here, but it didn't make sense to take chances.

Rapp grabbed the edge of the door and hung part-way out the side as they descended. The darkness was too deep to discern the charring on the walls of the stone buildings. The collapsed roofs and the inky graves beyond, though, were easy enough to pick out in the moonlight.

The Saudi did a respectable job of the drop-off and

Rapp slipped the face mask off the top of his head and over his face. Coleman's men spread out, looking a little less smooth than normal in the chem suits designed to protect them from biological threats. Rapp positioned himself at the right flank of the formation, searching the darkness for human shapes as the chopper started to climb.

The beat of rotors began to fade like they had in so many ops in the past, but then were drowned out by the deafening crash of an explosion. He instinctively threw himself to the ground and trained his M4 carbine on the source of the sound. The sky to the northeast was lit up, and he watched through his face mask as the helicopter broke apart and flaming chunks of it started to rain down on the desert.

Predictably, the shooting started a few seconds later.

A disciplined burst from a tango to the south landed a few feet to Rapp's right and he rolled in the opposite direction, getting to his feet and sprinting toward the village, finally penetrating into the narrow streets as rounds pounded a stone wall to the east.

"Give me a sit rep!" he said over his throat mike.

Everyone sounded off as uninjured, reporting opposition east, north, and south. Rapp dropped behind a rock wall but it turned out to be a bad position when what seemed like a .50-caliber round pulverized a stone two feet from him. He flipped over the wall, sweat already starting to soak him in the poorly ventilated hazmat suit.

"Mitch!"

It took Rapp a moment to realize the shout hadn't come over his earpiece and he followed it through an empty doorway to his right. Coleman was inside with his back to the wall next to a window opening, occasionally peeking over the blackened sill to make sure no one was moving in on them.

Rapp took a similar position next to the door, peering out as he called for an update from Coleman's men.

"We're just inside the southwest edge of the village and we're in a position to cover each other," Maslick said over the radio. "No one's hit yet but we're taking heavy fire from the south and we're seeing sniper activity to the north. The low ground to the west looks clear. Can you reach us? We can cover you and then get out down the slope on our side."

"Rocket!" Coleman shouted.

They both threw themselves to the ground, anticipating an impact on the heavy stone walls of the building. The projectile went wide, though, and instead exploded in a narrow street just to the east. Flame billowed through the windows and door but didn't reach either one of them. The smoke was another story. Suddenly Rapp was thankful for the fogged face mask.

"If these assholes could shoot straight, this would kind of suck," Coleman said, moving back to his position next to the window.

The former SEAL's muffled words were intended as a joke, but it was a pretty good description of their situation. The problem was that from what Rapp had seen, their attackers *could* shoot. They'd hit the chopper. Fire discipline was good—with controlled bursts only when a viable target presented itself. And while they continued to miss, they seemed to always go just a little wide to the east.

They weren't going for kills, he suddenly realized. They were driving his team west, trying to draw them into the low ground. And it was working. He already had three men on that side of the village, and both he and Coleman were in a position where the smoke and fire were encouraging them to re-form with them.

"Why didn't they take the chopper out while we were on it?" Rapp shouted over the sound of gunfire starting to pound the walls around the window Coleman was beneath.

"Maybe we caught them by surprise."

"You mean the force dug in around a burned-out village in the middle of nowhere?"

Coleman looked back at him through his face mask as chunks of shattered wood and rock rained down on him. "It does seem a little far-fetched."

"But they forgot to put men to the west."

"You're thinking ambush? That they're driving us there? Why? If they want us dead, why not just surround us and do it?"

The answer was pretty clear: Sayid Halabi. The son of a bitch was holding a grudge. He didn't want to kill Rapp, he wanted to capture him. He wanted to throw him in a hole and spend the next five years working him over with a set of pliers and a blowtorch.

And if that was true, it was their ticket out of there.

"We're going east," Rapp said into his throat mike.

Not surprisingly, Joe Maslick's voice came on the comm a moment later. "Did you mean west, Mitch? The heaviest fire is coming from the east and it'd leave us climbing toward shooters controlling the high ground."

"You heard me. East. Come right up the middle of

the main street on Scott's orders. Leave your hazmat suits and face masks on. I repeat, biohazard protocols are still in effect. Understood?"

The response sounded hesitant but there was no question that Maslick, Wicker, and McGraw would follow his orders to the letter.

"What are you thinking?" Coleman said as Rapp slipped up next to him and took a quick look outside. The flames had managed to find fuel and the smoke was combining with the condensation on his face mask to make it hard to see.

"Halabi figured I'd come and he left men with orders to capture me. But they don't know which one of us I am because of the suits."

"So we're going to charge a bunch of guys dug in above us because you think he ordered them not to kill you?"

"You got it."

Coleman looked up at the missing roof and the flames starting to lap over it. "That's a lot to hang on a hunch."

Rapp nodded and moved to the door. "I'm going. If I'm still alive in fifty yards, follow me."

Before Coleman could answer, Rapp slipped out and started sprinting along the edge of the street. Incoming fire was intermittent and, as he'd hoped, always led him by a few yards, trying to drive him back. Another rocket was fired and he was forced to drop, but it struck a building well ahead. Halabi's men were playing it safe. None of them wanted to go back and give their dear leader a bucket containing what was left of the prize he so desperately wanted.

Rapp leapt back to his feet, charging through the

scattered flames left by the RPG and starting up the slope on the east side of the village. He could make out five separate guns all sparking in the darkness ahead of him. Despite that, he fought his natural instinct to zigzag and vary his pace. Unpredictability was a good strategy when faced with an enemy that wanted to kill you, but counterproductive when facing an enemy dedicated to near misses.

He heard gunfire erupt from behind him and looked back to see four figures in hazmat suits falling in with him. The guns in front went dark, as did the sniper going for long shots from the south. Halabi's men had finally figured out what was happening and were having to recalibrate.

Rapp put the shooters to the north and south out of his mind for the time being. He could see lights coming on in his peripheral vision and assumed they were headlamps being used by the men as they ran to reinforce their comrades to the east. They were hundreds of yards away, though, crossing moderately difficult terrain. It was unlikely that they would figure in the fight over the short term.

Human figures rose up from the earth about fifty yards ahead, their outlines just visible in the moonlight as they began to charge. Based on the way they were holding their rifles, it appeared that they were planning to use them as clubs.

Completely insane, but pretty much what Rapp was counting on. While these men were a serious step up from the average terrorist psychopath, they were still ISIS. And that meant they'd follow the man they believed to be God's representative on earth right off a cliff. In fact, they'd be happy to do it. More virgins for them.

The men coming in from the sides started shooting again, but were still making sure not to hit anything. Coleman's team engaged them while Rapp focused on the men coming at him. Individual rounds from his M4 dropped the first two and left two remaining. They were running crouched now, zigzagging to reduce their chance of being hit. Rapp, still on a collision course with them, fired on the run at the man to the right. It took nearly his full magazine, but he finally spun him around with an impact to the right side of his chest.

Less than a second later, he collided with the last man. They went down locked together, starting to roll back down the slope. Some of the rocks beneath them were sharp and while the chances that Rapp had any deadly germs stuck to his chem suit were low, he wasn't anxious to puncture it.

He managed to arrest their momentum but ended up with Halabi's man on top. Predictably, he went straight for Rapp's mask so he could get a look at who he was fighting and thus determine the rules of engagement. While Halabi's orders would have been to keep Rapp alive, he doubted Coleman and his men would receive the same courtesy.

Rapp grabbed the man's finger just before it went under his faceplate, wrenching it hard enough to feel it snap. When he jerked back in pain, Rapp scissored a leg up and used it to slam his opponent to the ground. After a brief struggle, the CIA man managed to get hold of one of the rocks he'd been worried about a few seconds before and slam it into the man's forehead.

He was just getting back to his feet when a man went streaking by—undoubtedly Wick, a fast and light sniper who would be anxious to set up in the high ground before the men approaching from the north and south could close in.

Rapp let Coleman and the rest of his men pass by before he started up, protecting their flank. A few quick bursts in the direction of the headlamps emptied what was left of his mag. There wasn't much chance of hitting anything, but he might be able to persuade them to slow down.

By the time Rapp made it to the top of the slope, Wick already had his McMillan TAC-338 rifle set up on a bipod and was sighting through the thermal scope. He pulled the trigger and a single round exited the barrel.

"Hit."

A second shot followed three seconds later.

"Hit. They're taking cover."

Rapp lay down among Coleman and his men, glancing behind him and seeing a barely perceptible band of light on the horizon.

Rapp wiped the dust from his faceplate and watched the jet's angle of descent steepen. Contrails appeared, followed by a massive wall of fire rising from the earth. Another jet dropped a similar payload, spreading the firestorm.

Unfortunately, the air support had nothing to do with him. The Saudis had finally gotten around to incinerating the village, which was about four miles back now. The sun was still low on the horizon, but the heat was already starting to climb. In another hour, running in the chem suits they were still wearing would no longer be doable.

Rapp picked up a set of binoculars and scanned across the six ISIS operatives pursuing them, finally settling on a man using his hand to shade a similar set of lenses against the sun. They were persistent and well organized, but seemed content to prosecute their chase from just out of rifle range.

His earpiece buzzed and he picked up the satellite call. "Go ahead."

"Do you see the Saudi jets?" Claudia said.

"They're hard to miss."

"According to the pilots, you've got two groups coming in on you. One from the northeast and the other from the southeast. As many as twenty vehicles in total. Another seven vehicles are coming in from the west to reinforce the men chasing you."

That explained why their pursuers were keeping their distance. Halabi had called in the locals still loyal to him. Probably nowhere near the quality of the men they'd been dealing with so far, but it didn't matter. The terrorist leader's plan to capture him didn't really demand crack troops. Just a lot of warm bodies willing to turn cold in an effort to overwhelm them.

"ETAs?"

"Call it twenty-five minutes for the forces approaching from the east. A little longer for the western reinforcement because now they're going to have to go around the fire."

"Can the Saudis take them out?" Rapp asked.

"Irene's working on it and she's gotten the president involved. He's tried to contact the king directly, but he's sick and not taking calls. I don't think they're going to help us, Mitch. The people Irene has reached out to are angry that the Agency's operating in the area without notifying them and they're throwing up a bunch of red tape."

The fact that the two jets had turned back toward Saudi Arabia suggested that she was right. Yet another pain-in-the-ass development in what was turning out to be a serious pain-in-the-ass day.

"Mitch? Are you still there?"

"I'm here."

"What can I do to help?"

"You tell me."

When she spoke again she sounded like she was on the verge of breaking into tears. "I . . . I don't know."

"No problem. Can you do me a favor?"

"Of course. What?"

"Make us a reservation at that new Japanese place in Manassas for Saturday. I've had sushi stuck in my mind all day."

She actually managed a choking laugh. "You're getting better at this relationship stuff. I appreciate the effort."

"It's going to be fine," he said and then cut off the call.

When he walked back to Coleman and his men, he found them all crammed into a sliver of shade provided by a boulder.

Bruno McGraw was the first to speak. "What's the plan, boss?"

"We take off the monkey suits."

That order was met with more enthusiasm than probably any he'd given in his career. The strict protocols necessary for the safe removal of the suits felt painfully slow, but after ten precious minutes, they were down to their custom desert camo. Despite the fact that temperatures were already hovering around ninety, Rapp felt like he'd just plunged himself into a frozen lake.

He squinted into the sun and pointed at two dust plumes now visible to the east. "Twenty vehicles total with an unknown number of men. ETA to us is about fifteen. Seven more vehicles coming in from the west to reinforce the men chasing us. ETA's probably around twenty-five minutes."

"What about the Saudis?" Coleman asked.

"Forget them. We're on our own."

The mood that had been elevated a moment before by the removal of the chem suits started to slide again.

"We're limited on ammo and water," Rapp said. "And there's nowhere around here to get more."

"The nearest village is a long way away," Maslick pointed out. "And there ain't much in it."

"We could reverse course and charge the guys coming up behind us," Wick suggested. "If they still don't want to shoot us, it'll be easy to whack them and take their gear."

Rapp shook his head. "If they're smart—and I think there's a good chance they are—they'll just run and lead us straight into the reinforcements coming in behind them. If you figure five men per vehicle, we could be facing a force of over forty men. They'll blitz us and absorb whatever casualties they have to."

"And even if we kill them all," Coleman said, "by the time we do, we could have as many as another hundred men on top of us from the east."

"Well, we can't wander around on foot in the flats," Wick said. "They might just be a bunch of pricks in pickups but that's still cavalry as far as I'm concerned.

And who's to say those are the only people coming to the party? There could be another fifty vehicles gassing up somewhere."

Rapp nodded. They were trapped on a narrow plain with a steep rocky slope rising about five hundred yards to the north and an equally steep and rocky one descending the same distance to the south.

"Seems like an easy decision," Coleman said. "We climb. We'll be way faster than the guys on foot, it'll give us the high ground, and it'll neutralize the advantage of the trucks."

"What then, though?" Rapp asked. "You saw the map. That slope tops out into a mesa that's about a quarter mile square."

"Chopper extraction?"

"Based on what I'm hearing, I don't think we can count on it."

The group fell silent as Rapp walked back to a vantage point that allowed him to see the men digging in to the west. He scanned with his binoculars again, and again found a man scanning back. Rapp lowered his lenses and let him get a good long look at his face.

"You all are going up the ridge to the north."

"What do you mean 'you all'?" Coleman replied. "What are you doing?"

"I'll head down the slope to the south. They don't care about you. Their orders are to capture me or die trying."

"Screw that," Coleman said, and his men mumbled their agreement with the sentiment. "We're not leaving you to roll down a canyon with a hundred guys coming in on you."

"You have your orders."

"Kiss my ass, Mitch. You don't give orders anymore. The Agency pays me and you don't even work there. As far as I can tell, you're just an unemployed tourist."

"Then let me put it this way," Rapp said, starting to gather his gear. "I'm going south and I'm shooting anyone I see behind me. If it's one of you guys, I probably won't go for center of mass. But I'm gonna make it hurt."

CHAPTER 11

Victoria Schaefer leaned out the window and once again squinted into the sunlight. Nothing had changed. It probably hadn't for hundreds of years. Three- and four-story buildings rose across from her, separated by narrow dirt and cobble paths. Beyond, she could see the land drop off steeply and the terraced mountains beyond. The splashes of vibrant green created a stark—and strangely beautiful—contrast with the reddish brown that had made up her universe since arriving in Yemen.

For what must have been the thousandth time, she studied the sheer drop from the tower they were locked in and for the thousandth time calculated it at just over fifty feet. The nearest building was only about ten feet away, but instead of the empty arched window frames that dominated the village's architecture, it presented a blank wall. Signs of humanity were fleeting, and over the past few days she'd become convinced that all were men loyal to Sayid Halabi. What had happened to the original inhabitants, she could only imagine.

Schaefer turned and focused her attention on the room that they were imprisoned in. The entire space was no more than fifteen feet square, with rock walls and two heavy wooden doors. One led to the stairway they'd been brought up and the other was a mystery. The ceiling was supported by beams that had been darkened by what she suspected was centuries of cooking fires. Good for hanging yourself from if it became necessary. And it appeared that it might.

Since their star turn in Halabi's video three days ago, they'd had no contact with anyone. A water jug, now almost empty, had been provided but no food. The bucket they used for a toilet was in the far corner and was in danger of overflowing. She wanted to dump it on an unsuspecting scumbag who wandered beneath their window, but Otto kept stopping her. Always the voice of reason.

The worst, though, were the nights. The cold wind flowed freely through the windows, and the uninsulated stone turned the room into a meat locker. They slept—probably only a few minutes a night—huddled together in a corner. Gabriel Bertrand had finally gotten his chance to grind up against her but didn't seem to be enjoying it as much as he'd expected.

She turned her attention to the Frenchman, who was sitting with his back against a wall and knees pulled to his chest. She'd been doing her best to ignore him, and he took her flicker of interest as an invitation to speak.

"They're going to just leave us here to starve."

He was already cracking. Hunger, lack of sleep, and uncertainty were potent weapons against anyone. But they were particularly potent against a man who had led a charmed life since the day he was born. The only son of a wealthy Parisian family, he'd been gifted with an exceptional mind and spent his entire adult life coddled by top universities. His research in Yemen had been the hardest thing he'd ever done, and he wouldn't have lasted an hour if he hadn't been certain it was his path to blazing academic glory.

Otto Vogel, on the other hand, was an almost perfect counterpoint to the French scientist. He was sprawled on the floor, deftly spinning a twig on the tip of his index finger. As always, his armor seemed impenetrable.

"Anthrax isn't that dangerous," Bertrand continued as she turned back to the window. "And they filmed us. Why? So they can put the videos out on the Internet to scare people. But that will backfire, yes? People will be frightened, but they'll also be wary. If they have symptoms, if they come into contact with some unknown substance, they'll go to the doctor and get antibiotics. And the governments of the world can't allow the manufacture of weaponized anthrax. They have to come. They have to rescue us."

The suggestion that they should build a bioweapon to bring about their rescue prompted Victoria to look at him over her shoulder. He averted his eyes.

"I didn't mean it like that."

Vogel stopped spinning the piece of wood, a rare glimmer of anger crossing his face. He'd had enough of the Frenchman within an hour of their first meeting and now he was reaching his limit.

"The Americans were motivated to find Osama bin Laden, too. How long did that take? And even if they are able find us, what is it you think they're going to do? Send soldiers to assault this mountain in order to save us? Risk their men's lives and maybe give Halabi a chance to escape to save three people?"

"What are you saying?"

"I'm saying that they'll blow the entire top of this mountain off. You'll hear a slight whistle and then you'll explode into—"

"Otto!" Schaefer interjected. "You're not helping."

He frowned and went back to spinning his stick.

"They aren't going to be satisfied with making movies and they're not going to give us a choice," Bertrand said. "How long can we hold out? They'll starve us. Freeze us. Torture us. And finally, they'll kill us."

In truth, none of that would be necessary, Schaefer knew. It wouldn't take much more than a mild rash to get Bertrand pumping out every dangerous pathogen he knew how to create. Trying to get him to grow a backbone was a waste of time. As she saw it, there were two paths ahead of them. The first was to throw the man out the window and let his incredible knowledge of microbiology die with him. Undoubtedly, Otto would enthusiastically sign on to that strategy, but to her it was just an abstraction. She'd never knowingly harmed anyone in her life.

That left only one option: convincing him to focus that magnificent brain on something other than the hopelessness of their situation.

She sat next to the Frenchman and motioned Vogel over.

"Listen," she said, speaking quietly in case there were listening devices. "We're scientists, right? There's a lot of equipment in that room, and we can probably ask for more if we play our cards right. All we need to do is figure out how we can use it to get ourselves out of here."

"Agreed," the German whispered.

"Agreed?" Bertrand said, the volume of his voice high enough that Victoria clamped a hand over his mouth.

"Don't talk, Gabriel. Think. Gas? Poison? Explosives? You keep telling everyone you're a genius. Prove it."

Sayid Halabi climbed the stairs with Muhammad Attia hovering directly behind. The voices of his prisoners had dipped to below what his microphones could pick up, suggesting that it was time to pay them a visit.

Undoubtedly, they'd begun plotting. They would pretend to cooperate and use the equipment he gave them to create some kind of weapon. Perhaps a disease that they inoculated themselves against. Perhaps a poison. Perhaps even a way to contact the outside world. It was to be expected.

He pulled back the bolt and opened the door, watching the three Westerners leap to their feet as he entered.

"How long will it take to make weaponized anthrax in a quantity sufficient for multiple large-scale attacks?" he said.

They looked at each for a moment before the woman answered. "None of us have ever made anthrax. We have nothing to do with bioweapons research. Do you have an Internet connection? You can look it up and see that I'm telling the truth."

The Frenchman kept glancing over at her, drawing

strength from his unwillingness to look weaker than a woman.

"Dr. Bertrand?" Halabi prompted.

He drew back at the sound of his name. "It's . . . It's not as easy as you think. That's why no one uses those kinds of weapons. It's not just that you could infect your own troops, it's that nature tends to take its own path. It's impossible to control and impossible to predict. And anthrax has its own unique problems that make it hard to weaponize. It—"

"I can assure you that I'm not stupid," Halabi said, cutting the man off. "We know that anthrax can be weaponized because it's been done before. By the Russians on a large scale and in 2001 by an American scientist with a background similar to yours. Now tell me how long and what additional equipment you will need."

None answered.

"Muhammad . . ." Halabi said.

Attia pulled a pistol from the holster on his hip and fired a single round into the German nurse's chest.

Victoria Schaefer managed to catch him before he hit the floor and Halabi watched a scene play out that was identical to the one with her translator. She tore open Vogel's shirt, looked at the wound over his heart, and realized that she was powerless.

This time, instead of running, she lunged with surprising force and speed. It wasn't enough, though. Attia caught her and dragged her toward the door at the back of the room. She screamed obscenities and fought violently enough that Attia was struggling to keep hold of her as he slid an ancient key into the lock. She actually managed to inflict a superficial wound on his neck before they disappeared across the threshold.

Her shouts and the sound of her beating futilely against Attia continued and Halabi examined Bertrand's reaction. The Frenchman's eyes flicked back and forth from the body on the floor to the open door the woman had been forced through. He was a surprisingly simple and transparent man. He showed no more empathy for his comrades than he had for patients. Instead, he seemed entirely focused on calculating how this affected his own situation.

The sounds of struggling faded and finally went silent. The woman, just out of sight in the room, would now be secured to the table at its edge. She managed to shout a few more epithets, but then her words became screams. Within a minute, there seemed to be nothing but her terror, pain, and hopelessness bouncing off the stone walls.

"How can you stand there and do nothing to stop this?" Halabi asked Bertrand. "What was it you said earlier? Anthrax isn't even dangerous. And, as you suspected, I've released videos with my plans. The Americans will know what's coming and be vigilant."

Bertrand didn't respond. He seemed to be slipping into shock as the screams of the woman echoed around them.

"I need to generate fear, Doctor. That's all. My goal is to convince the Americans that there's a price to be paid for continuing to create instability and suffering in the Middle East. We don't want to be murdered for our oil. We don't want our democratically elected governments to be overthrown and violent dictators to be inserted. In short, we don't want to live like you and we don't want to be your slaves. We just want to be left alone to find our own path."

It was a sentiment that he would undoubtedly be sympathetic to, because it had largely been gleaned from his own naïve political posts on Facebook. Still, he didn't answer immediately, holding out until the woman's screams took on a gurgling quality.

"I'll do it."

Halabi nodded and shouted to Attia in Arabic. "Finish her!"

A gunshot sounded and Halabi put a comforting hand on Bertrand's shoulder. "I'm sure she appreciated your mercy."

CHAPTER 12

"**T**HESE images are *garbage*, Irene!"

Scott Coleman had recon photos that covered a radius of twenty miles around the place where he'd split from Rapp, but they looked like they'd been taken through the bottom of a dirty Coke bottle.

"The wind's kicking up and the satellite can't penetrate the dust," Kennedy explained.

He ran a hand over the hazy eight-by-tens arranged on Shamir Karman's desk, leaving a streak of blood across them. The bandage on his forearm was so tight he could barely feel his fingers, but the wound just wouldn't stop seeping. It was hard to complain, though. He was lucky his arm was still attached. The fight to get back to Al Hudaydah had been nastier than he'd counted on.

Rapp had been right about most of the ISIS forces focusing on him, but that still left three vehicles full of terrorist pricks to come after Coleman's team. The climbing had been steeper and looser than it looked and they'd gotten pinned down in a cliff band about thirty yards up the slope.

With the crack troops concentrating on Rapp, the less disciplined fighters had unleashed as much ammo as they could in his team's general direction, underestimating how good their cover was. After ten minutes of setup, his guys had started to return fire—single rounds aimed at carefully selected targets. About half the ISIS force went down in the first two minutes, but then the rest got wise. After that, the skirmish had turned into a stalemate that wasn't broken until well after sunset. The injury to his arm, a set of bruised ribs, and a self-sutured gash over his kneecap were souvenirs of the two hours he'd spent silently climbing back down the dark slope.

The remaining ISIS forces had assumed Coleman would go up and try to escape over the top, leaving them completely unprepared when the four Americans walked into their camp with silenced pistols. Things had gotten a little hairy when the inexperienced force panicked and started shooting wildly in every direction, but eventually they all ended up dead.

By then, though, it was too late to do anything for Rapp. More ISIS troops had joined the hunt and there were headlights spread out in a search pattern that was probably five miles wide. Worse was the fact that a few of them noticed the shooting behind and reversed course to provide support for their comrades.

Piling into the ISIS pickups and turning tail was one of the hardest decisions Coleman had ever made. But with that many enemy fighters and no idea where Rapp was, there had been no other option.

"Screw the photos," Coleman said, sweeping them off the desk. "They're not going to tell us anything we don't already know. Mitch is out there and there's only so far he could have gotten in the last . . ." He paused and looked at his watch, cursing silently. ". . . forty-three hours. All we need is air support from the Saudis and to bring in—"

"It's not going to happen, Scott."

"What do you mean it's not going to happen?"

"America's role in the Middle East in general—and Yemen in particular—has come under a lot of scrutiny since the presidential primaries started. Christine Barnett is on the attack and everyone else is in defense mode. Getting anyone to authorize an operation in Yemen and trying to get any meaningful cooperation from the Saudis at this point is . . ." Her voice faded but the message was clear.

"So after everything Mitch has done for the president, America—and even Saudi Arabia—this is how they repay him? By abandoning him in the middle of the Yemeni desert? Because the optics might not be great inside the Beltway?"

"I'm afraid optics are all that's left inside the Beltway," Kennedy said. "But I'm not completely powerless. Not yet. I have a chopper pilot on his way to you and I'll find a way to borrow an aircraft. I've also contacted a number of private contractors who have worked with either you or Mitch in the past. We're bringing them in—"

"When?" Coleman said, cutting her off for perhaps the first time in his life.

"You should have one chopper and as many as ten men within thirty-six hours."

He did the math in his head. "By then he'll have been out there for more than three days with nothing but a half-full CamelBak, an M4, and a couple of spare mags."

"Christine Barnett has everyone on—"

"I don't give a shit about that crazy bitch!" he shouted but then lowered his voice after realizing he'd just yelled at the director of the CIA. "I'm sorry, Irene."

"I'm as frustrated and angry as you are, Scott. And I'm doing everything I can."

"I know. Keep me posted," he said and then disconnected the call.

He lowered himself into the chair behind him and looked down at the useless photos scattered across the floor. That was it. Mitch Rapp had been abandoned. And not just by the American and Saudi politicians. By him. He should have told Rapp to shove his orders up his ass. He should be out there fighting with him. And if necessary dying with him. One last charge into a barrage of ISIS bullets would be a hundred times better than sitting in this room doing nothing.

His sat phone rang and he declined the call when he saw that it was Claudia. What could he tell her? That Mitch was somewhere in the desert with every ISIS fighter in Yemen either searching for him or on their way to search for him? That instead of helping, his team was sitting around with their thumbs up their asses?

"You should talk to her."

Joe Maslick was sitting on a stool in the corner of the tiny room, feeling as helpless as he was. The others were checking their weapons or catching some shut-eye on the building's bombed-out second floor, waiting for word that they were going back into action.

Coleman nodded and was about to reach for the

sat phone when the door leading to the office started to swing inward. Instead of the phone he grabbed the SIG P226 next to it, while Maslick retrieved a similar weapon from his holster.

The man standing in the threshold had a bearded face almost completely obscured by the scarf wound around his head. Only two bloodshot eyes and the sun-damaged skin around them were visible. He was dressed in traditional Yemeni garb but it was so caked with dirt that it was impossible to even guess at the original color of the cloth.

He ignored the two men aiming guns at him, fixating on the bottle of water on the desk. Coleman watched as he pushed the scarf away from his mouth and drained the bottle in one long pull.

It took the former SEAL a few seconds to conjure the expected nonchalance. "What took you so long?"

Rapp tossed the empty container on the floor and used the back of his hand to wipe the mud from his lips. "Stopped for lunch. Can I assume we're blown here?"

"Yeah. Four Americans in camo showing up at the restaurant hasn't been great for Karman's cover."

He nodded. "Tell him to gather up his people and get us some vehicles. We'll wait until dark and then make a run for the Saudi border."

CHAPTER 13

SAYID Halabi began to stand, but the pain in his damaged spine prompted him to abandon the idea. Instead he settled back behind the desk that dominated the room. A Panasonic Toughbook computer sitting in front of him was connected to a series of satellite dishes that beamed signals horizontally for kilometers before finally pointing skyward. Maps of the Middle East, Europe, and America hung on the walls, allowing him to visualize how the world would be affected by his plans.

Thousands of miles to the west, Irene Kennedy was sitting at a similar desk, with a similar computer, considering similar maps. All more grand and sophisticated, of course. But fundamentally the same. If he was going to defeat America, he would have to learn to think like the woman charged with protecting it. Strategize like her. Use the high-tech tools at her disposal with equal dexterity.

During his time convalescing from the injuries Mitch Rapp had inflicted on him, he had come to accept that ISIS would never be a military force to rival the West. With that acceptance, though, had come the realization that it wasn't necessary. The era of traditional armies was over and had been for decades. For all its size and sophistication, even the American military was capable of little more than a lengthy string of elaborate failures.

The world was now defined by a complex web of interrelated cold wars. External battles between the Europeans, Americans, Russians, and Chinese raged just beneath the surface. But even more important were the internal battles—between the individual countries that made up the EU, between political parties, between races and economic classes.

The United States was as weak as it had been in human memory. Its people were unconcerned with anything but their own selfish needs and had turned their political system into just another source of cheap entertainment. Its defenses were still built around standing armies that had become little more than a way for the military-industrial complex to enrich itself. America's ability to adapt and reinvent itself had been stripped away by politicians who had trained their constituents to view change with fear and anger.

God had provided him with the right weapon at the right moment in history. Now his primary mission was to use America's internal tumult to keep Irene Kennedy and Mitch Rapp blinded, and to ensure that when the moment came, America would be too fractured to react. The world would be left rudderless.

So far, it had been child's play. Christine Barnett had latched on to the anthrax videos immediately, using them to attack her political opponents and the CIA instead of concerning herself with defending her country. Even more interesting was her willingness to go beyond accusations of incompetence and to insinuate that the Alexander administration's activities in the Middle East had brought about this attack.

Halabi had thought Barnett was going too far and might suffer backlash, but he'd been proven wrong. In an America trained to react only to partisanship, her message was finding an audience. It was human nature to hate the traitor more intensely than the enemy, and in America the two parties were increasingly using the language of treason when referring to each other. It had gone so far that an enterprising businessman was printing T-shirts that read "I'd Rather Be ISIS Than . . ." and then finished half with "Republican" and half with "Democrat." To Halabi's great amusement, he was having a hard time keeping them in stock.

He reached out and retrieved a worn notebook from his desk, flipping absently through it for a few moments. Gabriel Bertrand's elegant scrawl was all in French but it would have been equally incomprehensible in English or even Arabic. The complex analysis of the Yemeni respiratory disease contained in the text was currently being translated and put into layman's terms by a young Egyptian doctor.

The man's report would be delivered later that week, but Halabi didn't need it to know that the book contained the blueprint for overthrowing the world order that had persisted for centuries. That Gabriel Bertrand had unknowingly revealed the secret to inflicting suffering and death on a scale unimaginable in the modern era.

Muhammad Attia appeared in the doorway and

Halabi returned the book to his desk. "What of Mitch Rapp, Muhammad?"

The man's brow furrowed, but he didn't speak.

The reaction was no surprise. Attia had always opposed his master's focus on the CIA man but hesitated to give voice to that opposition. Finally, he spoke.

"Our last confirmed contact with him was almost twenty hours ago."

Halabi leaned forward in his chair. "Does that mean you believe him to be dead?"

"No."

"Then I don't understand. He's one man alone in difficult, unfamiliar terrain. On the other hand, your highly trained men have now been joined by what? Two hundred additional fighters and more than thirty vehicles?"

Attia nodded.

"Your silence isn't an answer, Muhammad."

Finally, a hint of resolve became visible in his disciple's expression. "No one has even seen him since he descended into the canyon. Or, better said, no one who's survived. Twelve of our men are dead, including three of mine. He seems to be targeting our crack troops and leaving the others alone to the degree possible. He kills them, strips them of their food, water, and weapons, and then fades back into the desert."

"He'll become exhausted," Halabi said, the volume of his voice slowly rising. "He'll get sick or injured. He can't last out there forever. Bring in more local men loyal to us. Overwhelm him. Trap him like the animal he is."

"Trap him?" Attia said, the frustration audible in

his voice. "We can't even *find* him. All we can do is make guesses based on the pattern of bodies he leaves behind. It's likely that he buries himself during the day to sleep and moves only at night. And he has an endless supply of food, water, and ammunition because it's being provided by his victims."

"The desert will—"

"The desert will do nothing!" Attia said, daring to interrupt him. "This isn't a hardship for him. It's his home. He's spent his entire adult life fighting in places just like this one. He could live out there for weeks. Perhaps months. Killing our people when they present an opportunity or when he needs supplies. But he won't have to, because his comrades won't leave him out there forever. They'll find men loyal to him and they'll find aircraft. When that day comes, our men will die without ever having laid eyes on Mitch Rapp. What is it you tell me every day? That with a thousand good men, you could bring America to its knees overnight? But you can't find a thousand good men. And now you're going to leave the few you *have* managed to find to be picked off one by one by a man who America's next president will likely put in prison."

Halabi felt the familiar hate well up inside him but then it faded into an unfamiliar sense of confusion and uncertainty. Had he fallen into the same trap that had snared him so many times before? Rapp's life had been his for the taking in that village. But instead of ordering the helicopter destroyed on its way in, he'd insisted on Rapp's capture. Why? Did it further the pursuit of Allah's will?

No.

He had failed to kill God's greatest enemy on earth

because of his own desperate need to take revenge. To see the CIA man broken and groveling not at God's feet, but at his own.

Halabi understood now that Rapp wouldn't be caught in that desert, that God had put him beyond the reach of his men as a punishment. Once again, he could feel God's eyes on him. This time, though, they radiated something very different from the love and approval that he had become accustomed to.

"Pull our men out, Muhammad."

"All of them? There's no reason not to leave the local—"

"All of them. It's no use."

Attia gave a short, relieved nod before speaking again. "I assume you agree that we have to move out of Yemen immediately? It's unlikely that Rapp could have interrogated one of my men before killing him, but it's possible that he's learned about this place. Can I begin preparations to move our operations to our secondary site in Somalia?"

Halabi nodded and the man turned, disappearing through the door.

More retribution from God. They would trade a mountaintop fortress surrounded by people sympathetic to his goals for a maze of caverns surrounded by men whose allegiances changed like the direction of the wind.

Halabi closed his eyes and once again envisioned the dangerous path to victory. The greatest obstacle ahead wasn't the U.S. military or Irene Kennedy or even Mitch Rapp. It was his own arrogance.

Finally the ISIS leader pushed himself to his feet and limped to the far wall. There he retrieved a whip consisting of various chains attached to a worn wooden handle. He swung it behind him, feeling the metal bite into his flesh. The blood began to flow and the pain flared, but God remained agonizingly silent.

CHAPTER 14

RAPP accelerated out of the trees and onto a flat summit bisected by a newly paved road. Below he could see the widely spaced dots of porch lights and, in the distance, the glow of Manassas reflecting off low clouds.

Their escape from Yemen had been surprisingly uneventful other than the number of people involved. Predictably, Shamir Karman had become emotionally attached to a number of his employees and had refused to leave them behind. It had taken a little creativity, but they'd managed to cram everyone into a five-vehicle motorcade and avoid getting strafed by the Saudi air force. By now Karman would be installed in a New York condo and the others would be getting fast-tracked through immigration.

Coleman and his men were at Walter Reed getting their wounds checked for the various antibiotic-resistant infections making their way around Yemen. And, of course, grumbling about the fact that Rapp's two days fighting his way through the desert had left him with nothing more than a moderate sunburn.

Empty lots started to appear on either side of the road, all owned by people loyal to Rapp. Near the center of the private subdivision, he passed a couple of completed foundations and a house surrounded by a yard strewn with toys and sports equipment. With all those kids, Mike Nash's place was always either descending into anarchy or recovering from it.

Creating a neighborhood full of shooters had been his brother's idea and, as usual, it had been a solid one. While the fortress of a house Rapp had built was capable of repelling pretty much any attack that didn't involve artillery, the fact that any fight would be immediately joined by a bunch of former SEALs, Delta, CIA, and FBI added to the deterrent.

And so he finally had a place he could let his guard slip a little bit. Maybe relax and have a couple of beers in a chair that wasn't backed up to a wall.

Or not.

Sayid Halabi was alive, pissed, and had apparently been doing some deep thinking. His propaganda videos were beautifully produced and perfectly targeted. His men were well trained and well disciplined. His use of technology was cutting-edge.

He seemed to have lost interest in futile attempts to take and hold territory in favor of embracing the concept of modern asymmetrical warfare. He'd identified the internal divisions tearing America apart and was using fear—amplified by Christine Barnett— to widen them.

It was hard not to give the terrorist piece of shit credit. The rage gripping Barnett's constituency seemed to become more powerful and more deranged every day. Her followers didn't seem to think Sayid

Halabi carried any of the responsibility at all for the bioweapon he was cooking up. They were far more interested in blaming America's foreign policy for provoking jihad, the president's party for not anticipating the threat, and the CIA for not making it magically disappear. Trying to find a news program that even touched on the subject of stopping ISIS was an exercise in futility. All they were talking about was how Halabi's videos were affecting the presidential primaries and how an attack might reshape the general election.

He used the controls on the steering wheel to turn up the stereo, filling the interior of the Dodge Charger with Bruce Springsteen's "The River." Not the most uplifting song, but it took him back to a simpler time. A time when America's enemies were external and could be eradicated with a gun.

A traditional red barn appeared on his left and shortly thereafter the white stucco wall surrounding his house began to emerge. Dim spotlights illuminated the copper gate, but also something else. A lone figure sitting on the ground next to it.

Claudia.

She didn't seem inclined to get up as he approached, so he stopped and stepped out of the vehicle. Despite the cloud cover, it was a beautiful night. There was a light breeze from the north and temperatures were hovering in the mid-seventies. Even so, she had her arms wrapped around her knees, pulling her thighs to her chest as though she was freezing. His headlights combined with the spots, reflecting off tears running down her cheeks.

He wasn't sure what to say. She'd been in this business a long time and knew the realities of his world. The likelihood of him living long enough to buy a set of golf clubs and retire to Florida was fairly low.

"You did everything you could," he said, finally.

"Which was nothing. No one returned our calls, Mitch. And the few who did gave nothing but excuses."

He pressed his back against the wall and slid down next to her. "At the end of the day, I'm at the sharp end of these operations. And I'm comfortable with that."

"Comfortable being abandoned by the country you spent your life fighting for?"

He considered her question for almost a minute before speaking again. "It's nice out there at night. You wouldn't believe the stars. And the quiet."

She just stared straight ahead, unable to meet his eye.

"In a way, I like it," he continued. "Being alone is simple. I like the freedom of knowing that I don't have anyone to rely on and no one's relying on me. There's a clarity to it that you can't get anywhere else."

She laughed and wiped at her tears. "You should never tell a psychiatrist that. They'll lock you up."

"Probably," he said. They sat in silence for a few minutes before she spoke again.

"It was a trap, Mitch. Halabi went after you specifically."

"Seems like."

"What terrifies me is that he didn't want to kill you. That he was willing to lose good men to capture you. I try not to, but I can't stop thinking about what would have happened if he'd succeeded. What he would have done to you."

Rapp shrugged. "There's no point in dwelling

on things that could have happened. You take what lessons you can from them and you move on."

"And what did you learn out there, Mitch?"

He looked over at her. "I feel like we're beating around the bush here. If you have something to say, say it."

"Okay, I will. It's getting bad here, Mitch. America's changing. I think maybe you don't see it, because it's your country. But I do."

"It's just politics," Rapp said dismissively. "I've been dealing with this crap my entire career."

"No. It's more than that. You weren't here to see the brick wall Irene and I hit trying to get help for you. Most people believe that Christine Barnett will be America's next president and they're focused entirely on dealing with that fact. A lot of good people are getting out and a lot of bad ones are moving up. People are paralyzed. They don't know who they should ally themselves with. What positions they should take. No one can figure out exactly what she wants."

"Power," he said, standing and holding a hand out to her. "That's all any of them want."

CHAPTER 15

WHEN Irene Kennedy entered the Oval Office, the meeting's other attendees were just settling into the conversation area at its center. President Alexander was the first to notice her and he strode toward her with a hand outstretched.

"Irene. It's good to see you. As always."

His years in Washington had done nothing to diminish the southern gentleman in him, though they both knew he was lying. When they got together outside of their normal schedule, it meant something had gone wrong. A nuclear threat. A terrorist threat. A Russian leader gone mad. Or, in this case, a psychotic fundamentalist building a biological weapon.

"I think you know Senator Barnett?"

The handshake between the two women was coldly mechanical and accompanied by what must have been Barnett's thousandth attempt to stare her down. As chairman of the Senate Intelligence Committee, Kennedy was forced to interact with her much more than she would have liked. Barnett was a woman whose only true human emotion seemed to be ambition.

She was interested solely in information that could advance her status, increase her personal wealth, or destroy the careers of her rivals. Everything else was just noise to her. And that laser focus had worked. It was almost certain that she would be the next leader of the free world.

"And I assume you've met Colonel Statham?" Alexander continued, picking up on the tension between the two women and trying to diffuse it.

"Of course," Kennedy said, turning with a genuine smile toward the army officer. Despite being a bit overweight and barely five foot four, he was in many ways the Mitch Rapp of deadly diseases. Statham had spent his career seeking out the most terrifying pathogens Mother Nature could dish out. Everything from Ebola to plague to rabies. He had endless stories about things like extracting a foot-long worm from his own leg, being swept over a waterfall while trying to reduce his runaway fever in an Asian river, and being chased through the bush by a hippopotamus. Not surprisingly, he was extremely popular at cocktail parties.

"Gary," she said as he took her hand warmly. "I thought you were in Africa."

His eyes lit up at the mention. "We're working on an Ebola vaccine. Just initial testing, but it's promising."

"Are we ready?" Alexander said, clearly feeling one of the microbiologist's infamous digressions coming on.

"Yes, sir," Statham said.

"Then you have the floor," he said, motioning for everyone to sit.

"I didn't bring the ISIS videos because I figure

everyone's watched them too many times already. My team's gone over them with a fine-toothed comb and, combined with the Agency's analysis, I think we have a pretty good idea of what happened."

"And?" Christine Barnett said, already starting to sound impatient. Undoubtedly, she was looking for ammunition for another attack on the administration of the man sitting next to her.

Despite this, neither Alexander's expression nor his body language even hinted at his deep hatred for Barnett. He'd resigned himself to the fact that she would likely be his successor and he was committed to doing his best to make sure she was prepared for the job.

And while Kennedy admired his effort, she also understood that it was a waste of time. The presidency demanded less a specific skill set or background than it did a type of person. Unfortunately, Christine Barnett would never be that woman.

"Doctors Without Borders was working on an outbreak of a very dangerous SARS-like virus in the village," Statham continued, unflustered. "The three medical personnel that Halabi snatched had stopped the spread and had victims corralled in a building that they'd converted into a treatment facility. It's clear that ISIS knew about it and they sent extremely well-trained and well-prepared troops. Even our Delta guys were impressed by their plan and how it was carried out."

"What plan?" Barnett said.

"I was just getting to that. If you combine all the existing videos into one timeline, you can get a pretty good blow-by-blow. All of Halabi's men were wearing protective gear and they nailed all the doors in the village shut, starting with the treatment facility. They didn't touch anything and after the villagers were sealed up, they burned the buildings."

"Are we certain there were no survivors?" President Alexander asked.

"As certain as we can be," Kennedy responded. "As you know, Mitch took a team there and confirmed that the entire village was burned. Also, there's a significant amount of open desert around it, making it unlikely that a hypothetical survivor could have reached the next-closest population center. Having said that, we're monitoring all of them for unusual activity that could suggest the illness has spread."

"Is there any point to sending another team to have a more in-depth look?" Alexander asked.

She shook her head. "The Saudis obliterated that village five days ago."

"Nothing's certain in this business," Statham interjected. "But with the fire, the protocols used by ISIS, and the isolation, I think we probably dodged this bullet."

Barnett actually laughed at that. "So we don't have to worry about some village in the middle of nowhere with the flu. All we have to worry about is that ISIS now has a sophisticated bioweapons lab manned with Western experts. Is that how you define dodging a bullet? What were those people doing in a terrorist-controlled area of Yemen anyway?"

"Putting themselves in harm's way to help sick people and make sure a potentially catastrophic disease didn't spread," Statham said, no longer able to hide his irritation.

"It's a nice sentiment, but now look where we're at. If we hadn't allowed those—"

"They're from an NGO," Kennedy said, cutting her off before she could sidetrack the meeting. "Two of them aren't even American citizens. We weren't in a position to tell them where they can and can't help people."

"Well, maybe we should have been," Barnett shot back.

"Agreed. But your committee has been reluctant to support our operations in Yem—"

"I was told that Sayid Halabi was dead," she said, the volume of her voice rising. "If I'd known he was in Yemen looking to build a biological capability, I wouldn't have taken that position."

Kennedy wanted to remind her that the Agency had never confirmed Halabi's death and, even if it had, he was only one of a countless number of dangerous jihadists now taking cover in Yemen. But what was the point? This wasn't about truth. It wasn't about protecting America. It was about her installing herself in this office.

The uncomfortable silence that ensued was finally broken by Statham.

"Since you mentioned Halabi's biological weapons capability, let's talk about it for a second. The main purpose of those videos was to look scary. Basically, a lot of fancy stainless steel equipment and three people wandering around in biohazardy-looking clothes. But the truth is, most of that stuff has nothing to do with the production of bioweapons."

"What about the latest video?" Barnett said. "The one I just got a few hours ago? Halabi says he's got Gabriel Bertrand producing a half ton of anthrax."

"That video does suggest that he has the capacity

to produce anthrax, but not in anywhere near those kinds of quantities. It's just propaganda."

"Whether it's a little anthrax or a lot doesn't matter," Barnett said. "People are terrified. And they should be. It's this government's duty to protect the country from these kinds of threats. And despite the billions we squander on homeland security, I have to spend my days sitting around watching a video of Sayid Halabi building bioweapons."

"How long before he has enough anthrax to attack us?" Alexander asked in an uncharacteristically subdued voice. He looked exhausted. Not only from his seven-plus years in office, but from the knowledge that everything said in this meeting would be used against him and his party in the evening news cycle.

"It depends on how much he plans on smuggling in," Statham said. "The amount necessary for a small-scale attack might already be available."

"Casualties?"

"Limited. Any biological weapon is serious and terrifying, but anthrax is hard to deploy. You have to get the granules small enough for inhalation and keep them from clumping. And then the victim actually has to breathe them in. It doesn't spread from human contact and it doesn't scale up well."

"The Russians did it," Barnett said.

"The *Soviets* did it," Statham corrected. "They bred a very deadly spore capable of being deployed as an aerosol. When it got through their lab's filtration system, it killed more than a hundred people. But we're talking about a massive effort by a major world power. This is different. Think about the Aum Shinrikyo cult in Japan. They put an enormous amount of money, expertise, and effort into trying to do the same thing and ended up abandoning the effort in favor of sarin."

"I keep being told not to worry about ISIS and I keep getting burned," Barnett said.

Kennedy frowned but, again, kept her mouth shut. The number of written warnings her office had provided about ISIS in Yemen would fill a good-size closet.

"The bottom line," Statham continued, "is that Halabi could kill a lot more people with a bomb or mass shooter. And it would be a hell of a lot less complicated."

"But not as terrifying," Kennedy said, turning her attention to Barnett and locking eyes with her. "The upcoming election's widening the already dangerous divisions in America. He understands that the fire's already raging and now he's passing out gas cans to anyone willing to use them."

As expected, Barnett glared back. What wasn't expected, though, was the nearly imperceptible smile.

"Irene," the president said, again trying to cut through the tension between the two women, "do we have any idea where Halabi and the French scientist are now?"

"That's why I was a little late arriving," Kennedy said. "We had a geological appraisal done on a cave wall visible in the last video. The general consensus is that it's consistent with what you'd find in Somalia. Unfortunately, a country where we have even fewer resources than in Yemen."

Again, Barnett laughed. "It's my understanding that we don't have *any* resources in Yemen. From what I've been told, Mitch Rapp rolled into Al Hudaydah and started throwing his weight around, then flew into an ambush. We were forced to start mounting a rescue operation and in the process our operation's cover was blown."

It was a skillfully conceived piece of spin, typical of her and her office. Nothing she said was an outright lie, but it managed to tell a story that was more or less the opposite of the truth.

"The only lead we had was that village," Kennedy said calmly. "Mitch went in knowing full well that an ambush was possible. A chopper pilot was killed and Mitch spent two days fighting his way out of the desert. I wonder if you'd have done the same for your country, Senator?"

"I've devoted my entire life to public service," she shot back.

"And I'm sure we're all very grateful for the sacrifices you've made," Kennedy responded, but she was already starting to regret the exchange. All interactions with this woman were a bad combination of dangerous and a waste of time. Barnett placed everyone in two columns: useful to her and dangerous to her. Kennedy's designation had been determined long ago.

"And what exactly is Mitch Rapp's status with regard to the CIA?" Barnett asked.

Kennedy was surprised by the question. They were talking about a potential biological attack on the United States. What did Mitch's employment details matter? She glanced at the president but he seemed to be content to give Barnett some leash. Instead of intervening, he was scrutinizing the woman as though she were a toddler trying to learn a new skill.

"I'm not sure what you're asking, Senator."

"Does he work for you?"

"He no longer works directly for the government, if that's what you mean. He's a private contractor."

"Contractor," Barnett repeated. "Is that a way of saying that what little oversight we once had over him is gone?"

An expression of resigned disappointment appeared on Alexander's face and he finally stepped in. "I think we're getting a little off topic here, Gary. As much as I hate to even contemplate this attack happening, what if it does? What are we doing to get ready for it?"

"The most important thing we can do is get the facts out there and keep the hysteria down. Though that's easier said than done with everything getting stirred up by the media and the—" He managed to catch himself before saying *politicians*. "Uh, the medical community is prepared and looking for potential infections. If anything, we're going to end up with an overreaction. People thinking they have anthrax when they don't. But that's not a serious problem."

"Irene?" the president said.

"We're marshaling what resources we can in Somalia but, as I said, they're limited. And obviously we're coordinating with other areas of Homeland Security to do what we can to keep any biological agent from ever making it into the United States."

Joshua Alexander nodded. There wasn't much more he could do. He was at the end of his last term in office and it was likely that this disaster would land in his successor's lap. On one hand, he was incredibly thankful for that. Eight years in this job was enough for anyone and too much for most people. On the other hand, the idea of Christine Barnett taking the reins was terrifying.

"I want daily progress reports from both of you. And if anything significant changes, contact me immediately."

Kennedy and Statham—two of the most competent and reliable people he'd ever worked with—nodded and stood. After a few strained pleasantries, his three guests began filing out. Before Barnett could fully turn toward the door, though, Alexander put a hand on her shoulder.

"Could you hang back for a minute, Christine?"

When they were alone, Alexander indicated toward the sofa Barnett had been sitting on. The senator looked a bit suspicious, but she sat and watched him take the chair opposite.

"I don't agree with the way you're running your campaign, but I'm a big boy and I understand that what you're doing is effective." He pointed to the Resolute Desk. "And that pretty soon that'll probably be yours."

Barnett tried to keep her expression neutral, but she was clearly pleased to hear that assessment from the leader of the opposing party.

"It's important to understand," Alexander said, speaking deliberately, "that the job of *being* president has very little to do with the job of *running* for president. When you sit down in that chair, you've won. There's nowhere else to go. You'll be there for a few years and then you'll retire and end up a few pages in a history book. While you're in this office, though, it can't just be about politics. You have the lives of three hundred and twenty-five million people in your hands."

Barnett nodded, considering his words for a few seconds before standing. "You rule your way, Mr. President. And I'll rule mine."

CHAPTER 16

"I CALL her Betty, Mitch. Doesn't she seem like a Betty?"

Anna ran one of her tiny hands along the sheep's woolly back. It nuzzled her briefly and then went back to whatever it was that it found so fascinating in the dirt.

The sun was directly overhead and the humidity kept pushing higher, creating a haze on the mountains around them. The barn they were standing next to was designed to be shared by the homeowners in the subdivision and had been set up with stalls for horses.

Rapp's plan had been to rip them out in favor of a gym and shooting range. Unfortunately, Scott Coleman and his wily seven-year-old co-conspirator had commandeered the space while Rapp was in Iraq. He'd left for Baghdad with visions of a thirty-foot climbing wall and returned to a petting zoo.

"That animal's not a pet, Anna. Wouldn't a better name be something like Shank? Or maybe Stew?"

She spun, pressing her back against the sheep and

spreading her arms protectively. "Betty's not dinner! And neither is Jo-Jo or Merinda!"

"He's just being a grouch," Claudia said. "Look how fluffy they are. Maybe we could shear them and make him a nice sweater instead."

Anna's eyes narrowed suspiciously and she pointed to another knot of animals near the south fence line. "The goats aren't fluffy."

"But they eat grass," her mother assured her. "We won't need to mow anymore."

Rapp frowned. Was he really destined to live in a subdivision with thirty people and two hundred ungulates?

"Scott told me people have ostriches."

And a flock of eight-foot-tall flightless birds.

"They make really big eggs," Anna said, picking up on his reaction. "You can have them for breakfast. Mom could make like a gallon of that eggs benny dick sauce."

"Benedict," her mother corrected.

Rapp's phone rang and he glanced down at the screen. "I've got to take this. Why don't you go see how Cutlet's doing?"

"Her name's not Cutlet!"

"Vindaloo?"

Anna wagged a finger at him in a gesture she'd picked up from her mother and then ran off to join her new friends.

"Hello, Irene," Rapp said, fighting off a vague sense of disorientation. Having one foot in two completely different worlds took some getting used to. But learning to switch immediately between them was even harder. "How'd the meeting go?"

"Not as well as I'd hoped."

He watched Claudia follow her daughter across the grass. She looked like a French fashion magazine's idea of a cowgirl. Spotless jeans and work shirt, straw hat, and a pair of boots that suggested ostriches weren't just good for eggs.

"What'd Gary say?"

"The anthrax threat is real. Halabi just needs a way to smuggle it in."

"Take your choice," Rapp said.

"We're ramping up border security on every point of entry in the country, but it's not an easy thing to intercept. We're not talking about a large package or a package with contents that would look particularly remarkable."

"I assume we still don't know anything about Halabi or the lab's location?"

"Probably Somalia. That's it."

"I killed a bunch of his people and he's going to have to replace them. Maybe we could get to him that way. I can go back and—"

"No, you can't."

"What?"

"Christine Barnett's blaming you for failing to kill Halabi in Iraq and then blowing the cover of our operation in Yemen."

"She was *opposed* to that operation in Yemen. And she made us starve it to the point that it was useless."

"I'm pretty sure that's not how she's going to portray the situation."

The malleability of truth was another disorienting thing that had crept into his world. There were hours of video and thousands of pages of documents demonstrating Barnett's history of opposing U.S. operations in the Middle East. But it didn't matter. All she had to do was get on TV and deny it. For her supporters, history would be erased.

"Barnett sees the intelligence agencies as a check on her power," Kennedy said. "And she's going to do everything she can to either weaken us or turn us into part of her political apparatus."

"What about Alexander?"

"He's reconciled himself to her being president and doesn't want to make any more waves than he has to. This election is tearing the country apart as it is."

"Rolling over for her isn't going to pull the country together."

"To be completely honest, I also think he's concerned about becoming a target once he's out of power. At this point, I think he'd be happy to just ride off into the sunset, never to be seen again."

"So he's going to leave us hanging just like any other politician."

"Yes. The only difference is that he'll regret it."

"Doesn't mean much when you're swinging from a rope."

"Maybe not. But I'm more sympathetic to his position than you are. He's a fundamentally decent man in an impossible job."

Rapp moved into the shade of the barn. "I don't work for the Agency anymore. Seems to me that there's no law against a private citizen and a few of his friends going on vacation in Yemen or Somalia. And if in the course of that vacation Sayid Halabi were to get shot in the face or beaten to death with a hockey stick, no harm done, right? Better to stop the anthrax there than to hang your hopes on some TSA guy stumbling on it in a piece of luggage."

"That's the real reason I called, Mitch. President Alexander knew you'd say something like that and wants to impress on you that it's a nonstarter. He and his party are in defense mode right now and he doesn't want any explosions that Barnett could use to strengthen her position."

"You've got to be kidding me."

"I'm not. Do you see them yet?"

"See what?"

"Wait for it. They should be almost there."

Rapp looked around him and finally spotted what she was talking about. Two black SUVs with heavily tinted glass rolling up the street. They approached close enough to get a good view of his house and then parked by the still-unfinished sidewalk.

"They're FBI," Kennedy explained. "Alexander ordered round-the-clock surveillance on you to make sure you don't cause him any trouble."

He stared at the vehicles for a few seconds before responding. "So after more than twenty years that's how it is."

"I'm sorry, Mitch. And even though I know you won't believe it, so is the president."

He stepped out of the shade of the barn and started toward Claudia and Anna without bothering to look back.

"Good-bye, Irene."

CHAPTER 17

THE sandy earth allowed Sayid Halabi to move silently, even with the knurled walking stick that he now relied on. The cave's ceiling was low enough to brush the top of his head, a sandstone slab decorated with crude drawings that had been forgotten for thousands of years.

It was a less comfortable and versatile location than the one he'd been forced to abandon in Yemen, but in many ways far more secure. The area was remote enough to avoid prying eyes, but not so remote that the movements of his men would seem unusual. The cavern itself was in a strong defensive position with deep chambers and multiple widely spaced exits. Most important, though, Somalia's unfamiliar operating environment would degrade Mitch Rapp's effectiveness.

A glow ahead began to overpower the dim LEDs spread out on the ground, and Halabi increased his pace slightly. When he reached the end of the corridor, he stopped and silently scanned the semicircular chamber beyond. The nonessential scientific equipment had served its propaganda purpose and had been abandoned in Yemen. The lab was now less impressive to look at, but also far more functional— a space designed for nothing but the production of anthrax.

Photos of it had already been disseminated on the Internet, transforming the general threat to a specific one. Western experts had immediately identified the facility's purpose and capabilities, providing ammunition to the politicians and media companies. The airwaves were now filled with the most sensational and lurid depictions of a large-scale anthrax attack. Partisan disputes continued to grow in intensity, with Christine Barnett spinning the threat into a purely political issue.

America was nearing complete paralysis. Politicians were focused entirely on the battle for the White House. Homeland Security executives were scrambling to position themselves to survive the change in administration. And the American people were turning increasingly inward, focusing on imaginary internal enemies while largely ignoring the external forces bent on their destruction.

Halabi watched silently as Dr. Gabriel Bertrand moved from a stainless steel incubator to the table next to it. If it hadn't been for the stone walls, he could have been at home in France. The cool, dry environment inside the cave left his clean-shaven face without a hint of perspiration. Carefully combed hair hung just above the collar of a spotless lab coat and crisply creased slacks covered what was visible of his legs.

All very much intentional. The Frenchman had been provided a place to wash, living quarters far more luxurious than even Halabi's own, and a beautiful young Yemeni girl who had been instructed to attend to his every need. The more he had, the more he had to lose.

From Halabi's perspective, it was an unfamiliar and rather intolerable situation but one without a viable alternative. The physical coercion he would have normally used would be counterproductive in this case. While the anthrax was a simple matter, Bertrand's role going forward was to become increasingly critical and complex. He needed to be healthy and clearheaded to complete the tasks ahead of him.

"I understand you've made a great deal of progress," Halabi said, moving out of the shadows.

Startled, Bertrand spun, pressing his back against the table and staring silently as Halabi approached.

"Am I correct that your first batch of anthrax will be ready for deployment later this week?"

The Frenchman nodded numbly.

"And you're aware that the effectiveness of our attack has bearing on your situation here? That I expect a number of Americans to be infected?"

"I can't guarantee that," he blurted. "I don't know how you're going to deliver it and to whom. And if people know they're infected they can get antibiotics to cure—"

"I'm not concerned about whether people are cured. Only that they contract the disease. I'm interested in causing panic, not in a specific death toll."

He didn't respond and Halabi smiled. What wouldn't this man do to protect his own life and comfort? Perhaps it was time to find out.

"Come with me, Doctor."

"Where?"

Halabi ignored the question and started back down the narrow corridor. Only a few seconds passed before the Frenchman's footsteps fell in behind. The circuitous route finally took them out into the starlight and they used it to cross to another cave entrance two hundred meters to the north. Halabi motioned the Frenchman inside and they began to descend.

"Where are you taking me?" he asked again, the numbness in his voice now replaced by fear.

This time Halabi answered. "To see if you can help me with a problem that's arisen."

They'd barely penetrated twenty meters when they came upon a computer monitor resting on a boulder. It was connected wirelessly to a camera set up in the depths of the cavern. Halabi pointed to the monitor and Bertrand's eyes widened as he looked at the two women depicted on it. One was lying motionless on a cot, so still that it was unclear if she was alive. The other was convulsing with a coughing fit violent enough that it caused her to vomit.

"One of my men was infected with the virus you were studying. Before he died, he infected his family. These are the two that are left."

It was a lie, of course. One of the infected villagers had been secretly taken from the makeshift infirmary before it was burned. She had died more than a week ago, but not before Halabi had used her to infect the martyrs on the computer screen.

"What about your other men? Or people you came across during the journey here?" Bertrand said, his fear turning to something verging on panic.

"We had no contact with locals on our way here and none of my other men are showing symptoms."

That was in fact true. They had been extraordinarily cautious transporting the infected villager there. Only one of his men—wearing the appropriate protective clothing—had come into contact with her, and she had traveled in a sealed van along roads far from population centers. The vehicle had subsequently been incinerated and the man who had handled her was quarantined in a separate cave system. Without symptoms thus far, thank Allah, but he would stay there another two weeks in an abundance of caution.

"It is impossible to overstate how dangerous this virus is," Bertrand said. "Are you certain none of your other people are showing signs of infection? And do you have a record of who your man and his family came into contact with after exposure? Have any of them left the area? Can you get in touch with them?"

The Frenchman continued to talk, but Halabi ignored his words in favor of his tone. It was impossible not to savor the horror and desperation in it. Impossible not to revel in the fact that soon the entire world would share that horror and desperation.

"What can you do to help them," Halabi said, silencing the man's babbling.

"Help them? What do you mean?"

"It's a simple question, Doctor."

"Nothing. There's no cure or way to attenuate the effects of the virus. The only thing you can do is try to keep the victims breathing and hydrated, and possibly use antibiotics to ward off secondary infections. Then you wait and see if they survive long enough for their immune system to react."

"We have ventilators and IVs, as well as basic protective clothing. What we don't have are people with medical training." Halabi paused for a moment. "Other than you."

He examined the French scientist as he stared at the screen. What would the man do? Would he put himself at risk to help these people? Two apparently innocent women?

The answer came a few seconds later when Bertrand began slowly shaking his head. "Basic protective clothing isn't enough. You'd need state-of-the-art equipment and to follow very precise procedures. Otherwise there's a chance that we could lose containment."

"So we should let them die?" Halabi prompted. "Alone and suffering?"

"If this got out, there'd be no way to stop it. We could be talking about millions—maybe *hundreds* of millions dead. And why? Because one of the gloves you gave me had a hole in it. Or one of the shoe covers I wore wasn't properly disposed of."

"We're completely isolated in a sparsely populated region of Somalia," Halabi pressed, now just goading the scientist. "My men would gladly die for me and I'm willing to order them to seal us in these caves should the illness spread. Not only would it die here with us, but it would likely be centuries before our bodies were even found."

Bertrand's only response was to turn away from the monitor and stare off into the darkness of the cavern.

Halabi had wanted to get a measure of the man and that's exactly what he'd accomplished. The people depicted on that computer screen were nothing to him. Two poor, uneducated peasants who lived and would die like so many others before them. Anonymous and irrelevant.

Of course, Bertrand would care more about the outside world. But how much? What would he sacrifice to save millions of strangers and the morally bankrupt societies that they comprised? Discomfort? Perhaps. Pain? Doubtful. Death? Almost certainly not.

When Halabi finally led the Frenchman out of the cavern, he looked utterly broken. Any illusions he might have had about himself had been stripped away and now lay dying with the people in that chamber.

CHAPTER 18

I T was still impossible to believe this was really happening.

Holden Flores was crammed into the trunk of a mid-1970s Cadillac—the only vehicle the Drug Enforcement Administration could find with enough space for his six-foot frame, body armor, and weapon. Air was provided by a few holes drilled in what turned out to be less than optimal places. The only comfortable position he'd managed to work out covered about half of them, leaving him with a choice between agonizing leg cramps and suffocation. So far he wasn't sure which one was worse. More experimentation would be necessary.

Not that he had any real right to complain. He was only a few years out of college and everyone knew shit rolled downhill. Besides, a car trunk wasn't the craziest place a DEA agent had ever hidden. Not even close. That honor would probably go to a porcelain clown statue outside of Albuquerque back in the 1990s. What made Flores's situation unique was less the Caddy itself than where it was parked. Not in a remote desert clearing near the border. Not in some dilapidated neighborhood full of meth labs and gang-bangers.

No, he was in the bottom level of a parking garage serving San Ysidro's newest boutique mall. Above him was a tastefully laid-out selection of fair trade coffee, locally made jewelry, sustainable clothing, and all manner of gluten-free, vegan, organic snacks. Normally, not his thing but after four hours in a trunk, a soy hot dog with some ethically produced sauerkraut was sounding pretty good.

Flores started getting lightheaded and he slid his ass off the ventilation holes, feeling a trickle of cool air as he glanced down at his phone. The screen was linked to cameras hidden throughout the space and he scrolled through the feeds. Tesla? Check. Another Tesla? Check. Spotless minivan with a sticker suggesting it had been converted to run on recycled cooking oil? Check. Young, affluent couple pushing a baby jogger toward the elevator? Check and check.

What wasn't visible was the improbably long tunnel leading from this garage to a far less impressive building on the other side of the Mexican border. In fact, it was so well hidden that no one in Homeland Security's entire network had ever found even the slightest trace of it. The tip had come from NASA, of all places. They'd been testing a new geological survey satellite when they'd stumbled upon an underground anomaly that traced a perfectly straight line from San Ysidro to Tijuana.

At first they'd thought it was a glitch in their equipment. Once that was ruled out, they started searching for evidence of a disused sewer line or power conduit. When that turned out to be a dead end, a tech in Houston had made a joke about it being a drug tunnel. Apparently, someone there had taken the idea seriously enough to send a few screen shots to her cousin at DEA.

And now there he was, sweating his ass off with a spare tire wedged against his spine. Probably because of some forgotten mine or collapsed well that would have been easy to check out with a little cooperation from the Mexican authorities.

Unfortunately, the chances of that happening were right around zero. Relations with America's southern neighbor were at an all-time low. The constant background noise about immigration, trade, and drugs had been bad enough, but with the upcoming election, it was all blowing up. Everything was about blame and politics. Us versus them.

Even the solid Mexican law enforcement guys were now either sitting on their hands or, worse, actively undermining DEA and ICE operations. They figured why should they die in gangland executions because the Americans like to get high, eat tacos, and have their lawns mowed on the cheap.

Flores watched the screen of his phone as a maintenance guy appeared on the north camera. It would have been nice if he'd been one of theirs, but they'd run into a suspiciously solid wall on that front. Normally, those kinds of jobs were abundant in this area and the DEA sent various applicants with nicely fabricated résumés. Not so much as a call back.

That had left them with a pretty complicated surveillance environment, but they'd finally figured out the narco trafficker's system. How were they getting in and out of the tunnel with enough product to make this enterprise worthwhile?

A fucking car elevator.

The very thought of it made Flores a little queasy. Not the elevator specifically, but everything around it. This mall had been built by an American-Mexican consortium. The city had provided incentives and tax credits. When it opened, the mayor and Arnold Schwarzenegger had cut the ribbon. That's right, Kindergarten Cop himself had shown up to open a drug trafficking front partially paid for by the state of California.

The maintenance man paused, glancing around in a way that was suspicious enough to get Flores's attention. This section of the garage was as far as you could get from the elevator leading up to the mall. Lighting was worse than in other areas and there was a slight choke point that formed a bit of a psychological barrier for all but the most intrepid parkers, mostly those who wanted space to let their overpriced rides breathe and to reduce the possibility of a door ding.

After confirming he was alone, the man slipped into a spotless Ford Escape and pulled it out of a space along the wall. Flores felt a burst of adrenaline and disbelief when the floor behind it dropped six inches and slid back. A moment later, a van rose from the ground so fast that it was almost thrown in the air when the platform reached ground level. But only almost. Clearly the weight and speed had been calculated to make sure it just bounced silently on well-oiled shocks.

And all this had happened with the Ford situated in a way that would completely block the view of anyone approaching. Fortunately, the DEA had managed to mount a camera on an overhead pipe, allowing everyone to watch this magnificent operation in full HD.

The van began pulling smoothly off the platform and the elevator immediately dropped again, allowing the asphalt cover to begin sliding back into place.

That, however, was exactly what this operation was designed to prevent. There was no practical way to get into that tunnel from the U.S. side once the cover was closed. It would take serious construction equipment and approvals that wouldn't go unnoticed by the drug lords. At best, everyone would be long gone before the DEA could get access. At worst, they'd blow it up and cave in half the town.

Everything had to go right and, for once, it did.

The Tesla directly across from the elevator was on remote and its DEA controller floored the accelerator. It collided with the van, forcing it back until its rear end dropped into the gap in front of the closing cover. At the same time, Flores leapt from the trunk, listening to the crunch of metal as the cover slammed into the rear doors of the van.

He sprinted to a predetermined position behind a pillar as the two men in the van struggled to open doors that had been jammed by the flex of the overloaded vehicle as it had dropped over the edge. The sound of distant screeching tires could be heard from above, suggesting his backup was on the way. Power should have already been cut to the passenger elevator leading to the garage and the lane down to this level would now be blocked by a Special Response Team.

"DEA! Put your hands where I can see them!" Flores shouted, aiming his weapon around the pillar.

There had been no way to put more men than him on this level. There were only so many 1970s Caddies you could pack into mall parking without someone taking notice. And while he agreed with that assessment, it didn't do anything to make him feel less alone. Particularly when the men, instead of following his orders, hunched forward and reached for the floorboards.

Flores held his fire. Maybe they were just scared and dazed from the impact of the Tesla. They could be cartel enforcers, but they might also just be twenty-dollar-an-hour drivers. No need to have soldiers pilot your transport vehicles. In fact, it would be worse, right? They'd look suspicious.

Unfortunately, his theory fell apart when the men's hands reappeared holding MP5s.

The weapon in Flores's hand wasn't what he would have liked. Something terrifying like the DEA's Rock River LAR-15. Or maybe a Daniel Defense DDM4 with a sweet integrated suppressor and an oversize mag. Nothing shouts *down on your knees* like thirty rounds of .300 Blackout ready to rock.

Instead, he had a punk-ass grenade launcher filled with tear gas rounds. The first two shots went in quick succession, and he pulled down the full face mask he had riding on top of his head. The gas was made even more effective by the confined, poorly ventilated space. Within a few seconds it was already getting hard to see.

That didn't bother the men in the van, though. They just started shooting on full auto through windows they'd unwisely rolled down. The haze around him lit up with the barrel flashes and Flores dropped to his stomach, covering his ears. Those assholes' eyes and noses would feel like they were on fire by now and it would be getting hard for them to breathe. At this point, they wouldn't be able to pick out targets smaller than a battleship if they were standing on a mountaintop on a clear day. He just needed to avoid getting tagged by a ricochet.

The guns went silent and he could hear shouting in Spanish as the men hunted blindly for fresh magazines.

Flores's position on the concrete was right where he wanted to be but he couldn't stay. His backup was going to come around that corner in a few seconds and by then the assholes in the van might have reloaded. If they weren't deaf from the shooting they'd done already, they could aim by sound at the approaching car. Not high percentage, but that didn't mean they wouldn't get lucky.

Flores toggled his throat mike. "I'm going for the van. Don't shoot me."

He pulled his sidearm and ran through the gas mostly by memory. It took less than five seconds to make it to the van's open window but he was having a hard time picking out what was going on inside. The click of a magazine being driven home made it fairly obvious and he slammed the butt of his pistol into the side of the driver's head. He slumped unconscious onto the steering wheel and Flores aimed his pistol at the man struggling to get the passenger door open.

"Hands up, dickhead!"

The man froze, trying to decide what to do. There weren't many options. He was out of ammo, blind, and his breathing was coming in choking gasps.

Flores's backup came around the corner and skidded to a stop. Doors were thrown open and shouts drowned out the quiet hiss of one of the canisters still spewing hesitant streams of gas.

Confronted with all that, the man in the passenger seat finally raised his hands.

Flores kept his weapon trained on the drug runner's head as his team started moving cautiously toward the vehicle.

Holy shit. I'm a total badass.

CHAPTER 19

RAPP'S limousine eased beneath the hotel portico behind a lemon yellow Lamborghini and an SUV adorned with an improbable amount of chrome. He watched a woman struggle from the low-slung sports car with the help of the doorman and then teeter toward the entrance tugging at a miniskirt that seemed to be half-missing.

"I'll get out here," he said, reaching for the handle.

"It'll just be another moment," his driver responded. "I can get you under cover and to the doors."

He appreciated the man's professionalism, but it was eighty-three degrees beneath a clear dark sky and the doors he was talking about were less than twenty yards away.

"I think I can make it."

Rapp stepped out under the watchful eye of a group of young people standing at the edge of the parking lot. He was wearing the new suit he'd found hanging in his closet and a clip-on tie that was signed on the back by some Italian guy. His hair was tied back and his beard trimmed, but that still left enough of his features obscured that they initially thought he might be a celebrity trying to fly under the radar.

By the time he made it to the sidewalk they seemed to have concluded that he was nobody and were turning their attention to an approaching Ferrari. Rapp entered the lobby and found a similarly well-groomed Scott Coleman motioning him toward a private elevator near the back.

"Thanks for bailing me out at the last minute, Mitch. The job offer in Iraq came out of nowhere. It's going to be really good for the company's profile but I need to be there personally and we're stretched a little thin."

Everything he was saying was complete bullshit, Rapp knew. This was almost certainly part of a plot by Claudia to convince him of the benefits of the private sector and to get his mind off the Agency, anthrax, and Sayid Halabi.

His initial reaction wasn't just to say no, but to say *hell* no. Then he'd remembered that those words had never come out of Coleman's mouth in their entire relationship. Even when the job description ended with "and then we'll probably all die," the former SEAL charged in without question. How could Rapp do any less?

"Why don't I just go with you to Iraq," Rapp suggested. "Mas or Bruno can handle this."

Coleman smiled as he used a key to access the elevator. "I can't put you on a protection detail, Mitch. My client would end up getting killed by someone trying to get to *you*."

"Uh huh," Rapp said, following his friend into the elevator and resigning himself to the fact that there was no escape.

"Trust me, you don't want to go to Iraq. I guarantee you this is going to be the best job you've ever had. KatyDid bought up the entire top floor and they've locked themselves in the presidential suite."

"A venereal disease bought up a hotel floor?"

"That's chlamydia. Katydids are grassh—" He fell silent before finishing his sentence. "For God's sake, Mitch. It's what the press call Didier Martin and Katy Foster."

"Who?"

Coleman looked at him sideways as they began to rise. "Martin is pretty much the biggest singer in the world. He's been a household name since he was, what? Fourteen? His girlfriend Katy is an actress and model. Probably the most popular person on social media for two years running. I mean, I know you spend a lot of time in caves, man. But come on."

"What's this to me?"

"That's the best part. All you have to do is sit in a comfortable chair outside their door. They never leave the room. Basically, they eat, screw, get high, and watch TV. Almost always in that order. Two days from now, he's doing a concert and once he leaves the hotel, the venue's security takes over. And for this—wait for it—I'm jacking him for fifty grand a day."

"Visitors?"

"Not unless Martin calls you and tells you they're coming. Oh, and don't go inside unless he specifically tells you to. And if he does, don't talk to either one of them unless they ask you a question. Also, it's better if you don't look at them directly."

"Seriously?"

"Doesn't matter," Coleman said as the elevator

opened and they stepped out. "He's not going to call, and the only time you're going to lay eyes on them is when you turn them over to stadium security. No one's going to try to kill them. No one's going to shoot at you. Just sit in the comfy chair, play Angry Birds on your phone, and collect twenty grand a day."

"I thought you said you were charging him fifty."

"I gotta cover my overhead," Coleman said and pointed to a chair set up next to a set of opulent double doors. Rapp lowered himself into it.

"What do you think?"

"It actually is pretty comfortable."

"Here's the key to the elevator and a key to the room that you won't need. Enjoy and don't forget to remind Claudia to water my plants. I'll see you when I get back in a couple weeks."

"So that's the chef's salad to start, the filet with french fries instead of baked potato, and a Coke." The room service guy lifted a silver cover off the plate and snapped out a napkin before dropping it in Rapp's lap.

"Did you forget the cheesecake?"

"Of course not. It's on the lower shelf. Best in the city. Did you want this on Mr. Coleman's account or on the room?"

"Definitely the room," Rapp said, reaching for his silverware.

"Anything else I can do?"

"Put a thirty percent tip on there for yourself."

"Thank you very much, sir."

Rapp expected him to disappear down the hallway like Coleman had a few hours ago, but instead he just stood there.

"Problem?"

"What are they like?"

Rapp shrugged and cut into the steak.

"Didier's music makes my ears bleed, but Katy . . ." His voice faded for a moment. "That woman is *smoking* hot. Wouldn't it be nice to be in there with her instead of out here?"

Rapp shoved the bite of steak into his mouth and grunted noncommittally. In truth, he had no idea what either one of them looked like. Though it probably wouldn't be a bad idea to check Google since he was supposed to be protecting them.

The man stared at the doors longingly for another couple of seconds and then started back for the elevator.

Rapp watched him go and then returned his attention to his filet. It was good, but not good enough to distract him from the fact that his life suddenly felt foreign to him. Normally, he savored boredom. It generally went hand in hand with his time between operations, and it gave him a chance to sleep, heal, and plan the next mission. This was different. He wasn't tired, he didn't have any injuries, and there *was* no next mission.

A stream of screamed curse words managed to filter through the door, breaking the hours of silence. He ignored them, taking a thoughtful sip of his Coke.

The fight against Islamic terrorists had been, in many ways, easy. The enemy was a bunch of religious fanatics perpetrating unprovoked attacks on civilians with no real purpose other than to create suffering. There were white hats and there were black hats. And while the tunnel was long, it was also straight. When you killed all the people in the black hats, the job was done.

The muffled crash of shattering glass became audible as he popped another piece of steak in his mouth.

Now the operating environment was changing. More and more, threats seemed to come from within. He'd been dealing with corrupt politicians his entire life, but there had always been the cover of a few good ones. Now they were running for the exits. In a few months, Christine Barnett could be the president of the United States. Kennedy would be out, as would pretty much every other person he respected in Washington.

What then? Comfortable chairs in hotel hallways?

The crash that came next was a hell of a lot louder—like a piece of furniture being thrown through a plate glass window. Had to be something else, though. Architects had gotten wise to celebrities throwing things through penthouse windows and had made them shatterproof.

Rapp leaned back in his chair, chewing thoughtfully.

Where did he fit into a world where the definition of "enemy" was becoming a constantly shifting matter of perspective? Where people were judged by their words and not their actions? Maybe nowhere. Maybe it was time to hand things over to the younger generation.

The next time the woman screamed, it wasn't to swear. Her voice was filled with fear and pain, and was partially drowned out by an enraged male voice making incoherent accusations. Rapp frowned as he sliced off another piece of steak. It was a perfect example of everything he'd been thinking about. He was happy to risk his ass saving people from ISIS or the Russians or al Qaeda. But when had he signed on to stop people from inflicting wounds on themselves?

Finally, the sobbing started. Terrified and barely audible through the door, it sounded so pathetic, Rapp figured it'd calm things down. Instead, it had the opposite effect.

Listening to that asshole tear around the room made Rapp think about other people he'd tried to protect over the years. And about how many were dead now. The innocent women and children guilty of nothing but being born in the wrong part of the world. The men who just wanted to make a life for themselves and their families but who found themselves conscripted into terrorist groups. The soldiers who did everything they could with the shit sandwich they'd been handed.

And now here he was sitting in some swanky hotel listening to two pampered screwups try to kill each other. They might as well have been spitting on those people's graves.

When something hit the door hard enough to knock off part of the molding, Rapp finally stood. His preference would have been to let them finish each other off, but one of them ending up dead wasn't going to reflect particularly well on Coleman's organization. He owed the man too much to let his company's name get splashed across every newspaper in the world.

Rapp tapped his key card against the lock and pushed reluctantly through the door. The scene inside was pretty much what he'd expected. Martin was in the middle of the room in his boxer shorts, high as a kite and slurring some nonsense that Rapp didn't bother to listen to. His pale skin was covered in tattoos and a baseball hat turned sideways completed the impression of a suburban kid playing gangster.

At his feet was a skinny young girl wearing nothing but panties and a cut-off T-shirt. She was beautiful in that over-the-top reality star kind of way, but the blood flowing from her nose and the heavily dilated pupils didn't enhance the package. When her gaze shifted to Rapp, Martin spun.

"What the fuck are you doing in here?" he screamed.

"I keep asking myself that."

Rapp was surprised when the little prick grabbed a lamp and rushed him. He deflected the lamp with one hand and rammed the other into his stomach, leaving the singer spewing his dinner all over the marble floor.

Then it was the girl's turn. She leapt to her feet with energy Rapp would have bet she didn't have and mounted a similar charge. This time he just stepped aside. Her momentum took her right past him but then she hit the vomit. Her feet went out from under her and she landed hard, cracking the back of her head on the tile.

Rapp looked down at them for a few seconds and then went back out into the hallway, closing the door behind him. He sat and pulled the cheesecake from the lower shelf of the cart before digging his phone from his pocket. Coleman picked up on the first ring.

"What? Why are you calling me?"

"There's been a problem," Rapp said through a mouthful of dessert.

"You didn't kill them. Please tell me you didn't kill them."

"No, I didn't fucking kill them." He paused to swallow. "But you might want to call an ambulance."

CHAPTER 20

WHILE his objective was still within sight, the vantage point from which Sayid Halabi was viewing it had changed significantly. The Western-style office he'd constructed in Yemen had been left far behind. He was now sitting on a broken stool behind a desk constructed of scavenged plywood. Lighting was minimal—an exposed bulb dangling from a spike driven into the rock overhead. It provided barely enough illumination to see a map of North America similarly anchored to the cave's wall. The few creature comforts they'd managed to bring into Somalia had been given to the Frenchman to keep him motivated.

In many ways, Halabi welcomed the change. The laptop on his improvised desk remained turned off. His worldly belongings were contained in a modest wooden crate in the corner. A prayer rug, faded and worn, was neatly rolled at his feet. The austerity made him feel closer to God, though he recognized that the sensation was a false one. In order to succeed in a world ruled by the enemies of Islam, he would have to return to the sophisticated tools they so deftly wielded. But for now, he'd allow himself to revel in the stillness.

He pushed himself to his feet and limped over to the map. It was difficult to make out detail in the dim light so he leaned in close, examining the line depicting the border between the United States and Mexico.

America's refusal to deal with its addiction to narcotics and cheap labor was yet another gift from God. Instead of creating a coherent framework to provide those products and services, the very country that demanded them insisted that they be illegal. Predictably, the result was a spectacularly profitable black market that had generated a smuggling infrastructure unparalleled in human history.

Halabi had recently partnered with a Mexican drug cartel that was desperate for a reliable Middle Eastern heroin supplier. It was a business he knew well, having used the trade to destroy the lives of millions of Westerners while using the profits to wage war on their countries.

In their first, tentative transaction, a small package that supposedly contained heroin had been hidden in a shipment of Mexican cocaine four days ago. The stated goal was a proof of concept—to ensure that Esparza's cartel could circumvent border security and deliver the package as promised to one of Halabi's representatives in California.

The weaponized anthrax that the package actually contained would then be deployed where it would have the biggest impact: politicians who backed Middle East intervention, business and tech leaders, the celebrities who were worshipped as though they were gods. And, of course, Mitch Rapp.

Delivery vectors would be far more sophisticated than the anonymous delivery of suspicious white powder that the Americans had experienced before and were expecting again. Careful profiles had been made of desirable targets, with ones that were difficult to access being ruled out. In truth, though, he'd been forced to discard surprisingly few. Politicians and captains of industry tended to be creatures of habit, and with America's low unemployment, getting ISIS operatives into kitchens, behind service counters, and even in the business of repairing sensitive HVAC systems was laughably simple.

More complicated, but in the end perhaps more fruitful, were the celebrities. Physical access to them, their food, and their homes tended to be more difficult. In the end, though, the answer had been obvious: identify the ones who were drug users and infiltrate their supply chain.

If all went well with the anthrax delivery, shipments of actual Afghan heroin would ensue, cementing his relationship with the Esparza cartel and providing a reliable means of getting whatever and whomever he wanted across the U.S. border.

Halabi stepped back from the map, continuing to contemplate the blurry image and wondering idly where the anthrax was now. An empty Mexican desert? Hidden in an innocuous vehicle waiting to cross a U.S. checkpoint? Already in California and on its way to his representative there?

How long until he saw the fruits of his labor? Reports of famous and powerful Americans being rushed to hospitals. Images of men in hazmat suits searching opulent mansions, glass office towers, and cordoned sections of the Capitol Building. Distant shots of elaborate funerals and furtive video of intensive care units.

Of course, Christine Barnett would not be targeted. She was too useful. He relished the thought of her using the attacks to further undermine the intelligence agencies that were her country's only hope. She would turn the American people against them, replacing their leadership with people whose only qualification was loyalty to her. Soon the organizations that had been America's first line of defense would exist only to protect and augment her power.

Muhammad Attia appeared at the cavern's entrance and pointed to the computer on Halabi's desk. "You have a call from Mexico. It's urgent."

The ISIS leader nodded and Attia disappeared again.

Even deep in the Somali cave system, it was impossible not to turn his gaze upward when he turned on the device. The assurances he'd been given by his communications experts were of little value. No one could fully grasp the evolving technology of the Americans. It was a never-ending arms race—terrorist groups discovered how to hide their networks and the Americans learned how to find them.

Unfortunately, the only way to know for certain where that arms race stood was to test it. To flip a fateful switch and wonder if somewhere overhead a warning light had begun to flash in one of America's drone fleet.

Halabi returned to the stool, reminding himself that his future was in God's hands. Only Allah had the power to decide whether he lived or died. Whether he would usher in a new age or disappear in a cloud of fire and dust.

He entered his password and waited for the secure call to connect. When it finally did, the accented voice of Carlos Esparza filled the confined space.

"Have you been following the news?"

"Of course."

The delay created by the signal bouncing all around the world was infuriating, but unavoidable.

"Did you see the DEA grandstanding about their big bust in San Ysidro?"

"The shopping mall," Halabi said. He'd made note of the story in passing but was more focused on the presidential election and the coverage of the anthrax threat. "Why should this be of interest to me?"

"Because your product was in that shipment."

Halabi felt the breath catch in his chest.

"Hey. You there?" Esparza prompted. "This connection isn't worth shit."

"You told me you had the most sophisticated smuggling network in existence. That the Americans—"

The Mexican talked over him, causing their voices to garble for a moment. ". . . kidding me? We had a German-engineered tunnel running to a mall with a fucking Whole Foods. Do you have any idea how hard it is to get those holier-than-thou vegan pricks to open a store in your property?"

"The engineering of your tunnel and your tenants aren't my concern," Halabi said, beginning to sweat despite the cool temperatures. "The fact that you lost my product is."

"Cost of doing business."

The ISIS leader opened his mouth to speak but then

caught himself. Esparza believed that the package he'd been given was nothing but a trivial amount of heroin. A display of concern and irritation would be expected. But outright anger might be met with suspicion.

The scientific equipment necessary to make another batch of anthrax was there with them in Somalia. In the end, though, the anthrax was little more than a distraction designed to keep Irene Kennedy blinded and the American people at each other's throats. It was the fatal blow that mattered.

"I have people that you've assured me you can get across the border," Halabi said finally. "They're not as easily transported as a small package of heroin and they're not as expendable."

"Stop breaking my balls," Esparza responded. "Have you not been paying attention? It took *NASA* for those assholes to find my operation. Fucking NASA. Your people will be fine. In fact, it's getting easier to smuggle people every day. That nut bar putting out those anthrax videos has border security pulling resources from human trafficking and focusing on intercepting product."

"And if I send you another package? Can I expect you to lose it again because of this increased focus?"

"Remember what I said about those assholes needing NASA to do their job for them? That intercept was a fluke. I've got a thousand ways across the border, and I hired a kid from MIT to tell me if we've got any more orbiting telescopes getting into our business. Send me another package and I guarantee it'll get through."

"What will happen to the heroin?"

"What heroin?"

"*My package that was confiscated,*" Halabi said, trying to control the frustration in his voice.

"Who gives a shit? I told you already. These kinds of losses are just the cost of doing business. Once we get this partnership up and running, your problem won't be interceptions, it'll be what to do with all the money you're making."

"You didn't answer my question."

"You want an answer? Fine. Nothing's going to happen to it. Those DEA pricks will take some pictures of themselves with it to try to convince people they're actually earning their paychecks and then they'll put it in an incinerator and it'll all just go up in smoke."

CHAPTER 21

IRENE Kennedy had been directed to a conference room instead of the Oval Office, where she usually met the president. She'd been told nothing of the meeting's agenda, nor why it was urgent enough to force her to cancel a long-planned meeting with the director of the Mossad. Unusual enough to take note of, but hardly unprecedented. The president of the United States could call meetings however and whenever he wanted.

When she entered, she saw Christine Barnett sitting near the back of the long table that dominated the room. She didn't rise, instead glaring at Kennedy and giving her an almost imperceptible nod. In contrast, the other man in the room strode over to take her hand. Robert Woodman had been the director of the DEA for just over two years but Kennedy didn't know him particularly well. He was something of an enigma in Washington—a former lawyer who had known the president since college but who had few other contacts inside the Beltway. His leadership at the DEA had been competent, but cautious. Her gut feeling was that he was a smart, patriotic man who just didn't have much passion for his organization's mission.

"It's good to see you, Bob," Kennedy said, still in the dark as to the purpose of the meeting. Of course, she'd been briefed on the well-publicized bust in San Ysidro, but that was very much outside of her sphere of influence. When the army's diminutive bioweapons expert entered, though, her heart sank.

Gary Statham's face held none of the warmth or inquisitiveness that it normally did. He remained silent as he shook hands with Kennedy and Woodman. A moment later, he was seated at the table, staring down at it as though it held some secret.

When the president entered, Kennedy chose a seat as far from Christine Barnett as possible. Not only because of her personal distaste for the woman, but in hopes that some physical distance would keep the senator focused on the subject at hand and not her hatred of the CIA.

"I'm sure all of you are aware of the recent drug bust at that mall in California?" the president said.

"It'd be hard to miss," Barnett said, responding to what was obviously a rhetorical question. "What's next? Are we going to find levitating subterranean trains? The fact that our borders—"

"I'm sure we're all looking forward to you solving America's drug problem," Alexander said, cutting her off. "Robert? Could you bring us up to speed?"

Woodman nodded. "The truck that came through that tunnel was carrying roughly four hundred kilos of cocaine in two hundred separate packages. As a matter of procedure, we select a random sampling of them to test for purity, contamination, and to get an idea of where it came from. When our analysts opened the bags, it was clear that one of them didn't contain cocaine or any other narcotic. In light of everything that's been going on, we closed it back up and called Gary's people."

The president turned his attention to the army colonel, who immediately picked up the narrative.

"It contained anthrax," he said simply.

"How much damage could it have done?" the president asked.

"That depends on how it was deployed. To be clear, there's no way to make this some kind of weapon of mass destruction. It can't, for instance, be put in a crop duster and flown over New York. And with all the publicity, I imagine anyone opening an envelope full of suspicious powder would get in touch with the authorities pretty quickly. Having said that, Gabriel Bertrand knows what he's doing. This is finely ground, weapons-grade stuff. Obviously it could be put in food or drinks, but a much worse scenario would be if someone who knew what they were doing got it into a building's ventilation system. You wouldn't know it until people started coming down with symptoms and then it would be too late for many of them."

"How many casualties are we talking about with the quantity that was found?"

"The nature of this pathogen is that most of it is going to be wasted. Absolute worst case, you could have seen as many as a couple of hundred people infected, with casualty rates probably around fifty percent."

"Are we just going to assume that package is all that's out there?" Barnett interjected. "The fact that the DEA tripped over this one doesn't mean there aren't a hundred more that made it through." She pointed to a vent near the ceiling. "It could be coming through there right now."

"I don't think so," Statham responded. "Based on the equipment we've seen in the ISIS videos, this is about all the product they could have produced in the time they've had."

"What if they have equipment that wasn't in the videos?"

"Unlikely," Kennedy said. "Halabi is going for maximum emotional impact. He knows that the strength of anthrax as a weapon isn't its ability to generate a high body count. It's its ability to generate fear. Showing off his biological weapons capability is in many ways more important than the attack itself."

Barnett laughed. "That's what I'm supposed to tell my constituents?"

"Senator," the president cautioned, but Barnett ignored him.

"Are we at least assuming that Halabi's making another batch? And that we can't count on NASA to find it for us again?"

"I am," Statham admitted.

"Then what are we doing about it?" the president said. "Irene?"

"Since he can't go for big numbers, I think we can count on Halabi focusing on high-value targets. Politicians and business leaders concentrated in technology and defense. Maybe even celebrities. Among other things, we've already spoken with potential targets about securing the ventilation systems in their buildings. We've also tried to get our political leadership to randomize their habits, particularly where they eat and shop. We'll go back and impress on them again the importance—"

"So are we going public with this?" Barnett interrupted.

"I'd strongly recommend against it," Robert Woodman replied. "Based on what our informants are saying, the talk south of the border is about the loss of the mall, not the coke. That's about what we'd expect with a twelve-million-dollar bust like this. The lack of concern about the contents of that truck suggests that either the traffickers aren't aware that the anthrax was in their shipment or they assume we won't find it."

"You're trying to tell me that the drug traffickers don't know what they're transporting?" Barnett said incredulously.

"It actually makes perfect sense," Kennedy responded. "There's no profit in terrorism, and they run the risk of bringing an enormous amount of heat down on themselves. A likely scenario is that one of Halabi's Middle Eastern drug operations has partnered with a Mexican cartel and he slipped the anthrax into that shipment."

Woodman nodded in agreement. "We're trying to trace back the owners of that mall but, as you can imagine, it's a web of shell corporations and foreign partnerships. Based on the ambition of it all, we believe that it was a joint project between a number of different trafficking organizations. We've seen them spread their risk like that before on big projects. Also, we have the two men who were driving the van in custody. We're interrogating them and hoping to figure out which cartel they're working for. Bottom line is that if we go public with the anthrax, everyone in the supply chain is going to scatter. Our chances of tracing this package back to its source will go to zero before the first news show even finishes its report."

"Is your interrogation getting results?" Barnett said.

"Not yet. These are hard men, Senator. And the consequences of them talking to authorities is high. But we're continuing to work on them."

"I feel safer already," Barnett said sarcastically.

"If you have any thoughts on a course of action, Christine, I'd love to hear them," Alexander said.

Typically those kinds of questions had the power to shut her up for a while. Barnett was a prodigy at tearing down the efforts of others, but her policy proposals tended to be smoke and mirrors—designed more to pump up her base than to actually solve the complex problems facing America. This time, though, she wasn't so easily silenced.

"Get the hell out of the Middle East. That's my thought. We're spending the better part of a trillion dollars a year on a military that can't win wars against insurgencies and won't fight nuclear-armed countries— basically everyone we'd ever want to fight. The record's clear. Vietnam. Iraq. Afghanistan. We're not gaining anything. We're just whacking away at a hornet nest and then acting surprised when we get stung."

"I think that's a naïve view," Kennedy responded.

The senator's eyes narrowed at the insult but Kennedy couldn't bring herself to care. In the very likely event that Barnett became president, her first order of business would be to put someone loyal to her in as head of the CIA. And more than that, she'd almost certainly try to make an example of Kennedy by tying her up in years of bogus Senate investigations. There was little Kennedy could do or say at this point that would make her future any darker.

"Sayid Halabi's endgame isn't to use anthrax to kill a few hundred—or even a few thousand—Americans," Kennedy continued. "And while I agree that he wants us out of the Middle East, it's not so he can create a peaceful Islamic paradise there. No, he needs a refuge to build his capability to make war on the West. We learned this lesson in Syria, where we left a vacuum that ISIS exploited, and we've just learned it again in Yemen. Don't be fooled, Senator. Halabi will offer easy, seductive solutions and short-term political wins. But he won't stop until he's destroyed or we are. And in a world of runaway technology and political division, it might be us."

CHAPTER 22

ONE last shove and the massive filter finally snapped into place. Rapp stepped back, wiping the sweat from his forehead and examining his handiwork. According to Gary Statham, the upgrade would filter most biological agents, complementing the existing system designed to combat gas attacks. The drawback—and there always seemed to be one—was that the motors in his ventilation system would no longer be powerful enough. Based on the manufacturer specs, they'd burn out after less than forty-eight hours under the additional load. So they'd have to be replaced, too.

Rapp tossed his screwdriver on a greasy rag and took a seat on an ammo box. The safe room hidden in his basement was about the size of a single garage bay. Constructed entirely of reinforced concrete and steel, it included two huge batteries for storing energy from the rooftop solar panels, filtered water drawn from a well beneath the building, bunk beds, and a full bathroom. The cheerful yellow on the walls was a gift from the interior designer he'd hired to deal with the details of the house. She'd said something to the effect of "if the wolves are at the gate, a little hygge will go a long way." What that meant, he had no idea.

Based on the theory "two is one and one is none," he'd had the space ridiculously overbuilt. At the time he'd figured the most dangerous thing he'd have to face was a coordinated attack by a well-trained, well-armed terrorist cell. In that scenario, all he really needed was solid blast resistance, a few weapons, and breathable air. The food, bathrooms, and well water were complete overkill in a neighborhood where a bunch of Arabs shooting rockets would be dealt with pretty quickly.

Now, though, it all seemed ridiculously inadequate. At this point his best-case scenario was that Sayid Halabi had weaponized anthrax and that Rapp was number one on his hit list. Worst-case was . . . What? Sayid Halabi was a terrorist piece of shit, but it would be a mistake to deny that he was a brilliant and ambitious one.

So now Rapp had biofilters in place and the already confined space had been turned claustrophobic by boxes of provisions stacked to the ceiling. Still, he only had enough to keep the three of them fed for five months and his goal was six. So much for the shower. And he might have to give up the minigun. It wasn't the most mobile or practical weapon in his arsenal and took up a lot of space. Having said that, there were some problems that could only be solved by six thousand rounds per minute.

He heard footsteps above and reached for a beer while Claudia came down the ladder.

"You here to help?"

"I don't think I'm qualified," she said. "But I know a very good psychiatrist who is."

"Funny."

"Every reasonable report I've seen says that the anthrax isn't a large-scale threat, Mitch. I agree that he'll try to target you if he can, but it looks like you're preparing for the apocalypse down here."

Rapp took a pull on his beer. "I don't trust him. Anthrax is easy to produce. He could have hired a third-year biology student to make it. But he didn't. He took Gabriel Bertrand. My gut says there's more to this than the anthrax."

"What?"

"I don't know. But what I do know is that the U.S. isn't ready. If Halabi's figured out a way to hit us with something big—something biological—what's our reaction going to be? The politicians will run for the hills and point fingers at each other. And the American people . . ." His voice faded for a moment. "They faint if someone uses insensitive language in their presence and half of them couldn't run up a set of stairs if you put a gun to their heads. What'll happen if the real shit hits the fan? What are they going to do if they're faced with something that can't be fixed by a Facebook petition?"

"Then what are we doing here, Mitch? I have a house in South Africa that no one knows about. Let's go there. Make a life for ourselves and never come back."

"What are you talking about?"

There was a glint of sympathy in her eyes that bordered on pity. Like she was talking to a child who'd lost his favorite toy.

"The country you love is gone, Mitch. Christine Barnett is going to be the next president and she hates the CIA. She hates *you*."

He opened his mouth to respond, but she kept talking. "Look at yourself. You're not twenty-five anymore. You've been stabbed, shot, blown up. And nobody cares. Everything you've done, everything Irene's done. Barnett sees your success and the loyalty people have to you as a threat. She'll drag you in front of congressional hearings and twist your words and actions. Politicians who've never sacrificed anything for America will question your patriotism. Their followers will post lies about you on the Internet and the Russians will amplify them. Then the media will smell ratings and join in. They'll call you and Irene traitors and cowards and demand that you be prosecuted." She waved a hand around the room. "How is your fancy bunker going to protect you from that? Halabi doesn't need to kill you or anyone else. He just needs to keep fanning the flames that have taken hold here. Then you'll destroy yourselves."

"That was quite a speech," Rapp said when she finally fell silent. "Been practicing long?"

She ignored his jibe and dropped onto a box of dried pinto beans. "This is a battle you don't know how to win, Mitch. For the first time in your life, it's time to retreat. Let's go so far away that you'll be forgotten. You've earned that."

"Listen to what you're asking, Claudia. You want me to let myself be run out of my own country by a politician and a terrorist."

"It's over!" she said, the volume of her voice rising in the tiny space. "Not only have you been told to back off, there are guards parked in our neighborhood enforcing it! And Irene's next. After her, it'll be everyone else. Everyone who won't bow down and kiss Christine Barnett's ring."

"What do you want me to say, Claudia? That you hitched your wagon to the wrong man? I've been telling you that from day one."

"Don't you dare try to take the easy way out of this conversation."

"Then what? You tell me what you want to hear."

"I want to hear about our future, Mitch. I want to hear about the path forward that you see but I'm blind to. Where will we be in a year's time? Here? Barricaded in this room? Sitting with Irene in a Senate hearing? Meeting with the team of lawyers trying to keep you out of jail?"

His phone rang and he glanced over at it. The number was immediately recognizable but not one he would have expected to see. President Alexander's encrypted line.

"Don't even *think* of picking that up while we're fighting."

She would have been surprised to know that it never crossed his mind. While Claudia could be a monumental pain in the ass, she was one of the few people in the world who actually gave a shit about him. She wasn't there to bask in his notoriety or for protection or to use him as a weapon. She was just . . . there.

"We could have a life, Mitch. If you get bored, you can do some jobs with Scott. You could finally get your knee worked on. Heal. Maybe do a triathlon again." She leaned forward and gazed intently at him. "I admire everything you've done. You're the best at what you do. Maybe the best who ever lived. But there has to be an end to it one day. And that day seems to have come."

A ringtone sounded, but this time it wasn't his cell. He glanced at a bank of security monitors and saw one of the FBI agents charged with surveilling him. He was standing at the front gate, repeatedly pressing the call button. After thirty seconds or so, it became clear that he wasn't going to give up.

Rapp stood and opened the intercom. "*What?*"

The man's expression turned a bit sheepish. "The president requests that you take his call, sir."

Then he got in his SUV and drove off. But not back to his normal post at the edge of the road. Instead, he and his colleagues disappeared down the hill.

Rapp's cell started ringing again and this time he picked up. Claudia normally left the room when Irene or the president called, but this time she stayed put.

"Yeah."

Normally, his greeting would be one more respectful of the office, but on that particular day he couldn't conjure it.

"Has Irene briefed you on the latest developments?" Alexander asked.

"Why would she? I'm out and you posted guards to make sure I stay that way."

Alexander ignored the comment. "The DEA found a shipment of anthrax mixed in with the drugs they confiscated at that mall in San Ysidro."

"Nice work. Give Bob Woodman my compliments," Rapp said, hovering his thumb over the disconnect button.

"It's just blind luck that we intercepted it," Alexander rushed to say. "NASA stumbled on it. And it's even luckier that one of the random samples they took was from the package containing anthrax."

He could feel Claudia's eyes drilling into him. "That's very interesting, sir, but with all due respect, what's it to me?"

"We're not going public," the president said, clearly committed to dragging this out for some reason. "The hope is that we can trace the drugs back to the traffickers Halabi's using."

"Good luck," Rapp said, but again Alexander spoke before he could disconnect the call.

"You understand my position, don't you, Mitch? A few days ago, Halabi's anthrax was nothing but a bunch of propaganda videos on the Internet. On the other hand, I see Christine Barnett as a clear and present danger to the country. Now the situation's changed. We've been attacked with a biological weapon and it's not going to be the last. All other considerations—including doing something that could inadvertently help Barnett get into the White House—are secondary. And that's the kind of playing field you work best on."

"Is it? Next year you'll be playing golf and signing a multimillion-dollar book deal. Irene and I will be running from five different Senate investigations."

"Maybe. But you're not going to turn your back on your country. And neither am I."

Before he could answer, Claudia did it for him. Her shrill scream nearly shattered his eardrums in the tiny bunker.

"He doesn't want your fucking job!"

Both he and the president fell into stunned silence

as she climbed the ladder and disappeared through the hatch.

Alexander was the first to speak. "Is that true?"

Rapp sat back down. In many ways everything Claudia had said to him that day was right. America was tearing itself apart with hate and rage that had no basis in reality. Christine Barnett would be the next president of the United States and come out gunning for Rapp, Kennedy, and anyone else she couldn't control. What Claudia couldn't see, though, was that America's core was unchanged. The United States was a country of extremes. It had moods. Phases. Eras. But in the end, it always eventually got its shit together and remembered what it was.

"Mitch? Are you still there?"

"Yeah, I'm here. But I've got a question."

"Ask it."

"How much is it worth to you?"

"What do you mean?"

"We had a conversation just like this one a while back. You made it clear that it was my neck on the chopping block, not yours. I'm not in the mood to play that game again."

"I assume you have demands?"

"You assume right. I want a pardon."

"You haven't done anything yet."

"Then just start it with 'I pardon Mitch Rapp' and end it with your signature. The middle can be blank. And you should probably leave a fair amount of space."

When Alexander spoke again, his voice had turned a bit cold. "Anything else?"

"A letter saying that you were kept fully informed of my actions and approved of all of them."

"Are you actually going to?"

"What?"

"Keep me informed."

"No."

"Then how can I sign documents like that?"

"That, sir, is not my problem."

CHAPTER 23

THE road's dirt surface was rutted to the point that Rapp could barely get the SUV to forty miles per hour. In the east, the rising sun was illuminating the mountains and creating a blinding glare on his windshield. The desert in this part of California didn't look much different than Yemen beyond the addition of a few scattered cactus and Joshua trees.

After another ten minutes and two dry river crossings, a building started to separate itself from the heat shimmer to the north. No photos had been available, but it was pretty much as Claudia described—a dilapidated wood and stone structure that had served various purposes over its sixty-year history: storage facility for the forest service, barracks for construction crews, and a temporary holding facility for captured illegal immigrants. Now some of the windows were missing glass, part of the roof was bowing, and the chain-link fence surrounding it was streaked with rust.

The two Mexican traffickers caught at the San Ysidro mall were being held there, but they couldn't be kept incommunicado for much longer. The cartels had eyes and ears everywhere and this would already register as unusual to them. A few more days would blow past unusual and move into the territory of suspicious.

There was a partially collapsed wall about twenty yards from the fence and he pulled into the shade it offered. Claudia hadn't called yet, so he grabbed a greasy paper bag from the passenger seat and got out, jumping up onto the vehicle's hood and lying back against the windshield.

The Coke he extracted from the bag was a little warm, but the burrito wasn't bad. He watched the sun climb into a cloudless sky as he chewed, finally turning his attention to the building when a man in his early thirties appeared and approached the fence. They looked at each other for a moment and then Rapp went back to his breakfast.

According to the intel he'd been provided, the man's name was Holden Flores. He was a relatively new recruit to the DEA, well liked and in possession of a spotless record. It had been he who'd captured the two men being held in that building and for his first time at bat, it had been a solid performance.

A tiny dot became visible in the sky to the south and Rapp shaded his eyes to watch it approach. The radio-controlled plane set a course straight for him, finally circling at an altitude low enough to show off its six-foot wingspan, cerulean paint scheme, and video equipment. Apparently the cartels had started using these things to keep their eye on American law enforcement.

By the time he finished his burrito, another man

had appeared at the fence. Thomas Braman was in charge of this operation and his reputation was more mixed than that of the young man he was now barking at. Not completely useless, but one of those arrogant government assholes who reveled in throwing around whatever scrap of weight they had. This was just the kind of situation that would drive a man like Braman crazy. He hadn't been told about the anthrax, he had no idea why he'd just spent the better part of a week living in an abandoned maintenance building, and he was completely in the dark as to the identity of the man lying on the SUV outside his gate.

Apparently he'd already called headquarters demanding information nine times and was currently dialing for an even ten. Rapp watched him jab Flores in the chest while he waited for the line to connect. A moment later he was pacing across the dusty enclosure, pointing in Rapp's direction as he spoke urgently into the phone.

Rapp went back to watching the drone, following it lazily for a couple of minutes before his own phone rang. The number that came up was a string of zeros ending in the number four, indicating an encrypted call from Claudia.

"Yeah."

"I have them."

"And?"

"One blank pardon and one letter saying that the president is aware of and has approved all of your actions. Both with original signatures."

"Any loopholes?"

"They were too complicated for my English but Scott read them . . ." She paused a moment to recall his exact words. "He said you could 'drive-by a bunch of nuns and walk.' I'm not sure what that means exactly, but I gather it's what you wanted."

Rapp nodded. "And he's got them now?"

"Yes."

Coleman was going to put Rapp's presidential get-out-of-jail-free cards in an airtight lockbox that would then be buried somewhere along the remote trail system they ran on. Alexander was a decent enough man for a politician, but it didn't stretch the imagination to think he might get cold feet and want those documents back.

"And you're set on your end?" Rapp said.

"Yes," she said reluctantly.

"Then let's do it."

He hung up and slid off the hood, striding toward the gate. Flores just watched and Braman disconnected his call, moving to within a couple of feet of the chain link.

"What's your name?"

"Mitch."

"You got ID?"

"No."

This was just a bullshit dance and everyone knew it. Braman had been told someone of Rapp's description was coming and that once he arrived, it was his operation. But the DEA man wasn't going to cede authority without at least a show of defiance.

Rapp pointed to the chain around the gate and Flores unlocked it, letting him through.

"Anything I should know?" Rapp said as he walked toward the building with Braman hurrying to catch up.

"They're typical cartel soldiers. We're in the process

of interrogating them, but they're not talking. They know their rights. And they know that if we keep them here much longer without charging them, their lawyers are going to eat us for lunch."

They entered the building and Rapp looked around the room he found himself in. Debris had been pushed to one side and the floor had been swept to the degree possible. To the right was a smaller room stacked with rusted tools and, incongruously, millions of dollars' worth of cocaine.

"Are they down there?" Rapp said, pointing to a narrow hallway.

"Yeah. But I don't know what you're going to do with that information. I told you, we've been interrogating them nonstop since we got here, and tomorrow we have orders to get them and their product into the system. I don't know where the hell you came from, and frankly I don't care. But I guarantee you've never dealt with psychos like these. They're the kind of people who throw bags of human heads into nightclubs. And they know exactly what's going to happen to them if they say one word to us. So you're wasting your time. And worse, you're wasting mine."

Rapp nodded and started down the hallway, pushing through a metal door at the back. The room on the other side was probably twenty feet square, furnished with a single chair and illuminated by sun filtering through holes in the roof.

The two men handcuffed to an overhead pipe were pretty much what he'd expected. Muscular, late twenties or early thirties, with tattoos visible through sweat-soaked shirts. Their shoes were missing and they had a few minor scrapes, probably from their capture and not their interrogation.

The younger of the two had hard eyes, but the older one had crazy eyes. He lunged pointlessly in Rapp's direction, before being stopped by his handcuffs. The motion was violent enough to open a cut on his right wrist and the blood began sliding down his wet forearm.

"Fresh meat!" he shouted in heavily accented English. "Another DEA pussy? You got a woman at home? Would she like a real man? How about a daughter? You know I like them young. I show them a real good time before I slit their throats. We know who you are, little boy. We're watching. We're always watching."

"Shut the fuck up!" Braman shouted, trying to take control of the situation.

"Your family's first," the man said, fixing on him. "You think we don't know where they live?"

The DEA man couldn't hide that he was a little unnerved by the man's words. And, in truth, he had every right to be. The cartel's use of drones, hackers, and highly paid informants made it pretty credible that they really did know where his family lived. To date they hadn't acted much on that kind of information on the U.S. side of the border, but it was just a matter of time.

As the drug trafficker's diatribe slipped into unintelligible Spanish, Rapp turned toward his compatriot. The younger man's resigned expression suggested that he figured his future was pretty well laid out: Keep his mouth shut. Go to jail for a few years under the protection of cartel-sponsored gangs. Lie around, lift some weights, eat three squares a day, and finally get out and go back to work.

When he eventually got around to meeting Rapp's eye, though, he seemed to recognize that his situation had changed. He wasn't sure how yet, but he looked worried. Maybe this wouldn't be as long a day as Rapp had expected.

"Let me go," the crazy one said, switching back to English and refocusing on Rapp. "You could both just say I escaped. Then my friends won't have to visit your families."

Rapp thought about the offer for a moment and then retreated back through the door. Flores jumped to his feet when he entered the outer room, but Rapp went straight for the storage area. He had to climb over the coke and a few shovels, but he managed to retrieve a large bolt cutter that he'd noticed earlier.

When he returned to the interrogation room, Braman looked at him like he was nuts. "What kind of idiots is Washington sending me? If you're too scared of this guy to be here, then go back home to the suburbs."

The cartel man's face broke into a smug smile when Rapp lifted the bolt cutters toward his handcuffs.

"Stop!" Braman said, reaching for his sidearm.

Rapp opened the cutters, but at the last second diverted them to the man's wrist. They were likely too old and dull to cut through the steel of the cuffs, but they didn't have any trouble taking off a hand.

The man screamed and dropped to his knees as Braman drew his pistol. The problem was that the DEA man wasn't sure whom to point it at, and his hesitation gave Rapp time to swing the bloody bolt cutters into the weapon. It flew across the room as Rapp slammed his foot into Braman's chest, sending him toppling back through the door.

The DEA man just lay there on the floor, staring wide-eyed while Rapp slammed the door shut. As anticipated, there was no way to lock it from the inside, so he slid a rubber doorstop from his pocket and shoved it under the gap in the bottom.

When Rapp finally turned back around, the small room looked like a slaughterhouse. Blood had spattered the walls and was pooling beneath the man staring at his severed hand.

Then he was in motion. Rapp dodged right when he lunged, letting him pass by and collide with one of the room's concrete walls. The second attack came almost immediately and was accompanied by a moaning scream that didn't sound entirely human. This time Rapp went left with roughly the same result.

Someone started banging on the steel door from the outside but the specially designed doorstop didn't budge. The cartel man's attacks continued for another minute or so, becoming slower and clumsier as the blood loss took its toll.

Finally, he couldn't rise. He tried to crawl in Rapp's direction but only made it a few feet before collapsing facedown on the floor. The pounding on the door stopped around the same time, undoubtedly because Braman was on the phone, desperately trying to connect with the DEA director's office.

The sudden silence was surprisingly pleasant, and Rapp wiped some of the blood off the only chair in the room before sitting.

The surviving cartel man looked a little shell-shocked.

"How's your English?" Rapp said.

The man's eyes locked on his colleague and the blood flowing from the stump where his hand had been a few minutes before. "It's good."

"All right then. Let's talk about how the rest of the afternoon's going to go. You're going to die. There's nothing that's going to change that. If you tell me everything I want to know, it'll be quick. If you don't, I'm going to use those bolt cutters to remove your balls. And if you don't tell me after that, things are going to get serious. Do you understand?"

"Don't tell him anything!" the man on the floor gurgled.

Rapp retrieved his Glock from a holster hidden beneath his shirt and shot him in the temple.

"Do you understand?" he repeated, laying the weapon in his lap.

The man managed to nod.

"Good. What's your name?"

"Miguel Arenas."

"There was a specific package in that shipment of coke, Miguel. It was different than the others. What do you know about it?"

When Arenas responded, his voice sounded a bit distant. Exactly what Rapp had been going for. People facing certain death tended not to concern themselves with their professional obligations or the problems of their multimillionaire employers.

"There was one packet with markings that could be seen with black light. We were told to separate it out and deliver it to a different contact."

"Who?"

"I don't know."

It was undoubtedly true. Cartels ran a lot like the CIA—need to know was one of their main mantras.

"You have a description though, right? You had to be able to identify him to meet him."

"Six feet. Dark hair and skin. Beard. He doesn't speak Spanish." The man nodded toward his dead friend. "That's why Paco and I were chosen for this job. We speak good English."

"Where?"

"In the desert. The coordinates are on our phones."

The NSA had the phones, but hadn't been able to crack them yet.

"What's the password on your phone?"

"Calvillo386. All capital letters."

"When are you supposed to meet?"

"Four days ago."

Rapp swore under his breath. Not that he was surprised, but he'd been hoping to get lucky. The goal had been to deliver a package of harmless simulated anthrax to the contact and then follow him as he distributed it to his network. And if it hadn't been for all the grab-ass going on in Washington, he might have had time to pull it off. Now, though, he was screwed.

"What cartel do you work for?"

"Lacandon."

"Any other orders?"

"No. Just make the delivery and cross back into Mexico."

Rapp picked up his pistol. "Then I only have one more question. Head or chest?"

The man sagged against the handcuffs securing him to the pipe. "Head."

Rapp aimed and squeezed off a single round. Predictably, someone started pounding on the door again, but it lasted only a few seconds.

He leaned back in the chair, contemplating the two dead men. As usual, options were pretty much nonexistent. He was either going all in on this thing or he was getting on a plane to South Africa with Claudia and letting the world go to shit without him.

Maybe she was right. Maybe it was inevitable. He and people like him had managed to hold back the tide for this long, but the modern world was generating too many threats coming from too many different directions. Eventually he or someone else was going to miss. Did it really matter if it was now or a year from now? Maybe it was time to hit the reset button on the world. Make people see that there were consequences to their actions. Make them remember what they had and value it enough to protect it.

Who was he kidding?

He dialed Claudia and, not surprisingly, she picked up on the first ring.

"Are you all right?" she asked in a tone that was impossible to read. The hat she was wearing now was that of Scott Coleman's logistics director, and it meant her personal feelings for Rapp had to be temporarily put aside. At least that was the theory.

"Yeah."

"How did it go?"

"We're shit out of luck on the meet. It's come and gone."

"You weren't able to get anything on the contact?"

"He didn't know anything. The password on one of the phones is Calvillo386 in all caps. It has the coordinates of the meeting place. Worth checking out, but I'm guessing you'll just find a piece of empty desert."

"What about the cartel they work for?"

"Lacandon. Do you know anything about it?"

"Of course."

It was to be expected. She'd made extensive contacts in the underworld during her time working with her husband in the private contracting business.

"Don't keep me in suspense."

"It's operated by Carlos Esparza."

"Never heard of him."

"Years ago when he was still an up-and-coming trafficker, one of his competitors tried to hire my husband to deal with him."

"He didn't take the job?"

"No. Even by cartel standards Esparza is extremely violent and volatile. He's also smart and obsessed with security. I was struggling to even locate him, let alone get enough information to plan a successful hit."

"So you decided the risk and amount of work weren't worth the reward?"

"We probably would have come to that conclusion. But about a month into our initial legwork, Esparza caught up with our client."

"And?"

"Our best information was that he tortured him and his family for months and then ground them up and fed them to his men."

"Outstanding."

"He's our nightmare scenario, Mitch. Some cartel leaders get where they are because they're careful and methodical. He's the opposite. His success is based on the fact that he's unpredictable and brutal. The smaller operations are afraid of him and the larger ones don't think it's worth going to war with him. And he's greedy to the point of self-destructiveness. He wants to run the biggest cartel in the world. Be the richest and most powerful man in the world. Based on my research into him, nothing will ever be enough."

"Okay. Get me whatever updated information on him you can."

"Mitch . . . This isn't going to work. The plan you've come up with isn't a plan. It's—"

"If you have any better ideas, I'm listening."

"You know my answer to that."

"I'm not walking away, Claudia. But you're free to. Anytime you want."

"You say that so often, sometimes I wonder if it's what you want," she said coldly.

He considered his next words more carefully than he would have thought given his current situation. "It's not what I want. But I understand what I'm dragging you into here. You like to control things, and this isn't that kind of an operation. If it goes to shit, I don't want it to blow back on you and I don't want to leave you thinking it was something you did or didn't do."

She was silent for long enough that he started to wonder if they'd been disconnected. Finally, she responded.

"I don't want to be involved. I admit that. But I'm not going to trust your life to someone else. There's no room for error here, Mitch. Nothing can go wrong. Not one thing."

And yet something always did.

"Where do you stand on your end?" he said, changing the subject.

"I spoke with your brother. He said he can bankrupt you and involve you in as many illegal financial schemes as you like."

"Will it look real?"

"He says yes, but he asked me to tell you that you're an idiot, suicidal, and that whatever you think you owe to America, you've already paid back a hundred times over."

"But he'll do it?"

"He said he'd handle all the arrangements personally."

Rapp nodded. Steven was a financial genius who hadn't made a mathematical error since he was seven years old. And as an added bonus, he liked his big brother and would be disappointed to see him made into hamburger patties.

"Mitch, I still think we should bring Irene in on this. With her power and experience we could be much more thorough."

"No. She'd shut us down the minute she heard the plan. And even if she didn't, she'd be obligated to tell the president. With everything that's going on in Washington, I don't trust him. We'll hold her in reserve. Nothing we do is going to fool her. She'll know what's going on and she'll be there for us if we need her."

"What about Scott and his men? We need them to get talk going in the spec ops rumor mill."

"No problem. Tell them whatever you need to."

Coleman and his boys were one hundred percent loyal and none of them gave a flying fuck about what was going on in Washington. They'd gun down everyone in Congress before they left him hanging.

"Even if everything goes right, Mitch . . ." Her voice faltered.

"It'll be fine. All I have to do is be convincing."

When she came back on she spoke so softly he could barely make out her words. "Not too convincing, though, right, Mitch? Not too convincing."

CHAPTER 24

"IF I didn't know better, I'd think there was a god," Senator Christine Barnett said.

Her campaign manager looked up at her with a deep frown.

"What?" she said.

"I've warned you about this before, Senator. . . . If you ever slip and someone records you—"

"It wouldn't matter."

"You're not bulletproof."

"Pull your head out of your ass, Kevin. I hired you for your cynicism and now you're finding Jesus on me?"

"I'm not finding Jesus. But there are people out there who have. And you need their votes."

She smirked and started pacing around her office again. "You're thirty-five years old and already living in the past. The American people don't give a shit about God. They don't care about the environment or the deficit or health care. And they couldn't find Iraq or Yemen on a map."

"What do they care about?" Gray said coldly.

"Should it worry me that I'm having to tell you?"

"Anytime you think you can find someone better, I'll be happy to step down."

Barnett was always on the lookout, but the truth was that there wasn't anyone even close. She wasn't sure if that spoke to Gray's brilliance or the fact that everyone else out there was a drooling idiot, but at this point it didn't matter.

"What they want—what they thirst for—is to hurt the people they hate. They don't want a politician droning on about unemployment. They want a general. They want to blindly follow someone who can provide them an enemy and lead them to victory against that enemy. Someone who can give their lives purpose." She leaned back against her desk and glared down at him. "If you spend your time and my money finding ways to help people, we're going to lose this election. But if you can find me ways to inflict damage, we're going to run away with it."

"And you think making anthrax your signature issue is the right weapon?"

"I'm not sure yet. It has potential, but like all good weapons it's dangerous if you don't use it right." She smiled, recalling yesterday's meeting. "You should have seen Irene Kennedy. She was sweating bullets. And Alexander just looked lost. He's done and just wants to avoid any fireworks on the way out. The DEA head, though . . ."

"Woodman?" Gray said.

She nodded. "He doesn't seem stupid. We should be reaching out to him and letting him know there's a place for him in my administration if he plays ball."

"Agreed. I'll take care of it."

"The question is whether we leak the fact that the

anthrax made it across the border. Then we'd have a clear message: Sayid Halabi isn't bluffing and we can't keep counting on blind luck and NASA. Next time this administration lets someone stroll over the border with a bioweapon, people are going to die."

"I'd advise caution, Senator. If that leak were ever traced back to you—"

"Then we'd have to make sure that doesn't happen. It's not the first time we've leaked something and it's never been tracked back to us before."

"What about the fact that we'd be jeopardizing an ongoing terrorism investigation? ISIS will pull back if they know we're onto them. Halabi will disappear and they'll switch to another smuggling route. Our chance of stopping them will be even worse."

"That's the story Alexander and that bitch Kennedy will tell, but no one's going to listen. After the fact, it'll just sound like an excuse. What the American people would take away is that the White House and CIA were keeping a serious threat secret so they wouldn't look bad during the election season."

"What if this goes beyond politics, Senator? What if our actions actually *do* help the terrorists?"

She shrugged. "How would that hurt me?"

"I don't understand."

"You read the briefing. It's anthrax. It can't be used as a weapon of mass destruction. We're talking about a few high-profile targets. Hysteria grows and Alexander's administration gets the blame."

"People will die."

"According to Gary Statham, fewer than a hundred. What would be much worse for us is if Alexander's people actually succeed. What I don't need to see on television is a bunch of spec ops guys busting up terrorist cells. Or even worse, one of them putting a bullet in Sayid Halabi. That could give Alexander's party a bump at the worst possible moment."

"And what do you think the chance of that is?"

"Of them pulling off something big? Low. And even lower now. My understanding is that Mitch Rapp is out. Alexander's afraid of letting him off the leash during the election cycle."

Gray didn't look as happy about that as he should have.

"Relax, Kevin. I've got Secret Service and thirty private contractors working my security."

"Yeah, *your* security. But nobody's looking for suspicious white powder in my mailbox."

She waved a hand dismissively. "ISIS isn't going to bother with you."

"You have no idea what ISIS is going to bother with."

"Fine," she said. "Figure out what security you're comfortable with and set it up. Happy now?"

Based on his expression, happy was an overstatement. But he gave a short nod. "So what do you want to do, Senator?"

She fell silent for almost a minute as she considered the question. "Right now? Nothing. But we need to be ready. Start looking into how we can leak with zero chance of it being tracked back to us. If I decide to move on this, I want to be able to move fast."

"Fine," Gray started. "But laying the groundwork is very different than acting on it. We've got a lead in the primary that's looking unassailable and your numbers against your likely opponents in the general are just about as good."

"Don't start resting on your laurels, Kevin. We need to stay on the offensive."

"Are you sure? Risk and return, Senator. What we don't need right now is an unforced error."

"Hell yes, I'm sure!" she said, the volume of her voice rising. "Those poll numbers aren't worth the paper they're printed on. People will say they'll vote for a woman, but when they actually get in the booth, will they? Or will I go into the general with a twenty-point lead and come out giving a concession speech? When Election Day comes, Alexander, his party, and whatever idiot they run against me have to have been destroyed. Do you understand me? When we're done with them, their own mothers are going to question voting for them. And if you're willing to do what it takes to get me there, then you've got a very bright future ahead of you. If you're not, then not only will I replace you, but I'll make sure you never work in politics again. Am I being clear?"

"Senator, we—"

"Am I being clear?"

Gray stared back at her for a couple of seconds, but finally diverted his gaze and stood. "Crystal."

CHAPTER 25

A FEW hard kicks got the sticky rubber doorstop free and Rapp pulled the door open. Thomas Braman and Holden Flores spun toward him, along with another man who hadn't been in evidence when Rapp arrived. All had donned bulletproof vests and the new man was holding a Remington 870 shotgun. Flores immediately put his hand on his sidearm but didn't draw it, instead leaning left to get a look at the blood-splattered room and the two corpses. For a second it looked like he might throw up.

Braman's eyes remained locked on Rapp, but most of his attention seemed to be focused on the phone plastered to his ear. It wasn't hard to guess what was happening on the other end: absolutely nothing. His bosses in Washington would be hiding in their offices while their assistants provided excuses and transferred him to another unavailable executive.

And Braman, while a pain in the ass, wasn't an idiot. He knew that the music was winding down and that he was going to be the only one left without a chair. If he stopped Rapp and that created a backlash from the White House, he'd be crucified for not following orders to hand over authority. On the other hand, if he let Rapp walk, he could be charged as an accessory to the murder of two Mexican nationals.

Welcome to the current state of American politics, Rapp thought. Everyone who didn't have a place at the very top of the political food chain was expendable. No loyalty. No gratitude. No courage. Braman was an arrogant prick looking to move up in the world, but there was nothing in his record that suggested he'd ever screwed his men in pursuit of that goal. He probably figured he'd been an honorable soldier in the war on drugs and didn't deserve to be hung out to dry for something that wasn't his fault.

And he was right.

Rapp passed silently by them, leaving bloody footprints on the concrete floor. He pushed through the door and felt the morning heat hit him. The sky was devoid of clouds and bleached yellow by the dust and the sun. Despite the situation, he had a sudden craving for an icy beer. Something to help him contemplate a future that was now so dark he couldn't even penetrate its edges.

The DEA men spread out behind him, and for the better part of a minute he stood there listening to Thomas Braman desperately try to get someone to take his call. The man's voice rose to a shout, dominating the small enclosure as Rapp watched the cartel's surveillance drone circle overhead. Whoever was operating that plane had already been taking particular interest in this situation and now he had a blood-splattered man staring up at his cameras.

"Don't even think about transferring me again," Braman said. "If he's in a meeting, get him out!"

This wasn't how this was supposed to go down. He'd figured on waiting until they were on the dirt road leading out. There was a dry wash that he'd identified as being a perfect spot for what had to be done. He'd purposely bog the truck down, and then when the DEA men were gathered in a tight group looking at the buried tires, he'd make his move. It would be about as controllable a scenario as he could create.

Now, though, he had the drone overhead and the three DEA men standing right behind him. Braman, the most experienced, had a phone instead of a gun in his hand. A glance back confirmed that Holden Flores had his hands at his sides instead of on his weapon. The other DEA man still had the shotgun but was holding it across his chest aimed at the sky.

Bird in the hand.

"Don't hang—!" Braman fell silent for a moment. "Shit!"

Rapp waited until the man was consumed with redialing before he turned, walked a few steps, and slammed a fist into Flores's jaw. The kid crumpled, but before he even hit the ground, Rapp had drawn his Glock and pumped a round into the sternum of the man holding the shotgun. He jerked back and fell, his weapon bouncing from his hands and spinning through the dirt.

Braman dropped his phone and went for his pistol, but then went down when he took a bullet to the chest.

Rapp kicked the weapons away from the men and surveyed their condition. Flores was out like a light, so Rapp started with the first man he'd shot, rolling him on his stomach and using the flex cuffs hanging from his bulletproof vest to bind his wrists behind him.

Out of the corner of his eye, he saw Braman starting to reach for his weapon.

"Don't do it, asshole . . ."

When he didn't listen, Rapp shot him in the ribs. That seemed to put an end to his plans.

The drone swooped in even closer when Rapp started dragging the men inside the building. Flores didn't regain consciousness, but the other two moaned and swore under their breath at the pain of being moved. The ballistic vests had saved their lives, but between them they had more than a few broken ribs and probably one cracked sternum.

Braman was last, and by the time Rapp dropped him into a puddle of blood in the interrogation room, he'd gotten enough wind back to make some fairly graphic accusations regarding Rapp's mother. He fell silent when Rapp hovered the barrel of his Glock an inch from his forehead.

"I don't need your commentary, Braman—I just need the drugs. I'm having a few financial problems and this is going to take care of them."

"Screw you!"

Rapp had to admit that this guy was starting to grow on him. Despite that, he slammed the butt of his Glock into Braman's nose and walked out, bolting the steel door behind him.

Rapp straightened, stretching his back and looking around him at the cluttered storage room. Fortunately, it had a set of rolling doors that the DEA had put back in working condition. He'd been able to back his SUV up to them and load about five hundred pounds of coke, which was now covered by a dirty tarp weighted down with a couple of shovels. In the unlikely event he got pulled over, he'd just look like he was on his way back from Home Depot.

He finished changing into clean clothing while the dull ring of metal started on the other end of the building. Apparently, at least one of the three DEA men had recovered enough to free himself and go to work on the door imprisoning them.

Rapp slipped into the vehicle and pulled out, accelerating to a speed that allowed him to crash through the chain link gate. Not surprisingly, Carlos Esparza's surveillance drone wasn't far behind.

CHAPTER 26

SAYID Halabi shut down the computer on his improvised desk, watching the cave descend into gloom as the screen went black. He had scoured every report about the drug operation at the San Ysidro mall and found nothing even hinting that something unusual had been found among the confiscated drugs. Now most of the stories were about the sophistication of the tunnel structure and the profitability of the narcotics trade.

It was exactly what Carlos Esparza had told him to expect. A few of the individual packages would be randomly selected for testing and then the entire shipment would be destroyed. The chances of the brick containing anthrax being chosen were diminishingly small. But small was very different than nonexistent.

If the bioweapon *were* found, it was extremely unlikely that the discovery would be reported to the public. Kennedy would maneuver from the shadows, using the information she gleaned from the intercept to trace the bioweapon back to its source. And when she succeeded, she would send Rapp. It was how they operated. And it was how so many of his brothers had been martyred.

The Frenchman was completing another batch of anthrax, but Halabi had begun to question whether it had ever been important. He'd told himself that it was a necessary distraction to keep Kennedy blind to his real goal.

But was it?

He wanted so desperately to outsmart Irene Kennedy. To outfight Mitch Rapp. To ensure that the American people knew, as they slowly suffocated, how easy it had been to defeat them. He wanted Kennedy and Rapp to understand that he had been pulling their strings the entire time. That they had been the defenders of the walls when they had finally fallen.

Ironically, the semidarkness allowed him to see with unprecedented clarity. In Yemen, he'd already made the mistake of not striking when the moment was at hand. Allowing Rapp to escape had been an inexcusable tactical error, and he wouldn't compound it by underestimating the threat the man posed. Halabi knew that every moment he hesitated was a moment the CIA man could use to destroy him.

The cave that housed the weapon that would annihilate the West was within the reach of America's specialized weaponry. A single bombing run could incinerate the deadly virus incubating in his people's bodies. And he would likely die with them, arriving at the feet of God having failed once again.

There was no choice but to accelerate his timetable forward. Rapp was coming. He could feel it. Speed was the critical component now. Not complexity.

Halabi reached for the notebook at the edge of his desk, opening it and running his fingers across Gabriel

Bertrand's elegant script. He had read the annotated Arabic translation that had been prepared for him, but there was something about seeing the original that created a compelling sense of history. Would this book one day be enshrined in a holy site commemorating the fall of the West?

Bertrand called the disease he'd discovered Yemeni acute respiratory syndrome, a laughably innocuous name for something that was about to reshape the world. Symptoms typical of a mild flu tended to appear within two days of exposure. Onset was fairly slow, with the illness generally not turning severe for another five days. For those who reached that point, around seventy percent would be dead within a week, a mortality rate thirteen times higher even than that of the Spanish flu, which decimated the world population in the early twentieth century.

Even more unusual was how easily it spread. Under normal conditions, the pathogen could survive on surfaces for as much as seventy-two hours. And, according to Bertrand's extensive calculations, even relatively trivial contact with the virus produced an infection rate of over fifty percent.

It was incredible how clumsy and ineffective the armies of the West now seemed. In comparison to the weapons created by God, they were nothing. Even the nuclear arsenals that so terrified the world were pitiful by comparison. Used against a major population center, they could achieve little more than a sudden blast, a few hundred thousand casualties, and a lingering radiation zone that could be easily contained or avoided.

The careful and purposeful release of YARS would

spread through the highly mobile and densely populated West like a wildfire. Casualties would be tens—
perhaps hundreds—of millions. The highly integrated
and interdependent modern world would collapse as
the specialized people who kept it running fell ill.

The medical system would be the first to be over-
whelmed as workers abandoned it out of fear of being
infected. Then law enforcement, who were critical to
holding back the violence and avarice simmering just
beneath the veneer of Western civilization.

Power grids would falter, as would the elaborate
transportation systems that brought food and other
critical products. Militaries would be called back
from their imperialist missions in the Middle East
and Asia to try to control the upheaval, but their close
living conditions and contact with the public would
make them even more susceptible than the general
population.

Even after the contagion had run its course, the
long-term effects would be immeasurable. The West's
entire economic system, based on the slow growth of
populations, would collapse. Homes, businesses, and
entire cities would be abandoned. Open democracies,
utterly incapable of returning their countries to order,
would be replaced by insular dictatorships.

Of course, the death toll in the Middle East would
be significant as well, but the effects would be less far-
reaching. Larger cities like Cairo and Riyadh would
be wiped out, but they had become godless cesspools
and deserved their fate. Disconnected rural areas
would take fewer casualties and were far less reliant on
the complex web of technologies that kept the modern world functioning. Once free of the oppressors

and colonists, the Muslim people would unite in the service of Allah. They would wage jihad on a mortally wounded West and extend the new caliphate across the globe.

The law of God, and not that of man, would once again reign supreme.

CHAPTER 27

THE GPS on Rapp's phone called out the next turn and he veered left onto a dirt track that wound through Joshua trees and flowering ocotillo. There was still about an hour of sunlight, which would be just about what he needed.

It was a little more than a mile to a stucco building whose ochre color and organic shape allowed it to blend into the desert landscape. Probably a little bigger than he needed and in terrain that was a little more open than he would have liked, but beggars couldn't be choosers.

He stepped out of the SUV and glanced at the sky, struck by the irony that it was his turn to worry about overhead drones. Nothing. The cartel's model plane had followed him from the DEA outpost to the pavement but had been behind when he'd accelerated to highway speeds.

Rapp retrieved a remote from a lockbox near the front door and used it to access the garage. Mixed in among the beach chairs, mountain bikes, and coolers were a number of brand-new shovels and picks, as well as a locker filled with enough military-grade weaponry to take over a small African nation.

He pulled the SUV in and entered the house to see if Claudia's thoroughness extended to the fridge. As expected, it did. One of the benefits of having a French logistics coordinator was that you always got the good stuff. High-end cheese, homemade pasta sauces, fresh bread . . .

And alcohol-free beer.

He swore under his breath and explored the house while dialing his phone.

"Are you there?" Claudia said, by way of greeting.

"Yeah."

"What do you think?"

"Could be worse. The walls are thick and the windows are either glass block or barred. Power's off-grid and batteries are topped off. Kind of a complicated interior layout, which would work for me if I was planning on staying inside, but I'm not. It'd be too easy to get trapped in here and a few Molotov cocktails would be enough to set the place on fire."

"It was the best I could do at the last minute. You said you wanted remote and it doesn't get much more remote than that."

"Since I can't stay in here, where do I go?"

"Scott's men have you set up on the perimeter. There are diagrams on the tablet on the counter. The usual password."

"What about the DEA guys?"

"I called in an anonymous tip to the police. They're on-site now and have called ambulances for three injured men. So at least we know they're all alive."

He'd been careful with the placement of his shots

and had chosen frangible ammunition that would hit like a ton of bricks but not penetrate their vests. Of course, the science of shooting people in the torso and not killing them was a fairly inexact one. In fact, he might have just invented it.

Rapp grabbed one of the nonalcoholic beers and sat down at the kitchen table. "Any luck setting up a drug deal?"

"No bites yet, but I set a good price and the word's getting around. I wouldn't be surprised if we have at least one offer by tomorrow morning."

He nodded and took a pull on the watery beer substitute. Claudia was using her old contacts to let people know that a couple hundred kilos of high-quality coke had just come on the market. The fact that the seller was an unknown necessitated a discount deep enough to get fringe players involved. The sale, though, wasn't the point. The goal was to get enough chatter going that Carlos Esparza found out that his stolen product was on the auction block.

While it was true that government confiscation was just another cost of doing business, the theft and attempted resale of his property was an entirely different animal. When a government agent turned criminal, the rules changed. The kid gloves came off and Rapp would now be treated just like anyone else who had stolen from the cartels.

"Do they know where I am? I lost the drone when I got on the highway."

"I imagine they have a pretty good idea. They have people all up and down these roads that they could have called on. And I wouldn't be surprised if they're doing something similar to what I just did—looking online for properties that were recently rented for the short term. I'm still gathering intel on Esparza's cartel, but it seems to be much larger and more sophisticated than when Louis and I dealt with them. About half their business is in marijuana trafficking, though, and they're getting hurt badly by legalization."

"So a perfect candidate for a business partnership with Middle Eastern heroin traffickers."

"Very much so. The cartels see this as their primary avenue for growth. As the U.S. cracks down on oxycodone, those addicts are looking for a replacement. Esparza's cartel is targeting the middle-class suburban market—painkiller addicts who have no contact with the underworld or drug dealers. He seems to be trying to create a reliable product that looks and works very much like pharmaceutical-grade oxycodone. But for his plan to work, he needs a reliable supply of high-quality opiate."

"That actually sounds like a pretty solid business plan. You should turn Steven on to it. He'll probably want to buy stock."

"Like I said, Mitch, Esparza's a psychotic. Not an idiot."

"And how's *my* life going?" he said, changing the subject.

"Poorly. Your brother's put you at the center of a massive web of illegal and collapsing investment schemes. You've got inexplicable inflows and outflows of tens of millions of dollars, a huge mortgage on your house, and involvement in a Russian real estate scam that implicates you in the death of Tarben Chkalov. Many of these things are actually real and currently under investigation by the authorities in various countries. What Steven's managed to accomplish in such a short time is incredible. He's a true genius. Did you know he can multiply four-digit numbers in his head?"

"Yeah. He's always been able to do that. Who knows about this?"

"I've anonymously sent files to the FBI, CIA, SEC, IRS, and a few congresspeople, including Christine Barnett."

"So, in a nutshell, I'm broke and under investigation for a bunch of illegal activities that I'm not smart enough to understand."

"Yes. But that's not all."

"No?"

"No. When I found out what you've been up to, I drained what few bank accounts you had left and ran. I'm now hiding out in southern Texas, fearful of your reprisal."

"That *is* pretty bad," he said, feeling more ambivalent than he should have about Claudia and Steven's thoroughness. His survival unquestionably depended on the convincing destruction of his life, but hearing it laid out in black and white was pretty sobering.

"There's more."

"More?" he said, feigning enthusiasm. "Really?"

"I'm not alone here in Texas. I left you for another man. In fact you know him. Scott Coleman. After working so closely together, a relationship evolved between us. He's here now ready to protect me should you ever find us. In fact, he and Anna are out back grilling dinner. Would you like to talk to him?"

"No." Rapp looked around the empty kitchen, trying not to think about her and Coleman flipping steaks while he waited for either the FBI or a cartel hit squad to show up on his doorstep.

"Mitch? Are you still there?"

"Yeah."

"You asked me to do this to you."

"I know."

"And the moment you shot those DEA agents, you passed the point of no return. There can't be any holes in your cover or questions about your motivations."

"It had to be done," he reassured her.

"No, it didn't," she said, some of her carefully constructed calm starting to crack. "We could have—"

"Claudia . . . Not now, okay? I don't have much light left and I have a lot of work to do. For all I know, Esparza has fifty men sitting at the end of my driveway waiting for sunset."

"I'm sorry, Mitch. I shouldn't have said anything. I was being selfish."

"Don't worry about it. We'll talk later."

He disconnected the call, wondering if what he'd just said was true. If they would ever talk again.

Rapp tossed the bottle into the sink, hearing it shatter against the porcelain. He'd made his decision and there was no changing it now. Time to focus.

CHAPTER 28

IRENE Kennedy felt her pace slow as she approached Senator Barnett's office. The emergency meeting was originally scheduled to take place in the White House but when rumors about Mitch Rapp had begun circulating, the location had abruptly changed. And when those rumors had turned toxic, the president suddenly discovered a conflict that wouldn't allow him to attend. Not surprising, but disappointing. And a bit foreboding.

She passed through Barnett's outer office and was motioned to an open door at the back. Inside she found Barnett standing in the middle of the imposing space, speaking quietly with the head of the DEA.

Her handshake with Woodman was tense and perfunctory, but Barnett dispensed with the pleasantry entirely, instead walking to a small conference table. Kennedy was surprised, having assumed that the politician would take a position of authority behind her desk. The purpose of the move became clear when Woodman took a seat to the right of her.

The only remaining chair was a rather austere wooden one directly across from them.

The battle lines had been drawn.

"When was the last time you spoke to Mitch Rapp?" Barnett asked.

"I'm not sure exactly. A few weeks? Around the time the president asked him to stand down."

Barnett made a show of writing her response down. "You're certain?"

"If you need a precise date and time, I can check my phone records and provide you with one."

She didn't seem that interested. "Are you aware that Mr. Rapp was sent to interrogate the two men who smuggled the anthrax across the U.S. border?"

"Sent? By whom?"

"I assume by you."

"I can assure you that isn't the case, Senator."

"So you're saying you had no involvement in those orders?"

"I think we've already established that."

Clearly Barnett was less interested in what was happening with the DEA and ISIS than she was with understanding who could be blamed and how it could help her quest for the presidency.

"Are you aware of what happened during Rapp's questioning of the two suspects?"

"I'm not."

It was actually true. There was a significant amount of loose talk swirling around the Beltway, but it would have been unnecessarily dangerous for her to look into it. For the first time in her career, ignorance seemed to be the best course.

"The police received an anonymous tip about gunshots at the facility where the men were being held. When they arrived, they found the suspects dead and three DEA agents gravely wounded."

Barnett leaned back in her chair, a satisfied smile exposing overwhitened teeth. She motioned to Woodman, who finally got an opportunity to talk. He didn't seem happy about it, though.

"Rapp tortured at least one of the suspects and murdered both. Then he attacked my men and stole a significant portion of the narcotics being held on-site."

Kennedy paused to consider what she had just heard. Conclusions weren't hard to come to. Rapp had wanted answers from those drug traffickers that the DEA weren't able to get. A murkier question, though, was on whose authority? Was he working under political cover that she wasn't aware of. The president had gone directly to him before. Was this another case of that?

"Are your people going to be all right?" Kennedy asked finally.

"They sustained substantial injuries, but I'm told they'll recover."

"Thanks to their body armor and training," Barnett cut in. "Otherwise they'd be in the morgue with those two suspects."

Woodman's face was expressionless. He knew full well that if Rapp had wanted those men dead, they would be.

"Please continue, Bob."

His expression suggested continued reluctance. What was causing that reluctance, though, was difficult to say. Even if Kennedy had known the man well, it was hard to predict how someone would react to a situation like this. He was smart enough to know that something didn't smell quite right. But he was also smart enough to know that Barnett was likely to be his boss in a few months.

"Rapp also said something."

"Yes?" Kennedy prompted.

"That he had financial problems and needed the drugs to settle his accounts."

"Are you aware of Mr. Rapp's financial situation?" Barnett interjected.

Kennedy folded her hands in front of her on the table. "Yesterday, my office received a file that seems to detail a number of financial improprieties on Mitch's part. It's my understanding that the FBI and IRS received similar files. Of course, we're looking into the allegations, but they're complicated and far-reaching, so I don't have anything to report yet."

"Financial improprieties," Barnett repeated incredulously. "My people's initial review of that file suggests something more like an organized crime syndicate that would put Al Capone to shame."

It was an exaggeration, but not an outrageous one. The maze of hidden accounts, foreign partnerships, and shell corporations had almost certainly been created by Rapp's brother Steven. And if that was the case, it would take years—perhaps decades—to get to the bottom of it. His gift for complex financial transactions rivaled his older brother's abilities with a gun.

The question was why? Rapp had very little interest in money and was already worth millions—as was

Claudia Gould. Why had he created a phony financial crisis and then purposely told the DEA that he was stealing the drugs to deal with that crisis? The answer was as obvious as it was dangerous. He was trying to make contact with the cartel that had smuggled the anthrax and infiltrate them.

"As I said, Senator, we're looking into the allegations. But I'd urge caution. That file gives every impression of having been compiled by a hostile foreign government."

Of course, that was completely nonsense. The faint whiffs of Russia and Iran were much more likely Claudia's doing. She was an extremely clever woman.

"An ad hominem attack, Dr. Kennedy? I would have thought that was beneath you. It doesn't matter *where* the information came from, only whether or not it's true. And even if it isn't, Mitch Rapp murdered two drug trafficking suspects in cold blood as well as—"

"They weren't drug trafficking suspects, Senator. They were transporting a bioweapon across the U.S. border. The rules of engagement are different for men like that."

Barnett laughed. "Ah, yes. That's the comic book, isn't it? Mitch Rapp, the great patriot, desperately interrogating two hardened terrorists in order to save us all. Don't insult my intelligence, Doctor. The questions Rapp was asking those men had nothing to do with America. More likely he wanted to know how to get top dollar for the coke he stole and how to stay ahead of the cartel he stole it from. And now while you sit there trying to spin the situation, he's using the skills you taught him to disappear."

She didn't respond, prompting Woodman to speak up.

"We have two separate informants saying that an unknown party has put word out on the street that he's got a couple hundred kilos of quality product and he's looking to unload it fast. There's no question in my mind that this is your man, Irene. There's a possibility that we can track—"

Barnett put a hand on his arm, silencing him. Clearly, she believed that any information Kennedy gained in this meeting would be passed on to Rapp. The human species' ability to believe whatever it wanted was truly incredible. Barnett would overlook everything Rapp had done for America and believe any attack on him—no matter how far-fetched—without question.

"I think we've said enough on that subject, Bob."

And then something completely unexpected happened. Woodman glanced at Barnett and moved his hand to scratch his left temple. When he was sure the senator wasn't looking, he raised his middle finger.

Kennedy barely managed to suppress her smile. The DEA chief would be fully aware of what went into creating an undercover legend sufficient to get close to a major cartel. At a minimum, he would keep his mouth shut. With a little luck, he could be counted on for some minor assistance if it could be kept under the table. Kennedy gave him a nearly imperceptible nod as Barnett started into one of her infamously indignant speeches.

"It's hard for even me to believe that this is happening, Dr. Kennedy. The two men that Mitch Rapp murdered were our only lead in finding Sayid Halabi and intercepting the next package of anthrax that's probably already on it's way. This is your fault and the fault of your agency. The fact that for twenty years you haven't noticed that you have a psychotic working for you is hard to believe. That you didn't notice the multimillion-dollar house of cards he'd built, though, frankly suggests more than incompetence."

And there it was. Barnett was going to play this as complicity. She was going to drag Kennedy in front of an endless string of congressional hearings in an effort to find something that could be used to prosecute her criminally. And to send a message to anyone else who might be feeling defiant.

Barnett let the accusation hang in the air, hoping to coerce Kennedy into responding to it. Instead the CIA director reached for her briefcase and stood.

"If there's nothing more, I obviously have a lot of work to do."

She turned and went for the door, barely getting her hand around the knob before Barnett spoke again.

"Have you heard about Rapp's partner Claudia? Apparently she left him for Scott Coleman and they're now in hiding because they're afraid that he'll kill them."

The malignant glee in Barnett's voice was clearly audible and Kennedy took comfort in it. The senator wasn't as calculating as she was given credit for. At her core, she was at the mercy of her infinite greed for power.

This was going to get ugly and no one was going to escape without getting bloody. But, as Stan Hurley had been fond of saying, it's not how you play the game, it's whether or not your opponent ends up dismembered in the woods.

CHAPTER 29

*W*HERE *were these assholes?*

It was Rapp's second night sleeping in a foxhole stacked with five hundred pounds of coke. And while the drugs themselves were surprisingly comfortable, the impermeable tape wrapped around them left him wallowing in a shallow pond of sweat.

Even worse was the tree above him. Coleman had undoubtedly chosen that location for the additional cover the foliage provided, but hadn't considered the sizable spines that constantly dropped from it. So while he was all but invisible and had a good line of sight to the house, his back and ass were covered with tiny, infuriatingly itchy wounds.

How hard could it be for Esparza to find him? Maybe Claudia had overestimated the capabilities of his outfit. At this point, she'd dropped enough hints to lead a nine-year-old to his door.

Rapp looked past the offending tree at the stars and then glanced over at the vague outline of the house. It contained a comfortable bed, a well-stocked fridge, and satellite TV. Just twenty-five yards of dead-flat terrain away.

When he was in similar holes in the Middle East, he never thought about creature comforts. He was almost always in the middle of nowhere, often surrounded by people who had never even seen a microwave or automatic coffeemaker. But lying there within earshot of the air-conditioning unit somehow made every cactus spine, scorpion, and tarantula that much more irritating.

Not that there was anything he could do about it. Esparza's men were coming and there was no way to be certain from what direction or in what kind of numbers. The design of the house made it more of a trap than a viable defensive position, and if the team the cartel sent was smart enough to surround it, he'd have a hell of a time fighting his way out. Particularly if they brought anything heavier than the expected handguns and assault rifles.

He moved the M4 carbine to one side and tried to find a slightly more comfortable position. Six more hours to dawn. With a little luck, he could get some sleep.

The quiet crunch of tires or approaching footfalls that Rapp expected didn't materialize. Instead, two massive SUVs roared up the road and skidded to a dramatic stop in front of the house before firing up their light bars. He pushed himself to his elbows, peering over the top of the hole as an improbable number of men poured from the vehicles. Despite all the weapons and the glare of the lights, it had kind of a clown car quality to it.

They started firing at the house on full automatic as one of the vehicles' powerful sound systems started blasting something that to Rapp's ear sounded a little like polka music. He reached for his rifle and slid into a position that allowed him to keep an eye on his six, concerned that the fireworks at the house had been designed to cover the approach of foot soldiers from behind.

He decided he might be overestimating the enemy when one of them abandoned his position behind the SUVs and sprinted toward the front door. His comrades didn't have time to divert their fire and the man was cut down before he could even make it to the porch. His body skidded to a stop by the porch steps as the others focused their fire on the windows.

In a somewhat better-organized move, two men pulled a tactical battering ram from the back of one of the vehicles and managed to lug it onto the porch without getting shot. They struggled to coordinate their efforts, but on the second swing the door flew open. When they disappeared inside, their comrades reluctantly stopped shooting.

Everything went silent, but it lasted only about five seconds. A muffled explosion flashed in the empty window frames and Rapp figured it was from the grenade he'd wired across the hallway. Though it could also have been the mine he'd put under the carpet behind the sofa. It was pretty obvious in good light, but with all the dust and half the bulbs shot out, you never knew. These assholes didn't seem to be the sharpest knives in the drawer.

That assessment was confirmed when the men reacted to the explosion by running to the windows and door in order to randomly spray the interior. The fact that one or both of their men might have survived the blast didn't seem to concern them.

Some were running out of ammo and struggling to get new mags in weapons that they clearly weren't familiar with. Rapp considered picking off a few with his silenced Glock, but it seemed unnecessary at this point. Better to just settle in and watch the show.

Two more men ran inside, but the ones shooting through the windows didn't seem aware of it. Rapp assumed they'd get gunned down in a few seconds but he was proven wrong. The garage door suddenly billowed outward, sending a cloud of dust drifting lazily through the spotlights. One of them had gotten far enough to find the charge he'd hidden beneath the owner's stash of lawn furniture.

Rapp took the foil off a home-baked cookie and shoved it in his mouth as a man with an impressive collection of tattoos finally managed to get everyone to stop shooting. A moment later, all that could be heard was the polka music and the dull hum of a model plane circling above.

The tattooed man started shouting at someone standing near one of the windows and pointing at the doorway. Rapp didn't speak Spanish, but it wasn't hard to figure out what was being said. Tattooed Guy wanted Guy By The Window to go inside. And Guy By The Window, not being quite as stupid or high as some of his companions, wanted to stay where he was.

The conversation ended abruptly when Tattooed Guy shot the man in the chest. That lit a fire under the others, and a few moments later, three men were crossing the threshold. Their cautious movements suggested that the group's initial enthusiasm was fading.

Rapp finished his cookie and reached for a box of Pop-Tarts. Popcorn probably would have been more appropriate, but how could Claudia have known?

Four relatively uneventful minutes passed before an explosion blew off part of the back of the house. He'd gotten pretty artistic with that charge. It had been hidden in an AC vent with the tripwire woven through the top of a shower curtain.

It took another three minutes or so before the surviving two men reappeared in the doorway and began giving their report. Again, Spanish fluency wasn't necessary to understand what they were saying. They'd found neither the man nor the coke they'd come for.

There were five men left outside and their discussion quickly went from heated to a full-blown shoving match. For a moment, Rapp thought they were going to start shooting at each other, but he didn't get that lucky. Tattooed Guy managed to get control and dialed a phone while the others huddled in tight around him. They looked like they were working out the next play in MS-13's annual football scrimmage. Did these people receive no training at all?

Rapp picked up the suppressed M4 and fired at the tightly grouped men on full automatic. Not surprisingly, they were all down before half his magazine was expended.

He stepped out of the hole, ducking under various low-hanging tree branches as he approached the men on the ground. All were dead or headed in that direc-

tion so he glanced up at the circling drone and raised
one of his hands, palm up. The sentiment would be
clear in any language.

Is that all you've got?

One of the men on the bottom of the pile started
moving and Rapp shot him in the side of the head. He
wasn't going to get anywhere with these soldiers. That
had already been proved during his interrogation of
the men the DEA had picked up. He needed to talk to
the man in charge.

Rapp walked over to the nearest SUV and turned
off the music. At this point, there wasn't much he
could do other than load the product and drive
off in one of Esparza's pimped-out vehicles. If that
didn't piss the man off enough to reach out, nothing
would.

He was about to climb in when the ring of a cell
phone became audible. Rapp had to search through
the pile of men, but finally found the phone in Tattooed Guy's lifeless hand. The blood on the screen
confused its touch sensitivity but Rapp finally managed to pick up.

"What?"

The screaming on the other end started with what
he assumed was a stream of Spanish epithets.

"Speak English, dipshit."

"I'm going to carve you up and feed you to my dogs,
you . . ."

The sentence devolved into Spanish again.

"Who is this?" Rapp said, crafting his tone to sound
vaguely irritated. "Lorenzo Varela? Why don't you
shut the fuck up and let the big boys work."

The name belonged to the leader of an upstart cartel

run by a college-educated kid from Mexico City. Just the kind of guy someone like Carlos Esparza would despise.

"Varela? You stupid piece of shit! This is Carlos Esparza!"

Rapp didn't respond immediately, instead glancing nervously up at the drone. "Bullshit."

"You want me to prove it? How about I send a hundred men with pliers and blowtorches up to you? I'm going to—"

And more with the Spanish.

Rapp waited for the cartel boss to run out of oxygen before he spoke again. "Look, man. The DEA said this was Varela's shipment. They didn't say anything about you."

More Spanish. Rapp was starting to regret not paying more attention in high school.

"I don't want a war with you, Carlos. I just needed some money to disappear with. Your product's in a hole to the northeast of the house. Why don't you send some guys over to get it."

"And are you still going to be there when they show up, *pendejo*?"

"I could be, but I don't think you can afford to lose any more men."

"Fuck you!"

Rapp didn't respond immediately, making a point to look thoughtfully up at the drone he hoped Esparza was watching from in real time.

"Maybe we can make this work for both of us," he said finally.

"What?"

"I need money and to get as far from U.S. law

enforcement as I can. And you clearly need men who can tell one end of a gun from the other."

Esparza laughed hard enough that Rapp thought he might choke. "You just stole my drugs and killed eighteen of my men. Now you're asking me for a job?"

"Why not? I said I'd give the coke back." He thumbed at the bodies behind. "And you're suddenly light on personnel."

"Then why don't you get on a plane to Mexico and we can have a talk face-to-face."

"Okay."

Esparza started laughing again, this time sounding less enraged and more incredulous.

"What's so funny?"

"You're either crazy or you've got balls too big to fit on a plane."

"Probably a little bit of both," Rapp said honestly.

CHAPTER 30

NORMALLY Rapp slept like a baby on planes. Today, though, he was in an economy class seat wedged between a woman who weighed north of three hundred pounds and a man who let out brief, choking snores every twenty seconds or so. If he'd been on a C-130 over Afghanistan, he'd be spread out on a pile of cargo netting, dead to the world.

It wasn't just the seat, though. That imaginary C-130 would land in a country where he'd spent much of his adult life. In the Middle East, he knew the players, had access to highly trained backup, and spoke the language. He understood the culture and had a deep understanding of his enemy's capabilities and motivations.

When he touched down this time, he'd have none of those advantages. His Spanish was barely good enough to order a Coke. And worse, this wasn't one of the simple search-and-destroy missions he'd become so good at over the years. Killing Carlos Esparza wasn't the objective. In fact, the opposite was true. He needed to ingratiate himself with the man. To use him to learn about the ISIS network and follow it back to Sayid Halabi.

Unfortunately, endearing himself to people had never been Rapp's forte. Kind of the opposite, actually.

Not that any of this was likely to matter. Esparza was probably just flying Rapp to Mexico so he could put a bullet in his head personally. The timing was kind of a shame. He finally had the blank presidential pardon he'd always dreamed of, and instead of taking it out for a spin, he was going to end up buried in the jungle.

And while that was all bad, it wasn't enough to keep him awake on a plane. No, that went deeper, to a question that was easy to ask but hard to answer.

What the hell was he doing there?

He'd given Claudia's diatribe more thought than she'd probably give him credit for and come to the conclusion that she was largely right. Christine Barnett was going to be the next president of the United States and she'd use that position to destroy him and anyone else who refused to kneel.

Best-case scenario, Rapp would survive this mission and be forced out of government service by her. Much more likely, though, was that Barnett would dedicate a significant amount of government resources to seeing him and Kennedy enjoying adjoining cells in a maximum security prison.

And it wouldn't exactly be hard. Rapp had just killed—technically murdered—two drug smugglers, and forced his brother to create a web of illegal transactions that spanned the globe. Even if Steven sat down in front of a Senate panel and demonstrated that it was all smoke and mirrors, it wouldn't be enough.

Rapp would end up being used as a weapon in Christine Barnett's war against the intelligence and law enforcement communities that she saw as a check on her power.

The plane finally touched down, and Rapp remained in his seat while the rest of the passengers rummaged around in the overhead bins. He'd leave the plane without the carry-on he'd brought. It was just a prop to make him look less suspicious to the people at the airline desk. At this point, his only meaningful possessions in the world were a fake passport, a GPS watch, a phone, and a wallet containing five hundred U.S. dollars and a couple of high-limit credit cards.

When Rapp stepped into the terminal of Angel Albino Corzo International Airport, he immediately noticed the man flicking his gaze nervously from his phone to the crowd. He likely had nothing but a hazy drone photo to work with, so Rapp decided to help him out. He adjusted his trajectory toward the casually dressed Mexican and pointed to the exit.

"That's me. Let's go."

The man led Rapp out of the building and they crossed to the parking area under clear skies and temperatures in the mid-nineties. Rapp's thin linen shirt was already starting to soak through by the time they reached a large black SUV parked at the far end of the lot.

Tinted windows made it impossible to see inside, but when Rapp climbed in the back, he found pretty much what he'd anticipated. Two men who looked like former Mexican soldiers frisked him and shoved him to the floor, pulling a cloth bag over his head and closing a set of handcuffs around his wrists. He resisted his natural urge to snap their necks. Driving around in an SUV full of corpses asking random people if they knew where Carlos Esparza lived wasn't going to get him very far.

It was impossible to measure the passing time, partially because his watch was secured behind him and partially because the warmth and vibration of the vehicle's floorboard finally put him to sleep. For some reason, lying there with two cartel killers' feet on his back was a lot more relaxing than the time he'd spent getting sucked into his own mind on the flight. There were no longer options to consider. No secondary concerns. No political agendas. His only job now was to survive long enough to find Sayid Halabi and kill him.

The trip started out on smooth pavement, eventually degenerating into rough asphalt and then a dirt track that jerked him fully awake. In the last half hour or so, they crossed two streams deep enough for water to seep under the door and a few ruts that seemed even deeper.

After what Rapp guessed was somewhere between three and four hours, they finally came to a stop. He was immediately dragged from the vehicle and shoved to his knees on the damp ground. Voices speaking Spanish swirled around him for a few minutes before the bag was pulled off.

He squinted into the filtered sunlight and counted eight guards within his field of view. All were wearing camo, all were armed with AKs, and all had the look of former Mexican cops or army. Nothing special, but head and shoulders above the men he'd killed in California.

Much more interesting was the house intermittently hidden by the jungle in front of him. From the exterior, it had the look of a primitive village, with clapboard sides, scavenged materials, and a roof of corrugated tin and palm fronds. From the air, it would be completely indistinguishable from the other tiny villages in the area, but from where Rapp was kneeling, it was quite the architectural marvel. Massive windows revealed a luxurious modern interior of marble and glass. A swimming pool was hidden under a roof held up by pillars designed to look like trees. Behind and to the north, some kind of crop—food, not drugs—had been planted in a way that suggested subsistence farming.

A man in slacks and an open-collared shirt appeared from the house and approached to within ten feet of Rapp. He was probably in his early thirties, with vaguely stylish glasses and an expensive haircut. Certainly not Esparza. More likely some kind of business advisor. Rapp ignored him, craning his neck to get a better feel for his operating environment. It wasn't too complicated. Jungle. Men with guns. Big house.

Another five minutes or so passed in silence before a second man appeared. He was probably in his mid-forties, with medium-length hair that was a little wild, a gold and diamond watch that looked like it weighed as much as a brick, and clothes that seemed to have been chosen based on the number of digits on the price tag. It was one of the strange things about these cartel bosses. They spent half their time obsessing over accumulating obscene amounts of money and the other half trying to figure out what to do with it.

"We had a bet whether you'd come," Esparza said in solid English. According to Claudia he'd spent a fair amount of his youth in Arizona.

"Who won?"

The man just smiled and pulled a gold .44 Magnum Desert Eagle from his waistband. He aimed it at Rapp, who began instinctively running through the sequence of moves necessary to survive: Drop the cuffs that he'd picked in the first few minutes of the drive there. Roll forward, letting the round go harmlessly over his head. Get hold of the man, disarm him, pull him in close enough that no one would dare take a shot . . .

That was a good way to kill Esparza and escape into the jungle, but Rapp had to remind himself again that that wasn't why he was here. He was here to make friends and figure out how to get close to Sayid Halabi.

"Seems like we've both gone through a lot of trouble for you to just shoot me," Rapp said.

"Oh, I'm not going to shoot you. I'm going to torture you. For months. Until there isn't anything left of you that can even feel pain. Until you don't even know you're *human* anymore. Then I'm going to feed you to my dogs."

"I feel like that would be a mistake," Rapp said, slipping the cuffs off and getting to his feet.

The familiar sound of weapons being slammed to shoulders momentarily drowned out the hum of jungle insects. Esparza thrust his weapon out in front of him but wouldn't allow himself to take a step back in front of the men. His assistant, who was apparently less concerned with machismo, retreated a few feet.

"You're pulling in what?" Rapp said, dusting off

his pants. "Seventy-five million a year on a gross of a hundred and ten?"

Claudia had given him the number, and based on Esparza's expression she'd gotten pretty close. "You're heavily extended in pot, but legalization in the U.S. and Canada is starting to bite. So, you're looking to replace that business with Middle Eastern heroin. You want to take advantage of the crackdown on oxycodone and replace the pharmaceutical industry as the supplier of choice. The bottom line is that you want to move up and you figure this is the play that can get you there."

Rapp fell silent and was surprised when the next man to speak wasn't Esparza but the preppy sidekick. His accent was more highbrow.

"And what do you think of that plan?"

"I think you've got a good shot," Rapp responded. "But it's going to be complicated. Not only because the DEA knows the cartels are going to take this opening, but because working with the Arabs can be . . ." His voice faded for a moment. "Let's say challenging."

"I have hundreds of people on my payroll," Esparza said. "Police, intelligence operatives, judges, military officers. And I have enforcers. You're not the only man in this business who's good with a gun."

Rapp looked around him at Esparza's guards. "Are you sure? From where I'm standing, your talent pool looks a little shallow."

Esparza aimed directly between Rapp's eyes, but again his assistant cut in again.

"I assume you think you have something to offer us?"

"I can provide extensive knowledge of the operations of the U.S. government. CIA, NSA, FBI, and DEA. You name it. Even the White House."

"I have contacts in these places, too," Esparza said, not wanting to be upstaged.

"I also have a lifetime of experience dealing with the Middle East and speak native-level Arabic and fluent Dari. Those are pretty dangerous waters, and I know how to navigate them. You're not just having to get around the Agency and the U.S. military. They're the least of your problems. You've got a hundred different terrorist groups, tribes, and other factions—all of whom are involved in pissing contests that go back a thousand years. And if you manage to cut through all that, then it's going to be time to deal with the Pakistanis and the Russians."

"And you expect me to believe that a crooked cop can, as you say, navigate those waters?"

"Better than anyone on the planet."

"Better than anyone on the planet?" Esparza mocked. "You're confident for a dead man."

"What's your name?" the assistant asked.

"Mitch Rapp."

It clearly didn't mean anything to the man, but Esparza's face went blank for a moment before he burst out laughing.

"This is your story," he barely managed to choke out. "That *Mitch Rapp* stole drugs from DEA and then came here to ask me for a job? For a moment, I thought you had balls. But now I see that you're just crazy."

He summoned one of his guards, but then held out a hand when Rapp spoke again. Apparently he was finding the whole thing pretty entertaining.

"You say you have highly placed contacts. Use them. My story isn't going to be hard to confirm. Unless I miss my guess, this is blowing up all over the Beltway right now. And if you find out I'm lying, it's just as easy to start cutting me up tomorrow as it is today."

CHAPTER 31

AFTER almost two days, Rapp had his accommodations feeling pretty homey. The rusty steel cage itself measured about six feet long by three feet wide, by four feet high. It was located back far enough into the jungle that he could see the dim glow of Esparza's complex in the evening but nothing more than foliage during the day.

He'd managed to pull up the tall grass that grew around the cage and use it to create a fairly comfortable surface to stretch out on. A stick secured to one of the bars above him created a convenient stream of drinking water when it rained, which seemed to be about two hours every night. Bugs were plentiful, but a little too juicy and a touch bitter. Better than the lizard he'd caught last night, though. That thing had been dead hard to choke down. The bottom line was that the Lacandon jungle didn't seem to have anything with the pleasant texture and slight nuttiness of an Iraqi scorpion.

He'd been stripped of everything he'd brought with him and was now wearing a bright orange jumpsuit reminiscent of the ones ISIS passed out to their beheading victims. It was soaked through to the skin and covered with mud, but the material was still capable of keeping him comfortable through the relatively warm nights.

So he wasn't going to starve or freeze. The question was no longer whether he could survive out there; it was how long he was going to have to do it. So far, no one had come to visit and while the cage's lock was old and unsophisticated, it was solid. In the end, it might be boredom that got him.

Based on the temperature and the sound of the jungle, it was probably an hour from dawn when he heard soggy footsteps coming in his direction. Someone to let him out, hose him off, and give him a job? Someone to put a bullet in his skull? In the end, there wasn't much he could do about it either way. He had to fight his instincts and remain passive. He was there to win a popularity contest, not perform a bunch of executions.

The man who appeared wasn't Esparza, which was probably a good sign. If it was going to be the bullet in the head or the blowtorch, the cartel leader would want to do it personally.

He stopped in front of the cage, backlit by the light bleeding from the compound. A little shorter than Rapp, with a scraggly beard and a gut straining against grimy fatigues. Weaponry consisted of an AK slung over his shoulder and a Bowie knife sheathed on his right hip.

"What?" Rapp said.

The gun came off the man's shoulder and he leaned

it against a tree before using the knife to hack off a thick branch. When he returned, he came a little closer, but stayed out of reach.

"California," he managed to get out through a barely comprehensible accent. "My cousin."

The fact that he then shoved the branch through the widely spaced bars and into Rapp's ribs suggested that one of the corpses currently ruining Claudia's Airbnb rating had been a relation. Rapp feigned pain, covering his side and cramming himself into the back of the cage.

As anticipated, the display of weakness encouraged the man. He rammed the branch in over and over as Rapp slapped ineffectually at it. The fact that this asshole hadn't been smart enough to trim the leaves was making it impossible for him to build enough momentum to do any real damage. He seemed to real-ize this and instead of stepping back to fashion a more effective weapon, he decided to go for a gravity assist.

He took a step forward and went in from the top, jabbing Rapp in the chest. The force increased a bit, but was still nowhere near what would be necessary to cause injury. Having said that, the guy seemed to just be warming up, and lying in the mud getting poked with a stick was already getting old.

He was now only about a foot or so out of reach. The opportunity was there, but Rapp couldn't decide if it made sense to take it. Esparza's assistant was probably still checking out his story and getting too aggressive might be a mistake. On the other hand, letting himself get trapped in a cage for days on end might suggest that he wasn't worth hiring.

Rapp suspected he was just talking himself into it,

but he quickly decided that killing this piece of shit was definitely the right course of action. He waited for the stick to come down again and instead of slapping it away, he grabbed it and pulled. The already off-balance man pitched forward, struggling to keep his footing in the slick mud.

His right leg came into range and Rapp yanked it through a gap between the bars. The cartel enforcer made the mistake of bending at the waist to try to free himself and Rapp got hold of his beard, using it to slam his face into the top of the cage.

Unfortunately, there wasn't enough leverage available to do any real damage. A thumb in the eye socket was an option, but sound was the main problem at this point. Rapp managed to use his beard and hair to spin him around and clamp a hand over his mouth. At that point, it was just a matter of getting hold of the knife.

Ten more seconds and it was over. Rapp kept the back of the man's head pinned securely against the bars as blood cascaded from the gash in his neck. When he finally went still, Rapp let the body slide into the mud and turned his attention to the lock. The mechanism wasn't particularly sophisticated, but the overall build quality was depressingly solid. Prying it open with the knife wasn't going to happen and a search of the dead man turned up no keys. Just a half a pack of cigarettes and a lighter.

Rapp needed something stiff enough to work the lock mechanism but soft enough that he could fashion it with the knife. Materials at hand were limited. Rocks were hard, but not easily carved into a pick. The jungle foliage was easy to carve, but too flexible to move the heavy tumblers.

He pulled off one of the man's boots and pried apart the sole, hoping to find some kind of plastic stiffener, but it was just rubber and leather.

Why did everything have to go the hard way?

He pulled the man's leg inside the cage and yanked back on it, using one of the bars as a fulcrum. The quiet snap of bone sounded immediately, but he kept pulling until the jagged fracture popped through the skin.

Surprisingly, the knife was razor sharp, and it took only about fifteen minutes to fashion part of the man's fibula into the appropriate tools. Once the lock had dropped off, Rapp swapped clothes with the corpse and shoved it in the cage. It wouldn't fool anyone who was really interested, but it'd be enough for someone casually glancing through the trees as they passed.

A quick recon of the compound confirmed his first impression—minimal physical or electronic security, but a lot of armed guards. None looked particularly attentive, but their sheer number made getting by them unlikely even in the remaining darkness. Quietly killing a couple more was definitely doable, but how high a body count could you run up in a popularity contest? It wasn't really his area of expertise, but he guessed that anything over zero was a move in the wrong direction. So he waited.

Dawn brought what he was looking for: a fairly sloppy changing of the guard. Taking advantage of a temporary gap along the northeast corner of the compound, Rapp slipped out of the jungle and through a door partially hidden by foliage.

It opened to a storage room and probably provided access for deliveries. Past the well-stocked shelves was another door that led to a spacious industrial kitchen.

There were a couple of pots steaming on the stove but no sign of the cook, so he crossed the tile floor into an airy dining room.

Human activity continued to be nonexistent as he crossed a surprisingly tasteful living room and entered a hallway at the back. Most of the doors were open and led to stylish bedroom suites that looked like they'd never been used.

He slipped into one of them and locked the door. A quick search turned up a closet full of designer clothes, some of which still had the tags hanging from them. As luck would have it, he and Esparza were around the same size. The loafers looked a little small but would undoubtedly be more comfortable than the guard's damp, torn-up boots.

The bathroom was behind a massive stone barrier that doubled as the headboard of the bed. The back wall was constructed entirely of glass and looked out into dense, flowering jungle. Rapp spotted a switch set apart from the ones for the lights and flipped it. The glass turned opaque.

This was more like it.

CHAPTER 32

RAPP pushed his hair from his face and examined himself in the still steamy bathroom mirror. With a belt, Esparza's designer slacks stayed up and the fact that he wore his shirts loose allowed them to accommodate Rapp's broad shoulders. The loafers were definitely on the tight side but that was probably a good thing—they'd stay on if he had to run. But that wasn't the goal. If there was any running happening today, his mission had failed.

Satisfied that he was appropriately groomed for a job interview, Rapp strode back out into the hallway. It was still empty and he headed unchallenged toward the large, palm-frond-covered terrace he'd noticed when he arrived.

On his way across the living room, a plump woman in her fifties appeared from a door to the right. She stopped short, giving him a quizzical look as she wiped her hands on an apron that appeared to have seen some serious action. Just the person he was looking for.

"Breakfast?"

Her eyes narrowed as she tried to decipher what he'd said.

"Comida?" he managed to dredge from his memory.

That got a nod.

"Cómo se llama?"

"María, señor."

"María. Café?"

That got another nod, but he wasn't through his Spanish repertoire yet.

"Huevos rancheros?"

"Sí, señor."

"Perfecto. Y orange juice." He pantomimed holding a glass. "Uh, naranja. Sí? Muy grande. Mucho hielo."

"Entiendo. Tortillas de harina o maíz?"

He had no idea what she'd just said, but on the subject of food his instinct was to just agree with whatever this woman recommended. "Sí."

She didn't seem to fully understand his response, but he wasn't worried. "Dónde está Señor Esparza?"

She pointed. "En la terraza."

Esparza was right where María said he would be, sitting at a table with a plate of fruit and a newspaper in front of him. The entire terrace—including the fountain and massive fireplace—were shaded and protected from overhead surveillance by foliage. The bugs were a little thick, but at least they weren't for breakfast anymore.

The cartel leader didn't look up until Rapp sat down across from him. His confused expression only lasted a split second before recognition set in. He looked like he was about to shout for help from the surrounding guards, but Rapp spoke first.

"I figured you'd probably heard something back from your contacts by now."

There was a place setting in front of him, so Rapp shook out the cloth napkin and set it on his lap.

Esparza was frozen, eyes flicking to the knife near Rapp's right hand. His body language suggested he was going to throw himself backward and call in a little machine gun fire, but then María appeared with a cup of coffee and a pitcher of icy, fresh-squeezed orange juice.

"Gracias," Rapp said, accepting it with a disarming smile. Esparza's desperation to escape seemed to wane as Rapp poured himself a glass of juice and downed it in a few gulps.

"I see you're making yourself at home," he said, examining the clothes Rapp was wearing.

"I figured you wouldn't mind," Rapp responded, testing the coffee. Not surprisingly, it was top-notch. "What have you been able to figure out?"

Esparza remained silent for a few seconds before finally speaking. "That it's possible you're who you say you are. There's a surprising amount of information available on the recent activities of Mitch Rapp but getting confirmation is difficult. My assistant is supposed to have a more thorough report for me this morning."

María returned with the huevos rancheros and Rapp dug in as the cartel leader looked on.

"It appears that you stole a fair amount of money over your career."

"Stole, my ass."

"So you deny the accusations your government is making?"

"I took money from terrorists and the people who funded them. I've been hanging it out there for America for twenty fucking years and my annual salary wouldn't cover the clothes I found in your guest bedroom. And what if one of my enemies came after me and I had to run? You think the politicians would help me out? I sure as hell wouldn't bet my life on it. So, sure. I had a few rainy day funds."

"Invested stupidly, apparently."

"I got some bad advice. Not really my area of expertise."

"A man with friends like yours could make these kinds of problems go away with the snap of a finger."

Rapp shoveled another forkful of María's amazing eggs in his mouth and shook his head. "*Could* is the operative word there, Carlos. Past tense. President Alexander isn't going to get anywhere near a scandal during this clusterfuck of an election. And Christine Barnett wants nothing more than to hang me up by my balls."

"An uncomfortable position."

"You think?" Rapp said, letting the volume of his voice rise. "I've been shot, stabbed, set on fire, and blown up. Twice. All in the defense of the Stars and Stripes. And all I asked in return was enough money to survive my retirement." He was almost shouting now, demonstrating the kind of passion that a man like Esparza would appreciate, but not so much that it would worry the guards. "But what am I looking at instead? A jail cell and a piece-of-shit president who's never lifted a finger for anyone but herself."

It was pretty much a retread of all the things Claudia had been telling him, but there was no reason it wouldn't work as well on Esparza as it had on him.

"And your woman? My people tell me she left you for a friend of yours."

"Her boss and my backup man Scott Coleman," Rapp spat out. "Who knows how long that's been going on? Turns out that when the money and power goes away, so do they."

"It seems you'd want to kill them," Esparza said, interested enough to keep probing, trying to find a crack in Rapp's story.

"I wouldn't mind. Believe me. But Scott's a dangerous son of a bitch and the Agency's going to be looking for me to make a move like that. For now, I'm just going to have to let it go. When all this dies down and I get my feet under me, though, you can bet your ass I'm going to be paying them a visit."

Esparza fell silent, watching the man in front of him. As insane as it seemed, all indications were that he really was Mitch Rapp. And that created both opportunities and dangers that he never thought he'd be contemplating. Over the years, he'd managed to put many important people on his payroll. But Mitch Rapp? None of his competitors—even those with revenues that would get them on a *Forbes* list—had anyone who could compare.

Vicente Rossi appeared, took a few steps across the terrace, and stopped dead. It was an understandable reaction, but one that Esparza couldn't be seen sharing. Instead, he cut a slice of the pineapple on his plate and casually waved his business advisor over.

"I don't think formal introductions have been made. This is Vicente."

Rapp nodded in the man's direction but otherwise didn't acknowledge him.

"What do you have for me?" Esparza said, taking a bite of fruit to cover his nervousness. He had killed countless men. Tortured them and their families. Built a cartel that commanded fear and respect that far outstripped the scope of its operation. He refused to allow his fear of this unarmed American to show.

Rossi, still standing, had no similar qualms. "Perhaps this is something that would be better done in private?"

Had he discovered something that would cause the CIA man to go for the knife still within his reach? Esparza met Rapp's dead gaze, refusing to turn away. "Now."

Rossi gave a reluctant nod. "I'm satisfied that this is indeed Mitch Rapp."

It wasn't a surprising conclusion at this point, but still the cartel leader felt a surge of adrenaline. "And the DEA men?"

"We were able to get people into the hospital where they're being treated. There's no question that they were shot, but because of their body armor, their injuries are relatively minor." He paused. "Unlike our men, who are dead."

Esparza leaned back in his chair, gazing up at the younger man. The reason the DEA men had survived was obvious. There would have been no reason for Rapp to antagonize the Americans any more than necessary. And the reason so many of his men were dead was equally obvious.

"Did my men talk?" Esparza asked.

Rapp shook his head. "That's why I didn't know the shipment was yours. My compliments on your management style. I took off one of their hands with a set of bolt cutters and they were still more afraid of you than they were of me."

Esparza smiled at that. In the end, he and Rapp were much alike. Two predators who got what they wanted. "Go on, Vicente."

"Mr. Rapp seems to have left his official capacity at the CIA some time ago to pursue what appears to be a vendetta in Saudi Arabia, though it's impossible to know how much Agency involvement there was. Irene Kennedy is quite clever at covering her tracks. He was recently in Yemen, most likely working as a private contractor in her employment."

"And now?" Esparza said.

Rossi seemed reluctant to continue but understood that he had no choice. "The allegations of long-term financial impropriety combined with the shooting of the DEA agents and the murder of two Mexican nationals has very much changed his status. Not surprisingly, everyone is backing away from him as quickly as they can."

"Including Kennedy?"

"Unclear. But her ability to support him at this point is nonexistent. People are abandoning her almost as quickly as they are Rapp. If Senator Barnett wins the presidency it's hard to see how she'll escape being indicted."

"So you can see my problem," Rapp interjected. "And why your organization is an interesting solution. Half those politicians would be dead if it weren't for me. But now they're turning on me without a second thought. You, on the other hand, have a reputation for loyalty and rewarding competence."

Esparza watched María approach and begin collecting their empty plates. "I think you'd find working for drug traffickers much more predictable than working for politicians."

"I don't doubt it."

"Why don't you go with María. Since my men can't perform the simple task of keeping you in a cage, you might as well stay in the house."

Rapp stood and Esparza studied his confident gait as he retreated across the flagstone patio.

"Thoughts?" he said when the CIA man had disappeared through the glass doors.

"Kill him now."

The cartel leader laughed.

"I'm serious, Carlos. You can't trust this man."

"Didn't you just tell me that you confirmed his story?"

"He and Irene Kennedy have the capacity to create any illusion they want."

"But why? I think your lack of balls might be clouding your vision, Vicente. The CIA doesn't give a shit about drugs, other than maybe to sell them to finance their black ops. And I think it's unlikely that the rise of Christine Barnett is just a trick to allow Mitch Rapp to infiltrate a medium-sized Mexican drug operation. And then there's the matter of the DEA agents. Even with the vests, one could have easily been killed. The Americans don't take those kinds of risks. And they don't torture drug traffickers to death."

"But—"

"The timing of this couldn't be better for us, Vicente. We're in a dangerous position because of the loss of the San Ysidro mall, and there's no question that someone like Rapp could help with the Arabs. He speaks their language. He understands how they do business and what scares them. . . ."

"The timing of this couldn't be better for us," Rossi repeated. "You don't find this at all suspicious? That a man dedicated to fighting Middle Eastern terrorists arrived on our doorstep right after we sent through our first shipment of Middle Eastern heroin?"

Esparza frowned and took a sip of his coffee. "Heroin has been flooding out of the Middle East for years. Between that and Saudi oil, the Americans finance virtually every terrorist operation in the world. And even if they *did* care, why would they come after us? There are cartels with longer-standing relationships with the Arabs."

"What about our exposure to American retaliation?" Rossi countered. "Mitch Rapp probably has more ugly secrets in his head than anyone but Irene Kennedy herself. You say the CIA doesn't care about us and you may be right. But the day they find out we've taken on Mitch Rapp, we move directly into their crosshairs."

Esparza nodded thoughtfully. This was perhaps the most compelling argument for killing Rapp. The risks of having him there were incredibly high. Probably too high.

Rossi sensed that he'd gained an advantage in their discussion and decided to press. "I can figure out how to deal with heroin, Carlos. There are a lot of Arab immigrants in Mexico, some of whom are already involved in the drug trade. We can hire as many as we need."

Esparza tapped his index finger absently on the

tabletop. Summarily executing Mitch Rapp seemed like an incredible waste. Both of talent and opportunity for sport.

Everyone he hired into a position of authority had to pass a test. Depending on the specific demands of the job, that test might relate to skill, toughness, loyalty, or intelligence. Some were relatively easy. María had been hired based on her ability to make food indistinguishable from Esparza's own mother's. For others, failure had meant death.

"We'll test him," Esparza said, finally.

"Carlos, I don't—"

"Relax, Vicente. We'll create a test that's impossible for him to survive. Do you have no curiosity at all? No interest in seeing Mitch Rapp in action? In seeing what he would do and how long he could last against impossible odds?"

"What if he beats those odds?"

Esparza considered the question for a moment. "Then we'd have to consider the possibility that the rewards of employing such a man might be worth the risks."

CHAPTER 33

RAPP followed two armed guards through the house in the direction of the front door. With the exception of his phone, all the possessions he'd arrived there with had been returned. The green cotton slacks and brown shirt supplied by Claudia had been cleaned and pressed but would still allow him to blend into the jungle if necessary. The gray trail-running shoes were less stylish, but sturdy, light, and possessed a tread designed for soft surfaces.

The barking of dogs became audible when they stepped into the humid morning, ahead and to the right but hidden in the foliage. They skirted the clearing that stretched along the front of the house, staying beneath the jungle canopy in an effort to foil possible overhead surveillance.

The scene they finally came upon was, unfortunately, about what Rapp had expected. Two dirt bikes and three 4x4s sprayed with matte camo paint—one with a mounted machine gun heavy enough to nearly bottom out the suspension. The sixth and last vehicle was a spotless Humvee painted British racing green. Like Rapp's clothes, designed to blend in anywhere.

Seventeen men were either in the vehicles or standing around them. All were wearing full camo and equipped with assault rifles, sidearms, and light packs with water bladders. The exception was Esparza himself, who was wearing his typical five grand worth of designer linen. The only obvious change was that he'd traded his calfskin loafers for a sturdy pair of hiking boots.

Worse were the six dogs. In Rapp's estimation dogs were usually smarter than their human masters and always more motivated. The mix of breeds was designed more for intimidation than tracking but despite being heavy on the Rottweilers and pit bulls, the pack would still be effective. Particularly if they managed to catch what they were chasing. In this case, him.

"Everyone who works for me has to pass a test first," Esparza said, speaking in a voice loud enough to be heard over the frenzied dogs. "This will be yours."

"You're getting a little ahead of yourself, aren't you?" Rapp said. "We haven't talked money."

The man bristled, unaccustomed to being challenged. But none of his men seemed to speak English, so he was the only one who registered Rapp's attitude.

"How much do you think you're worth?"

"Two hundred and fifty grand seems about right."

The cartel leader laughed. "A quarter million a year? I don't even pay Vicente that much."

"A month, Carlos. Two fifty *a month*."

The cartel leader's bemused expression spoke volumes. He was going to agree. But probably not because he was willing to pay that amount. More likely, he'd created a test that he was certain Rapp wouldn't survive.

"Done," he said, pointing to a primitive road leading into the jungle. "All you have to do is make it to a small village twelve miles to the north. Actually, *village* might not be the right word. It's just three houses. But one of them has a covered porch and operates as an informal restaurant for the local farmers. Meet me there and you'll get your first month's payment."

Rapp was fairly sure he knew the place—a crossroads where the crappy dirt road met a slightly less crappy dirt road that ran from east to west. The bulky GPS watch on his wrist contained a color screen and was full of topographical maps that he'd downloaded during his layover in Mexico City. And while the tiny screen didn't have the resolution to depict buildings, the distance and direction was right, and businesses tended to set up at crossroads.

"What if I don't make it?" Rapp said.

"Then you'll be dead."

Rapp scanned the men around him again. Some were overweight, others looked like the run-of-the-mill psycho cartel enforcers, and a few looked like solid former Mexican soldiers. All the gear was well maintained and top-of-the-line. They had weapons, vehicles, dogs, and the home field advantage. In his column, the heat wasn't too bad this time of the morning and the sky suggested rain was coming. Likely a lot of it.

"Do I get a head start or does everyone just start shooting now?" Rapp asked.

"Ten minutes."

"That seems light."

"This isn't a negotiation," Esparza responded, retrieving an old-fashioned stopwatch from his pocket and making a show of clicking the button on top. "Your precious minutes are already running out."

Rapp toggled the timer on his own watch and started to run. The roadbed was soft and a little slick, limiting him to a seven-minute-mile pace. The goal was a stream just over a mile from there. Based on what he'd been able to make out on the topo, it was steep and narrow enough to neutralize even the dirt bikes, and the reliable water supply gave him a decent chance of running into a human settlement where he could scrounge supplies.

The critical component at this point was to stay ahead of his pursuers until the rains came and reduced the effectiveness of the dogs. Probably doable as long as the handlers kept hold of them. If they got close enough to release them, though, things were going to get exciting.

He notched his pace upward to the very edge of what the surface would safely allow. The idea that Esparza would live up to his word on the ten minutes seemed a little far-fetched.

After six minutes of running, he activated the screen on his watch to check his position with regard to the stream. In the end, it turned out to be unnecessary. The water from recent rains had swollen it to the point that it had washed out part of the road. Rapp slid down an embankment into the muddy creek, alternating between it and the banks, depending on which maximized his speed. After about a hundred yards he heard the distant whine of the dirt bikes starting up. The timer on his watch read eight minutes and four seconds. Frankly, a minute longer than Rapp had figured. Apparently, that was what passed for honor among thieves.

If they weren't complete morons, it would take only about three minutes before they found the place where he'd ducked into the jungle. At the pace he'd set, his footprints were clearly visible, though it would be impossible to determine whether he'd headed upstream or downstream. Best bet, the dirt bikers would radio it in and split up to chase. The dogs would be put in vehicles and driven to the place where Rapp had abandoned the road. So call it another five before he had an organized chase coming up behind him.

Not surprisingly, the microscopic topographical map hadn't provided a very accurate picture of the terrain. Instead of narrowing into a tiny scar cut through the jungle, the stream kept getting wider, deeper, and more powerful. Cascades that were half waterfall and half mudslide fed it from the canyon walls, making it increasingly hard for Rapp to keep his footing.

Overhead, the clouds were building, but at a pace that was slower than he'd hoped. The rain he was counting on to save his ass from the dogs seemed a long way off.

When the pack become audible again, they were going nuts. The question now was, would their handlers try to keep them under control or would they let them run?

The answer came about a minute later when the sound of their barking suddenly diminished. They were no longer straining against their handlers. They were loose.

The jungle at the edges of the now thirty-foot-wide river was too dense for a human to move through, but the dogs would manage it pretty well. Rapp abandoned the shallow water on the right bank and went for the deeper center. He selected a thick, leafy tree from the floating debris and tangled himself it in. A branch behind his head kept his nose and mouth out of the water while the rest of him floated along beneath the surface.

Because he'd traveled mostly in the water, the dogs wouldn't have much to work with. They'd have to move along both banks, trying to pick up a scent. As long as the river kept moving and he stayed submerged, he'd probably be all right.

Probably.

After an hour of floating along at a less than thrilling three or four knots, the situation started to deteriorate. On the positive side, his femur wasn't yet a dog toy. On the negative side, it was potentially a few seconds from becoming one.

There were two pit bulls on the east bank, staying roughly even with him. They seemed to sense that their prey was close but hadn't yet focused on the tree he was hidden beneath. A Doberman was on the opposite bank, hanging a bit farther back with its handler alongside. Two soldiers were visible in the shallow water to the west, scanning the dense jungle around them with assault rifles gripped tight.

One got a call on his radio and he spoke into it for a few seconds. His words were unintelligible, but his tone and gestures weren't hard to decipher. They figured Rapp was in the river because the dogs couldn't pick up his scent, but they had no idea where. The response was also audible, a static-ridden jumble of anger and frustration from Carlos Esparza. He wouldn't be too worried yet, but he'd be looking up at the same darkening clouds as Rapp was.

When the clouds finally opened up, they did so with no warning at all. One minute Rapp was floating along with an overheated Rottweiler swimming about ten yards in front of him and the next he was fighting to breathe as water came at him from every direction.

The shouts of the soldiers were swallowed by the downpour, as were their outlines. Shots rang out but it was impossible to know if they thought they'd spotted a target or were just using the sound to locate each other. The Rottweiler, again proving its intelligence, made a beeline for the nearest land bank as the river began to swell.

Rapp stayed put, struggling against a current that kept pushing him under. He was finally forced to unhook his feet from the trunk and let them dangle in the deepening water. His head was still among the tree's leafy branches, but now high enough to get a few breaths between waves crashing over him.

From the impact of the stationary objects he was colliding with, he could tell that the speed of the water had picked up significantly. He held on, knowing that he was leaving his pursuers well behind. Soon, though, it became too dangerous. The water was filling with larger, more jagged debris, and the current was becoming impossible to fight. Ahead, the channel narrowed enough to give him a shot at reaching the east bank.

Despite his having a gift for swimming that had helped him win the Iron Man in his youth, the fifteen-foot trip turned out to be harder than it looked. He took a few good hits from deadfall, one particularly large tree sending him to the bottom and dragging him across the rocks for almost a minute.

When he finally came up, he found himself only a few yards from the edge of the jungle. A few hard strokes put him in range of a partially submerged tree and he managed to use it to pull himself to safety. After crawling onto the muddy bank, he lay there vomiting what felt like a tanker truck full of muddy water. Finally, he pulled himself beneath a bush, using the leaves to protect himself from the pounding rain while he got his breathing under control.

Images of carving Carlos Esparza's heart out with a dull stick flashed across his mind, but he reminded himself again that wasn't the mission. No, that'd be too easy.

Rapp had been out of the water for just over two hours when the dogs became audible again. Someone on Esparza's team was a pretty functional tracker and was using his canine teammates to maximum effect.

A temporary hole in the cloud cover had tipped the advantage back to the chasers, leaving Rapp with very little time. The handlers would soon get close enough to release the dogs again and then he'd have five hundred pounds of muscle, teeth, and claws bearing down on him like scent-seeking missiles.

He was currently lying in a large field of surprisingly healthy-looking coca plants. Typically, the Mexicans imported their coke from farther south, but Esparza seemed to be trying to integrate his supply chain. The plants were harder to spot from the air than marijuana, but it was doubtful that anyone was even trying. With the relationship between the United States and Mexico being what it was, the government would probably be happy to overlook this fledgling cash crop.

The compound in front of him contained four modest buildings—most notably a two-story structure that seemed to be the Mexican answer to a barn. It would have come off as a typical subsistence farm if it weren't for a few details to the contrary. The coca plants were a pretty clear tip-off, obviously. As were the well-camouflaged fifty-five-gallon drums that likely contained the chemicals necessary to refine Esparza's experimental crop. Most interesting to Rapp, though, were the two guards.

Both were armed with AKs, but older and more poorly maintained than the ones carried by the men pursuing him. Neither had sidearms, opting instead for knives sheathed on their hips. One was sitting on a log with his back to Rapp at a distance of about fifteen feet. The other was twenty feet farther, leaning against the barn and facing his companion. Every once in a while they spoke to each other, but neither seemed particularly interested in the conversation. Other than that, there was no sign of personnel or activity.

The sound of the dogs was getting closer. When they were released, it would be a matter of minutes before they were on top of him. And this time, he didn't have a whole lot to work with to escape them. While he'd made significant progress toward the village that was his objective, he was currently stuck in relatively flat terrain with no rivers nearby. The patch of blue sky above him was shrinking fast, though, suggesting the weather might be turning back in his favor.

No more time for fancy strategies or precision. It was time to pull out the hammer.

He dug the toes of his shoes into the soft earth, putting himself in a position similar to that of a sprinter in a starting block. He wanted to wait until the man against the barn wasn't looking in his direction, but the strained barking of the dogs suddenly became less frustrated. They'd been turned loose again.

He shot forward, snatching the knife from the first man's belt and dragging the blade across his throat. The guard near the barn grabbed his weapon and leapt to his feet just as Rapp threw the knife. While it was still in the air, the man caught his foot on something and pitched forward. It changed the range between them just enough that instead of penetrating his chest, the blade hit hilt-first.

Again, Rapp charged, but he was forced to drop and slide when the man got his finger on the trigger. A spray of rounds filled the air over his head as they collided. The guard's feet went out from under him and they wrestled for control of the weapon. Rapp had nearly gotten into a position to choke him out when he heard something burst from the coca plants behind him. He stopped fighting and let the guard roll on top of him just as the Doberman reached them. The man screamed when it clamped its jaws around his shoulder, and Rapp slid from beneath him as more crashes sounded.

The AK was out of reach and there wasn't time to go for it. Instead Rapp bolted for the barn with an unknown number of dogs chasing. He sprinted through the door, leapt over some rusting fifty-five-gallon drums, and landed three rungs up a ladder that led to a loft. There was no time to climb, so he just jumped, using his momentum and arm strength to flip himself onto the rickety platform.

At least one dog slammed into the base of the ladder, and Rapp heard the claws of others as they tried desperately to reach him. Rapp immediately got into a position that would allow him to kick any that made it to the top, but, as impressive as they were at moving through the jungle, climbers they were not. Every few seconds, a paw or snout would appear, but then it would disappear again as the dog lost purchase and fell back into the crazed pack.

Once he was reasonably satisfied that none were going to get lucky, Rapp looked around him. No weapons or even respectably sharp farm implements were in evidence. Instead, the space was neatly stacked with duct-tape-wrapped bricks. He ripped one open and tried a small sample of the cocaine he found inside. Apparently Esparza's botany experiment was succeeding. It was seriously good shit.

Rapp moved back to the edge of the loft and the sight of him got one of the pit bulls excited enough to make the top rung. Rapp kicked it in the side of the head, sending it cartwheeling back into the pack completely unfazed.

He ripped open the kilo brick in his hand and then did the same to a few others. While he was working, two more dogs took a shot at climbing the ladder. Their muzzles, necks, and chests were covered in the blood of the guard they had just torn apart.

All six were now present—enough that they could functionally climb on top of each other to try to get at him. It was an unexpectedly effective strategy and their barking turned deafening as Rapp kicked at them.

There was a brief lull as a falling Rottweiler knocked them back and Rapp took advantage of it to chuck the open kilo bags on top of them. They were momentarily enveloped in an impressive cloud that, when it dissipated, left them all a ghostly white. Predictably, their barking and attempts to get to him increased in intensity. He started to regret the light running shoes he'd chosen as he kicked at them, trying to protect his ankles from fangs coated in foaming saliva.

As the coke went to work on them, though, they lost their focus. Some started fighting. Others just ran around in circles or attacked the walls. One bolted out into the rain that had started up again.

While they were distracted, Rapp went to a window on the eastern edge of the loft. He stood to the side of it, gently pushing the wood shutter open and taking a look outside. The downpour had reduced visibility to less than twenty feet.

He climbed down the front of the building with the water pounding on him from above. About halfway to the ground, the force of it became too much for the slick handholds he was improvising and he lost his grip. Fortunately, the landing was soft—about three-quarters mud and one-quarter what was left of the guard the dogs had taken out. Rapp scrambled for the AK and, when he found it, ran for the cover of the coca plants.

CHAPTER 34

" . . . I couldn't make as much. You didn't give me time."

Sayid Halabi looked over his laptop at Gabriel Bertrand standing in the rock archway. The package in the Frenchman's hands seemed to glow in the dull light. Vacuum packed and covered in duct tape, it was indeed smaller than last time. The anthrax it contained could be augmented with other materials to mimic the kilo packages expected by the Mexican smugglers. And, with luck, it would be deployed in America to some minor effect. But the handful of victims it would produce no longer mattered.

Halabi continued to silently watch the scientist as he shifted his weight uncomfortably from one foot to the other. The goal had been to keep him ignorant of the reality and scope of the upcoming attack, using him only to fill in critical pieces of information not available elsewhere. But this was now impossible. The complexity of accelerating the timetable on a biological attack of this scale made continued efforts at subtle manipulation impractical. Halabi would get only one chance. If he failed and was discovered, the entire world would line up against him. Militaries and intelligence agencies that had spent decades battling each other would join forces, coordinating their massive resources with the goal of exterminating both him and the organization he led. The next week would decide whether ISIS reshaped the planet or disappeared from its surface.

"It will be enough," Halabi said finally.

The Frenchman approached cautiously, leaving the anthrax on the plywood desk. He was a comically weak man. Ruled by cowardice and arrogance. Devoid of a belief in anything greater than himself. But unquestionably in possession of a magnificent mind.

Bertrand had written extensively on the history of contagions spanning from early Egypt to the outbreak of SARS in the modern era. He'd studied the spread of pathogens, examining how they initially took hold, modeling their paths, and scrutinizing their aftermath. Even more interesting, he'd done a great deal of work detailing how epidemics of the past had been made worse and how those mistakes had the potential to be repeated on a much grander scale in the future.

Halabi rotated his laptop so the man could see the screen. "Do you know what this is?"

Bertrand squinted at it for a moment and then shook his head.

"It's a population map of the United States, with transportation infrastructure overlaid—airports, bus and train routes, major highways . . ."

Not surprisingly, the man didn't understand. And there was no delicate way to remedy his ignorance.

"I intend to infect five of my men with the virus you discovered in Yemen and transport them across the U.S. border," Halabi said bluntly. "From there, they'll spread the disease throughout the country and the industrialized world."

Bertrand's expression went blank. "I . . . I don't understand. What are you saying?"

"I don't know how I can be more clear."

He stood frozen for a time before taking a few stumbling steps back. "You . . ." he stammered. "It's . . . It's not possible."

"It's not only possible, it's quite simple. YARS is extraordinarily contagious, so infecting my people will be a trivial matter. And I have a group of smugglers in Mexico willing to transport them across the border."

"You can't do that."

"I assure you that I can, Doctor. In fact it's already in motion. I just need you to help me with a few final details."

Bertrand squinted through the semidarkness as though he were looking at a child unable to grasp a simple concept. "This isn't anthrax. It's a highly contagious, extremely deadly disease with no effective medical treatment. Even Spanish flu . . ." His voice faded for a moment. "In 1918 and 1919 it killed more than thirty million people worldwide."

"I'm aware of the history of the Spanish flu," Halabi said calmly.

"All evidence suggests that this disease is even more contagious and has a significantly higher mortality rate. Add to that the rise in long-distance travel and the increase in the world population, and you could be talking about casualties in the hundreds of millions."

"That's my estimate as well."

Still, Bertrand's' expression suggested that he believed he wasn't being clear. "This can't be controlled. It won't just kill people you think are your enemies. It won't be just Americans. Or Christians. It'll come here. It'll spread across the Middle East. It'll kill your men, members of your family. Maybe even you."

"If that's God's will."

"Are you out of your mind?" the Frenchman said, finally starting to grasp what they were talking about. "If it was God's will, he'd do it himself. This isn't a bullet or nerve gas or even a nuclear bomb. You can't target an opposing army or country. You can't predict what it will do. And you can't stop it once it's started. It's impossible to win because winning doesn't exist."

"You're wrong, Doctor. With its complexity, interconnectedness, and reliance on technology, the industrialized world will completely collapse. It won't just be disease that kills them. It will be starvation. Cold. Darkness and chaos." He waved a hand around him. "Certainly, millions will die in this part of the world, but that isn't enough to destroy us. It's the way we've lived for millennia."

Bertrand took another step back. "You think . . . You think you can level the playing field?"

Halabi smiled. "I'd forgotten that idiom. Thank you. It encompasses my goals perfectly. The West's financial, human, and military resources will simply cease to exist. As will their desire and ability to interfere in the affairs of others."

The Frenchman had finally retreated far enough that his back hit the cave's stone wall. He seemed to be trying to speak but found himself unable to do so. Halabi filled the silence.

"As I said, infecting my men and getting them into America is relatively simple. As is selecting the cities they'll be sent to. Based on population density, location, and airport activity, the obvious choices are Chicago, Houston, Los Angeles, New York, Seattle, and Atlanta. My men will have no problem finding menial work—cleaning, food service, and the like. The details, though, are somewhat more difficult. How would this best be done? Transportation hubs seem obvious. But what about theaters where people are in very close contact and the virus wouldn't be subject to direct sunlight? What about cashiers who handle money for hundreds of customers a day? And what about when my people begin displaying symptoms? Perhaps nightclubs where the disorienting environment would make those symptoms less noticeable to the people around them?"

"Are you . . . Are you asking me to help you?"

Halabi ignored the question. "Another issue is how to protect my American disciples who will be hosting these people. They're all anxious to be martyred, of course, but it seems that it would be most advantageous not to infect them until my other people are near death. That would create a second wave of infection before the CDC and other authorities fully grasp what's happening."

"I made the anthrax," the Frenchman responded.

"And that was probably a mistake. But if you think I'm going to help you do something like this, you're insane."

"Am I?"

"Yes," Bertrand responded. "Once this is put into motion, I'll no longer be of any use to you. You'll kill me. And even if you don't, there's a good chance the disease will."

The scientist fell silent and looked around him, peering into the shadows as though there was something meaningful hidden there. Halabi had seen it many times before. He was experiencing the confusion that all nonbelievers suffered when they realized their lives would soon end. The only thing ahead of him now was a dark, empty eternity.

"Come," Halabi said, standing and walking past Bertrand into the passageway. With no other option, the Frenchman followed. As they approached the end of the corridor, two men appeared and dragged him into a chamber to the left. A strangled scream rose up and then died in Bertrand's throat when he saw what was waiting for him.

Much of Victoria Schaefer's body was rotted away and what was left had been mummified by the dry conditions. Her face was mostly skeletonized, with missing cheeks exposing the roots of her teeth and empty eye sockets staring out through strips of leathery skin. In truth, it was only her clothing and long blond hair that identified her.

"No!" Bertrand finally got out.

Halabi's men forced him onto the table next to the corpse and secured him there with straps. His screams quickly turned to convulsing sobs and he began begging pathetically in French.

Halabi approached and leaned over him as one of his men ignited a blowtorch. Bertrand's face and the rotted one next to it turned bluish in the light of the flame.

"Now let's discuss the fine points of my plan."

CHAPTER 35

CARLOS Esparza glanced back at the terrified family behind him and slapped a hand on the table. "Otra cerveza!"

They were huddled near the kerosene lamp throwing shadows across what passed for a kitchen. This was the building that was Mitch Rapp's goal, an improvised restaurant that was little more than a clapboard shithole with enough solar panels sufficient to keep a refrigerator running. Outside was a broad porch where local farmers gathered on weekends, but now the plastic furniture on it was in danger of being washed away by the pounding rain.

The husband retrieved a beer, but Esparza shook his head and pointed to the man's fifteen-year-old daughter. She took the bottle and approached hesitantly, holding it out in front of her.

She was a sexy little thing, with thick hair, coffee-colored skin, and a body that was still a bit awkward. He gave her a hard swat on the ass when she put the beer on the table and then watched her scurry off. Normally, he'd be laying plans to have her brought to his compound for a few interesting evenings, but tonight she was nothing more than an afterthought. Something to briefly distract him from the matter at hand.

They'd begun Rapp's test at 9 a.m. and it was now 3 a.m. the next day. One of the dogs had been recovered but the others were still on the loose, running off thousands of dollars' worth of his product. The heavy rains and loss of their tracking ability was allowing the CIA man to move through the darkness with impunity—an opportunity he was taking full advantage of.

At least seven of Esparza's men were dead. Some from bullets, others from knife wounds, and one who had been found with a tree branch wedged in his eye socket. So much equipment had been stripped from the bodies that it seemed certain Rapp was creating caches in the jungle. Preparing to survive and fight for as long as was necessary to reach his objective.

A burst of automatic fire erupted outside and Esparza swore loudly before edging toward the open doorway. He had four vehicles at the crossroad out front, two of which were idling with their headlights on. The rain had slowed and there was enough illumination to see the five men who had taken refuge behind them. All efforts to bring in further reinforcements had gotten bogged down in the mud miles from there.

The shooting stopped and, predictably, the shouting started. Fucking idiots. If they saw or heard something, it was a guarantee that Rapp wasn't there. Terrified for their own lives and enraged at the loss of their comrades, they'd begun shooting at ghosts and fighting among themselves. Exactly what the CIA man wanted.

Esparza stayed hidden behind the doorjamb as he scanned past the vehicles into the darkness. Was he kilometers away, planning his next move? Had he decided to run and take his chances as a fugitive? Or was he out there just beyond the circle of light?

The sound of a struggling vehicle became audible to the east and Esparza reluctantly crossed the wood deck, descending into the mud. Headlights began playing off the trees as his men dug in further. As though Rapp would just get in a car and drive up the road to them.

Idiots.

He took a position in the middle of the crossroad, shielding his eyes as the pickup drew near. One of his enforcers was driving and there were no passengers. At least no living ones. The vehicle stopped and Esparza looked at the man in the bed. He was stretched out in a bloody pool of rainwater, with his throat slashed from ear to ear.

"Find this motherfucker and bring me his head!" Esparza screamed as the rain gained force again. "Do you understand? Bring it to me now!"

No one moved. Finally, one man inched forward. "The dark and the rain are working against us, señor. Maybe we should try to get back to the compound. It's supposed to clear tomorrow and when the sun—"

Esparza pulled a pistol from the holster on his hip and shot the man in the chest. "Does anyone else have something to say?"

None seemed to, so he stalked back toward the building and the cold beer waiting for him there. How much was he paying to be surrounded by a bunch of weaklings? If this was the best they could do, he was a dead man. The other cartels would run over him like he wasn't there. Rapp was *one man*. One fucking man bumbling through jungle terrain he knew nothing about.

He stepped back onto the porch and went for the open doorway. Maybe he'd invite the girl to join him for a drink. His anger and nerves were building to the point that his head was starting to pound. It seemed almost certain that she could find some way to help him relax.

When he entered, Esparza saw a man in fatigues sitting at the table where he had left his beer. He was backlit by the kerosene lamp, but wore an immediately recognizable bandolier. Hand-tooled leather with a holster on one side and a similarly ornate scabbard for his silencer on the other. Pedro Morales had always seen himself in the romantic terms of a nineteenth-century Mexican bandit. But he'd served Esparza well. That is, until his naked body had been found in a ditch six hours ago.

"So if I remember right," Mitch Rapp said, "our agreement was for two hundred and fifty grand a month."

Esparza noticed that the holster was empty and Morales's nickel-plated Colt Government Model 1911 was lying on the table inches from his hand.

"That's your agreement with *me*," Esparza said, having a hard time thinking clearly under the American's stare. "But I'm not sure about my men. You've killed a lot of their friends."

Rapp remained motionless for a moment but then

began screwing the matching silencer onto the pistol. He stood and Esparza silently cursed himself for his own stupidity.

Rapp walked past him and the cartel leader heard the sound of his footsteps on the wood porch. He didn't bother to turn, though. It was clear what was coming. His words had condemned what was left of his men to death. They'd see the camouflage-clad man coming from the restaurant and assume he was one of theirs.

Esparza could shout a warning of course. Or even pull out his own weapon and shoot. But then his role in this would fundamentally change. At that moment, he was the man with the job and money Rapp so desperately needed. All it would take was one sound, though. One wrong move. And then he would become just another of the CIA man's victims.

So he remained silent, imagining the scene playing out behind him. The silencer and the rain would keep his men from knowing what was happening until two of them were already dead. One more would die in the ensuing confusion. And the last would be shot in the back as he fled in panic.

Esparza's gaze moved again to the family huddled at the back of the building. They flinched noticeably at a brief burst of automatic gunfire outside. A lone shout rose above the rain and then everything went silent until the sound of footfalls on the porch became audible again.

"You're running out of guys, Carlos."

CHAPTER 36

"To be clear, this isn't a formal hearing," Senator Christine Barnett said, doing a good job of sounding magnanimous. "We're here to talk without cameras and get an understanding of where we stand in this matter."

Despite her empty assurances, this felt very much like a formal hearing to Irene Kennedy. Barnett was in an elevated position flanked by congresspeople loyal to her. A number of aides were ensconced behind them and the gallery was scattered with people Kennedy assumed were political operatives.

"As you answer our questions, Dr. Kennedy, please keep in mind we're performing our own investigation into these matters."

The implication, of course, was that she'd lie. And that was exactly what she was there to do, but not for the reasons Barnett thought.

Kennedy leaned into the microphone on the table in front of her. "Thank you, Senator. I'll keep that in mind."

Kennedy's initial reaction had been to find a way

to avoid this kangaroo court, but it had been impossible. Barnett's power was growing, and with it the upheaval inside the Beltway. Predicting people's shifting loyalties was becoming impossible as they positioned themselves for what was to come next.

"What was your involvement in sending Mitch Rapp to California to interrogate those drug traffickers?"

Word was that Barnett's inquiries into that subject had hit a dead end. The further she tracked the chain of command back, the murkier it got.

"As I've told you in the past, I had no involvement."

"If you're denying that it was you, then who was it?"

It was a question that literally might be the most dangerous in the world. According to Scott Coleman, the president of the United States had not only personally given the order, but had also signed papers giving Rapp carte blanche.

Again, Kennedy leaned into the microphone. "I don't know who authorized Mr. Rapp's involvement, though my people are continuing to look into the matter. Has your office's investigation been able to shed any light on the issue?"

"I'm asking the questions in this hearing!"

Kennedy poured herself a glass of water. The truth was that this meeting served no real purpose. It was a fishing expedition. Barnett was trying to find something explosive for the very public hearing she was undoubtedly planning. But she wasn't going to get it.

"Let me make another clarification, Senator. Mitch Rapp doesn't work for the Central Intelligence Agency and hasn't for some time. He functions as an independent contractor. The last contract the Agency had with him was in relation to tracking Sayid Halabi in Yemen."

"Is it possible that he acted alone?" another one of the senators offered.

The fury registered on Barnett's face before she could prevent it. She was there to gather ammunition against Kennedy and the intelligence community as a whole, not just one man.

"It's absolutely possible," Kennedy responded, deciding to take the gift. "Mr. Rapp is well known in the upper echelons of law enforcement and intelligence. He could have used his reputation and contacts to convince people that he was operating under the authority of the CIA when that in fact wasn't the case."

"In order to murder two drug traffickers, shoot three DEA agents, and steal millions of dollars' worth of narcotics," Barnett interjected.

"That appears to be correct, Senator."

It was an uncomfortable position for Kennedy. Any defense of Rapp could weaken the undercover legend he'd created and get him killed. She wasn't just there to stand by and let the Senate throw Mitch Rapp under the bus. No, she needed to be behind the wheel pushing the accelerator to the floor.

"And this all relates to his illegal financial dealings?" Barnett said, continuing to probe.

"Our investigation is in its initial stages, but that also appears to be correct. Mr. Rapp had a number of foreign accounts and investments of questionable legality. One of his main investments—a financial services company in Poland—collapsed and came under the scrutiny of EU officials. That created a cascade effect."

"Meaning the house of cards he'd built came tumbling down, prompting him to steal those drugs in order to put together enough money to run."

"That's a reasonable conclusion based on the facts that we have at this time, Senator."

"Where did he get all the money to invest, Dr. Kennedy? And how long have those investments existed? We all know what the man does for a living and we're now very aware that he doesn't have any qualms about shooting innocent people."

"If you're suggesting he was taking contract killing jobs on the side, Senator, I doubt that's the case. Much more likely, he simply siphoned funds from the terrorist organizations he broke up. They themselves have extremely complex financial structures and it wouldn't be hard to hide those kinds of transactions."

"But this house of cards he built," Barnett said, still trying to find her footing. "It was constructed while he was officially working for the CIA. Isn't that right? While he was under your supervision."

Kennedy took a sip of water and focused on staying in character. Avoiding personal responsibility and abandoning Mitch Rapp were two things antithetical to who she was. But, for now, there was no other way.

"Obviously, I'm the director of the CIA, so everything that happens there is within my purview. Having said that, the monitoring of our agents is largely the responsibility of an independent division within the Agency. They work under a very specific set of parameters, all of which were adhered to in this case. The problem seems to be that Mr. Rapp covered his tracks extremely well. His money was held in countries that we have a hard time seeing into, and his ownership interests in foreign businesses were hidden behind a maze of offshore shell corporations and partnerships."

"So, you're saying that, as the director of the CIA, you take no responsibility for any of this?"

"The Agency's oversight infrastructure works independently from the office of the director. That independence is critical to their success and credibility. In light of what's happened, though, I'd agree that the system needs to be reviewed."

Christine Barnett entered her office, nearly catching Kevin Gray's leg when she slammed the door.

"*Backstabbing bitch!*"

"Calm down, Senator. It may—"

"Calm down? What the hell are you talking about, Kevin? Everyone in town whispers about Irene Kennedy like she's Joan of Arc. We went in there counting on the fact that she'd fall on her sword for her lifelong friend, the great Mitch Rapp. And what do we find out? She's just another politician covering her ass."

"We've still got—"

"And then that dipshit Hansen hands her the keys to the handcuffs!" She imitated the man's buttery drawl. " 'Is it possible that he acted alone?' "

"Mitch Rapp was the CIA's top operative for years, Senator, and in that time he stole millions of dollars. The fact that he was technically a contractor when he murdered those two men—"

"Were you not listening, Kevin?"

"Of course I—"

"Rapp killed two *terrorism suspects*. And his money didn't come from stealing from the government, it came from stealing from extremists. Why would voters give a shit about that?"

"He didn't kill those men to stop a terrorist attack, Senator. Like you said in your last meeting with Kennedy, he probably did it to figure out how to get top dollar for the drugs he was going to steal. And he didn't take the money from those terrorist organizations to starve them of funds. He took it to line his own po—"

"Too complicated!" she shouted. "The average American is barely smart enough to tie his own shoes. Do you really expect them to follow complex motivations and offshore shell corporations? In order for them to know who to hate, we need to tell them in a way they can understand. A strong, simple narrative. One sentence. No words more than two syllables."

"We weren't going to get hold of the news cycle anytime soon anyway. This morning's school shooting is sucking all the air out of the room."

"How many kids?"

"It's bad. Twenty-one dead and another seven wounded."

"So we get backseated and the anthrax story—"

"—was already starting to fade," Gray said, finishing her sentence. "The videos ISIS is putting out are just remixes of footage everyone's seen before."

"If we're going to keep people focused on this administration's inability to protect them, Halabi's going to need to get off his ass and do something more than make movies."

"I'm not sure we should be wishing that on ourselves, Senator."

She dropped into the chair behind her desk. "Don't turn into a Boy Scout on me again, Kevin."

"You're way out in the lead, Sen—"

"I don't want to be in the lead!" she shouted. "I want to win the election in such a landslide that everyone in Washington drops to their knees and kisses my ass. Do you understand?"

Judging by his expression, he didn't.

Kevin Gray was a hell of a political operative but, like everyone in his profession, he saw the winning of the presidency as an end, not a beginning. A seat in the Oval Office was a guarantee of pomp and circumstance, but not the guarantee of real power that most people suspected. As a woman, she'd have to fight for that. She'd have to tear it from the hands of the powerful men who had dominated the country since it was founded.

"The shooting of those DEA agents got some coverage," Gray said. "But because they survived and the identity of the shooter hasn't been released, not as much coverage as we hoped. We could leak that the perpetrator was a former CIA operative and that he also murdered two drug traffickers. Maybe hint that Kennedy could be involved. Everyone knows how close she and President Alexander are. It could get us—"

"Absolutely nothing," Barnett said, finishing his sentence. "In the current news cycle, that story wouldn't make an AM radio station in Bumfuck, Kansas."

"Then we wait," he said, not bothering to hide his frustration. "When things slow down, a story like that could get some traction. No question it'll get the attention of conspiracy theorists and Russian Internet trolls. They're always looking to give the Agency a black eye."

"We're losing control of this thing, Kevin. We've got a story about incompetence and corruption in this administration that we can spin into full-on hysteria. We can't let it get hijacked by some basement dweller who walked into a school with a gun. We're going to end up spending the next month running in circles debating gun control."

"I don't know what you want me to do," Gray said. "I can only work with what I've got."

She remained silent for almost a minute, calculating the pros and cons of every possible action. Finally she spoke.

"For now we forget about trying to tie Rapp to Kennedy. Instead we leak that the DEA intercepted the anthrax. We show the American voter that this administration allowed ISIS to transport a biological weapon across the U.S. border and the only thing that saved us was dumb luck. We tell them that Halabi's making another batch and that the administration has been keeping it secret from the American people. That Alexander's preventing our citizens from taking steps to protect themselves because he doesn't want to look bad in the press."

"I strongly disagree with that course of action, Senator. Leaking a former CIA agent's involvement in what happened in California is one thing. But this is an ongoing terrorist investigation. That's why the administration is keeping it secret—they're trying to track the supply line back to Halabi. If he discovers that the authorities know about the anthrax he could—"

"He could what? Run? How does that hurt me? The last thing I need is Alexander standing on a podium saying that he tracked down Halabi and put a bullet in his eye."

"Senator, this is—"

"Shut up and do it, Kevin."

"It's going to take some time. We'll use the same procedures as before, but this leak is a whole other level. If it were ever traced back to us . . ." He fell silent, leaving the ramifications to her imagination.

CHAPTER 37

"IT'S all opportunity now," Esparza said, swerving his custom Humvee around a rut in the dirt road. "Your politicians are just actors. They shout all day about drugs and illegal immigrants but they don't want to fix the problem. They just want to keep their voters angry while not pissing anyone off by taking away their coke or maid. All that shit you talk about us up north . . . separating children from their parents, the wall . . . it's a perfect storm. It puts our politicians in a position that they have to push back. And that doesn't just mean they look the other way. These days I've got more government assistance than I know what to do with. I mean, I pay. Don't get me wrong. And the last local government piece of shit who turned on me got to watch my guys gang-rape his daughter. But even if I didn't do any of that, a lot of our bureaucrats would screw the Americans for the hell of it."

Rapp focused on the edges of the jungle from the passenger seat. In all likelihood it didn't contain any imminent threats, but there was no way to know that for sure. He had no sense of his operating environment, no sense of Esparza's position in the current drug trafficking hierarchy, and no idea what was happening in America or the rest of the world.

"So you're looking to take the opportunity to expand," Rapp prompted. Esparza had been running his mouth nonstop for the entire drive, but so far hadn't said anything useful. Mostly bragging about his business genius and the meteoric growth of his operation.

"Hell yes, I'm going to take advantage. The Arab heroin is going to be big for us. The American government's doing its normal screwup job dealing with your oxycodone problems—half because your politicians are morons and half because they've got their heads completely up the pharmaceutical companies' asses." He paused for dramatic effect. "And you saw the coke plantation."

Rapp just nodded. He'd spent the better part of the week roaming around Esparza's compound, eating María's food, and drinking fresh-squeezed fruit juice. He had no access to phones, television, or computers. Discussions with Esparza tended to be centered on his excessively ambitious business plans and his passion for young girls. Unfortunately, the former subject tended to be overly vague and the latter overly detailed.

"That crop has been even more successful than we thought," Vicente Rossi said from the backseat. "It's obviously a long-term investment but within ten years we expect to have converted it into a significant profit center."

Again, Rapp didn't respond. The trail that led to Sayid Halabi was getting colder every day. He just didn't have the patience for this undercover shit.

"You didn't bring me out here to talk about profit centers," Rapp said finally. "Where are we going?"

Esparza glanced at his assistant in the rearview mirror. An out-of-character nervous tic.

"A meeting."

"Details, Carlos. Give me details."

The cartel leader's jaw tightened in anger, causing his response to sound a bit strangled. "We negotiated the terms of it more than a month ago, but since then things have gone to shit. The asshole we're going to see is named Damian Losa. He's an arrogant, aristocratic prick who's huge but flies way under the radar. He's doing probably a little over a billion U.S. dollars a year gross between blow, heroin, and weed. And that doesn't include his above-board businesses. He's got car dealerships in Iowa and factories in England. Son of a bitch gives money to museums and shit."

"What's he to me?" Rapp said.

When Esparza didn't answer, Rossi stepped in. "Losa was one of the main investors in that mall in San Ysidro. It's one of a number of projects financed and operated by a cooperative of cartels presided over by Mr. Losa. His idea was to reduce the fighting between individual organizations by creating joint enterprises. As you can imagine, he isn't happy about it being discovered."

"Didn't NASA find that tunnel?" Rapp said. "How can he blame you for that? Shit happens."

Again Esparza didn't respond, instead concentrating on avoiding the branches on either side of the dirt track.

"The construction of the San Ysidro mall was overseen by our organization," Rossi said.

"So? From everything I heard, you knocked it out of the park. The DEA was talking about that tunnel like it was the eighth wonder of the world."

"Yes," Rossi said, drawing out the word. "But the mall was meant to be a money-laundering operation."

Rapp considered that for a moment. "So you're telling me that the tunnel was something you added without telling Losa and the other cartels?"

"That's correct."

"So a megamillion-dollar money-laundering operation just went up in smoke, a number of American politicians have been exposed for taking cartel money, and a huge number of offshore corporations are now being investigated because you decided to add a smuggling operation on the down low."

"I think that's a fair summary," Rossi said in a tone that suggested he'd disapproved of their little improvisation. "We—"

"It was sitting there like a fat whore!" Esparza shouted suddenly. "If I don't take opportunities like that, someone else will. Where would that leave me?"

"Alive," Rapp said, turning his attention back to a jungle that was suddenly looking a lot more threatening than it had thirty seconds before. "Tell me about the meet."

"It's in a natural clearing in neutral territory. The land around it is mostly open and we've had drones flying overhead for two days now. No suspicious activity. Each of us can bring two men. It'll be fine. And this'll give you an opportunity to get a good look at Losa."

"Why?" Rapp asked, though he suspected he knew the answer.

"Because you're going to kill him. He's not going to let this go and I'm not going to wait for one of his people to slit my throat in my sleep. We need to move first."

"Are you saying you want to do this today? At the meeting?"

"No. The area's controlled by another cartel that's guaranteed our safety. If we move against him here, we might not make it home. Next month will be soon enough."

"Next month," Rapp repeated.

"Is that a problem? I hired a miracle worker, right? Isn't that what you told me? You didn't think I was paying you three million dollars a year to eat my food and work out in my gym. My *private* gym."

Rapp let out a long breath. This was bullshit. He was getting no closer to Halabi and now he was being driven into a possible ambush orchestrated by a man who sounded more like the CEO of General Motors than a drug lord. Time to end this.

He reached for the Glock 19 he'd been provided, keeping his movements slow and casual. He'd find a place for them to pull into the jungle, locate a quiet spot, and go to work on these two pricks. Rossi would crack at the first face slap and, for all his swagger, Esparza wouldn't last much longer. In an hour, Rapp would be using the late cartel leader's bejeweled sat phone to send Irene Kennedy everything the two men knew about ISIS.

"But first I need some help with the Arabs, " Esparza said.

Rapp hesitated, finally withdrawing his hand from the weapon and returning it to the armrest.

"I'm listening."

"The first shipment from our Middle Eastern supplier got confiscated in the mall bust. It was actually part of the shipment you stole—a dry run to show them what our distribution system could do."

"And?"

"The towelheads have access to good product but they're complete assholes to deal with. They don't understand shit about the smuggling business and got all twisted up over us losing their package."

I'll bet they did, Rapp thought.

When Esparza spoke again, his voice had lost some of its bravado. "Look, this heroin angle could mean a lot of money for me, and with what happened in San Ysidro, it needs to work."

"Meaning?"

"Meaning, you understand them, right? You speak their language and everything."

"Yeah."

"Then you could explain that what happened is just part of doing business and that no one else could do any better. Make sure they're not trying to find another organization to partner with."

After a week of feeling Halabi slipping away, Rapp could suddenly picture his head in the sights of his Glock again. "Sure. I could fly over and tell them how things work in the real world. Maybe help coordinate their shipments."

"That won't be necessary," Rossi said, leaning up between the seats. "They're flying in a representative with another small shipment."

"Right. All you need to do is talk his gibberish, kiss Allah's ass, and whatever else it takes to get his confidence. This time the product will get through. I guarantee it."

Rapp nodded and further relaxed his gun hand. While it wasn't Sayid Halabi's home address and a spare cruise missile, it was enough to work with. Esparza and Rossi had just earned themselves a temporary reprieve.

Esparza pulled into a gap in the foliage that looked like it had been recently cut. Beyond there was a small clearing with three men visible in the shade of its northern edge.

"That's him," Esparza said, without looking. "In the middle."

Damian Losa looked to be in his mid-fifties, with a trim waist, nice but not over-the-top clothing, and immaculate gray hair. The men on either side of him were just muscle, but even at a distance it was clear they were high-class muscle. Probably Eastern European. Almost certainly former spec ops. Whether there were a hundred more like them in the trees was yet to be seen. Relying on Esparza's surveillance team wasn't all that comforting but there wasn't a choice at this point.

They got out of the vehicle and Esparza indicated for him and Rossi to hang back while he started for the center of the clearing. Losa began to do the same but then one of his men grabbed his arm. Rapp moved a hand closer to his weapon, but it seemed that all he wanted to do was whisper in his boss's ear. He gave a brief response before walking to meet Esparza.

The conversation seemed to go about the way Rapp had imagined. Esparza was animated, waving his hands around and speaking in a loud voice, while Losa nodded and answered too quietly to be heard at a distance.

More interesting was that one of Losa's guards had broken away from his companion and was edging around the clearing. Again, Rapp moved a hand toward his weapon, but then the man got close enough to make out his features.

"How've you been, Andraž?"

"Good, Mitch. Mr. Losa would like a word with you after he's finished."

"Why?"

He just shrugged and started back the way he'd come.

The discussion between the two cartel leaders went on for another fifteen minutes before Esparza spun and began stalking back in their direction. Losa, on the other hand, stayed put and turned his gaze toward Rapp.

Screw it. Why not?

He started forward and Esparza waved him off. "We're leaving."

Rapp ignored him and passed by without speaking. When he got close to Losa the man offered a hand and he took it.

"Andraž recognized you," he said in lightly accented English. "I heard about your problems in America but I'm surprised to see you here. Can I assume that the drugs you stole belonged to Carlos?"

"Yeah," Rapp said, glancing back to see Esparza glaring at him and questioning Rossi in a low voice.

"And what exactly is your interest in all this?"

"I don't understand the question."

"I think you do."

Clearly Losa wasn't buying the legend Rapp had created to explain his sudden entry into the narcotics business.

When he stayed silent on the subject, Losa just smiled. "Even if everything you've done recently is a smoke screen, I believe that Christine Barnett's animosity toward you is real. You're going to have a hard time going back."

"Are you coming to a point?"

The man pulled out a business card and slipped it into Rapp's shirt pocket. "When you've killed Carlos—and I assume that will be in the next week or two—call me. I think you'd find working for my organization very rewarding."

Rapp nodded and turned, but then paused when Losa spoke again. "And if your friend Irene Kennedy finds herself needing to make a quick exit from the United States, my offer extends to her as well."

Rapp walked back to the Humvee thinking that maybe Coleman and Claudia were right. In the private sector all you had to do was stand around while people threw money at you.

"What the fuck was that all about?" Esparza said.

"He figures I'm going to kill you in the next couple of weeks and wants to give me a job after I do." Rapp slid into the passenger seat. "Now let's get the hell out of here before someone changes his mind and starts shooting."

CHAPTER 38

SAYID Halabi embraced the last person in line and stepped back as all six filed away. Allah had provided a rare overcast night, blinding any U.S. surveillance that might be overhead and extinguishing the stars. He was standing at the edge of the hazy ring of light created by a bonfire some fifty yards away. The light breeze swept the smoke toward him, bringing with it the sensation of warmth and scent of charred wood.

Near the fire a young girl lay on a cot, deathly still between violent coughing fits. From a safe distance, a man filmed the towering flames that framed her. He followed the embers swirling through the air for a moment and then focused on the six martyrs approaching the girl. Each wiped a hand across her face, smearing their fingers with saliva, blood, and phlegm, and then rubbing it into their eyes and noses.

When it was done, two of the men threw the cot and its dying occupant into the fire. Her screams filled the air for a moment before going silent forever.

Gabriel Bertrand looked on from beneath the tree he was chained to, watching in horror as the girl's body writhed and blackened. Finally, he turned toward the people stripping off their clothing and cleaning themselves with powerful disinfectants. Halabi didn't want them to leave a trail of disease that Western authorities could follow to him in Somalia. But more than that, he wanted the infection to appear in America as though it had come from nowhere. As though it was a punishment from God's own hand.

Tears reflected on the Frenchman's swollen cheeks and he began to sob. Whether he wept over his own fate or that of the world was impossible to know. Of course, he had broken easily. The removal of one of his fingernails had gained his cooperation and a few minor burns near his groin had ensured that it would be enthusiastic.

Halabi now had an optimized plan for spreading YARS throughout the West while sparing the Middle East to the degree possible. Individual targets had been identified, protocols had been refined, and timetables had been developed. Using software downloaded from the Internet, they had run a number of simulations based on different variables.

Even if nearly everything went wrong during deployment and the West's reaction was more robust than anticipated, the death toll would be no less than ten million, centered on major cities in America and Europe. If everything went to plan, though, the outcome would be very different. The disease would run out of control, creating a pandemic that would fundamentally change human existence for generations.

The computer application that they were relying on had originally been designed to research the spread of the Spanish flu. Comparing that disease with YARS was a fascinating exercise, as was comparing the world it devastated to the one that existed today.

The very name "Spanish flu" was just another lie foisted on the world by America. The truth was that the disease had first taken hold in Kansas City military outposts. It killed more U.S. troops during World War I than combat, spreading easily in the cramped conditions that prevailed on ships, battlegrounds, and bases.

The initial reaction of the medical community had been slowed by its focus on the war, but when the scope of the threat was recognized, the country had pulled together. Surgical masks were worn in public to slow the spread of the disease. Stores were prohibited from having sales to prevent the congregation of people in confined spaces. Some cities demanded that passengers' health be certified before they boarded trains.

There was no denying that the United States and its citizens had been strong in the early twentieth century—accustomed to death and hardship, led by competent politicians, and informed by an honest press.

So much had changed in the last century. The American people were now inexplicably suspicious of

modern medicine and susceptible to nonsensical conspiracy theories. They were selfish and self-absorbed,
willing to prioritize their own trivial desires over
the lives of their countrymen. Their medical system,
designed less to heal people than to generate profits,
would quickly collapse as it was flooded by desperate
patients and abandoned by personnel fearful of being
infected.

And during all this, America's politicians and
media would use the burgeoning epidemic to augment their own power and wealth. That is, until the
magnitude of the crisis became clear. Then they would
flee.

The sound of a truck engine pulled him from his
contemplation and he turned. His people, disinfected
and wearing clean clothing, climbed into the vehicle
and set off into the darkness. Halabi bowed respect-
fully in their direction, acknowledging their sacrifice and the enormity of the journey ahead of them.
After the long drive to Mogadishu, they would board
a private jet that would take them to Mexico. From
there they would be smuggled across the northern
border.

And then everything would change.

As he stared into the darkness beyond the fire, he
recalled the black-and-white images he'd seen of the
Spanish flu epidemic. The most striking, as always,
were those that contained children. Like the little ones
of the Middle East, they stared out from the photo-
graph with a mix of ignorance, hope, and misplaced
trust in the adults around them.

On a blurred portrait taken in a hospital ward,
someone had scrawled a nursery rhyme created by

minds too young to understand the collapse of their world but desperate to somehow acknowledge it.

> *I had a little bird,*
> *Its name was Enza.*
> *I opened the window,*
> *And in-flu-enza.*

CHAPTER 39

RAPP paused to check his reflection in the glass door before exiting onto the terrace.

The set of clippers provided by María only had one setting so his previously long hair was now a uniform three eighths of an inch. The beard was completely gone, leaving smooth, slightly pale skin in its wake. A pair of aviator sunglasses hid his eyes and the sun damage around them.

Combined with clothing loose enough to obscure his muscular physique, it was a pretty effective disguise. Esparza and his people had been warned not to use his name around the Arab who was about to arrive. There was a good chance Rapp had killed someone he knew at some point.

An SUV appeared to the west as Rapp came up behind Esparza and Rossi, who were already waiting. Their impeccable clothing and expectant expressions once again demonstrated the importance of this deal to them.

The vehicle pulled up and a man carrying a large courier bag immediately stepped out. Rapp remained outwardly serene but his heart rate notched higher.

He and Muhammad Attia had never been face-to-face but Rapp knew everything about him. His height and weight. His U.S. passport number. Even the name of his first girlfriend in high school. Attia's family had immigrated to America as refugees when he was still a toddler and done well for themselves, providing their son a life of middle-class security.

What had turned him against his adopted country was something that the Agency's psychologists speculated on endlessly. As far as Rapp was concerned, all that mattered was that he was a smart, fanatical son of a bitch who could blend effortlessly into American society. A man that Rapp had spent a lot of time trying to hunt down and kill.

Resisting the urge to jam a thumb into his eye socket, Rapp instead gave him a stilted greeted that would camouflage his real ability with the Arabic language. Westerners with native-level fluency were unusual enough that they tended to generate questions.

"I speak English," Attia replied.

Esparza smiled and offered his hand. "That's excellent. I'm Carlos. This is my assistant Vicente."

Attia shook hands a bit reluctantly, more interested in scanning his operating environment just as Rapp had been when he'd arrived.

Esparza pointed at Rapp. "Don't just stand there. Take his bag."

The cartel leader had been expecting all communication to have to be translated and was clearly enjoying being in a stronger position than expected. His curt order was intended as a reminder. *You work for me.*

Attia held the satchel out as Esparza put a friendly hand on his back. "Come. We have lunch prepared. I'm certain you're going to enjoy it." He glanced back at Rapp as they started toward a dining table decorated with fresh-cut flowers. "Take that to his room. And then you're dismissed."

Instead of going to Attia's room, Rapp ducked into his own and locked the door. A quick search of the courier bag turned up what he was looking for: a duct-taped package about the size of a building brick.

He laid it in the bottom of the bathtub before digging a box of scrounged supplies from beneath the vanity. The sunglasses, a pair of kitchen gloves, and a scarf tied over his nose and mouth was the best he was going to do for protection. Better than nothing, but he imagined that it would get a disgusted face palm from Gary Statham.

Using a pocketknife, he carefully peeled back the tape to expose a shrinkwrapped core. The color and consistency of its contents were exactly like the pictures he'd seen of the intercepted anthrax. Lady Luck was with him. Or not, depending on whether he started coughing up blood in the next few weeks.

He filled the bathtub and worked beneath the surface, slitting the plastic and emptying it into the water. When it looked pretty well cleaned out, he drained the tub and washed both it and the bag with a bottle of high-end tequila that was the most reliable disinfectant he'd been able to turn up. It took another ten minutes to mix a decent facsimile of the anthrax with stuff raided from the kitchen.

He was forced to replace the shrink-wrap cellophane from María's personal stash, but the original

tape was salvageable with the help of a little superglue.
It likely had hidden markings and their absence would
be noticed by men down the supply chain.

Finally, Rapp patted the package with a bath towel
and used a blow dryer to eradicate any remaining
moisture. The finished product wasn't bad. Someone
would have to be paying serious attention to attribute
the damage to anything more than normal wear and
tear.

He put it back in the bottom of the bag and then
carefully replaced the clothes and other items in the
order they'd been removed. Now all he needed to do
was take it to Attia's room, trace him back to wher-
ever he came from, find Halabi, kill him, and wipe out
his operation. Preferably before Attia's contacts in the
United States noticed they were trying to destroy the
great Satan with a mixture of flour, cornstarch, and
dried mustard.

What could possibly go wrong?

CHAPTER 40

"**I WANT** you all to look around," Christine Barnett said, gazing out over the crowd. "Let what you see really sink in."

As was their custom, they did as they were told. Almost two hundred people, mostly men wearing work clothes despite being unemployed, craned their necks to examine their surroundings.

The building was cavernous and filthy. Disused machines stood silent and rusted. Spotlights had been brought in and were focused on the stage, leaving her audience illuminated only by what sunlight could filter through broken windows.

America was booming economically. The stock market was rallying, unemployment was under four percent, and corporate profits were near record highs. But none of that mattered as long as there were a few crumbling factories and pockets of forgotten citizens like the ones before her. Their confused, angry faces made all those statistics meaningless. And more important, it made Joshua Alexander's affirmations of his administration's success look callous and out of touch.

When attention turned back to her, she leaned closer to the microphone. "We have the world's biggest economy. We have the most powerful military in history. We invented pretty much everything worth having. Cars. Electric light. Personal computers. Smartphones. The Internet. *We* push the world forward. *We* keep it safe. How did this happen? How did we *allow* this to happen?"

The inevitable applause started and she stepped back to gaze benevolently over the crowd. Of course, the answers to her question were well known. Mechanization had made many factory jobs obsolete. Others had inevitably—and, in truth, irretrievably—flowed overseas.

The world was changing at an ever-increasing rate and that was a trend that couldn't be stopped. These people were the ones who had been left behind. The ones who steadfastly refused to leave the dead cities they had been born in. The ones who saw themselves as America's backbone but who survived on government aid and disability checks. Drug addicts, drunks, and halfwits incapable of performing anything but the simplest of tasks.

Ironically, it was those self-destructive traits that made them so useful. Their inflated sense of worth and victimization was easy to manipulate. When asked what exactly it was they wanted, they either didn't know or weren't willing to make the sacrifices necessary to get it. What they did know—with burning certainty—was what they hated: the world that had stolen everything from them.

"You didn't lose your way of life," Barnett said. "It was *taken* from you. The incompetence and corruption in Washington has gotten so bad that an honest hardworking person can't succeed in this country. That's not the America I know. It's not the America we grew up in. The country I remember was one where being honest and hardworking *guaranteed* success. It guaranteed that you could provide for your families and that your children could expect to do even better."

She waited for another wave of applause to die down.

"Instead, we spend trillions sending our brave men and women to fight and die overseas. For what? To spread peace and democracy? The people in those countries don't *want* peace and democracy. And even if they did, why is this our job? Why aren't we using that money and our incredible military to fix the problems we have here? Why are we building bridges and power grids in Afghanistan while we watch ours fall apart? They told us these wars and all this nation building was going to keep us safe, but trillions of dollars later, it's done the opposite. Now we have a madman threatening us with a biological attack. And what's this administration's response? To keep doing the same things that haven't worked in the past."

She pulled the microphone off its stand and began pacing across the stage. "America's the strongest country in the history of the world. But even it can't take this kind of incompetence year after year. Nothing's unbreakable. So now it's up to us. This is a democracy. It's our responsibility to turn this around. To protect our country and change it back into one where good, hardworking people aren't taken advantage of. They're rewarded."

• • •

"You were on fire today," Kevin Gray said as Barnett slid into the back of the limo across from him. "Reactions look good."

"Are we going to get decent television coverage?"

"I'm pushing, but political speeches in Iowa aren't exactly ratings grabbers. One of the British royals just announced she's pregnant and President Alexander's out there stumping hard for your opponent. His rally in Texas was quite a bit more successful than we'd anticipated. After almost eight years, he can still pack 'em in."

"We've got to choke him off, Kevin. He's the past. We have to *own* the media on this. I don't want to see that man's face or hear his redneck drawl on any outlet in America."

"Alexander was the clear star of the show, Senator. But that's a good thing. You're not running against him. Col—" He caught himself before uttering the name of the man who was now almost certain to be her opponent in the general election. She'd forbidden the speaking of it out loud in her presence. "*Your opponent* looked like a sidekick."

"Where are we with the anthrax story?" she asked.

The glass separating them from the driver was soundproof, but Gray still leaned forward and lowered his voice. "Our contact in the press has the information. He's gone through it, and my understanding is that he's satisfied."

"So he's going to run with it."

Gray nodded, looking a little queasy. "In the next forty-eight hours, the equivalent of a nuclear bomb is going to go off in the press. Mexican cartels smuggling anthrax. NASA and dumb luck keeping it from hitting the street. A former CIA operative shooting DEA agents. It'll be splashed across virtually every news outlet in the world."

"And none of it can be traced to us."

"If anything, it's going to look like it came from somewhere inside the DEA."

"You're sure? That bitch Irene Kennedy has eyes and ears everywhere."

"She'd have to be psychic. I used a brand-new laptop running a secure, open-source operating system. Heavily encrypted email from anonymous account to anonymous account. And now the laptop's crushed and lying in a landfill."

Barnett nodded. In truth, the weak link was the reporter himself. Alexander and Kennedy would unquestionably accuse him of collapsing an ongoing terrorism investigation, but the clock was ticking. Even if they threw him in jail, he'd be watching the poll numbers and know that all he had to do was wait. In a few months Barnett would be president, Alexander would scramble for anonymity, and Kennedy would be on her way to prison.

Of course, it would have been neater to have the reporter killed after his story broke and to use his death to feed a conspiracy theory implicating the CIA. But that had the potential to light a fire that she didn't have the power to control.

At least not yet.

CHAPTER 41

RAPP stepped out of the air-conditioning and into the late morning heat. The sun was in the process of clearing last night's rain from the jungle, creating a palpable cloud of humidity. Esparza and Vicente Rossi were on the terrace, sitting at a shaded table.

Security was unusually heavy, with no fewer than twenty camo-clad men in view. Many were new, raided from other cartel operations to replace the men Rapp had killed. He memorized their positions and weapons as he strode toward the table. There was an empty place setting for him, but instead of sitting at it Rapp took a position that would allow him to keep his back to the building. He wasn't normally invited to these meetings and that, combined with the heavy security, was putting him on guard.

"Not hungry?" Esparza said, shoveling some pineapple in his mouth.

Rapp just shook his head and continued to watch the guards through dark sunglasses. They didn't seem to be paying much attention to him and most didn't look smart enough for tricks. If he was the target, he'd be getting furtive glances and Esparza wouldn't be sitting so close.

"Things keep getting worse for your friend Irene Kennedy. Our informants say there are a lot of rumors floating around Washington that she knew about your financial dealings and might have been involved."

"She can handle it. In the end, Irene always comes out on top."

"The story about what you did to those DEA agents still hasn't broken. Maybe I should send CNN my drone footage. Throw a little gas on the fire."

Rapp just shrugged. "Why am I here? Problems with the Arabs?"

There was a flash of anger in Esparza's eyes. He was a man accustomed to deference, but he was also a man backed into a corner. A corner that he thought Rapp could get him out of.

"If you're worried about losing that package again," Rapp continued, "I could take it over the border myself. I'll guarantee its delivery."

He made certain to sound bored at the prospect of acting as a delivery boy, but beneath his vague frown, he felt very much the opposite. If he could make contact with even one of Halabi's men in the United States, Kennedy could put multiple surveillance teams on him. Combined with penetration into phone and Internet communication, they could have eyes on the entire network within a week.

"Fuck the Arabs," Esparza said. "I should lose their shit again on purpose. Teach those whiny little assholes that they can't start crying like women every time the cops get lucky."

"Why don't I have a conversation with the guy that came in yesterday? I could give him a lesson on the facts of life."

"He's gone," Rossi said, searching Rapp's face for a reaction to his statement. The former CIA man didn't give him anything, keeping his expression dialed to bored irritation while running through a string of screamed curses in his mind.

"Back to the Middle East?" he said, sliding an empty plate toward him and scooping some bacon onto it.

"We're not that lucky," Esparza replied. "Those assholes won't stop riding me about their lost product. They're bringing men into a private airstrip about an hour from here. That asshole went to pick them up. He wants us to smuggle them into the U.S. to keep an eye on my distribution network."

Esparza slammed his fork down on the tabletop as his voice became a shout. "Piece of shit! He's bringing in men to watch *my* operation? They don't know dick about what I deal with here. They just run around the desert picking poppies and fucking goats. I have to deal with border security, the cops, the FBI, the DEA, and those pricks at the IRS. And if that wasn't enough, now I've got NASA poking its nose into my operation. Fucking *NASA*! What do these assholes think they're going to do about that? Attack Cape Canaveral on camels?"

Esparza's face had turned bright red and the sweat was starting to run down his forehead when he finally fell silent. The question seemed rhetorical but his intense gaze suggested that an answer was required.

"I don't know," Rapp said honestly.

Halabi would have already had a network in place for the first shipment of anthrax. Why bring in more people now? It was a huge risk with no apparent payoff.

"That's it?" Esparza said. "*I don't know*? You told me you were the world's great expert on these people."

"I can't read their minds, Carlos. When he gets back, hand him over to me. I'll get you your answers."

Esparza contemplated Rapp's clean-shaven face for a moment and then slid a manila envelope across the table. "We have bigger problems than a bunch of towelheads spying on my operation."

"What?" Rapp said, ignoring the envelope and instead stabbing a slice of pineapple with his fork.

"Damian Losa is trying to put the screws to me on this mall thing. He and my other partners already made enough off that deal to pay back their investment but now they want more."

Rapp opened the envelope and thumbed through its contents. Pictures of Losa, his houses, his security. Bios on his bodyguards, information on his family and the school his kids went to. Even a copy of the itemized bill for armoring his Range Rover.

"Not an easy job," Rapp said, speaking on automatic as his mind tried to make sense of Halabi's latest move. "Losa's got more security than the president."

"I'm paying you a lot of money and you don't do anything but eat my food and kill my men. Time to step up."

"You want it to look like an accident? Or would you ra—"

"I want a fucking *fireball*! I want people scraping him and his family off the sidewalk with a toothpick. I want to send the message that anyone who screws with me is a walking dead man."

"I don't do families."

"You work for me."

"It's unprofessional, Carlos. And I have a reputation to protect. If you want his wife and kids taken out, get one of your other people to do it. His oldest son's nine and his wife wears three-inch heels. You must have *someone* who can shoot straight enough to hit targets that slow."

Esparza opened his mouth to respond but Rapp cut him off. "I'll need a team. Two men should do it. I have people in mind."

"A team? That comes out of your pocket."

Rapp smiled and dabbed his mouth with his napkin. "Not how it works, Carlos. Expenses are yours."

"You're not the only killer in the world."

"Then bring in a second-stringer who'll work on the cheap. But if they screw up—if Damian Losa survives—he's going to come down on you like the wrath of God. You've got one chance at this and you can afford precisely a zero percent chance of failure. I—and only I—can provide that."

Esparza's temper flared again and again he managed to control it. The man was in an even tighter box than Rapp had imagined. Losa and the other cartels were breathing down his neck, his marijuana operation had hit serious headwinds, his cocaine cultivation initiative was years from providing any real benefit, and his foray into Middle

Eastern heroin was bogging down. The cartel leader was stretched to the breaking point and he knew it.

Before anyone could speak again, the sound of a motor started to separate itself from the hum of the jungle. The guards all straightened and pulled their weapons off their shoulders.

Esparza walked to the edge of the terrace, watching a white panel van approach from the west. It went as far as it could on the worsening road, finally pulling beneath the trees at the edge of the compound. Attia jumped out of the driver's side and went to the back, opening a set of double doors to let the passengers out.

Rapp took a position next to Esparza and examined them as they began filing up the road. Six in all, no fighters. Two were probably in their mid-fifties, another in his late teens. There was even a woman—hunched as she covered her mouth and tried to suppress a cough. These weren't people trained to keep tabs on Esparza's operation. They had been chosen for their ability to blend in—to move through America unchallenged. But to what end? Suicide bombers? That seemed a little mundane after all the trouble Halabi had gone through to hype his biological attack.

"These are the people they sent to spy on your ops?" Rapp said, trying to prompt Esparza to break his silence. When it didn't work, he pressed a little harder.

"These aren't traffickers. Look at them. There's something going on here and we need to figure out what it is."

"I don't give a shit what they look like. I just want this deal done."

"I don't think—"

"I didn't ask you what you think!" he shouted. "They told us we're supposed to keep our distance and that's what we're going to do."

"What do you mean 'keep our distance'?"

"I don't know. Maybe they think we're going to corrupt them. Give them a drink and some pork or something. Either way, no one's supposed to get any closer than ten meters and they wanted them to be housed as far from the compound as possible. Fuck 'em. I just cleared out the main equipment shed. If they want to sleep on the ground in there, let 'em."

Just as he finished speaking, one of the older men started coughing. It wasn't the light hack the woman had displayed a few moments before, though. The convulsions doubled him over. Two men grabbed him by the arms and kept him moving forward as the pieces began clicking together in Rapp's mind.

Halabi's men hadn't killed all the people in that Yemeni village like their propaganda films depicted. They'd taken them and used them to keep the virus alive. And now this innocuous group of people would be smuggled across the border where they'd infiltrate airports and stadiums and restaurants—anywhere people gathered in large numbers.

He remembered the briefing he'd gotten on the YARS virus before he'd gone to that village. The warnings about touching even the charred remains of the buildings. The fear in the voice of the famously unflappable Gary Statham.

"Mitch . . ." Esparza said. "Mitch!"

Rapp finally tore his gaze from the place where the Arabs had disappeared into the jungle, fighting to keep his expression neutral. "What?"

"Forget these pricks. They're just noise. Losa's the only thing you need to worry about right now. Once he's gone, I'll be back in the driver's seat."

CHAPTER 42

A HAND gripped Carlos Esparza's shoulder and gave it a weak shake. He came out of his light sleep but didn't bother opening his eyes. He could neither feel the heat of the sun angling through the windows nor hear the sounds of the staff preparing for the new day. It was still the middle of the night.

"Go back to sleep or get out."

The girl was young, beautiful, and blessed with an unusual level of sexual enthusiasm. Other than that, though, she was a complete pain in the ass. Sleep was hard enough to come by these days without some seventeen-year-old whore jabbing at him.

It seemed that everything that could go wrong *had* gone wrong over the course of just a few months. On the positive side, though, problems that arose so quickly could recede at a similar pace. He'd get the Arabs and their product into the United States without incident this time and then the heroin profits would start flowing. Rapp would deal with Losa. And then he would deal with Rapp. It would be a shame, but unavoidable. When Christine Barnett became president of the United States, she would make Rapp public enemy number one. It would be too much heat for his organization to bear.

The question was whether to kill Rapp or make a deal with the U.S. government to turn him over. His impression of Barnett was that she was even more corrupt and power hungry than the Mexican politicians he dealt with on a day-to-day basis. And while the mundane bribes he was accustomed to paying out wouldn't interest her, Mitch Rapp in chains was another matter. Certainly there could be little harm in having the gratitude of the world's most powerful leader.

He let his head sink deeper into his pillow, putting the matter out of his mind and starting to drift again. One problem at a time.

The hand gripped him again, this time tighter. He was about to swat at the girl but then heard a harsh whisper.

"Carlos! Wake up!"

The sound of Vicente Rossi's voice jolted him awake. What was the man doing in his bedroom? Instinctively, he reached for the bedside lamp, but Rossi slapped his hand away.

The girl next to him rolled onto her back. "Carlos, are you—"

Rossi lurched forward and clamped a hand over her mouth. "Be silent, bitch! Stay still and don't speak! Do you understand?"

Esparza saw the vague outline of her head move up and down before his assistant pulled back.

"What the fuck are you doing in here?" he whispered, trying to get control of the situation while his heart pounded uncomfortably in his chest. "Is it Losa? Are we—"

"Shut up!" Rossi said, pulling a phone from his pocket. The screen lit up, bathing the gaunt face of his assistant in a dull blue light.

"What—"

"Read it," Rossi ordered.

Esparza looked at the phone, scanning a headline about the interception of anthrax on the U.S. border. "A news story? You woke me up for this? What the—"

"Don't talk. Read!"

Esparza took the phone and scanned through the story, his anger flaring when he reached the part stating that the intercept had been made at the San Ysidro mall.

"Those motherfuckers," he said under his breath.

The Arabs he was dealing with weren't heroin traffickers. They were terrorists trying to use his network to smuggle a bioweapon into the United States.

"Tell the guards to go to the shed and kill every one of—"

"Forget the Arabs!"

Esparza fell into confused silence.

"You trusted Mitch Rapp enough to hire him based on one thing and one thing only. You believe that a man like him doesn't care about drug trafficking." Rossi tapped the screen. "But he does care about this."

Mitch Rapp stood motionless and listened to the jungle around him. The hum of insects. The quiet rustling of leaves created by a breeze too light to feel. The rhythmic dripping of water.

The only practical way out of Esparza's house

without being seen was through a narrow strip of bushes that extended all the way to the walls. Rapp had climbed out a window when two guards briefly abandoned their posts to share a cigarette. Slipping beneath the foliage, he'd spent the next hour and a half inching along the power conduit it hid. Finally, he'd made it to the jungle.

And that's where he was still, looking back at the dark compound. Esparza ran his security in two twelve-hour shifts, with all posts manned around the clock and three additional roaming guards at night. The problem was that none of those men were currently visible. All posts now appeared to be empty and everything was silent. On the surface, that lack of guards would seem to be a good thing. But it was unexpected. And he hated unexpected.

Coming up with a coherent strategy to handle this situation had turned out to be harder than he'd anticipated. His first plan had been to get to Rossi's phone, but it was an idea that didn't hold up under examination. Assuming he could get into Rossi's room undetected and assuming Rossi had a phone capable of connecting internationally without Esparza's authority, what then? Call Kennedy for the cavalry? Based on his last conversation with Esparza, she was fighting for her political life. And he wasn't in Iraq or Afghanistan. This was Mexico, a country that wouldn't take kindly to a bunch of U.S. troops rolling in unannounced.

Further, the threat he faced wasn't just a shed full of bioweapons; it was a shed full of bioweapons that could think and move on their own. If they made it out of here, the shit was going to hit the fan in a way that no one had seen for more than a century.

In light of all that, there was no point in trying to get fancy. Better to just shoot them all, close their bodies up in the shed, and set it on fire. Nice and neat on the bioweapon front but it did leave one small loose end.

Him.

He didn't need Gary Statham to tell him that if he went into that building and started splattering blood around, he had a high probability of being infected. So when this was over, he couldn't risk any human contact at all. No going back to the house. No fighting with guards. No getting to a phone. At best, his next two weeks would be spent living barricaded in a muddy cave in the mountains. At worst, his next two weeks would be spent dying barricaded in a muddy cave in the mountains.

Another careful scan of the compound didn't turn up any sign of the missing guards, so he started forward again. Staying silent in the dense foliage forced him to move at a crawl but he finally came alongside the shed housing the Arabs.

All the equipment and supplies the clapboard building had once contained were now piled haphazardly around it. Rapp dropped to his stomach and slithered across the damp earth, aiming for what appeared to be a small tractor stacked with rakes and shovels.

The tractor likely contained the gasoline he needed, but accessing it would be more than he wanted to deal with. Fortunately, just past a pile of rotting pallets, he found a much more convenient five-gallon gas can. A gentle nudge confirmed that it was almost full, prompting him to start screwing the suppressor to his Glock. Once secured, he weaved back through the equipment toward the front of the building.

The plan had been simple. Kick in the door. Shoot everyone inside using muzzle flashes for illumination. A little gasoline. A match. And then run for the hills.

Unfortunately, that plan broke down before he even made it to step one. When he arrived at the door, it was wide-open.

Rapp pulled his T-shirt over his nose and mouth before edging toward the threshold. He flicked a lighter, letting the brief spark illuminate the interior.

Empty.

The shooting started a moment later. He spun instinctively but then realized it wasn't coming from anywhere near him. Through the trees, he could see that the side of Esparza's home was lit up with the wavering light of automatic fire. And while it was impossible to determine how many guns, their location was easy to pinpoint. His bedroom.

Rapp retrieved the gas can, emptying its contents on the shed's exterior walls. When he reached the door again, he tossed the empty container inside and then circled again, this time with his lighter. By the time he was finished, the flames on the far side were already ten feet high.

The sound of gunfire at the house had stopped and the shouting had begun. He couldn't understand any of it, but the tone suggested that they'd finally realized they were shooting at an empty bed.

CHAPTER 43

"**B**ACK up, idiots!"

As the tight group of guards lurched back into the hallway, Esparza made sure to stay slightly lower than the men surrounding him. The one exception was Vicente Rossi, who looked like he wanted to drop to his knees and crawl.

The morons he was currently using for cover had fired on an empty bed, most completely emptying their clips in one terrified burst. Now they were retreating down the hall toward an exit on the south side of the compound. Everyone remembered what Rapp had done to their comrades and the few who had been unwise enough to leave themselves without ammunition looked like they were ready to break ranks and run.

"Stay together!" Esparza shouted. "If we separate, he'll pick us off one by one."

It was a lie, of course. Mitch Rapp had no interest in the guards that Esparza was using as a human shield. In fact, it was possible that he wasn't interested in any of them. It was the Arabs he wanted. The fucking lying towelheads who had—

The deafening roar of automatic fire suddenly filled the hallway and Esparza stumbled as the men in front of him began to fall. A few tried to return fire, but their position crammed together in the corridor caused them to jostle each other to the point that accuracy was impossible. Esparza could see muzzle flashes around the far corner of the hallway, but most of the body and face of the shooter was obscured. The men behind Esparza began to flee and he followed, shouting at them to cover him from the rear, to no effect.

The two guards just in front of him went down and he felt a searing heat in his right ear as a bullet grazed him on the way to tearing through another of his men.

The shooter—almost certainly Rapp—turned his attention to the overhead lights and Esparza was showered with glass as the corridor turned to shadow. Next to him, Rossi tripped but managed to stay on his feet as the men in front disappeared around a corner.

Instead of following, Esparza ducked into an expansive, unused library. He began shoving the door closed, but was stopped when Rossi slammed into it from the other side. The younger man fought his way through the gap, gasping for air as Esparza slammed the bolt home. Outside, everything had gone silent. Only the stench of gunpowder remained.

"It's not going to stop him!" Rossi said, stumbling down a short set of stairs that allowed him to reach the far side of the room. The floor had been sunken almost two meters in order to create a dramatic sense of space beneath an open-beamed ceiling. Walls lined with unread books towered over the only furniture in the room—an ultramodern acrylic desk and leather chair.

Rossi took cover behind the latter, his university-educated brain unable to comprehend that it would offer little protection.

Esparza was wearing nothing but a pair of sweatpants, loafers with no socks, and a shoulder holster containing his Desert Eagle. He pulled the weapon and aimed it at Rossi.

"What are you—"

Esparza fired a single round into the top of the chair, punching a hole in it and showering his assistant with vaporized leather.

"Go out there and talk to him, Vicente."

"No! He'll shoot me!"

"Why would he do that? He doesn't care about drugs, right? Just explain to him that we knew nothing about the anthrax. Find out what he wants."

"We just tried to kill him, Carlos. *You* just tried to kill him. He—"

Esparza fired another round into the chair, causing Rossi to dive to the floor. "Stop shooting!" he screeched.

"The next one's going in your face, you useless piece of shit! Now get out there!"

The younger man remained frozen for a moment but then seemed to process the fact that his boss wasn't bluffing. He moved reluctantly back up the stairs as Esparza watched over his sights.

"Mr. Rapp!" he shouted through the door. "It's Vicente. We just read the news about the anthrax. This is the first we heard of it. You must know that's true. Why would we get involved in an attack on America? All we want to do is provide a safe, high-quality product to people who want it. No different than your alcohol, tobacco, and pharmaceutical companies. We're in the business of making money. We talked about this. It's the only reason we're working with the Arabs."

"Open the fucking door," Esparza said, continuing to aim the pistol at Rossi. "Do it now."

The younger man complied, sliding back the bolt and letting the door drift back a few centimeters. When nothing happened, he pulled it fully open and took a hesitant step into the hallway.

"This is terrible for our business and we want to help you. We can—"

The sound of automatic fire erupted, drowning him out. Esparza jerked back with the pistol held out in front of him, but immediately recognized that Rapp wasn't responsible. If he'd wanted Rossi dead, it would have been a single shot between the eyes. More likely a guard who had glimpsed the American when he broke cover to make contact.

Rossi threw himself toward the door but missed and slammed into the jamb instead. The collision caused him to lurch back into the middle of the hallway, where he was hit by at least two rounds. The force of them spun him around and he landed flat on his back, staring sightlessly at the ceiling.

Esparza sprinted to the door, slamming it shut and throwing the bolt again. It wouldn't hold for long if Rapp got to it, but with the guard covering the hallway it would be enough. He retreated down the steps and cut left, feeling for a hidden switch behind a bookcase. Once toggled, the entire shelf assembly swung away. The hidden passage was something he'd insisted on not because he thought he'd ever need it, but because he'd always wanted one. Now it was going to be the thing that saved his life.

Esparza turned sideways, slipping inside and pulling the shelf back into position. The sensation of claustrophobia quickly took hold as he inched through the dim light sandwiched between concrete walls. The architect had insisted on shrinking the size of the passageway to provide a more elegant shape to the library and Esparza silently cursed himself for agreeing.

The sharp corner near the middle almost stopped him. His stomach had expanded over the past few years but panic and a lubricating film of sweat got him through.

Then the lights went out.

Esparza froze, the blood pounding in his ears interfering with his ability to pick something out of the silence. But there was nothing. No gunshots. No shouts. Just the labored rhythm of his own breathing.

In the end, it wasn't his ears that discerned something, but his nose. Smoke. A burst of adrenaline surged through him and he felt his mouth go dry. Had Rapp set fire to the house to flush him out?

He started moving again, panic starting to take hold. Finally, he reached the end of the corridor and searched blindly for the latch. Where was the fire? Where was Rapp? Had he gained access to the library and found the passage? Was he moving silently down it at that very moment? Maybe only a few meters away?

The latch! Where was it?

On the other side of that wall was freedom, Esparza told himself. Rapp, for all his skill, was just one man and the compound was enormous. He couldn't kill what he couldn't find.

His fingers finally grazed a recessed metal handle and he twisted it. The muted click seemed dangerously loud as he twisted his body into a position that would allow him to push the panel open a few centimeters. He was rewarded with a rush of humid, smoky air and the flickering glow of flames. Rapp was a formidable killer, but he wasn't a magician. There would be no way for him to know the passage was there. No way for him to find the exit behind the cascade of vines camouflaging it.

The truth was that while the CIA man had been admittedly good in the jungle, he was out of his element. He didn't speak the language, he wasn't familiar with the territory, and he had no backup or communications. Esparza, on the other hand, suffered from none of these disadvantages. All he had to do was get to his vehicle. Once out of immediate danger, he could call in reinforcements. This time Rapp wouldn't be up against a handful of men. He'd be hunted by military, police, and even local farmers. There would be no escape for him.

The cartel leader inched along the wall with his Desert Eagle held out in front of him. When he came to the edge of the vines, he was finally able to pinpoint the source of the smoke. It wasn't the house that was on fire, it was the shed where the Arabs had been housed.

Esparza finally broke cover near the east side of the building, weaving through widely spaced trees toward a freestanding garage fifty meters away. When he reached the side door, he pressed his back against the wall next to it. His hand was shaking and slick with sweat, but he finally managed to turn the knob. The door swung open on well-oiled hinges and he slipped inside. The dim outline of his Humvee was only a few meters away.

It was heavily armored, with bullet-resistant glass, run-flat tires, and a supercharged engine. There were no weapons Rapp could get his hands on that would be capable of stopping it and no vehicles in the compound that could chase it down.

He crossed the concrete floor in a crouch, peering through the SUV's windows to ensure that Rapp wasn't waiting for him inside.

Empty.

The wave of elation felt similar to the one he'd experience when he'd escaped the hidden passage. Maybe Rapp wasn't even hunting him. Or, better yet, maybe the traitorous piece of shit had been shot by one of the guards. Anything was possible.

Esparza climbed inside the vehicle, retrieving the key from a hidden compartment beneath the dashboard. The garage door was closed and it would take too much time to raise. While he was confident in the Humvee's armor, it made no sense to gamble his life on it. Better to just ram the door, spin the wheel, and present Rapp with nothing but a set of receding taillights. He twisted the key in the ignition and hovered his foot over the accelerator.

Nothing.

A second twist produced a similar result and he suddenly realized that the interior lights hadn't come on when he'd opened the door. He toggled the switch that controlled them to no avail.

His emotional state swung violently back to terror when he popped the hood and went around to look at the engine. The workings of car engines were a complete mystery to him, but the problem was still immediately evident. The battery was missing.

Esparza sank down behind the driver's-side tire, losing control of his breathing again. It was Rapp. The CIA man was toying with him, trying to make him panic. Trying to make him do something to reveal where he was in the sprawling compound.

Esparza left through the same door he'd entered, holding the gun shaking in his hands. He thought he saw movement in the wavering firelight but managed to keep from squeezing the trigger. Stealth was his only hope now. The slightest sound could lead to his death.

He crept into the jungle, moving through the wet leaves in search of the service vehicles parked seventy-five meters to the east. The darkness deepened and his eyes hunted for human shapes in the trees. Every few seconds he was forced to freeze when his mind tricked him: Rapp coming up from behind. Rapp in a tree waiting to drop. Rapp's mud-streaked hand snaking out from beneath a bush.

He made it to the access road and stayed near its edge, watching silently for movement. All but one of the vehicles—an open Jeep—was gone. Fucking cowards. The surviving guards had taken them and fled.

He remained perfectly still, scrutinizing the vehicle. Normally the keys were left in it, but were they there now? Rapp had no reason to have ever come back there. Would he even be aware that this vehicle storage area existed? No, Esparza tried to convince himself. The CIA man would focus on the compound and the more obvious escape routes.

He tried to stay put but with every passing second he became more impatient. The Jeep was right there. Only a few meters away. He'd drive it up the poorly maintained but passable dirt road that would eventually lead him to civilization. There he could gather his forces and plan his next move.

Finally, he jogged silently across the road and leapt into the lone vehicle. When he reached for the ignition, instead of finding the key he was hoping for, he felt something smooth and wet. Leaning forward, he was able to make out its vague outline. A severed hand still clinging to the key.

Esparza's ability to think abandoned him and he jumped from the Jeep, running up the road away from the compound. After less than twenty-five meters, a searing pain flared in his right leg and he collapsed in a shallow puddle. His mind was struggling to comprehend what had happened and he ran a hand down his leg, stopping at the shattered kneecap.

He screamed and tried to stand, but just went down in the puddle again. A moment later, something got hold of his ankle and began dragging him into the trees.

CHAPTER 44

"**W**E'RE safe."

The words coming over Sayid Halabi's headset were badly distorted but still intelligible. He let out a long, relieved breath, leaning back against the cavern wall and staring blankly into the semi-darkness.

He had more than a hundred people throughout the world monitoring the news twenty-four hours a day. Thank Allah they'd discovered the mention of the anthrax interception within minutes of its first posting and he'd been able to get through to Muhammad Attia.

"Esparza's guards didn't try to stop you?"

"We were scheduled to leave around sunrise. The fact that we left early didn't seem to concern them."

"Where are you now?"

"We're in the van on the 307 west of Juncaná. Our GPS says we're approximately nine hours from the warehouse where we're to pick up the truck. What are your orders?"

The plan was for them to drive to Córdoba, where

they'd transfer to a semitruck with a hidden compartment designed to smuggle them over the border. The question was how much had their situation changed? Was it necessary to radically alter his plans in light of this leak from the U.S. government? He could have Attia drop off individuals in various towns on the route north, but what would that accomplish? They didn't speak Spanish, they had no safe haven in or paperwork for Mexico, and they had only ten thousand dollars in cash among them. The disease would spread, but slowly and through a sparsely populated region thousands of kilometers from America's southern border. The world would recognize what was happening and would have time to stop it like they had SARS in Asia.

"What is the condition of your people?"

"Two are showing minor symptoms. One is fairly sick, but still able to function."

"Do you foresee a problem getting to the truck?"

"No. We have good roads and dry weather. Traffic is virtually nonexistent this time of the morning and we've seen no police. My only concern is that Esparza might have contacted his people. That his cartel might be working against us now."

Halabi stood and began limping back and forth through the small chamber. In fact, it was possible that Esparza still knew nothing about the anthrax report. And even if he did, why would he care enough to devote significant resources to finding Attia? Esparza's concern would be damage control—protecting himself not only from U.S. authorities who would label his cartel a terrorist organization, but from the Mexican government and other drug traffickers.

"What are your orders?"

Halabi didn't answer immediately, though his decision was made. In truth, it always had been. God had provided this crossroad in history—a span of a few short hours when a handful of people could dismantle everything the West had built over the last two thousand years.

The arrogance that had corrupted men's hearts would disappear. Once again, humanity would prostrate itself at the feet of God and beg for his mercy. Once again, they would understand that nothing they had done—nothing they had built—meant anything.

"We move forward as planned," Halabi said finally. "But be cautious."

"Understood."

Halabi disconnected the call and looked around him. They were already in the process of fleeing. While their communications were relatively secure, he couldn't risk trying to stay in contact with Attia from a fixed position. No communications were invulnerable, and there was no telling from day to day what new capabilities the Americans could bring to bear.

He walked to a plywood box on the floor and retrieved the pistol it contained. A Glock 19. The same model that Mitch Rapp used.

By the time he exited the chamber, the activity in the rest of the cave system had reached a fevered pitch. Evidence of their time there was being erased, equipment was being dismantled, and supplies were being transferred to trucks waiting outside. Once loaded, the vehicles would scatter, staying on the move for some time before crossing into Ethiopia. A storm system was forecasted, bringing periods of rain and critical cloud cover over the next three days. They would take advantage of it to foil Western surveillance before finally converging on a similar cave system to the west.

Halabi turned right when the corridor split, finally arriving at the chamber he sought.

Gabriel Bertrand looked very different than he had only a week before. The relatively opulent surroundings he'd been provided were gone now, replaced with . . . nothing. He was sitting in the dirt with one wrist handcuffed to a bolt driven into the stone. His body and hair were filthy, streaked with mud, blood, and what appeared to be his own excrement.

The man turned toward Halabi but his dull eyes didn't seem to understand what they were seeing.

"I thought you'd want to know before you die that the plan you devised is in motion." Halabi raised the Glock. "Nothing can stop it now."

CHAPTER 45

"**B**UT you're all right?" Kennedy said, her tinny voice emanating from the satellite phone lying on the Humvee's fender.

"Yeah," Rapp said, opening a cabinet at the back of the garage and fishing the vehicle's battery from it. "For now."

"And you're sure that anthrax shipment's been neutralized?"

On the floor near the open bay door, Carlos Esparza craned his neck, trying desperately to see what was happening. He was bound with items Rapp had found in a drawer—hands with a length of framing wire and feet with a colorful bungee cord. The bleeding in his leg had been slowed with a greasy rag and roll of duct tape.

"Yeah, but it doesn't matter. That was never Halabi's play—it was a diversion."

"A diversion? From what?"

"He didn't kill all those sick villagers in Yemen. He took at least one of them and used him to infect his people with YARS. You've got six of them headed for the border with Muhammad Attia."

There was a brief pause over the line. When Kennedy came back on, she sounded uncharacteristically shaken.

"I'm showing a roughly thirty-hour drive time to get from your position to Texas. Do you know where they are now? What their plans are?"

"No," Rapp said, finishing reinstalling the battery. "But I'm about to find out."

Esparza tried to scoot away, making it only a few centimeters before Rapp crouched down and grabbed him by the hair.

"I don't know anything about anthrax or Yemen!" he said in a panicked shout. "You know this. I just wanted to partner with—" His words turned to shrieks when Rapp clamped a hand around his shattered knee.

"The only thing that comes out of your mouth from now on is answers to my questions. Is that clear?"

"Yes! Yes, it's clear. But I—"

Rapp gave the wound another squeeze and once again the garage echoed with the man's screams.

" 'Yes' was the only answer required."

Esparza clamped his lips together, muffling himself.

"The Arabs, Carlos. Where are they?"

He looked legitimately confused. "What . . . What do you mean?"

Rapp reached for the man's knee again and he tried to jerk away. "Stop! You killed them! You burned them."

"I burned an empty shed. They were already gone when I got there. And so is the van they came in."

"I . . . I don't know."

Rapp retrieved a set of vise-grips off the floor and closed the jaws around the middle joint of Esparza's right index finger. He nearly choked himself screaming as the bone was crushed flat.

"Wrong answer, Carlos."

The cartel leader's face turned pale and his eyes started to roll back in his head as he teetered at the edge of unconsciousness. He'd undoubtedly done similar things to countless men, women, and probably a few children over the years. But he wasn't doing so well being on the receiving end. Rapp walked out of the garage and found a flowerpot that was partially full of rainwater. Emptying it onto Esparza's head brought him back around.

"Do you expect me to believe that your guards just let them drive out of here without your approval?"

"Why wouldn't they?" Esparza said, his voice barely a whisper. "I gave them a safe point of entry to Mexico and the contact information for a few coyotes who could help them cross the border. They said they wanted to handle the arrangements themselves and why wouldn't I let them? I didn't want them here. There was no reason for me to take on the risk of smuggling Arabs over the border. And I didn't want them in the U.S. watching my operation."

"Names, Carlos. What coyotes did you put them in touch with?"

"I . . . I don't know for sure," he replied, having a hard time getting in enough breath to speak. "Vicente handled those kinds of details."

Rapp pulled out his gun and pressed it to the man's head. "Then I don't need you anymore."

"Wait!" he shouted. "I have names. I have all of

them! I just can't tell you for sure which ones Vicente passed on. Please, Mitch. Please. Why would I lie? They used me. I want them dead as much as you."

Rapp holstered his weapon and went back to the Humvee to close the hood.

"Irene. What kind of help can you get me from the Mexican government?"

"I'm sorry, Mitch, but the answer is none. Even if our relationship with them was good at this point, the Mexican government is flooded with drug money. If we try to involve them, those coyotes are going to hear about it. And even if that wasn't the case, their local police don't have biohazard protocols in place. If they were to intercept Halabi's people, how many of their personnel would be exposed? Would we be able to stop them from putting Halabi's men in a crowded jail? What if they kill them in a public area and there's a significant amount of blood? What if they botch the operation and scatter them? The spread of the disease isn't stopped by borders. If this gets out it'll—"

"What about Gary Statham and his guys?" Rapp interjected.

"Are you suggesting we send a U.S. military force across the Mexican border?"

"From where I'm standing, it doesn't seem like a bad option."

"Even in the most cooperative political climate imaginable that would take weeks of negotiations. And that's not the environment we're working in. Mitch, it's a little after five in the morning here and the anthrax story is about to break hard. The White House is already all hands on deck trying to figure out how to mitigate the damage. In fact, I'm in a car on my way there now."

"Can I assume that Christine Barnett's people are going to be doing the opposite?"

"I think that's a safe assumption. When the morning news shows get into full swing, all hell is going to break loose inside the Beltway."

Rapp grabbed Esparza by the collar and dragged him toward the vehicle. The cartel leader started to cry out in pain, but Rapp clamped a hand over his mouth.

"What about Scott? Can you get him and his people over the border?"

"They're in Texas. Fully equipped and waiting for your orders."

"Brief them and tell them we're a go," he said, stuffing Esparza into the backseat. "And use whatever magic you've got left to get Gary's team in a position to move fast."

"I'll do what I can, Mitch."

He grabbed the phone off the Humvee's bumper and a roll of duct tape off the floor.

"I'm putting Esparza on."

Rapp leaned through the open rear door, pressing the phone to the cartel leader's ear and securing it there with a few winds of tape.

"There'll be a survey at the end of this call, Carlos. I suggest you make sure you have a very satisfied customer on the other end."

Esparza nodded weakly, looking increasingly dazed. Part of it was blood loss, but the other part was probably the shock from how fast his life had turned to shit. Only a few hours ago, he'd been lying on satin sheets with one of his underage whores, dreaming of the billions he was going to make in the heroin business. Now he was slowly bleeding out with a phone taped to his head.

"Mr. Esparza?" Rapp heard Kennedy say as he slammed the door and walked around to the driver's side. Her voice was firm, but soothing. Just the tone necessary to give the man the illusion of hope.

"I'm sure this has been a very difficult night for you, but I have some questions that need to be answered."

CHAPTER 46

"**T**HAT'S a lie!" Senator Christine Barnett shouted, wielding the television remote in her hand as though it were a weapon.

There was no doubt that she was right, Kevin Gray knew. The DEA man being interviewed could barely meet the interviewer's eye. But this was politics. Truth and lies were irrelevant. All that mattered was what people believed.

He had arrived at Barnett's house around 4:30 a.m., just as the Internet was starting to light up with rumors about an anthrax shipment being intercepted on the U.S. border. Now the sun was up and the newspaper article filled with the lurid details he'd leaked was in the wild. As expected, it had caught fire and was burning bright on virtually every news outlet worldwide. But like all infernos, it was proving impossible to control.

Joshua Alexander was once again demonstrating the political cunning that had made his meteoric rise to the presidency possible. He and Irene Kennedy weren't satisfied to absorb—or even deflect—

the political blow. They were trying to turn it to their advantage.

"Can we see?" the reporter said over the television's speakers.

The DEA agent grimaced in pain as he lifted his shirt and showed the deep bruising on his chest.

"So that's where the bullet hit your vest?"

He nodded. "One round here and another in my back."

"And you were sure the vest would stop the round?"

"Yeah," he responded, lowering his shirt again. "Well, pretty sure anyway."

"That seems like an incredible risk to take."

An uncomfortable smile played at the edges of his mouth. "The cartels have millions of dollars to spend on technology and they spend a lot of it on surveillance. In this case, it was something we could use. It can take years to penetrate a trafficking organization with an undercover agent, but with the biothreat we didn't have years. We had to make sure another attack wasn't carried out and try to trace the supply chain back to ISIS. Like the old saying goes, desperate times call for desperate measures."

Based on the reporter's expression, she had lost all objectivity. "I never thought I'd be sitting across a kitchen table from a card-carrying hero. But here I am."

The DEA man shook his head. "The American people pay my salary. It's the job."

Barnett started jabbing in the air with the remote again. "Look at that son of a bitch! He's eating this up! He and his people just went from being the morons who let someone walk away with their coke to being America's darlings."

Gray felt like he was going to be sick. He didn't have any idea how to talk his boss down and, for one of the first times in his career, he had no idea what to do.

Barnett began compulsively changing channels, finding pretty much the same story on every one. While she was distracted, Gray pulled the phone from his pocket and pretended to check texts. In reality, he was turning on a recording app.

Barnett landed on a station with a former FBI executive speaking to a roundtable of pundits. Even more ominous was the tiny picture-in-picture at the bottom right corner of the screen. It depicted people shuffling into the White House Briefing Room.

". . . next time you complain about paying taxes or start talking about how the government can't get anything done, I want you to remember those guys getting shot for the benefit of a cartel surveillance drone."

"So you're saying that CIA operative's financial problems—his motivation for stealing those drugs—were fabricated," the man next to him said.

"Of course they were. The Agency would have used the IRS, SEC, and probably a number of foreign intelligence agencies to create an ironclad legend for his guy. They had to make it *absolutely* convincing that he'd resort to something like this. After that, I can only speculate. My best guess is that he used this to make contact with the cartel that transported the anthrax and made a case for them to hire him. It's really incredible. This is dangerous to the point of being insane. I mean, we're talking a ninety-nine percent chance the cartel just tortures him to death for stealing their product."

"Bullshit!" Barnett shouted. "That asshole isn't just

coming up with all this on his own. He and Kennedy have been friends for years. She fed it to him and sent him out on a media tour."

"And where do you think this man is now?" one of the interviewers asked.

"Dead," the FBI man answered, genuine anger audible in his voice. "If he actually managed to succeed in getting inside that cartel operation, they would have executed him the second that story leaked."

"And our ability to track the terrorists and cartel operations died with him," the host said by way of a quick summary. "We're being told that the White House press conference is about to start."

The screen shifted to a view of the briefing room, and Gray watched Alexander's press secretary stride onto the podium.

"This is going to be short," he said and then began reading a prepared statement. "The events described in the *Post* this morning are largely accurate. We did intercept an anthrax shipment in San Ysidro and a CIA operative did assault three DEA volunteers in an attempt to infiltrate the cartel that had partnered with ISIS. What you don't know is that the operation was successful. Our man was able to access the top echelons of that cartel and was using those contacts to locate Sayid Halabi and the rest of the ISIS hierarchy. He was also able to thwart a second attempt to smuggle a quantity of anthrax across our border. However, as of this morning, we've lost contact with him and he's now presumed dead. Unfortunately, the information he was able to gather to date wasn't specific or conclusive. Having said that, our law enforcement agencies are doing what they can with it. Further, the FBI has picked up the reporter who wrote the article and are questioning him about his source. There's not much more to say at this point, other than to thank the men and women who have risked everything to keep this country safe. They won't be forgotten."

Hands in the audience immediately went up and he pointed to one of them.

"Do we know if we've intercepted all of the anthrax or if there could be additional attacks in process?"

"We're reasonably certain that the anthrax threat has been neutralized," Alexander's press secretary said. "But without a man inside, we can no longer monitor the situation on an ongoing basis."

He pointed again.

"Can you tell us more about the operations you're carrying out with regard to ISIS and the cartels?"

"No," he said and indicated another reporter.

"Was Christine Barnett aware of the existence of this undercover operative?"

Kevin Gray stared at the television screen and held his breath. The Alexander administration tended not to like to politicize these kinds of things. Would he stay that course?

"We had no choice but to brief the senator about the initial anthrax attack," he said, and Gray felt his heart sink.

Leave it there. Please, God, just leave it there.

"She was *not*, however, aware of the existence of our undercover agent. That information was shared on a need-to-know basis. For reasons that should now be obvious, we were concerned with leaks."

Gray squeezed his eyes shut and let out a long, shaking breath. There it was. The press secretary for the president of the United States had just implied that Barnett couldn't be trusted with sensitive information out of fear that she would leak it. And now that leak had happened.

He barely heard the rest of the news conference or Barnett's increasingly deranged ranting, only opening his eyes when the screen turned back to the round-table of pundits.

"They didn't say their man was dead," the host said. "Only that they lost contact with him."

The former FBI man shook his head in disgust. "Losing contact with an undercover agent almost always means the same thing. Take it from me—because of this newspaper article, that magnificent bastard is lying in a ditch somewhere with his throat cut." He leaned forward, planting both elbows on the table. "I've been enforcing the laws of this country my entire life. But as far as I'm concerned, the law is too good for the person who leaked this. Their head should be put on a pike and marched through the streets."

Barnett threw the remote at the television, missing by a couple of feet and hitting the wall instead. The TV went silent and Gray focused on not throwing up. Finally, he managed to speak.

"That's my head he's talking about."

"Quit whining," Barnett snapped back. "That computer operating system is a hundred percent secure. God himself couldn't trace it. What we need to focus on now is damage control. Where do we stand?"

"Where do we stand?" he said, squinting in her direction. "We stand in the middle of a complete clusterfuck. We were going to walk away with the nomination and were way ahead in the general election polls. You could have coasted right into the Oval Office. But that wasn't good enough for you. How long is that reporter going to hold out before he gives up his source? This isn't a story about the Alexander administration covering up their incompetence anymore. He got an undercover agent killed and collapsed a bioterror investigation. He—*we*—could actually be responsible for the U.S. getting attacked."

Barnett stared at him, the fury disappearing from her face in favor of a dead expression that was somehow much worse. Gray wondered if, for the first time in their relationship, he was seeing the real woman behind the façade.

Of course, she was bat-shit insane. The truth was that they all were now. There had probably been a time when politicians achieved this level of success because of patriotism or a deep sense of responsibility to their countrymen. But now it was just about power. In fact, crazy seemed to have become a prerequisite. The American people demanded it.

He suddenly wanted to disappear. To storm out of the room, get on a plane, and get the hell out of the country. To go to work for some multinational corporation marketing soap. Or perfume. Or blood pressure pills. To leave this life behind forever.

But he was scared shitless. The woman staring lifelessly at him from across the room was smart, ruthless, and driven. Even with everything happening—even if he walked out the door—she would likely be the next president of the United States. And the first thing she'd do with the power of that office was destroy everyone who hadn't supported her. Anyone she perceived as a threat. Would he end up in jail? In Guantánamo Bay? Drugged and seat-belted into a car careening down the side of a cliff?

"Okay," he said, struggling to keep his voice even as he recited his mantra. "There are no disasters. Just opportunities we haven't found yet."

Barnett's expression reverted to the more familiar—and now oddly comforting—one of rage.

"Where do we stand?" Gray said, repeating his boss's question of a few moments ago. "If anyone asks—and they will—you deny you had anything to do with that leak and point out that there isn't even a shred of evidence to the contrary. And the fact remains that the first anthrax shipment *did* make it across the border and it was pure dumb luck that it was found. On the other hand, criticizing guys who let themselves get shot to protect the country isn't going to poll well with anyone." He fell silent, rubbing his temples and trying to think the situation through. It wasn't hard.

"We only have one option, Senator. We play it down as hard as we can and try to change the narrative. Like you've said before, the public has the attention span of a goldfish. And this doesn't really have anything to do with you. You kept the anthrax intercept secret from the public against your will at the order of the president and on the advice of Irene Kennedy. As long as no one ties the leak to you, this'll eventually blow over."

"Blow over?" Barnett said. "You think I'm just going to let this go? Slink away and let Irene Kennedy make a fool out of me?"

"Ma'am, Rapp's dead and—"

"He's not dead!" Barnett shouted. "That son of a

bitch has more lives than an alley cat. He's alive and they're not telling us. That means he's out there, still working on this operation. Waiting."

"Waiting? Waiting for what?"

"For me to win the primary. Then, at just the right moment, he's going to reappear and save the day. Alexander and Kennedy will be heroes and I'll be standing there looking like a fool."

Gray just stared at her. How could he have not seen this before? The presidency wasn't an end for Barnett, it was a beginning. She wanted the power to close her fist around everything and everyone. She saw Kennedy and Rapp as beneath her—meaningless government workers who existed to do her bidding. Their defiance was stoking her hatred to the point that she was slipping into paranoia.

"Senator, the idea that Mitch Rapp is involving himself in some kind of complex political game is—"

"He sees me as a threat," Barnett said. "Just like Kennedy. They're going to use this to come after me. We have to find out what's happening in Mexico. We have to get ahead of it."

"We have no way of finding out what's happening," Gray said, becoming increasingly alarmed at Barnett's erratic demeanor. "No one's going to tell us anything, and if we try to twist arms at the intelligence agencies, it's going to go public and blow up in our faces."

"Not the *American* government," she said. "We can use our contacts in the Mexican government. They want us to get off their backs regarding immigrants and drugs, right? Well, as president, I can make that happen. And all I ask in return is a little cooperation and information."

"Now hold on, Senator. If Rapp's alive, it's possible that he's actually still on the trail of ISIS. We—"

"I'm not going to sit on my hands and see that son of a bitch shooting it out with terrorists on television!" she screamed.

Gray tried to stay calm, but he was starting to feel the honest-to-God beginnings of panic. This was the first time he'd ever seen Barnett under real stress. She'd lived a charmed life—an obscenely wealthy husband, children willing to toe her political line, and a career that went nowhere but up. What would happen when she got backed into a corner like all presidents did? What would happen if she was in charge when there was a real national crisis?

"We're in a hole, Senator. It's time to stop digging. This is about damage control now. You need to go out there and praise those DEA guys for their heroism. But then you remind voters that we can't count on NASA and government employees willing to get shot every time there's a threat to America. That this isn't a failure of the men and women in the trenches, it's a failure of leadership. Then we'll start talking about the economy. Or Russia. North Korea. Guns. It doesn't mat—"

"They're not going to allow it," she said, cutting him off. "This is going to be about a bunch of big strong men on the front lines while I'm back in my office hiding. The weak woman. I'm not going to let that happen, Kevin. We're going to get in front of this."

"That's crazy," he said, the words coming out of his mouth before he could stop them. "You can't control the Mexicans, Senator. They have no loyalty to you and no particular love for the U.S. right now. If you ask them to dig up information on Mitch Rapp, the first thing they're going to do is contact the cartels and—"

"Make it happen."

"Excuse me?"

"Call them, Kevin. Call the Mexicans. Find out what's going on. We can still head this off. If there really is something happening down there, we might be able to get the Mexican authorities to deal with it and keep Rapp and Kennedy from getting the win. If it works out, we might even be able to take some credit. Show the American people that I can stop threats *before* they make it to the United States."

Gray remained silent. He'd already allowed himself to be dragged into the leak that was turning into a disaster. He was already in deep and it was time to take his own advice and stop digging. The hole was starting to feel like a grave.

Gray picked up his coat and started for the door. "If you want to call the Mexicans, Senator, call them yourself."

CHAPTER 47

SCOTT Coleman let the minivan drift forward, coming to a stop again behind the Prius he was trailing. Farther up in line, an SUV was passing through the border checkpoint and into Mexico.

He had the windows down and was enjoying cool temperatures that wouldn't last long after the sun rose in about an hour. The news station playing on the radio was focused on the only story that anyone cared about—the anthrax that had crossed the border and the anonymous CIA operative who had been tracking it. The anonymous CIA operative that he was now on his way to meet.

"Mas is through," Claudia said, staring down at her phone from the passenger seat. "Bruno's next. He's three cars from the checkpoint."

Coleman wasn't particularly worried about the team getting across. While it was true that they were lone, dangerous-looking men in pickups and SUVs, they were completely clean. Perfect IDs, backdated resort reservations, and nothing in their vehicles but suntan lotion and swim trunks.

His situation was somewhat different. On the positive side, couples in late-model minivans tended not to raise a lot of red flags with border security. Less ideal, though, was the fact that they were carrying enough weapons to launch a pretty respectable coup attempt. Hidden beneath piles of luggage, for sure, but not enough to fool anyone who decided to do more than glance.

"Bruno's through," Claudia said, finally putting down her phone and looking up. "Mitch is on the road and he'll rendezvous with us at the airfield."

"Assuming we make it across the border," Coleman said.

"Are you worried?"

"Nah. God wouldn't let me get gunned down in an Izod shirt. He doesn't hate me that much."

Ahead, next to the open gates that led into Mexico, a green light kept flashing on and off. It was random and every once in a while it turned red, indicating that the car going through would be searched by customs. Normally the Agency would have rigged the game, but Kennedy was dead set against notifying the Mexican authorities. So they were just rolling the dice.

Claudia seemed to be feeling the pressure too, because she suddenly snapped a hand out and changed the radio station—as though listening to a news story about anthrax would give away their involvement with it. The green light flashed and the car two ahead rolled through. The Prius ahead of them was next, gliding through without incident. And then . . .

Green.

Coleman let out a quiet breath and pulled through,

but they weren't out of the woods yet. There was a secondary military checkpoint ahead specifically set up to look for weapons being transported into the country. According to Claudia's smuggling contacts, they were typically interested in pickups and SUVs piloted by one or two men between the ages of twenty-five and forty. However, if they spotted someone driving a larger vehicle that looked a little too innocuous, they sometimes pulled that over, too.

It was those same smugglers who had recommended the setup they were using. Red minivan loaded with options. "Baby on Board" sticker, but no baby. White couple, not too young, not too old. The smuggling Goldilocks zone.

And they turned out to be right. The soldiers by the side of the road didn't even look up as they passed.

Claudia turned the radio back to an analysis of the presidential nominations through the lens of the anthrax leak. Christine Barnett was fighting like a junkyard dog, of course, but the fact that she'd been out of the loop was making her look weak. There was also a fair amount of speculation flying around that she might have had something to do with the leak, but no evidence. The spin machines on both sides were running full speed and it was getting harder and harder to tease truth from bullshit.

Coleman tuned out the voices as he accelerated up the road. It was just a distraction at this point. His role in all this was simple: shoot in the direction Mitch told him to.

Claudia's phone rang and she picked up, channeling it through the vehicle's sound system.

"I understand everyone's through," Irene Kennedy

said over the speakers. Her voice was distorted by the encryption they were using, but still intelligible.

"Yeah, we're clear," Coleman said. "We'll make it to the airfield around eleven thirty tonight. Where do you stand?"

"Our worst-case scenario timing-wise is that the terrorists left Esparza's compound at one a.m. and are driving roughly thirty hours to the closest border checkpoint. If that's the case, they could be as far as Coatzacoalcos. Twenty-two hours from the border."

He consulted the GPS in his dash. "Then I'm starting to question our strategy, Irene. It looks like we're going to pass them on the road."

"We don't think so," Kennedy said calmly. "They appear to have contracted a smuggling organization and it's likely they're planning on changing vehicles. That's going to take time to deal with."

"Do we have a line on their coyotes yet?" Coleman asked.

"We're running down the names Carlos Esparza provided, but haven't come up with anything solid. We're also searching the roads in southern Mexico, but that's going to be low percentage. It's a lot of road and our satellite coverage is spotty."

"And if you do manage to find us a target?" Coleman said. "What are our marching orders?"

The fact that she didn't respond immediately worried him a bit.

"As of now, this is an unauthorized private operation on foreign soil. I've talked to the commander at Luke Air Force Base who's a personal friend of mine and he's agreed to put the appropriate aircraft on alert, but he isn't going to do anything more than that without a direct order from the president."

"Do you think you can get that?" Claudia asked.

"I'm meeting him in an hour, but a military incursion over the Mexican border involving a bombing run against a moving target is a big ask. The amount of ordnance necessary to ensure that the virus is completely eradicated is fairly shocking. I'm not hopeful."

"Great," Coleman said. "So you're saying we should just handle this on our own with a handful of people and a minivan with a few guns in it. And if we make the slightest mistake, no big deal. Only a few hundred million people will die."

"I'm doing everything I can, Scott. Alexander's a good man and he's been a good president. But politicians aren't built for these kinds of all-or-nothing decisions."

"What about going around him?"

This time the pause was long enough that Coleman thought they might have lost the satellite link. Finally she came back on.

"I had an informal conversation about that with a few highly placed people I won't name. What I can tell you is that no one has the stomach for what would essentially be a coup. In a way, it's comforting that our institutions are holding strong even in the face of something like this."

"It doesn't feel comforting from where I'm sitting, Irene."

"I know. And I'm sorry. Claudia? Are you there? How are you holding up?"

The question was understandable. While Claudia Gould was a logistics genius, she'd spent most of her career supporting her private contractor husband. Her definition of failure had involved things like missing the target, getting arrested, and not being paid. Now she was getting a crash course in the difference between that world and the one inhabited by Mitch Rapp.

Her eyes narrowed and the expression on her youthful face hardened. She had a daughter to protect and, at thirty-six, a life left to live.

"If you say we're the only people who can deal with this, then that's what we're going to do. Deal with it."

CHAPTER 48

RAPP stopped and examined the chain link gate illuminated in the Humvee's headlights. The sign on it was badly faded, but he could still make out the cheerful logo of a company that had once offered sightseeing flights over a nearby national park.

He dug a couple of antibiotic pills from his pocket and popped them in his mouth. A couple hours into his drive he'd spotted a pharmacy and made a quick stop. The man behind the counter had been oddly unfazed by Rapp's demand for an anthrax remedy, but in retrospect it wasn't so surprising. The American people were panicked over Halabi's threats and loved buying cheap pharmaceuticals in foreign countries. There was a good chance that he wasn't the first gringo to stop at that drugstore on his way home.

The bitter taste of the pills was strangely comforting. He had no idea if he'd inhaled any spores while emptying that bag into his bathtub, but chances were high. There was probably a reason the CDC didn't issue kitchen gloves and tourist bandannas as standard protective gear.

He spotted movement out of the corner of his eye and inched a hand closer to his Glock before registering the blond hair of Scott Coleman. The gate opened and he pulled through, idling while the former SEAL relocked the barrier and slipped into the passenger seat.

"I haven't talked to Irene in more than two hours," Rapp said, accelerating. "Give me a sit rep."

"We got here about a half hour ago and I have a chopper inbound. The tarmac's in worse condition than we thought so we can't land planes. We should be able to get two private ones in the air from the local airport, though. Irene's scrambling basically everyone the Agency has in-country—including a few people who retired down here. Not the most organized or well-trained force we've ever worked with, but at least we have warm bodies."

"And your team?"

"I left them closer to the border to form a defensive line. If we get a target, they'll be in a position to intercept from the north. But so far we've got nada."

A dark, wooden crate of a building appeared in the headlights and Rapp pulled around behind it, parking next to a minivan with a "Baby on Board" decal. There was a generator humming outside and a couple of extension cords running through the wall.

"What about Esparza?" Coleman asked, glancing at the empty backseat before jumping out.

"He didn't make it."

Technically accurate, but not the entire story. In truth, the man had stopped bleeding and was doing pretty well by the time he'd finished his conversation with Kennedy. When Rapp reached pavement, though, he'd decided that driving around with a bound cartel leader in the backseat was all risk and no reward. He'd pulled off into the trees and left Esparza there with his head twisted backward. With a little luck, his bones were already being picked clean by scavengers.

Coleman just shrugged and went for the building's only door.

The interior was painted in the same colors as the logo on the gate, but much of it was peeling or stained from leaks in the roof. Two windows had been covered in a mix of plywood and canvas to keep light from bleeding through and a bathroom with a collapsed sink was visible in the corner. Other than that there wasn't much—not even a table. The operation was being run from the floor.

Claudia was at the far end of the building, staring at a map and talking excitedly into the phone. "Where? Yes, I understand. And how good is this information? Fine. Yes. Get back to me as soon as you can."

She hung up and spun, fixing her almond-shaped eyes on him. The relief was clear in them but she let it show for only a moment. "We may have a functional lead. One of the coyote organizations Esparza gave us runs their operation out of a warehouse in Córdoba, southeast of Mexico City. That warehouse burned down three hours ago."

"Kind of weird," Coleman said. "But why risk setting it on fire and attracting attention? Are we sure it's not just a coincidence?"

"It's not a coincidence," Rapp said, running a finger along a map hanging on the wall. "The one thing we have going for us is that Halabi fucking *despises* the United States. I know this asshole better than he knows himself. This isn't about God. It's about him. He doesn't want to infect a bunch of coyotes with YARS and have them running around Mexico randomly spreading it. He burned that warehouse for the same reason he told Esparza to keep his men at a distance. Because he wants this to come from America. He wants everyone to think Allah himself slapped down on us. That *we* brought this on the world. Not Mexico."

"If you're right, then things might be finally moving in our direction," Claudia said. "The coyotes that operated out of that warehouse were a boutique organization specializing in smuggling contraband in refrigerator trucks. Flawless paperwork and hidden compartments that are almost impossible to detect without cutting the trailer apart."

"They're moving slower than we thought," Rapp said, continuing to study the map. "I'm guessing they stuck to back roads on their way to Mexico City and then hit traffic. After that, they had to load their people and fill the trailer with frozen food. Claudia, if we figure they rolled out of there around the time it burned, where could they be now?"

"Likely somewhere just to the east of Mexico City."

Rapp used a pencil to create an arc centered on that area of the map. Then he traced multiple similar lines above at roughly fifty-mile intervals, labeling each with a time.

He pointed to the gap between lines marked 12 a.m. and 1 a.m. "The way I see it, we have a fully loaded refrigerator truck somewhere in this band. Claudia, tell the Agency to create a map that'll give us real-time animation of the sections of road we need to focus on."

"That shouldn't be a problem," she said.

"Scott—what about the people you told me we have in-country?"

"I'll get Bruno, Wick, and Mas moving south. Two prop planes can be in the air in forty minutes searching the roads in your target area. And we've got around another twenty people spread out across the roads from the U.S. to Guatemala. Like I said, no one special, but all perfectly capable of looking for a truck. We've also got clear skies and some satellite coverage. But someone's going to have to tell us how to differentiate a refrigerated truck from a regular one."

Rapp nodded. "Claudia. Have Irene pull together all her Spanish speakers. If we spot a truck that looks like a good candidate, we'll phone in a plate number and description. Then Irene's people can call the company that owns it, confirm it's theirs, get a final destination, and make sure it's where it's supposed to be. How much time do we have?"

"If you're right about where they are now, it'll take them at least ten hours to cross into the U.S."

Rapp finally turned away from the map. There weren't many things that could make the sweat running down his back turn cold, but this was it. They were trying to cover thousands of square miles in a country where they'd never operated with a team made up of people who had little or no operational experience. No military support. No support from local law enforcement. And a Mexican government that vacillated between useless and openly hostile.

"Should we be putting U.S. authorities on alert that they might have to close the border?" Coleman asked.

Rapp thought about it for a moment and then shook his head. "Once that word goes out, how long until the press gets hold of it? We've already had one leak and we know how Halabi reacted. If he gets spooked and turns those people loose in Mexico, we're screwed."

"What about additional inspections for refrigerator trucks?" Claudia suggested.

"Same problem," Rapp said. "There's no way ISIS doesn't have people watching the border crossings, and it's hard to imagine they'd miss our guys going over every refrigerated truck with a fine-toothed comb. Halabi desperately wants to believe this is working. All we have to do is not convince him otherwise."

"So let's say we get lucky and find that truck," Coleman said. "We've got RPGs, but that's going to make a mess. We'll have half-burned bodies and thawing frozen food all over the place. There'll be civilians, cops, maybe army. Can we control that?"

Rapp didn't answer. He'd had a number of strategy sessions with Kennedy on his drive, and neither one of them had come up with a workable plan to keep this in Mexico. It went against every instinct he had, but he'd finally had to resign himself to the fact that the border was just a meaningless line on a map. Attia and the six terrorists he was transporting weren't the enemy. It was the billions of germs they carried.

"No," Rapp said finally. "We can't control it. And that's why we're going to let them through."

"Repeat that?" Claudia said, obviously thinking her less than perfect English had failed her.

"Gary Statham's got a team standing by in New Mexico. We need that truck to roll across the border without any fireworks. He'll be waiting for it on the other side."

CHAPTER 49

RAPP held the hand pump on top of a fifty-five-gallon fuel drum while Coleman worked it. Their pilot had the nozzle inserted in their rented chopper and was encouraging them with nonstop updates on their progress.

They'd set down on a remote dirt track fifteen minutes ago and, after a fair amount of searching, located the fuel cache left for them. The foliage was thicker and the terrain more undulating than Rapp had expected in this part of Mexico. Mountains were visible in the distance and they'd flown past cliffs that looked to be more than a thousand feet high. Population centers were pretty spread out and largely connected by two-lane rural highways. Road surfaces weren't bad, but inconsistent enough that the myriad transport trucks traveling over them were doing so at fairly conservative speeds.

The phone in his pocket started to vibrate, and he squinted at the screen through the midmorning sun.

"Go ahead," he said, picking up and leaving the former SEAL to complete the job.

"We've got a good candidate," Claudia said.

"Another one?"

They had nine cars on the road, looking for refrigerator trucks, supplemented by two private planes and the chopper they were currently refueling. At first he'd thought it wasn't enough, but now he was wondering if it was too many. Passing plate numbers and transportation company names to Agency analysts had turned out to be an inexact science. They'd already had three false alarms—one caused by some misfiled paperwork in Guadalajara, one by a simple transposition of a number, and one that probably was a smuggler, but not the one they were after.

"This is solid," she said. "We have circumstantial evidence that it originated in Córdoba around the same time that warehouse burned."

Rapp nodded. Soft, but at least it was something.

"Do we have anyone in contact with it?"

"One car ahead. He's stopped and will be in a position to get photos in about ten minutes."

"What about Scott's guys?"

"Bruno's about half an hour from the target. Mas and Wick are probably more like an hour and a half out."

"Understood."

"Gary Statham's waiting for your orders, and we have spec ops teams keeping a low profile at all the viable crossings. But this is starting to get tight, Mitch. Based on the maps we're using, Halabi's people could be within three hours of the nearest border. According to Irene, the president's starting to panic. He wants to close them."

Rapp looked out at the landscape surrounding

him. The plan was still to let ISIS roll onto American soil unchallenged. Once they were on the U.S. side, a sniper would pump a single round into the driver and the army's biohazard team would basically put a plastic bag over the entire site. On a gut level, it was a terrifying scenario, but it got better the more he thought about it. A semi at a border crossing was easily controlled—one car in front and one in back were enough to completely immobilize it. The driver was easily taken out and his body would be contained inside the cab. The likelihood that the people in back would have the ability to escape the trailer on their own was pretty remote, but even if they did, they wouldn't make it two feet before they took a bullet to the chest.

"Tell her to hold him off. Right now we're in reasonably good shape. We might not know for sure where Halabi's people are but we're fairly certain they're contained and all together. If we lose that, we're screwed."

"I'll relay the message."

He heard a shout and saw Coleman waving him over. They were done refueling and the chopper's blades were already starting to rotate.

"Send me the coordinates of that truck. We'll be in the air inside of two minutes."

"Did you say Grupo Amistoso?" Rapp shouted into the microphone hanging in front of his mouth.

Coleman, who was sitting next to him in the back of the chopper, gave him the thumbs-up. Rapp focused a pair of binoculars on a distant semi, but the trailer didn't carry the logo they were looking for.

"That's not it, Fred," he said. "We're still too far south."

"Roger that," their pilot said.

Coleman nudged him and slid a portable computer onto his lap. Rapp clicked on the file Claudia had sent and was rewarded with a series of high-resolution images depicting a truck driving along a straight stretch of highway. He enlarged one and focused on the windshield. Whoever had taken the photo was smart enough to use a polarizing filter, giving detail to the inside of the cab.

Muhammad Attia.

The surge of adrenaline that he expected didn't materialize. The opposite, really. All he felt was a profound sense of relief.

"This is our guy."

Coleman pumped a fist in the air.

"Fred, get eyes on him, but stay way back. We don't want to get made. We need to find out where the closest exits off that road are and make sure they're covered. Pull the planes back and keep our guy on the ground with him. Scott, what's Bruno's ETA?"

"Call it five minutes. Mas and Wick are still about an hour out."

"Okay. We need to line up people and vehicles along every possible path so we can keep staggering them. We're just here to keep an eye on him and stay invisible. Make sure everyone's clear. No interference and nothing that could call attention to us."

"Roger that," Coleman said before isolating his radio to start coordinating their effort.

Rapp responded to Claudia's email and then used his binoculars to scan the road again. Traffic was light—probably an average of two hundred yards between cars. The terrain continued to be rolling, with distant mountains now starting to soften in a dusty haze.

Another minute went by before their pilot's voice came over Rapp's headphones. "That's gotta be him at eleven o'clock."

He banked the chopper east so that Rapp could get a better look. Blue cab towing a yellow trailer with GRUPO AMISTOSO stenciled on the side. Exactly like the pictures.

Attia was staying just below the speed limit, driving smoothly and trying to keep a decent interval between his truck and the other vehicles moving in his direction. The closest was behind, a dilapidated sedan about three hundred yards back.

Rapp plugged his phone into his headset and dialed Kennedy.

"I understand the truck's been located," she said by way of greeting.

"Yeah. Southeast of Monterrey, Mexico, so he's going for one of the East Texas crossings. We're two and a half hours from the border by car. That can't be more than a few minutes out by jet. Get one over here."

"I'm afraid we're not going to be able to do that."

"Bullshit, Irene. This is a perfect scenario for us. He's a sitting duck and there's no one else close. We can slag that thing with zero civilian casualties and get our plane back across the border before the Mexicans even—"

"It's not the president, Mitch. He's authorized the strike."

"Then what are we waiting for?"

"I've had a number of demolitions experts and biologists looking at this. No one knows how much frozen food is in that truck or what kind. We also don't know what the false chamber those people are in is made of. That makes it impossible to be one hundred percent sure we can incinerate the trailer and its contents with no chance of flinging infected tissue away from the blast site. According to the notes we've retrieved from Gabriel Bertrand's university computer account, this disease likely started in Yemeni bats. That means we don't know if wild animals in Mexico could be infected and—"

"Have you run this by Gary?"

"Yes and he agrees. Letting the truck cross the border is still our best chance for containment."

"Shit," Rapp muttered, but it was lost in the drone of the chopper. Gary Statham was the best in the world at what he did. Questioning his knowledge of biological threats was like questioning Stan Hurley's knowledge of Southeast Asian hookers.

"Fine," he said. "I'm out."

"Wait, Mitch. There's something else."

"You've got to be kidding. What now?"

"I just got a call from a Mexican intelligence executive who I have a back channel to. His bosses have been asking about the possibility that the CIA is carrying out an illegal operation there. It seems that someone high up in the U.S. government has been calling and asking questions."

"What the *fuck*, Irene? You know where these leaks are coming from as well as I do. Shut them down or I'll fly to Washington and do it for you."

"Right now, you need to focus on that truck. My

concern is that these inquiries could get to someone being paid by Halabi. If that's the case, things could become very unpredictable very quickly. We can revisit the subject of what to do about the leaks later." She paused for a moment. "If there is a later."

CHAPTER 50

THE highway below Rapp was split now, with two lanes running in each direction and a broad dirt median between. Low, scrubby trees extended to the horizon and traffic remained light. The truck driven by Muhammad Attia was little more than a dot in his binocular lenses. Joe Maslick and Charlie Wicker were in separate vehicles about one mile and one and a half miles in front of it, respectively. Bruno McGraw was bringing up the rear, hanging back about three-quarters of a mile.

For one of the first times in his career, things seemed to be going too smoothly. The truck's last turn had put it on a highway that made only one border crossing practical. Gary Statham was currently loading his team on a transport and he'd guaranteed that they'd be ready when Attia arrived.

"Is he still holding his speed, Fred?"

"Yup. Two kilometers an hour under the limit. Slow and steady."

As expected. Attia didn't need to hurry. He just needed to avoid attracting attention.

"Scott. Give me an updated ETA."

"Some of those hills back there slowed him down a little. We're around an hour forty-five to Texas. Our guys at the border crossing are reporting light traffic and they're not anticipating any change to that."

Rapp glanced down at his phone. No messages. "Maybe we should have brought beer."

The former SEAL grinned. "Wanna bet? Your Charger would look good in my garage."

Rapp didn't respond, sweeping his binoculars east in an attempt to find a threat and again coming up empty.

The wisdom of not accepting Coleman's bet became clear nineteen minutes later when Claudia's voice came over the chopper's comm.

"The rumors spreading around the Mexican government have finally made the press, Mitch. A story just appeared online about the U.S. tracking an anthrax shipment across Mexico without the government's knowledge."

Rapp swore under his breath and glanced at his watch. The truck's time to the border had just gone under the hour-and-a-half mark.

"No need to panic yet," Claudia said. "It's one very speculative story on a pretty sensational Spanish-language site. All anonymous sources."

"Halabi's people aren't just going to be monitoring CNN," Rapp said. "And I'm pretty sure they know how to use Google Translate. If we found it, he's not going to be far behind."

"You're probably right," she admitted. "The question is when and what's he going to do with the information?"

"Mas," Rapp said. "Slow down. I want eyes on that truck. Wick and Bruno. Maintain your position."

"Roger that," Joe Maslick said. "But if I can see him, he's going to be able to see me. I won't be able to match his speed for long without making him suspicious."

Coleman turned his laptop toward Rapp and tapped a blue dot on the screen. It represented a vehicle their people had stashed in the trees just off the main road.

"Copy. We've got a car about twelve miles ahead of your position. You can pull off and make a switch. Bruno, when he does, you can close in and take over surveillance. From now until the border I want one of you close. Claudia, you're going to have to coordinate personnel and vehicle changes along the route."

"I'm already working on it."

"Mitch," their pilot cut in. "I'm seeing brake lights on the target."

"Is there an obstacle?"

"Not that I can see. Looks wide-open. Wait . . . He's turning into the median."

Rapp put the binoculars to his eyes as Fred Mason banked in an effort to keep their interval. All that was visible was a dust cloud. When the truck emerged, it had reversed course.

"The target has crossed the median and is accelerating back west," Rapp said. "I repeat, the target is now westbound. Bruno, cross over and get in front of him. Stay out of sight. Wick and Mas, cross over and get behind. Wick, close the gap and get eyes on him. Mas, you stay back far enough to keep out of sight. Claudia, patch in Irene."

A moment later, Kennedy's voice came on the line. "Go ahead."

"Looks like Halabi reads the news. Attia's jumped the median and he's headed toward Monterrey."

She started to speak, but Wick drowned her out. "I've got him in sight and he's hauling ass. Eighty-nine miles an hour by my speedo."

"Mitch," Kennedy said when she came back on. "Monterrey is an urban center with over a million people. Based on the satellite image I'm looking at, he can make it to the outskirts in less than thirty minutes. If he has a way to offload those people, they'll scatter and we'll never find them. Letting him reach Monterrey isn't an option."

Rapp considered her words for a moment. "We've got an RPG. We could go for the cab and crash it."

"That just puts us back in the situation that we talked about earlier. The scattering of Attia's potentially contaminated body parts. The chance of infecting animals. Possible damage to the trailer, blood, police, Good Samaritans . . ." Her voice faded for a moment. "The plan hasn't changed. We need to get that truck over the border and into the hands of Gary's team."

"From where I'm sitting, that's easier said than done, Irene."

"I'm going to call the president and see if there's anything he can do. But I'm not hopeful. Time is against us and his counterpart in Mexico is—"

"A scumbag with the IQ of a head of lettuce?" Rapp offered.

"I'm afraid so. I'll get back to you as soon as I can. In the meantime do *not* let that truck reach Monterrey."

She disconnected and Coleman spoke up. "He's got the hills in front of him. The first time he went over them, he was barely able to hold twenty-five miles an hour."

"Yeah, but we have the same problems at twenty-five miles an hour that we do at eighty-nine."

"We've got the chopper, a few guys, and some weapons," the former SEAL said. "If we disable the truck and take him out inside the cab, we could keep the cops and any bystanders back for a while. Maybe long enough for Alexander to explain the situation to the Mexicans?"

Rapp shook his head. It left too much to chance. The only thing more unpredictable than viruses was politics.

"Fred," Rapp said to their pilot. "Get us over those hills ahead. Let's see if we can find something."

Mason pushed the chopper to its less-than-impressive top speed while Rapp examined a tractor-trailer hauling pipes on the road below. Less than a minute later, they buzzed another semi, this one pulling a trailer emblazoned with the logo of a fast-food company.

"You got something?" Coleman said, recognizing his expression from years of working together.

Rapp remained silent, craning his neck to keep eyes on Attia's truck as it disappeared behind a rise.

"That one's not going to work," Rapp said, watching a tractor-trailer make its way up the steep slope they were hovering over. It was already more than a hundred yards into the climb and had barely slowed. Likely empty.

"We've still got the two we saw earlier," Coleman said. "Fast food and pipes."

Rapp nodded. "How's our fuel, Fred?"

"We've got another forty minutes in the air. Thirty if you count the time it'll take to get to our closest fuel stash."

The semi with POLLO FELIZ painted on the trailer reached the bottom of the hill and immediately started losing speed. "That's the one. Scott, what's Attia's ETA?"

"Call it just under five minutes."

"And we're still out of sight?"

"Yeah," Mason said. "As long as we stay low, he won't be able to see us until he crests that last rise."

"Okay, then let's do it."

Mason dove toward the truck, coming to a stable hover about five feet off the ground and thirty feet in front of it. The driver reacted immediately, slamming on his brakes and sounding the horn. The steep grade combined with the weight of his trailer allowed him to bring the vehicle to a full stop in seconds.

Mason dropped the chopper to within a couple feet of the asphalt and Rapp jumped out. The driver watched what was happening through his dusty windshield, not even bothering to lock himself inside the cab as Rapp ran toward it. He undoubtedly assumed this was a cartel operation and figured that complete cooperation was his only hope for survival. No point in dying over a bunch of frozen chicken.

Rapp yanked the door open and dragged the man out before taking his place behind the wheel. He'd never driven a truck exactly like it, but had extensive experience piloting similar rigs in Iraq and Afghanistan. Finding first gear wasn't as easy as he'd hoped, but once he did he was able to start the slow process of getting the loaded semi back up to speed. Mason climbed again and the truck's driver retreated to the side of the road with his cell phone already against his ear. Not that it mattered. One way or another, this thing was going public.

In his side-view mirror, Rapp saw an off-road pickup rolling up fast behind him. It moved into the left lane and slowed, coming alongside. Bruno McGraw leaned over the empty passenger seat and shouted through his open window. "You okay, boss?"

"Yeah. Go forward. Find me a place to turn around."

McGraw sped off as Rapp continued to push the semi's motor to its limit. He was almost to fifteen miles an hour when he saw Attia barreling toward the base of the hill. He hit the slope at almost ninety miles an hour, but the effect of gravity became immediately evident. His speed began to plummet as he closed the distance to the trailer Rapp was towing. When there was about a hundred yards between them Attia pulled into the left lane to pass, probably still traveling ten miles an hour faster than Rapp. By the time he'd made it to within twenty yards, that speed differential was almost cut in half.

Rapp kept his eyes glued to his side mirror, waiting for Attia to close to with ten feet before swerving in front of him and hitting the brakes.

Contact was almost instantaneous. Rapp was thrown back in his seat but managed to keep his hands on the wheel and his eyes on the mirror. Attia, now aware of what was happening, tried to swerve back into the right lane, but Rapp followed the move, gearing down and feathering the brakes.

They swerved along the road for another ten

seconds, slowing to four miles an hour before the pressure on the back of Rapp's truck disappeared. Attia had applied his own brakes and disconnected from him.

An assault rifle appeared through the terrorist's open window and Rapp's side-view mirror exploded, spraying him with shattered glass. Attia continued to fire short bursts as he drifted left, managing to get a few rounds into Rapp's cab and punch holes in the windshield.

Rapp had had about enough of their slow-motion car chase, so he twisted the wheel, bringing his truck to a halt across the road. Attia was forced to stop but now had a better angle. He took full advantage, forcing the CIA man to the floorboards as he emptied his magazine into the driver's-side door. Somewhere beneath the roar of the assault rifle, though, a deep thump became audible.

The sound of gunfire continued, but the ring of rounds hitting metal stopped. Rapp rose from the floorboard and spotted Coleman hanging out of the side of the chopper squeezing off careful individual shots in Attia's direction. The terrorist reloaded and trained his fire on the former SEAL. A moment later a smoke plume sprouted from the back of the aircraft. Mason lost control and the helicopter started to spin, slipping away from the truck.

Rapp escaped through the passenger door and landed shoulder-first on the running board before dragging himself behind the truck's front wheel. He barely made cover before Attia began spraying the cab again.

Rapp hadn't had time to take the truck out of gear

and it idled slowly toward the steep slope on the west side of the road. He pulled his Glock and paced the front wheel, dropping to the ground when the cab started to go over the edge. Dust kicked into the air as the trailer was jacked upward and dragged down the precipice. Attia lost sight of his target and stopped shooting. Rapp took his time, bracing the pistol with both hands from his location on the ground.

When the trailer finally cleared his position and began tumbling down the slope, he spotted the side of Attia's face around the front bumper of his vehicle. It was all Rapp needed.

A gentle squeeze of the trigger jerked the terrorist's head back and dropped him to the asphalt. He still had hold of the assault rifle and Rapp sprinted toward him, getting a foot on the weapon before he could lift it again. The bullet had grazed his cheekbone, leaving a deep wound that was bleeding profusely but not serious enough to rob him of consciousness. A sound that came out somewhere between a shout and a scream erupted from his throat when he recognized Rapp.

The CIA man pointed his pistol toward Attia's forehead, but then readjusted his aim to the man's chest before firing a single round. He'd already made too much of a mess as it was.

Rapp glanced down the slope and saw Mason trying to control his descent with mixed results. Wicker and Maslick were approaching from the east but Rapp waved them back. Attia was dead but maybe more dangerous now than he had been when he was alive. Despite the fact that his heart was no longer pumping, the wound in his face continued to pour blood—likely infected with YARS—onto the asphalt.

He leaned over the body, hesitating for a moment before grabbing it under the arms and dragging it back to the cab of the truck. By the time he got it inside, he was so covered in blood that he looked like an extra in a low-budget zombie flick.

"Wick!" Rapp said into his throat mike. "There's a shitload of blood on the road. You need to clean it up."

"Clean it up? With what?"

"How the fuck would I know? Maybe punch a hole in your fuel tank and use that. Call Gary and ask him what'll work."

"Roger that," came the unenthusiastic reply.

"Bruno," Rapp said, starting Attia's truck and putting it in gear. "Did you find me a turnaround?"

"About two hundred yards over the top of the hill. It's going to be about a ten-point turn, but we'll get it done."

"All right. Once I turn around, we're heading full-gas for the border. Bruno and Mas, you're blocking for me. Try not to kill any civilians or cops, but if you don't have any choice, do it. I'll take the heat for any casualties. Wick. Once you're done with that blood, head out into the desert and lay low until someone from Statham's team can pick you up."

He crested the hill and saw McGraw's truck parked sideways across the road, blocking oncoming traffic. Someone got out and motioned angrily at him but then thought better of it when McGraw pulled an HK416 assault rifle from the backseat and fired into the air.

"Scott!" Rapp said into his radio. "You dead?"

"Not yet, asshole. But we're down. Fred swears he can fix it. He says thirty minutes."

"You have fifteen. I want that fucking chopper in the air, do you understand me?"

"Roger that, Mitch."

The music that had been playing over the truck's radio suddenly went silent and a panicked Arabic voice came on.

"Muhammad? What's happening? Did we hit something? Was that shooting we heard?"

Rapp reached into his shirt pocket and retrieved a few antibiotic pills from a box soaked through with Attia's blood. He tossed them in his mouth, breaking them apart with his teeth and savoring the bitterness.

"Muhammad! Answer! Was that shooting?"

Of course that asshole Gary Statham would lecture him on how antibiotics didn't work against viruses, but screw it. The taste made him feel better. It was like soft body armor when the rifles came out. Sure, it wouldn't save you, but there was something strangely comforting about the weight.

CHAPTER 51

"**W**E'RE looking good," Joe Maslick said over Rapp's earpiece. "Road's pretty open and still no cops. ETA to the border at our current speed is approximately one hour, three minutes."

"Roger that," Rapp said, leaning forward over the truck's steering wheel and scanning the terrain surrounding the highway. Empty.

His speedometer was reading one kilometer an hour under the speed limit and he was keeping the vehicle steady despite increasingly powerful gusts coming from the south. Maslick was a couple of miles in front of him, completely out of sight. Bruno McGraw was visible in his side-view mirror.

The CIA had dedicated no fewer than three dozen native-level Spanish speakers to interfering with the police in the region. They were calling in false reports, scrambling communications, and impersonating officers in an effort to create confusion. It was a house of cards for sure, but one that only had to last for a little longer.

"We're back in the air," Scott Coleman said over a

spotty connection. "Sorry it's a little late. The damage was worse than it looked. If Fred's jury-rigging holds together, we should be able to get to you in thirty. If not, it's going to be another exciting landing."

"Copy," Rapp said.

A shrill ring filled the cab and Rapp glanced at the bloody sat phone lying next to Muhammad Attia's body. He leaned down to reject the call like he had four times before but then Claudia's voice came on the comm.

"Mitch. The NSA says Attia's phone's ringing again. They think they can trace the call. You need to pick up."

He rolled the window down a couple of inches before complying.

"Muhammad! Are you there?"

Even on speakerphone and mixed with the wind, Sayid Halabi's voice was unmistakable. Rapp had only heard it a few times, but the sound of it was indelibly burned into his mind.

He downshifted, increasing the engine noise and then shouting over it. "I'm here!"

"I can barely hear you. What's your status?"

It was exactly the question he wanted to hear—one that proved Halabi didn't know what was happening. Attia hadn't had time to get a call out and if the ISIS leader was tracking the truck via GPS, the slight detour toward Monterrey had been chalked up to a signal anomaly.

The Agency had been concerned that the people trapped in the trailer might be able to communicate out, but the risk turned out to be low. A couple of the CIA's tech geeks had physically closed themselves up in the back of a truck full of frozen food and confirmed that getting cell or satellite signal was virtually impossible.

"All is well," Rapp said in Arabic. "I'm about an hour from the border crossing."

"Why haven't you been answering my calls?"

Rapp found himself mesmerized by the man's voice—as though it were emanating from beyond the grave. He'd dropped an entire cave system on the ISIS leader and still he'd managed to survive. Would the NSA be able to locate him? And would Rapp live long enough to look into his eyes before putting a bullet between them?

"This is the first call I've received. It's possible that the cell coverage isn't as good as we anticipated."

There was a brief silence as Halabi processed what he'd heard.

"Very well. God be with you. Contact me when you're across."

It was incredible how much you could get away with in the modern world by using bad cell coverage as an excuse.

"God be with you," Rapp responded, though it seemed that Halabi had already disconnected. A moment later Claudia came back on.

"Mitch, do you copy?"

"Yeah. Was that long enough? Did they get him?"

"I'll try to find out, but in the meantime I have Gary Statham on the line. Can you talk to him?"

"Yeah, put him on," he said, rolling the window back up.

"Mitch? How're you holding up?"

"I'm covered in blood, I've got a corpse jammed

under the dash, and I forgot my driver's license. Other than that, fine."

"Understood. We're at the border quietly setting up. We don't want to tip off the Mexicans that it's not business as usual. The border's still open and operating normally. Still not too much activity and the Mexicans aren't stopping anyone leaving their side. When you get here, you'll just be waved through. Once you're on the U.S. side, stop. And whatever you do, don't get out of the truck."

"Roger that."

"Then we'll see you in about fifty-three minutes. Good luck."

"Mitch," Coleman said over the comm. "You've got a cop coming at you on the opposite side of the highway. ETA is about two minutes, but he doesn't look like he's in a hurry. Likely he'll just pass on by."

"Good to have you back. How's the chopper? Is it going to hold together?"

"Fred says fifty-fifty. But we're due a little luck, right."

Just over a half an hour to the border and everything was going as smoothly as could be hoped for. Gauges all looked good and the only vehicle visible was Bruno McGraw in his mirror.

"Cop just went by me," Joe Maslick said. "Still normal speeds."

The police cruiser appeared in the distance and Rapp followed it with his eyes as it passed and began to recede in his mirror. Then, after about a hundred yards, taillights flashed.

"Are you seeing this?" Rapp said.

"Yeah," McGraw responded as the police car crossed the median and began coming up behind them with siren wailing.

"Then deal with it."

His man drifted into the right lane in what appeared to be an effort to let the cop pass. But when it came even with the pickup, McGraw swerved left. The unexpected impact was enough to send the cruiser back into the median, where it flipped three times before coming to a rest on its roof.

"Claudia," Rapp said. "A cop just came after us and McGraw took him out."

"Copy that. We haven't heard anything over the police radios about you. Did you do anything to get his attention?"

"Negative."

"Then they may be communicating by cell phone, which is probably not a good sign."

"Looks like the Mexicans have finally decided to join the party," Coleman broke in. "You've got two more cruisers coming in on you from the east. They're still about five miles out but their lights are on and they're hauling ass. Hold on . . . Looks like they're slowing down. Yeah. They're crossing the median and setting up a roadblock. And you've got another cop coming up behind you. A ways back though and he's struggling to close the gap. You'll have a visual on him before you get to the roadblock, but I don't think he'll be on top of you yet."

Rapp glanced at his speedometer. Eighty-seven miles an hour. It was about all he was going to get out of the truck on this road. "Can I get around it?"

"That's a negative. They picked a place with rocky terrain and trees on either side."

"Mas!"

"I'm on it, Mitch."

When the roadblock finally came into view, it was chaos. Maslick had his pickup sideways in the road and was firing his assault rifle across the hood at the cruiser blocking the right lane. From that distance, Rapp couldn't tell what the cops were doing in response and at this point he didn't care.

"What the fuck?" he said over the comm. "I'm less than a minute out and I'm not planning on slowing down. *Get me through.*"

Twenty seconds later, he still didn't have a lane, but Maslick's rifle had been replaced with an RPG. There was a puff of smoke and then the cruiser on the left flew into the air on a pillar of flame. Rapp eased into that lane and maintained his speed as the dry brush in the median caught fire.

The cruiser was still hanging out into the asphalt, making it a tight squeeze. There was a deafening crash when his left fender caught the edge of the police vehicle's bumper, but he managed to hold the wheel steady.

"I'm clear," Rapp said. "ETA's coming down fast. Is Gary ready?"

"He says yes," Claudia replied over the comm. "But they're seeing some increased activity on the Mexican side of the border. Not sure what they're up to yet, but it's clear they know something's going on."

"Roger that. It's not much farther. We just have to hold this shit show together for a few more minutes."

He ignored McGraw as he passed, focusing instead on the police car that had appeared through the smoke and was overtaking him from behind. A moment later, though, Coleman's chopper became visible and the former SEAL opened up on the vehicle from above. It skidded off the tarmac and began spinning through the dirt, coming to a stop and staying that way. Whether it was damaged or whether the driver had decided he'd had enough was impossible to tell. Either way, he was out of the game.

The traffic started getting heavier and buildings began springing up on both sides of the road. He slowed, matching the speed limit. Cross streets started to split off the main thoroughfare and the increasing density of buildings made it impossible to see if anyone was going to pull out.

"So far, no stop signs, but if we run into any, someone's going to have to get control of the intersection so I can roll through. I can't risk a cra—"

Rapp fell silent when a light bar came on fifty yards ahead. The border patrol vehicle turned sideways in the road, blocking it at a choke point between two buildings. Rapp didn't even have time to give an order before McGraw swerved toward it. His brush guard connected hard with the cruiser's front quarter panel, spinning it completely around and through the front window of a shop to the left.

Unfortunately, it had a similar effect on McGraw's pickup. Rapp saw the air bags go off as the top-heavy vehicle teetered on two wheels before finally landing on its side. McGraw seemed unaffected, climbing out the open driver's-side window and firing his assault rifle in the air. The locals scattered, clearing a path.

Rapp shifted gears and slammed the accelerator to the floor. "We've lost Bruno. Mas, come around me. It's time to start breaking shit."

"Copy that."

Rapp had the semi up to almost fifty again when Maslick's supercharged Jeep Grand Cherokee passed and took a position twenty yards in front. He lay on his horn, and when that wasn't enough to clear the road, a nudge from his brush guard did the trick.

"I've got eyes on you!" came Gary Statham's excited voice over the comm. "There's a lot of activity on the Mexican side, but it's still disorganized. Just keep coming my way and don't—I repeat, *do not* crash that truck."

"Keep them off me, Scott."

"On it."

The chopper passed overhead with Coleman leaning through the open door firing at pretty much anything that moved. The border crossing was now visible and Maslick was driving like he was in a demolition derby. On the U.S. side, all the barriers had been lifted and what little backed-up traffic that existed was being waved through.

As Rapp approached, two Mexican border security vehicles started to pull out of their spaces to block him. Maslick sideswiped the front of both and then threw his vehicle in reverse, pulling it back and forth as they tried desperately to get around him.

Rapp swerved into a lane reserved for commercial trucks, aiming for the open gate that marked the border. Once through, he slammed on the brakes and downshifted, forcing the rig to a stop. A moment later, vehicles had pulled in front and behind, blocking him in. A few particularly stupid civilians were filming with their phones instead of fleeing, but a little automatic fire ran them off.

Men in hazmat suits appeared from nowhere, surrounding the truck with their weapons trained on him. One spoke into a microphone attached to a speaker on his hip.

"Do not exit the truck. Do you understand me, Mitch? *Stay in* the truck."

Rapp leaned his forehead on the steering wheel as people swarmed the vehicle, adding chocks to the wheels and disabling its electrical system. The AC went off and he was suddenly aware of the sun pounding through the windows.

"Mitch?" Claudia said over his earpiece. "Are you all right?"

He didn't answer, instead fishing the last two antibiotic pills from his pocket and tossing them in his mouth.

CHAPTER 52

THE truck's headlights created a circle of illumination that quickly faded into the blackness around them. Some three hundred meters ahead, Sayid Halabi could see two similar rings of illumination and he knew there were others behind. They had been on the road now for almost forty-eight hours, traveling by night and taking cover by day.

The landscape was wide-open and the skies had been clearer than forecasted, making their situation even more precarious. It was the reason he'd allowed his men to disperse and surrounded himself instead with local jihadists. The goal was to lose himself in the chaotic rhythms of a country that the Americans didn't understand.

He'd made the grave error of calling Muhammad Attia during the operation. And when the man hadn't answered, he'd compounded that error by calling again. And again. Finally he'd connected and spoken on a connection so filled with noise that the conversation was nearly unintelligible.

It was clear now that the garbled voice on the other

end of that call hadn't belonged to his loyal disciple. It had belonged to Mitch Rapp.

Halabi looked through his open window at the star-filled sky, searching for any sign of the Americans. They were out there somewhere. Watching, collecting data, calculating probabilities. Waiting to strike.

Only God could protect him now, but he wasn't sure that protection would be forthcoming. The YARS operation had expended every resource and burned every bridge in order to ultimately accomplish nothing. The truck containing his people had been stopped just across the U.S. border, sealed in plastic, and airlifted to an undisclosed location.

Irene Kennedy had skillfully disseminated the story that the trailer was filled with the radioactive components for a dirty bomb. It was a narrative that made locking down the area child's play. No one from the outside had any interest in approaching a contaminated zone, while the ones inside had every incentive to stay. The radiation source was gone and the government was promising testing and treatment for anyone exposed. In the unlikely event the virus had escaped the truck, it was containable.

Halabi glanced over at his Somali driver before staring off again into the darkness. Attia was dead. ISIS forces had been scattered and were now transforming into isolated criminal gangs. The highly trained group of men he'd surrounded himself with would spend the rest of their short lives being hunted by the world's intelligence agencies.

The other major threat to America, Christine Barnett, also seemed to be fading. Her attacks on America's intelligence agencies had been badly undermined by the heroism and competence displayed by the DEA, CIA, and army. For the first time in her political career, she was adrift.

Halabi closed his eyes for a moment, hiding from the reality of what he had done. He hadn't just failed to destroy the United States, he'd provided it with a tangible, terrifying external threat. The country that had been busy tearing itself apart would now turn away from imaginary dangers and focus on real ones. He had unwittingly provided the American people with the truths that their politicians and media had worked so hard to obscure.

Halabi retrieved a new phone from the floorboard, removing it from its packaging before just letting it fall from his hand. There was no one left to call. Nothing left to be learned. Details, strategies, and elaborate plans meant nothing. He knew that now. Mitch Rapp wasn't just the enemy of Islam. He was more than that. The forces of evil had chosen him. And now they were supporting him. Giving him strength.

Until he was dead, God's will could not be done.

Halabi understood that he was aging and injured. That he and his network would become the targets of a manhunt unprecedented in world history. He would never again have an opportunity like the one that he'd just allowed to wither. But he wasn't without resources. He still had benefactors and millions of dollars hidden in bank accounts throughout the world. He still had thousands of followers willing to die on his command.

There was no question that he was soon for the grave, but with his last breath he would drag Mitch Rapp in with him.

The poorly maintained roadbed became strewn with rocks and his driver was forced to slow, swerving through the obstacles. All sense of progress—already nearly nonexistent in Halabi's new reality—seemed to disappear.

A flash appeared ahead in the darkness, unmistakable but impossible to pinpoint exactly. A split second later, a bullet penetrated the windshield and slammed his driver back in his seat.

Halabi grabbed the handle and threw himself against the door but found it blocked. A barely visible figure leaned closer to the open window, his features gaining detail in the hazy artificial light.

Not a Somali bandit. His face was streaked with paint and his hair was covered with a sand-colored cap. What he couldn't hide, though, were his Caucasian features and bright blue eyes.

A pistol appeared and Halabi jerked back, raising an arm protectively as the man spoke.

"Mitch Rapp sends his compliments, motherfucker."

CHAPTER 53

RAPP lifted the remote control with difficulty, using it to increase the volume of the television bolted to the wall.

Senator Christine Barnett was jogging up the Capitol steps, besieged by reporters shouting questions, aiming cameras, and jostling each other with outstretched microphones. The press that she'd manipulated for so long suddenly seemed completely beyond her control.

". . . leak exposed a counterterrorist operation and allowed a serious threat to cross the border," someone shouted. "Is your committee going to investigate?"

"Of course," she said, looking haggard and uncertain. "This is an extremely important matter and it'll be fully vetted."

The authoritative rhythm of her speech was gone now. Her responses seemed canned. Fake.

"Now, if you'll excuse me," she continued, trying to pick up her pace without looking like she was breaking into a full run, "I have a meeting."

The screen faded back to an interview with a governor who was running a distant second to Barnett in her party's presidential primary. Rapp had met him on a number of occasions and in the scheme of things he wasn't that bad. A former army captain whose brain hadn't yet been completely scrambled by Washington.

"Your thoughts?" the host said.

"Obviously, there are a lot of questions here. About the leaks. About the senator's attacks on the CIA and DEA operatives putting their lives on the line to protect America. It's my understanding that the man who captured the ISIS truck and delivered it to the army may not survive. I wonder if she would have done the same for her country?"

"And the reports that her campaign manager Kevin Gray has resigned and is being interviewed by the FBI?"

"More questions," the man agreed. "If Senator Barnett intends to lead our party in the next presidential election, they're going to need to be answered."

They cut to a clip that Rapp had seen before and he hit the pause button to freeze Barnett's face in a deer-in-the-headlights expression that bordered on fear. It was his favorite shot of her.

He sank back into the pillows and focused on a ceiling that had become a little too familiar over the past couple of weeks. The room he was imprisoned in was about twenty feet square, constructed mostly of stainless steel and glass. Mysterious medical machines hummed around him, displaying vital signs and other information that confirmed he was still alive. As though the cracking headache and constant labor of getting air in and out weren't enough.

The illness had hit him thirty-six hours after he'd

been quarantined. It started with a single, innocuous cough and then progressed to a temperature north of 104, a respirator, and finally unconsciousness.

He heard a familiar hiss to his left and let his head loll over to watch Gary Statham come through the air lock in full biohazard gear.

"How're you feeling?" he asked while he checked the machines.

"Great."

"Happy to hear it. I didn't think you were going to make it."

"What're you talking about?" Rapp managed to get out. "You've been telling me I was going to be fine since I got here."

"I was lying. But today I come bearing good tidings. Your lungs and kidneys look good and we're not seeing any permanent damage. It's going to take a little time but you're going to make a full recovery."

"Is that straight? Or another lie?"

"That's straight," Statham said, turning toward the bed. He was a little hard to hear through the space suit. "You'll be back shooting people in the face before you know it."

"Outstanding," Rapp said, already a little out of breath from the conversation. It was hard to imagine even being able to get out of bed. Combat seemed a million miles away.

"Believe it or not, there are some people here who seem anxious to see you. Are you up for a five-minute visit?"

"Sure."

Statham clipped a microphone to Rapp's shirt and then disappeared back through the air lock. A few moments later, Claudia and Anna appeared on the other side of a long window to his right.

"They tell me you're going to be fine," Claudia said, sounding relieved, but still looking worried beneath the harsh fluorescent lights.

"Mom says you got the flu," Anna said, straining to get eye level with the bottom of the viewing window. "My teacher says they have shots for that."

Every time he came home from an operation the worse for wear, they had to come up with a cover story. And every time, his invented carelessness met with the girl's disapproval. Car accidents earned him admonishments about seat belts. Falls down stairs brought on scolding about proper lighting and sensible shoes. Now he was going to get the vaccine lecture.

"Maybe I need to start going to class with you," he said, thankful that the microphone made his voice sound stronger than it really was.

"You're older than my teacher! Can you play a game, Mitch? We brought an Xbox and they said they'd hook it up, but it might take a few days because of the Internet and stuff."

"Sure."

"What do you want to play?"

"How about one of those zombie games?"

"You always want to play the shooters because you always win!"

"This could be your year."

Her eyes narrowed.

"Let's not badger Mitch, okay, sweetie? He isn't feeling well and he's always nice to you when you're sick."

"Okay," she said, sounding a little guilty. Her eyes

disappeared as she dropped from her tiptoes, leaving only the top of her head visible.

A long silence stretched out as Claudia stared through the glass. She'd never seen him like this and it appeared to terrify her. He'd have said something to reassure her but he was still recovering from his extended conversation with Anna.

"Scott's here to see you. Should I tell him no? That you need to rest?"

Rapp shook his head. "I'm okay."

"Irene said she'd come tomorrow, when you're feeling a little stronger. She's working on a project she says you're going to like." Claudia patted her daughter's head. "Say good-bye."

"Bye, Mitch! I'll tell them to hurry with that Xbox!"

They disappeared and were quickly replaced by the slightly sunburned face of Scott Coleman. He'd been in a similar hospital bed after his run-in with Grisha Azarov and he seemed to be enjoying the tables being turned.

"You look like shit."

"Fuck you. How are the guys?"

"Good. Wick's just down the hall bouncing off the walls. He didn't catch it, but they want to keep him for another week to make sure. Mas made it over the border and he's home with a broken hand and a dislocated shoulder. Bruno's still in Mexican prison, but the diplomats say they'll spring him in the next couple of days. Doesn't really matter. The head of the most powerful gang there died in a freak drowning accident involving a toilet and Bruno's hands around his throat. Word is he's pretty much running the place."

Rapp just nodded as a broad grin spread across Coleman's face.

"He was there, you know."

"Who was where?"

"We tracked those calls from Halabi to somewhere near Hargeisa. They'd been holed up in a cave system there. By the time we found it they'd already taken off, but we had heavy overhead coverage and the Agency guys were able to run the timeline backward and piece together their movements from satellite photos. It wasn't easy. The weather was crap and the convoy kept breaking up and reforming."

"Is this story going somewhere?"

Coleman's grin widened further and he slapped a color eight-by-ten against the glass. The lighting was garish, a powerful flash in the darkness that illuminated a bearded man with part of his head missing. Rapp lifted himself off the pillows, forgetting the lines attached to him and locking on the image of Sayid Halabi.

"Don't worry," Coleman said. "I told him it was from you."

EPILOGUE

CHRISTINE Barnett used a key to unlock the office she kept in the southern wing of her Georgetown home. It was her private sanctum—a place that even her husband was prohibited from entering on the rare occasion he was in town. And now she needed it more than ever.

Barnett had barely slept in weeks, instead lying in bed hovering somewhere between dream and reality. Endless scenarios, dangers, and opportunities raced through her mind. The faces of allies and enemies floated in the darkness. She had lost control of her universe for the first time in her career and didn't know how to get it back.

Over the past weeks her poll numbers had plummeted enough to put her in a dead heat with her nearest primary challenger. Dramatic video of Mitch Rapp fighting his way across the border and then being surrounded by the army was still on every channel. The homeland security agencies she'd spent so much time railing against were now being deified by the American public.

Suddenly heroism and patriotism were generating better ratings than personal attacks and partisanship. The rage and negativity that she'd used to fuel her rise through the political ranks was faltering. The American people were looking for something new.

But what?

Kevin Gray wasn't returning her calls, and without him, her campaign's damage control strategy had never fully formed. More important, though, were his meetings with the FBI. She still hadn't been able to find out why he'd been interviewed or what had been discussed. It seemed unimaginable that he would have said anything about the leaks. He was smart enough to know that punishments for such things tended to be doled out to people on his level, not hers. But could she be sure of that?

No.

Her quest to become president was no longer about her thirst for power or the immortality that would accompany being America's first female president. It was about survival. She needed the full support of her party, the White House's ability to manipulate the press, and the authority to remove Irene Kennedy and her loyalists. Once ensconced in the Oval Office she would be untouchable. Until then she was vulnerable.

An increasingly familiar sense of fury and helplessness began to rise in her. She tried to swallow it, knowing that she wouldn't sleep at all that night if it hit full force. Six hours of staring into the darkness wasn't something she could afford. Her day started at 5 a.m. and wouldn't end until after midnight. During that time, she couldn't put a single foot wrong. One ill-considered word, one awkward pause, one unguarded facial expression . . . That's all it would take to put the White House forever out of her reach.

She sat down behind her desk and flipped on the lamp, squinting against the glare to take in the opulent room. As her eyes adjusted, they were drawn to something unusual in a rocking chair near the wall.

"Late night," Mitch Rapp observed.

Her body tensed and she drew in a breath to scream, but it got caught in her chest. His hair was close cropped and his normally full beard was short and neatly trimmed. The dark eyes were sunken and bloodshot, but still carried the intensity she'd grown to hate over the years. For some reason, though, it wasn't his stare that made the bile rise in her throat. It was the surgical gloves covering his hands.

She swallowed and finally managed to get out a panicked shout. "Help! Come up here now!"

The pounding footsteps of Secret Service agents on the stairs didn't materialize. All she could hear was her own breathing and the creak of the antique chair Rapp was rocking in.

"I didn't slip by them," he said. "They let me in."

Barnett remained frozen. This couldn't be happening. Even Mitch Rapp wouldn't dare. He wouldn't kill one of the front-runners in the U.S. presidential election.

"What do you want?" she heard herself say. "The directorship of the CIA? Homeland Security?"

He just rocked.

"Secretary of defense? Just tell me."

"I know you leaked the anthrax story that almost got me killed."

"That's not true! Who told you that?"

There was no way Rapp had proof. Even if Gray had talked, it would just be his word against hers. The laptop he'd used was brand-new and was now in pieces at the bottom of a landfill. The open-source operating system it ran had been confirmed secure by her husband's top people—some of whom he'd hired away from the NSA.

"There've been a lot of leaks over the years," Rapp continued. "And it's been hard not to notice that quite a few have helped you and hurt your opponents."

"Those have all been investigated and no one has ever even *suggested* that I was involved," Barnett said, starting to overcome her initial shock. She had to think clearly. Her life might depend on it.

Rapp smiled, but in a way that was so devoid of humor that it came off as more of a baring of teeth. Barnett went motionless as though she were faced with wild animal.

"You had us going for a while," Rapp admitted. "The NSA threw everything at those leaks and no one could trace them."

"Getting to the bottom of this will be one of my administration's top priorities," Barnett said. "There's nothing more important than the safety of this country and the men and women who ensure that safety."

This time his smile was even wider, causing Barnett to silently curse herself. She'd been a politician so long that she couldn't shut it off. The platitudes that were so popular with her millions of followers would be a joke to someone like Rapp.

"Do you want to know where you went wrong, Senator?"

"I have no idea what you're talking about."

"Kevin Gray. Brilliant guy, but a creature of habit. He always gets those new laptops at the same place. The Best Buy a few miles from his house. For the last two years, he's been buying ones custom built by us."

Barnett's mind began to spin as she tried to make the calculations she was famous for. How many leaks had she ordered over that time frame? How many had been carried out by Gray? Why hadn't Kennedy released this information long ago? Was it possible that Rapp was bluffing? Or had Kennedy been squirreling away the evidence to be used if Barnett ever reached the White House?

"I don't believe it," she said. "I don't believe Kevin would do that."

The only plausible way out was to shift the blame. To assert that Gray had acted alone. He already had the reputation as one of the most ruthless and ambitious campaign strategists in Washington. She could use that to create a portrait of a man who would do anything to win.

"If you provide my committee the evidence you have against him, we'll give it a full, bipartisan vetting. And if we find out he's leaked classified information, I'll be the first one to recommend prosecution."

Rapp reached into his jacket and Barnett's bladder almost let go. When his hand reappeared, though, it wasn't holding the infamous Glock, but instead a mobile phone.

"Like I said, a brilliant guy," he said, tapping the screen. "Brilliant enough to know you'd throw him under the bus."

"*Ma'am, Rapp's dead and—*" she heard Gray's recorded voice say over the phone's speaker.

"*He's not dead! That son of a bitch has more lives than an alley cat. He's alive and they're not telling us. That means he's out there, still working on this operation. Waiting.*"

"*Waiting? Waiting for what?*"

"*For me to win the primary. Then, at just the right moment, he's going to reappear and save the day. Alexander and Kennedy will be heroes and I'll be standing there looking like a fool.*"

"*Senator, the idea that Mitch Rapp is involving himself in some kind of complex political game is—*"

"*He sees me as a threat. Just like Kennedy. They're going to use this to come after me. We have to find out what's happening in Mexico. We have to get ahead of it.*"

"*We have no way of finding out what's happening. No one's going to tell us anything, and if we try to twist arms at the intelligence agencies, it's going to go public and blow up in our faces.*"

"*Not the American government. We can use our contacts in the Mexican government. They want us to get off their backs regarding immigrants and drugs, right? Well, as president, I can make that happen. And all I ask in return is a little cooperation and information.*"

"*Now hold on, Senator. If Rapp's alive, it's possible that he's actually still on the trail of ISIS. We—*"

"*I'm not going to sit on my hands and see that son of a bitch shooting it out with terrorists on television!*"

He fast-forwarded the recording.

"*Call them, Kevin. Call the Mexicans. Quietly. Find out what's going on. We can still head this off. If there really is something happening down there, we might be able to get the Mexican authorities to deal with it and keep Rapp and Kennedy from getting the win. If it works out, we might even be able to take some credit. Show the American people that I can stop threats before they make it to the United States.*"

By the time Rapp turned off the recording, enough blood had drained from Barnett's head that she had to steady herself against the desk. She wasn't just going to lose the primary. She was going to be held up as a traitor. She was going to be marched into court in handcuffs and convicted of treason. The fear she used to keep her enemies and allies in line would disappear. For the first time in her career the blood in the water would be hers.

Rapp stood and reached into his jacket again, this time retrieving a bottle of pills that he threw to her. She caught it and looked down at the label. Painkillers backdated to a minor surgery she'd had two years ago.

"That's a present from Irene Kennedy. It's the easy way out. For you and the country."

He went to the door but paused with his gloved hand on the knob. "Take the gift, Senator. Because if you don't, we're going to do it my way."

And then he was gone.

Barnett stared down at the bottle for a long time. Finally, she opened it and reached for a bottle of water near the desk lamp. She gagged on the first pill, terror causing her throat to constrict. After that, it was easy.

Pocket Books
proudly presents

TOTAL POWER

VINCE FLYNN

Available Now

Turn the page for a sneak peek at the latest
Mitch Rapp thriller by Kyle Mills, *Total Power* . . .

"**G**RACIAS," Rapp said, handing a ten Euro bill to the woman at the cash register. She doled out his change, and he wandered off to find a place to sit in the departure lounge. Only about half of the cafeteria tables were full, and he managed to secure one with a decent view of the people coming through security.

Jordi Cardenas and his people had delivered beyond all expectation, assembling detailed dossiers on every passenger and quietly upgrading the airport's security from barely average to state of the art. No one was getting so much as a squirt gun to the gates without their knowing about it.

Based on the information they'd gathered, there were three solid suspects in addition to the primary target, Hamal Kattan. All were youngish Middle Eastern men on trips that seemed out of the ordinary for them. One was terminating in Barcelona, while the other two were continuing to the US on the same flight as Kattan. A fourth man—from Pakistan—was a possibility but probably less than fifty-fifty. He had a history of international travel and was headed to Paris, where he had an apartment rented for the next two weeks.

Rapp gnawed off the edge of his ham sandwich and watched the people clearing security. Kattan and the men who were likely his escorts were already through and had spread out in the gate area on the other side of Duty Free. A group of Asian tourists was causing a bit of chaos at the X-ray machine but, with the help of their frazzled guide, finally pulled it together. They were followed by some vaguely annoyed-looking travelers who appeared to be local. Finally, the Pakistani appeared.

Rapp kept working on his sandwich as the man put his roller on the conveyor and passed through the scanner. Once again, Cardenas's team impressed. None displayed any more interest in him than they had in the Spaniards that came before. Behind the scenes, though, high-tech images were being uploaded to Langley for further analysis.

After retrieving his carry-on, the Pakistani directed himself toward the cafeteria. Rapp turned, watching him in windows that had been converted into mirrors by the darkness outside. His gut said that this guy wasn't involved, but he wasn't certain enough to bet anyone's life on it. His team would keep as close a watch on this Pakistani as they did the others.

The possible terrorist moved out of view, and Rapp turned his attention to his own reflection. His beard had been trimmed into something more respectable than his normal look—something Claudia disparaged as "man raised by wolves." His hair was similarly well put together, and green contacts were irritating his eyes. The straightforward disguise was rounded out by enough subtle foundation to lighten his deeply tanned skin.

He'd resisted that last one, but it was hard to complain. In order to camouflage Joe Maslick's two hundred and eighty pounds of muscle, they'd had to put him in a fat suit that expanded his girth to the point that he barely fit in a premium seat at the front. The pièce de résistance, though, was Charlie Wicker. Claudia's sense of humor probably had something to do with the fact that she'd decided to go with a gay theme. Whatever the motivation, it worked. No one would peg the diminutive guy poured into lemon-yellow jeans as one of the most dangerous men in the world. The other two had gotten off relatively easy. Bruno McGraw naturally looked like an American tourist and Coleman's blond hair and language skills made it easy for him to pass as German.

The music in Rapp's ear buds faded and a moment later was replaced by Claudia's voice. "They're all through. Jordi's people couldn't find any weapons on Kattan or the Pakistani. Two of the other men appear to be carrying custom firearms disassembled to fool the scanners. The third has a knife built into the frame of his carry-on. Take a look at your phone."

Rapp pulled up an email attachment that depicted the Airbus A320's seating chart. The tangos were marked in red with a symbol indicating the weapons they carried. His team's positions were noted in green.

"We did the best we could to seat the targets in good strategic positions, but Fred had the final word."

The Fred she was referring to was Fred Mason, Rapp's go-to pilot on any mission he could persuade him to participate in. The man could fly or fix anything from hang gliders to 747s and had nerves of steel. He'd be flying the plane that night and had seated the tangos where they would do the least amount of damage if they managed to get off an errant shot. It was an inexact science, though. Modern planes were crammed with critical wires, fluid lines, and computer circuits.

The intercom announced Rapp's flight, and he tossed what was left of his food before heading to the gate. They'd added a flight that was going out ten minutes before his and the boarding area was jammed with people trying to figure out what line they were supposed to be in.

Kattan elbowed his way back from the bathrooms, coming close enough that Rapp could pick up his nervousness. He was clutching a laptop case like it was a holy relic, and there was a bead of sweat running down his cheek. The little prick had wanted to play secret agent, and now he was discovering the weight of that game.

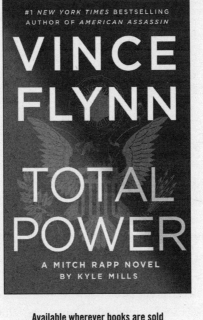